HOOSIER HOOPS
AND HIJINKS

Speed City Indiana Sisters in Crime

Edited by
Brenda Robertson Stewart and Tony Perona

Blue River Press
Indianapolis

Hoosier Hoops and Hijinks © 2013 Speed City Indiana Sisters in Crime

Library of Congress Control Number: 2013945327

Cover designed by Jennifer Rae Black
Packaged by Wish Publishing

Printed in the United States of America
10 9 8 7 6 5 4 3 2 1

Distributed in the United States by
Cardinal Publishers Group
www.cardinalpub.com

*This book is dedicated to all Hoosier basketball players,
whether they play in vacant lots, high school gyms,
college courts or professional arenas.*

ACKNOWLEDGEMENTS

The editors would like to thank the Speed City Indiana chapter of Sisters in Crime for their support and commitment to this project, Hank Phillippi Ryan for her generosity in writing the introduction and Adriane and Tom Doherty of Cardinal Publishers for their support. Most of all, we would like to thank the authors for their stories about Hoosier hysteria, hijinks and madness surrounding the game of basketball in Indiana.

CONTENTS

INTRODUCTION

Hank Phillippi Ryan

The seconds tick by. The suspense is unbearable. The pace is excruciating. The bad guys are on the hunt. The good guys are fighting back. Screams arise from the innocent onlookers—while uniformed law enforcement officers scramble to keep the peace.

A shot rings out!

Oh wait. No. It's not a thriller. It's the final buzzer.

You are about to be introduced to Hoosier Hysteria. It is not an affliction listed in the medical journals—though it is not only chronic, long-lasting and incurable, but it's also contagious.

The first symptoms? Calling "travelling" on innocent pedestrians. A longing for Friday nights in high school gyms. And inability to count by twos—two, four, six, eight—without adding "Who do we appreciate?" And the ability, even for the geometry-impaired, to gauge the arc of a perfect rainbow three-pointer. Soon you'll start picking your brackets, contemplating the Milan Miracle, discussing one-on-one versus zone. You learn there are no double entendres connected with French Lick. And you will rise in reverence when anyone mentions the name Larry Bird.

Yup. It's basketball fever. As only Indiana can provide it. Thank goodness there are no extant photographs of me as a Pike Junior High cheerleader, with a little white wool skirt and a bulky sweater with a fuzzy red P on the front. I learned to chant Dee-fense, even when, I now admit, I wasn't quite sure what that was. But you could not grow up happy in Indiana without being a player, a helper, a coach or a fan. Or all of the above.

But as you will read, sometimes Hoosier hysteria—on paper, only, of course!— turns a bit more sinister than a missed free throw or a blown overtime. What could be the true consequences, these stories ask, of rooting for the wrong team? Wanting to win just a little too much? Or making a wrong bet or keeping the teams' big secret?

It's only a game, you say? Don't you believe it. After that final buzzer, these stories reveal, it may be the games are only beginning. And they are games of revenge, of retribution, of collusion, of conspiracy, of greed and power and love and honor.

And murder.

When it comes to Hoosier Hijinks, not everyone plays by the rules. And that's what makes it irresistible.

— Hank Phillippi Ryan

Investigative reporter **Hank Phillippi Ryan** *is on the air at Boston's NBC affiliate. Her work has resulted in new laws, people sent to prison, homes removed from foreclosure, and millions of dollars in restitution. Along with her 28 EMMY's, Hank's won dozens of other journalism honors. She's been a radio reporter (at Indianapolis' WIBC), a legislative aide in the United States Senate, an editorial assistant at Rolling Stone Magazine, and began her TV career at WTHR in Indianapolis in 1975.*

The author of six mystery novels, Hank's won two Agathas, the Anthony, the Macavity for her crime fiction and The Mystery Writers of America's Mary Higgins Clark Award for The Other Woman. *She is the 2013 president of national Sisters in Crime and on the national board of Mystery Writers of America.*

THE ART OF THE GAME
Diana Catt

He'd held tickets for the same two stadium seats for ten seasons, but only used the one at the row's end. An empty seat on one side and an aisle on the other buffered him somewhat from the crowd. He wished he could isolate himself even more and often considered buying up more seats. But it wouldn't be necessary after this season. He'd found her again.

Arlie Messing's intense resistance training over the summer was paying off. New muscle mass affected more than her appearance. After the first three games of the season she was leading her team in scoring percentage and steals. Her junior year as a Purdue Boilermaker promised to be her best since senior year at Roncalli High School. Life was good.

Sometimes before dropping off to sleep, Arlie allowed herself the luxury of imagining her basketball future. An illustrious career at Purdue could open the golden gates to a spot with the Fever. Or maybe she'd be a coach. Professional women's team? College women's team? High school girl's team? Who knew what lay ahead. For right now, though, she was thrilled to fire up the Boilermaker steam.

The fourth game of the season, the first game at home, was approaching. Mackey Arena filled, and the crowd stomped and cheered with enthusiasm. Arlie's heart beat to the bounce of the ball and she immersed herself into the action. Her teammates worked their magic and the plays Coach called ensured their victory. The Lady Boilers rocked the night.

The next morning, Arlie was up early for her usual workout followed by team practice. She and her teammates were still riding high from the previous night's win when Coach had them watch a film of their next opponent, Bowling Green. Arlie felt the buoyant attitude of her teammates drop a notch as they studied the talent on the video. They ran their drills with the dedication to win.

When Arlie returned home, exhausted and ready to plop down in front of the TV, she found a mailing tube leaning against the front door. She opened the package, thinking someone had sent her the latest Lady Boilermaker poster. Instead, the roll of paper that shook out had her image hand-drawn in charcoal. It portrayed her sitting on the player's bench, with her long, dark hair pulled back and a towel draped around her neck. She held one end of the towel in her hand, ready to wipe off the tiny beads of sweat that dotted her forehead and upper lip.

Arlie stared in amazement, remembering the exact moment captured so precisely on the page. Her deep breathing to counter the last hard drive to the basket, the icy cold of the water she sipped, the coarse nap of the towel on her skin; the artist had captured her exact essence at that point in time. She glanced at the bottom for a signature. It was signed A Fan.

Sweet. If she bought matting and a frame, this would be a perfect birthday gift for her mom, her biggest fan. Arlie phoned David Pico, an art student friend.

"Hey, Picasso. I need your expertise."

"Anything for my favorite b'ball star."

"Somebody sent me a drawing. It's good. I'd like to send the artist my thanks, and I thought you might recognize the style. Got time to stop by, take a look?"

"Will you buy lunch?"

"How 'bout a cup of coffee?"

"I'm there in ten."

When David arrived, Arlie had coffee made and the sketch spread out on the dining room table. Her roommate, Jillian, was admiring it.

"A Fan? Why didn't they just sign their name?" Jillian asked. "Somebody has a crush on you, Chica." She held up her iPhone and snapped a picture of the sketch.

David whistled and picked up the sketch by the top corners. He studied the picture, then looked between the image and the model. "Not a beginner. Look at the shading and the detail. No accidental smudging from stray charcoal particles. I don't recognize the style, but I have a professor who knows all the local artists. He might know who drew this. Want me to show him?"

"He can check my facebook page," Jillian said. "I just uploaded it."

"Sure, but no rush," Arlie said to David. "I'm going to drop it off at Mickley's to get framed."

David continued to gaze at the sketch. "Let me mount it, Arlie," he said. "I've got a small project for my metallurgy class and I can use this for it. I think it'll make a splash."

"Hey, I don't want to impose. I can pay."

"OK, we'll work something out. But this..," he nodded slowly, "I've got just the thing. It'll be perfect, trust me. I'm the artist in your life."

"Well, looks like you've got competition," Jillian added with a shrug, pointing to the sketch. "Just sayin'."

There was a home game tonight and his excitement swelled as tip-off time drew near. He double checked his items: notebook, pencil, back-up pencil, binoculars, cash. He was ready to head out the door for Mackey. Then, one last glance at the faded sketch thumb-tacked to his apartment wall. The tilt of her chin, the way she held her shoulders for the pose with the ball resting on her hip, the contour of her biceps. Though she'd changed her number and uniform style, he'd found her. The changes were a message to him and he needed to let her know he understood.

Arlie was pumped for tonight's game, intending to earn revenge against Bowling Green. A former teammate from high school days, Vannie Lutteman, was one of BGSU's starting five. Arlie and Vannie fist bumped during warm-ups and Arlie'd felt a warm surge of her old Rebel pride. But, when waiting for the referee's whistle to start the play, she was all Boilermaker and ready to hammer down.

The teams battled for the lead throughout the game, which turned into a knock-down, drag-out overtime. Arlie took an elbow to the eye under the basket in the final seconds, but her shot tied the score. Then she hit the game winning free throw and the crowd went wild.

After the buzzer, Arlie's mom was immediately at her side and made her sit on the bench with an ice pack on her eye. The crowd was singing Hail, Purdue and swarming down onto the stadium floor. Arlie held the ice pack in place and accepted congratulations from fans, team mates, and opponents, especially Vannie Lutteman, who also hugged her mom.

Arlie and her mom ate at their favorite Italian restaurant after the game. She fielded questions from the staff about her eye and more congratulations on the night's win. The owner threw in an extra order of garlic bread sticks.

"Sure you don't want to stay over?" Arlie asked her mom.

"Not tonight. Maybe next time, though," Mrs. Messing said. "I have a couple of showings in Greenwood in the morning, and I'm meeting with a new client after that."

Arlie arched an eyebrow. "Sounds like you're busy. Real estate picking up then?"

"Not so fast in Indy, but there's a lot of activity in surrounding towns. Don't worry. I keep my schedule free for game nights."

The next morning, Arlie's left eye was nearly swollen shut. She loaded up on ibuprofen, completed her workout and went to practice. The eye throbbed. Her shots missed more often than hit. At the end of practice, Coach reminded her that the next game was only three days before the big tourney in South Carolina and handed her an ice pack.

When Arlie returned home, another mailing tube rested against the front door.

She shook out the rolled paper and held up the sketch, signed this time simply AF. It was a charcoal drawing like the last one, but with a dynamic touch of blood red. It depicted Arlie seated on the edge of her team bench, confetti strings atwirl in the air around her head. Her right eye was swollen. Red droplets spilled from a wicked, gaping slash over her eyebrow and rolled down next to the number five on the front of her uniform. Her face was contorted in pain.

Arlie drew in a breath and gingerly touched her tender, swollen eye. Not cut. No blood. Left, not right. She started to wad up the paper to throw away, but thought of David. She sent him a text message. Sketch #2 arrived. Come see.

Her phone chimed seconds later with the incoming message reply. B right there.

Thirty minutes later, David and Jillian studied the sketch spread out on the dining room table and compared Arlie's black eye to the damage illustrated in the drawing.

"Your big fan carried artistic license to a creepy level," Jillian said. "I thought this was an artist in love. Now, I'm not so sure."

"I showed the first sketch to Professor Mitchlin," David said. "He didn't recognize the style but he admired the skill."

"Show him this," Jillian said as she snapped a picture. "He might re-evaluate his opinion."

"The skill's still there. Look how the drops of red oil stand out against that charcoal," David said. "And look at the eyes. He's captured extreme pain in those eyes."

"But I wasn't in that much pain," Arlie protested. "And I didn't bleed. Wasn't even bad enough to stop the game. Where's AF getting this?"

"Maybe he's a masochist," Jillian said.

"I think you mean sadist," Arlie said.

"What's the dif?" Jillian said. "The guy's clearly disturbed."

"Maybe not disturbed," David said. "Maybe he was just afraid you'd been seriously hurt when you took that jab to the eye."

"And projected this? Why send it to me?"

David and Jillian both shrugged.

"Beats me," David said.

"Want to call the cops?" Jillian asked.

"Lord, no. It's just a picture. The coach would kill me if I got bad press for the team."

"Arlie, you busted up your eye late last night and this picture was already here this morning," Jillian said. "Not enough time for the mail. He delivered it. He knows where you live. Where we live."

"Everyone knows where we live," Arlie said. "You throw the biggest parties on campus. It doesn't mean I have a stalker."

"Want me to stay with you ladies?" David offered, rubbing his hands together. "I could crash on the couch. You could fix me breakfast. Massage my back in gratitude for my guard duty."

Arlie rolled her eyes. "Just show this to Teach. And don't worry, I don't want this one back."

He sat on the hard wooden chair and stared at the faded picture that held center stage on his wall and in his life. Number fifteen lived. And by now, she knew he'd found her.

The eye's swelling decreased and over the next few days shades of purple, green, and yellow appeared. With her vision returning to normal, Arlie's shooting percentages improved and she looked forward to the last home game before the tourney trip to South Carolina. On game night, in the locker room, Arlie slipped into her Lady Boilers number five and pulled back her hair into her usual pony tail. But when she glanced at herself in the mirror right before running out onto the court, she noticed the damaged eye in her reflection appeared on her right. It dawned on her suddenly that the sketch had been almost a mirror image. She recalled the ragged eye gash and the blood trail that the artist had drawn onto her jersey. Had AF hoped she'd feel pain? Was he out there watching her tonight? She tried to picture where he must have been sitting in the stadium to draw her from the perspective in the sketch. Then she shook her head. She had a game to focus on; couldn't let some crazed fan weird her out.

Once on the court, all thoughts, other than the task at hand, vanished. Arlie became the game; the ball, an extension of herself. She felt the special joy of an 'on' night—feeling to the bone that the shot would go in as she released the ball. When the buzzer signaled the end of the game, the Lady Boilermakers were on top. Amidst the cheering, as Arlie left the arena floor, she couldn't resist scanning the crowd. Was he there?

Arlie had invited David and Jillian to join her and her mom for Italian following the game. "Mitchlin thought he might know who did those sketches," David said after placing his order.

"What sketches?" Mrs. Messing asked.

Arlie threw David a scowl.

"What?" he asked. "Didn't you tell her?"

"Tell me now," Mrs. Messing said.

"It's no big deal, Mom. Just someone sending me drawings. It was going to be a surprise."

"Oops," David said. "I gave it away, didn't I?"

"She has a big fan," Jillian said. "One who likes to draw her at the game."

"Oh? I'd like to see them."

"I'm having the first one framed for your birthday. I got rid of the second. It, well, it wasn't as good."

Jillian held out her phone. "You can see them on here."

Arlie tried to grab the phone, missed and knocked over a glass of water. David laughed. "Not so graceful off the court, I see."

"Arliss Ann Messing," her mom said softly. "When did this happen?"

Arlie turned to her friends. "Thanks a lot, guys." To her mom she said, "It didn't happen like that. It was just a bump. No cut. You were there, remember?"

"But this shows you wearing number fifteen."

Arlie grabbed Jillian's iPhone and looked at the photo. "No, it's just hard to make out in this picture. See," she pointed to her jersey in the picture and showed her mom, "the artist drew a streak on my uniform next to my number five. But, I guess from here, it does look like a fifteen. Sort of."

"I'm staying tonight," Mrs. Messing said. "Don't even try to talk me out of it. Where are the sketches now?"

David had them both at his apartment. He'd finished framing the first, and had the second still rolled up in the mailing tube. He agreed to bring them over to Arlie's home for her mom to see as soon as they finished their meal.

"Want me to gift wrap number one?"

Arlie frowned and shook her head. "Just bring it over."

When David arrived with the sketches, Mrs. Messing was pacing the living room. David propped the framed sketch on a chair and started to open the mailing tube.

Arlie walked into the living room and gasped. "David, it's beautiful." The first sketch of Arlie sitting on the sidelines was bordered with a bold-red quilted silk, and framed with brushed silver that was embedded with long thin swirls of mirror in an intricate pattern. The final effect showed the viewer tiny fragments of themselves reflected at different angles.

"This needs candlelight," Jillian said. "Imagine thousands of tiny flickering lights coming from that frame."

"It's a gift for you, Mom. For your birthday."

"It is lovely, David," Mrs. Messing said, viewing the gift. "Thank you, Arlie." Then David emptied the second sketch out onto the table.

"Um, David?" Arlie drew out his name slowly. "How did this happen?" The red silk border of the framed sketch was the exact shade of the blood dripping from the wound drawn over Arlie's right eye in sketch number two.

He shrugged. "No idea. Just one of those weird coincidences, I guess." He compared the two colors more closely. "Red is, well," he paused, then shook his head and added, "This is odd, I gotta admit."

Late night notwithstanding, Arlie's next day began early as usual with her workout routine followed by team practice. When she returned home, exhausted and sweaty, she was surprised to see a Campus Police car in front of the house and David's bike on the lawn. She burst through the front door.

"Mom? Jillian? What's going on?"

"Another picture arrived while you were gone," Jillian said, meeting her at the front door. "Your mom called the cops."

Arlie covered her mouth with her hand and her eyes widened. "Why?" she asked.

"I also sent David to ask around – see if any of your neighbors saw who left it here," Arlie's mom said, joining Arlie and Jillian at the front door.

"Because of a picture? Come on, Mom, really? Where is it?"

"You don't want to see, Arlie. You and Jillian just get some stuff together. I'm putting you up in a motel for a few days."

Arlie was speechless for a moment and then turned to Jillian. "Did you see it?"

Jillian nodded. "She's right. You don't want to. I wish I hadn't."

"But, it was addressed to me, right? Who opened it?"

"I did," Jillian said. "Sorry, I couldn't wait. It's not like it was US mail or anything."

Arlie grabbed her roommate's arm. "Hand it over."

Jillian met her gaze, but caved a second later and handed over her phone. Arlie opened up the last photo taken and stared, not believing what she saw. This charcoal sketch bled more of the same shade of red that dotted number two and bordered number one. Again, the subject was seated at the player's bench. This time, however, her head was thrown back, mouth open in a scream, eyes staring overhead. A pearl handled knife, covered in blood lay on her lap. Her chest was bleeding from two open stab wounds positioned right above the number on her uniform. The AF signature hid beneath a pool of blood in the lower right corner of the sketch.

Arlie's hands began to shake and her voice quavered. "Who is sending me these? What kind of sicko is this guy?"

Two police officers entered the front foyer area from the dining room and were introduced to Arlie as Officers Purcell and Adams of the Purdue University Campus police. Officer Purcell, who appeared to be close to Arlie's and Jillian's age, carried two mailing tubes under his arm and looked at her face closely. "Seems like you're the one in the pictures, all right. Can you tell me what happened to your eye, Arlie?"

Arlie described how she was fouled at the game. "It wasn't like in the picture at all. I went up as another player was coming down. No cut. No blood. Happens all the time."

"Has anyone threatened you, Ms. Messing?" Officer Adams asked. He was old enough to be Purcell's father.

"No, never. It's just these pictures are getting…crazy. Kind of freaking me out."

"I think this latest picture is definitely a threat," Mrs. Messing said. "It's showing Arlie stabbed." Her voice rose in a reedy crescendo of emotion.

Officer Adams spoke to Mrs. Messing. "I'm sorry, Ma'am. Sending someone a drawing's not a crime. There's nothing we can do at the moment."

"But," Mrs. Messing said, "surely you can try to find out who's doing this. It's intimidation. This person is stalking my daughter."

Officer Adams nodded. "I can understand your concern, Ma'am. I have a daughter in college myself. But, nothing illegal has happened yet. These artistic types — sometimes they push the limits."

Young Officer Purcell pointed toward the front door. "That boyfriend of yours? David, right? He's an artist, isn't he?"

Arlie nodded. "He's a friend and an artist. So?"

"Thought so. Think he might know who's sending these?" Officer Purcell asked.

Arlie stared at the frosted window next to the front door. "He doesn't know."

"Maybe he did them himself? Did you think of that?" Officer Purcell persisted.

"That's crazy," Arlie said, returning her attention to the officer. "It's not David." But she thought about the perfect match of the red matting and the red blood. She thought about the second image showing her injury as a mirror of reality and all the tiny mirror slivers in the frame. Could she be wrong about him?

Just then David burst through the front door with a ten year old kid in tow. Arlie recognized the kid from around the neighborhood but didn't know his name.

"This is Doug," David said. "He saw the guy with the mailing tube, so I'm going to try the sketch artist thing."

"You saw the person who left this?" Arlie asked Doug.

The kid shook his head and looked at the floor. "I...I left it. But, I saw the guy who paid me."

Arlie cocked an eyebrow at Officer Purcell. It obviously wasn't David.

"Got any paper, Jillian?" David asked.

"You bet." She ran to her bedroom and returned with a notepad and pencil. David took the boy into the dining room and began asking descriptive questions. Arlie and Jillian stood in the doorway and watched them.

Officer Adams wiped his brow with a handkerchief. "This reminds me of a case we had here, oh, ten or twelve years ago. Before your time, Purcell."

Officer Purcell raised an eyebrow. "What was that?"

"Kid from somewhere in Southern Indiana came here to play basketball, like Arlie. She got a couple of drawings sent to her, too. Scared her so bad she packed up and quit school. Not my idea of a joke, I can tell you."

"Did you find out who sent them?" Mrs. Messing asked.

Officer Adams shook his head. "Never did, Ma'am. But now that I think back, she looked a lot like your daughter."

It wasn't long before David let out a low whistle. "Hey, I know this guy," he said.

"Who is it?" Arlie asked, darting into the dining room.

David turned his sketch around to show everyone. "Meet my art advisor. Professor Mitchlin."

Mrs. Messing looked triumphant. "He's going down. You don't mess with a Messing."

He balanced the pearl handled knife on his knees. A thousand times washed, a thousand times polished. He hadn't wanted her to leave. He hadn't expected her to control his thoughts for so long. Now, after all these years, she'd come back to the game. He realized she'd been playing him. His anger exploded and he hurled the knife toward the sketch he loved so completely. The knife buried to the hilt directly above the fifteen on her jersey. The thump of the impact echoed in his mind.

He stared at the sketch for several minutes, then rose slowly, deliberately from his seat and walked over to his work bench. He carefully chose the brush and the bold-red oil and turned toward the wall.

It was time to complete the picture.

It was time to end the game.

Bob Knight

Brenda Robertson Stewart

Robert Montgomery "Bob" Knight was originally from Ohio. He played basketball at Orrville High School and under Hall of Fame coach, Fred Taylor, at Ohio State University. Knight was a reserve on the team that included future Hall of Famers John Havlicek and Jerry Lucas. He graduated with a degree in history and government in 1962. He coached junior varsity basketball before accepting a position at Army in 1963.

Two years later, he was named head coach. One of his players was Hall of Fame coach Mike Krsyzewski. When Indiana University was searching for a new coach in 1971, they turned to rising star Bob Knight.

Knight endeared himself to Indiana fans with his disciplined approach to basketball and the high graduation rate of his players. Dick Vitale dubbed Knight "The General." In 1976, the Hoosiers were undefeated at 32-0 and crushed Michigan in the final NCAA championship game. Knight's Hoosiers would win two more national championships — in 1981 and in 1987. Knight led the USA team to gold in the 1984 Olympics with Michael Jordon on the team. He won eleven Big Ten conference titles and is only one of four coaches to win NCAA, NIT, and Olympic championships.

Bob Knight was elected to the Naismith Memorial Basketball Hall of Fame as a coach in 1991, his second year of eligibility. He told the committee to take his name off the list since he wasn't elected the first year he was eligible, but his request was denied.

Always a coach known for his quick temper, Knight was placed on a zero tolerance policy at Indiana University in May of 2000 following complaints against him. In September 2000, an incident allegedly occurred involving a student, and Bob Knight was fired by then president of Indiana University, Myles Brand. The next day, Knight said goodbye to 6,000 supporters in Dunn Meadow in Bloomington. He later took a position as coach of the Texas Tech University Red Raiders and in 2007 achieved his 880th career win passing retired North Carolina coach Dean Smith for the most career NCAA Division I men's college basketball wins.

SNOWPLOWED

Tony Perona

Indiana State Senator Garrett Snow wadded the No. 55 Baronville High School basketball jersey into a ball and tossed it in a high arc across the room. It landed in the middle of the wastebasket. "Nothing but net," he said quietly, though the door to his Statehouse office was closed. Looking up, he realized the mini-blinds to the windows in the hall were open. He rose from the chair and checked the view. No one there. Not unexpected, since the legislature was out of session. Relieved, he snatched the now-empty padded shipping envelope and stuffed it in the wastebasket on top of the gold and brown jersey.

He wasn't going to get worried about the numbers—his 55th class reunion was coming up and it had been 55 years since the kid from the rival high school who'd worn the No. 55 jersey hanged himself. Still, he wondered who was behind the mailing. He hadn't heard a thing about the suicide since he'd left Hampton High School.

If he had any regrets about his glory days in basketball, it was that he hadn't gotten a college scholarship or made the team at Indiana University as a walk-on. Not that it had hampered him. Life after high school had been a relentless, upward progression in business and politics. For years now he'd been the state senator for a district that included Fishers, one of the most affluent cities in Indiana.

He took some solace in the fact that his signature move at Hampton High had received its own name. It occurred during the sectional championship game. Garrett was assigned to guard the skinny, hot-handed forward, No. 55, who had single-handedly evened the game. With only minutes to go, Garrett and his teammates let the smaller man get into the lane and dribble for a

14

layup. Garrett, his big body only a step behind the shooter, went up with the guy and leveled him from behind. Sent him sprawling into the stands. Shook him up so much he could hardly shoot the final minute of the game. Garrett fouled out, but he became a local hero for executing the "Snowplow." Hampton High won the game.

Weeks later No. 55 was found hanging from the rafters of his family barn. Garrett knew the kid's name well, though he wished he could forget it. Al LeBlanc. Everyone clucked about how sad it was, and a few even questioned whether the suicide had been a result of what happened in the game. That line of thinking fortunately had never been pursued. Garrett refused to feel any remorse about the death. The game might have turned on that one act, but it didn't make him a killer. Why the kid decided to commit suicide wasn't his problem.

Not really. And certainly not without any proof. In 55 years, none had surfaced.

And now today he received this jersey in the mail.

Garrett glanced at his calendar. He had a two o'clock meeting with Charlotte Reinhardt, another Hampton High connection, and it was almost two. He barely remembered her. She hadn't run in *his* crowd. She'd been one of the artsy-fartsy types. *Charlotte Reinhardt? Please...* He rifled through more of his inbox, made sure there were no more padded envelopes. The phone rang and he picked it up. "Garrett."

"Senator, your two o'clock is here." Garrett recognized the voice of the head receptionist on the lower floor. He sighed. "Have my intern escort her to my office," he said. "She can wait if I'm not here." He hung up and went to the men's restroom down the short hall from his office. A janitor turned the corner ahead of him and preceded him through the door. It was a little brazen of the janitor to use the restroom in the office area, which was unofficially "staff-only." But how do you say that without coming off as an elitist?

The first thing Francine McNamara noticed when she and her best friend Charlotte Reinhardt entered State Senator Garrett

Snow's office was how cramped it was. The door opened into the middle of a small room, a rectangular table and four chairs to the right, the Senator's desk and a chair to the left. All were solid maple. The sense of claustrophobia extended to the walls, which were covered in framed, signed photographs. Snow certainly chummed it up with the famous—major political figures, professional athletes, and celebrities posing with him adorned the walls.

With only a little room for the women to move, Francine was tempted to sit but she wasn't sure of the protocol.

The short, thin intern provided no clues. "The Senator will be here in a moment," he said, smiling at Charlotte before he left. Francine thought he seemed nervous. She also noticed that he had virtually ignored her, making polite conversation with Charlotte as he led them up the stairs. She thought he didn't have much of a future at the Statehouse if he didn't overcome those shortcomings.

She watched Charlotte take in the room. "You'd think being a state senator for so long would get you something bigger than this," Francine whispered.

"Most of the other senators only have cubicles, so don't feel sorry for him," Charlotte said. "Anyway, I'm certain the walk-in closet at his palatial Fishers estate is at least twice as big as this. That probably compensates. I've known him since grade school, and he's always been the type to need compensating. I bet he has a small ..."

"... Remind me again why I'm here," Francine said, redirecting Charlotte's train of thought.

"You're here because old Gary needs to be put in his place over this single-class basketball nonsense, and I want a witness in case he's still the same bully my brother Mel and his friends came to know and hate."

Francine studied Charlotte's defiant posture. Though Charlotte was a good 6 inches shorter than her own 5' 10" height, she was stout and radiated a bulldog tenacity that made her formidable. The two inches of silver curls piled on her head by the beauty parlor helped, too.

Francine's large, dark-framed glasses slipped a bit on her nose. She adjusted them. "Mel seems to have done pretty well for himself, and that was a long time ago." Charlotte's younger brother, who was only a few inches taller than her and had been a string bean in high school, was now a successful character actor. He'd appeared in films with the likes of Sean Connery, Jane Fonda, and Dustin Hoffman.

"Some wounds never heal," Charlotte said, and for a moment her face became pained. Then she seemed to shake it off, like she needed to get down to business. "There's one more thing I should tell you about Gary. It shouldn't come up, but just in case something odd happens, you need to know that he liked to embarrass people. Sometimes he would stage improvisational skits, usually designed to make you the butt of a joke. He'd do it in a way that if you didn't go along, it made you look worse. Thank heavens he didn't have the video technology we have today."

Francine gave her a skeptical look. "He wouldn't do such a childish thing nowadays, would he? I mean, he's a state senator."

She patted Francine on the hand. "I'm sure he's grown out of it. I probably shouldn't even have mentioned it. But if something weird should happen, remember that it's me he's trying to embarrass, not you. So I'd need for you to play along. Just trust me to get him in the end ..."

Charlotte halted when the subject of her rants stepped into the room. Francine had seen him on television, but he was taller than she'd expected. Her husband Jonathan was six feet and Snow was surely a head taller than that. His build was square shouldered, and his reddish-blond hair, probably dyed, was buzzed short. He had wrinkles, but what really detracted from his rugged handsomeness was a jagged scar that ran across his cheek. It made him seem dangerous. Francine wondered what he'd done to earn the scar.

"Charlotte Reinhardt," Snow said, a politician's smile pasted on his face. "I couldn't believe it when my secretary told me you'd scheduled an appointment. It's been what, 50 years?" He tried to give her a hearty handshake, but she dodged it.

"Fifty-five. You would know that if you came to any of the Hampton High reunions, Gary," she said.

"Too many people live in the past. I've just never been one to dwell on past glories. And I go by 'Garrett' now."

"Mind if I sit down, Gary?" Charlotte asked, not waiting for permission but pulling up one of the solid maple chairs and easing herself into it. "I've always been curious. You were a big basketball star our senior year. Don't tell me you don't want to come back and relive some glory days."

"As I said, it's all in the past." He turned his attention to Francine. "Garrett Snow." He stuck out his hand.

When she moved to meet his grip, he engulfed her hand in his paw, squeezed too tightly and held on too long. *What is this, hand-to-hand combat?* She understood Charlotte's decision to dodge it.

"Francine McNamara. Nice to meet you," she said, though she didn't like to lie.

"So what can I do for you ladies?"

Charlotte leaned forward. "We're here to say that we don't approve of your continued persistence of this silly, single-class basketball nonsense. That action was settled more than fifteen years ago when the IHSAA voted to go to a multi-class format."

Snow folded his arms over his chest. "You didn't need to come all the way downtown to tell me that. You could have emailed or come to one of my forums with the IHSAA chief. Didn't we have one in Brownsburg? That's where you live now, isn't it?"

Francine was impressed he knew where they lived. But then, he'd probably researched Charlotte to find out if she was a constituent. Brownsburg was on the other side of Indianapolis from Fishers, so he didn't need to kowtow.

"Trying to rally public support for single-class basketball is nothing more than an opportunity for you to extoll the virtues of bullying," Charlotte said. "Your district covers one of the richest schools in the state. You regularly beat schools in your own class by huge margins. Going back to single-class is nothing more than legalizing bullying."

"Perhaps you're not aware of the Milan miracle ..."

Charlotte stood. "For Pete's sake, Gary, the Milan Miracle occurred in 1954 and has never been repeated. It's ancient history.

It's one reason the high school athletic association changed from single-class to multi-class. Large schools like Fishers and Carmel or even Brownsburg have resources available to them that smaller schools don't. Carmel's bench would blow a Milan out of the water today."

Garrett took two steps closer to the women. "I think we should let the voters decide that, don't you?"

The small room felt even smaller as he loomed over them, but Charlotte didn't flinch. "No, I don't. I think people who work with kids regularly and know the score should be the ones to decide matters like this. That's the purpose of the ISHAA."

Garrett's smile lost wattage. "Thank you for coming in, Charlotte. It was nice to see you again. I'll have my intern show you out."

"I'm not sure we've finished discussing this yet, Gary."

"Oh, yes we have." Snow buzzed for the intern.

A young man nearly as tall as Snow came in. His reddish-blond hair was clipped short like Snow's, and he had the same scar across his cheek. He wore chinos and a woven shirt under a blazer. If he'd been dressed in period clothes, Francine would have guessed he was Garrett's high school twin. He shut the door behind him. "Yes, Senator?"

Snow appeared startled. He stepped close for a better look. "You're not Al. Who are you?"

The young man frowned at Snow. "I'm Gary. I'm your intern cadet assistant. Are you okay today, Senator?"

"What the hell is going on here?" Snow hit the buzzer several times in annoyance. This time the intern who'd let them in originally opened the door. He was now dressed in a black suit and tie. He, too, closed the door behind him. "What can I do for you, sir?" he asked.

Snow exhaled in relief. "I thought I was going crazy, Alan. Would you please show these ladies out? And … Gary, too."

"I'll show them out," said the young Gary.

"I don't think so," Alan said. His eyes blazed in irritation at the other young man as he turned to Charlotte and Francine. "This way, please."

Young Gary cut in front of him and delivered a pancake block like he was an offensive lineman protecting the door and Alan was a defensive player trying to get through. Alan fell back against a chair and pushed it into the wall. His arms windmilled. They caught the edge of the table and scattered papers everywhere. Alan landed on his tailbone. He scrambled to his feet but Gary pancaked him again. This time his head hit the floor and he lay still.

"What are you doing?" Snow yelled. Young Gary eyed him with a mixture of surprise and confusion. Then he threw open the door and ran out of the office. The door slammed behind him

Francine straightened up in surprise. Her instincts told her to go help the intern, but she had a suspicion things were not as they seemed. She leaned her mouth to Charlotte's ear. "He didn't hit the floor that hard. Is this …?"

"Improv. Good thinking," Charlotte whispered back. "Remember, let me lead." She stepped back and pointed to the intern on the floor. "Good thing you're a nurse, Francine."

"Yes," Francine said, relieved to have a part she knew something about. "I am a nurse. I should look at him."

Charlotte nudged her toward the body.

"What's going on here?" Snow demanded.

Francine checked Alan's neck for a pulse. "He's alive," she said.

"Gary and I will go for help." Charlotte pulled on Snow's arm. She opened the door and pushed him out ahead of her. "Maybe you can catch your cadet assistant," she told him.

"He's not my cadet assistant!" Snow snapped at Charlotte but Francine saw something else in his mannerism. Snow was scared.

The last time Garrett Snow had heard the words, "cadet assistant," was at Hampton High, where the term had been used for upper class students who helped teachers for one or two semesters. It gave them a small measure of teaching experience, presumably to help them decide whether they wanted to pursue the profession.

But in the physical education department it worked differently. There, it was a way for jocks to get out of boring study halls. Garrett had become a cadet assistant to the basketball coach his first semester junior year. The coach taught PE. The thing Garrett loved most was that he was bigger and stronger than the incoming freshman boys, the largest number of whom hadn't hit their growth spurt yet. That gave him a certain physical advantage.

The first six weeks of the school year the weather was still good. "We'll take 'em outside, line 'em up, and play flag football," Coach Crumley said after lecturing the class on the rudimentary aspects of football. Crumley was a big guy, too, not nearly as tall as Snow, but heavier. Snow liked the Coach's wicked sense of humor. As a cadet assistant, he was supposed to be in the mix of students, "helping teach." Coach assigned the scrawniest freshmen the task of blocking Snow. Day after day, Snow enjoyed putting the freshmen on their backs.

It got even better during the second six weeks. That was mostly dodge ball. Those were the good old days, when there were no teaching standards for PE, at least none that bothered Coach Crumley. Snow could throw the ball so hard he'd leave welts on the freshmen. Al LeBlanc was one of them. Back then no one would have called it bullying. It was just part of gym class.

Garrett tried to recall the pleasure of seeing Al's face twisting with anger and frustration, knowing there was nothing he could do about it. For some reason, the face he kept seeing was that of his intern, Alan. Probably because both had the same first name. LeBlanc had disappeared before the third six weeks started, which was when they would have played basketball. Transferred to Baronville. The given reason had to do with Al's father moving closer to his job. But the real reason had been buried. Snow's father had seen to that.

Al had suffered some minor internal injuries from Snow's "teaching." The doctor believed in time they would heal, but he wanted regular follow-up visits Al's family couldn't afford. Al's father threatened to sue for the medical care. Snow's father, a politician who didn't need negative publicity, proposed an agreement. He would pay Al's bills in exchange for silence and no lawsuit. The doctor would give them all of the records and photos. Al's father also insisted a psychiatrist be engaged to treat his son for the trauma caused by "taking his lumps." Snow figured the move and the psychiatric care must've worked in some way, because LeBlanc played on the Baronville basketball team the next year. Until after the sectional. And no one could tie Snow to the suicide, not without a suicide note or the records from the psychiatrist.

Or a witness to the last time he'd seen LeBlanc.

Charlotte managed to get Snow into the hallway. She spotted someone in uniform down by the restroom. "Help!" she barked. As he hurried toward them, Charlotte asked Snow, "Did you see anywhere your cadet assistant could have gone?"

He seemed stunned by what was going on. "Stop calling him that. I've never seen him before, and I have no idea where he went."

"What is it, ma'am?" The man smoothed his mustache. He looked to be around 50, with salt and pepper hair that needed to be cut.

Charlotte nodded her head toward Snow. "We were in the senator's office and one of his assistants attacked the other one. The bigger one knocked the smaller one down, and he hit his head something awful. I'm afraid he might have a concussion. The bigger one ran off."

The officer activated the mike at his shoulder. "We have a reported assault in Senator Snow's office. I'm investigating now." He paused to ask Charlotte and Snow, "What did he look like?"

"He was tall," Charlotte said. "Like the senator here, only maybe not quite as tall. He was built like a house, too."

"Any distinguishing features?" He readied his finger at the mike button.

"He had a scar on his cheek. A long one."

The officer looked at Senator Snow's face, saw his scar. "Really?"

Francine worried when Charlotte left the room. Now it was just her and the intern, and she wasn't sure what was going on.

It might be improv, but what if it wasn't? Should she call 911? She checked Alan again. He wasn't limp like he would have been if he were unconscious. In fact, he was nearly as tense as she was. His pulse was rapid and his breaths were coming quickly, too, like hers. She wished Charlotte hadn't said anything about video. What if there were cameras?

Alan's suit jacket had fallen open, and she noticed that his shirt was too large and had a bulky layer underneath. She unbuttoned the shirt—no reaction from Alan—and pulled it to his side to see what he was wearing. It was an old basketball jersey, one from Baronville High School. The number on it was 55. She knew Baronville was near Hampton where Charlotte had grown up, but she didn't know it had a high school.

Alan stirred. "Chest hurts," he groaned. He settled back into his unconscious-appearing state.

As hard as the big assistant intern hit him, it ought to hurt, she thought. She loosed his belt buckle and pulled up the jersey. That was when she gasped. There were bruises all over his body. He looked like he'd been hit with something. She gently touched a bruise and the make-up smeared.

She looked at her finger. Alan muttered something.

"What?"

He muttered again. Francine looked around. Now she was sure it was some kind of skit. Were they being filmed? How long did she have to play this part? She bent down to hear him.

"Photos," he whispered, before becoming unconscious again.

A dozen things ran through Francine's mind. What did he mean by that? She checked again out of the corner of her eye for a camera, trying not to be obvious. She decided it could be anywhere. What did he mean by photos?

She reached for her purse and pulled out her iPhone and began taking photos of the bruises.

Charlotte led the officer back into Snow's office, Snow trailing behind them looking bewildered. Francine was leaning over Alan's body, which was not moving. She was snapping photos with her smartphone.

"What are you doing?" Charlotte asked.

Francine cleared her throat. She hoped she was being convincing. "Taking photos of this young man's body. It's covered with bruises."

"Bruises?" asked the officer.

"This is my friend Francine," Charlotte said. "She's a nurse."

"Retired," Francine replied. Then she wondered if she was allowed to say that, or if she should have been playing a nurse that was still licensed. She took a deep breath. "He keeps going in and out of consciousness," she said. "He took a bad fall."

"Twice," Charlotte added. "Gary flattened him like a Panini sandwich, and when he got back up, Gary did it again."

Alan's eyes fluttered and he coughed. Francine scooted back to give him room. The young man slowly propped himself on his side using his arms.

The officer pushed the table toward the windows so he could kneel next to him. "Are you okay, son?"

Alan shook his head. "I'm hurt."

The officer pulled out a notebook. "How did you get those bruises, son?"

Alan glanced at Snow, groaned, then laid back down and went into his unconscious state again.

The officer turned to Francine. "In your opinion, how did he get these bruises?"

Francine panicked. What was she supposed to say? She glanced at Charlotte, who seemed to be urging her on with her eyes, so she settled on answering like a nurse. That was all she knew about the role she was playing. "He seems to have been hit repeatedly."

He scribbled that in the notebook. "Up close, like with a fist or a hard object?"

Francine hated improv. Why couldn't he be asking Charlotte something? "No, this is more of a welt, like something was thrown hard at him from a distance."

"Like a ball?" The law man reached into the young man's suit coat and pulled out a wallet.

Francine shrugged. It was possible. And she liked sticking to short answers. "Yes, possibly a ball."

The officer found the young man's wallet. He read the name off the drivers' license and looked at Snow for approval. "Says his name is Al LeBlanc."

Al LeBlanc, thought Snow. The damn intern even looked like him. And what the hell was he doing wearing that damn Baronville jersey, the No. 55? What was going on? Who were these people, and what were they after?

"That's not his name. His name is Alan Thompson," Snow protested.

The officer put the wallet back in the suit coat. "Really? How long has he been working for you?"

"He's one of our semester interns. He's from Ball State. His last day is coming up. Or maybe it's today. I don't know. My secretary would, but she has the day off."

"So you don't know much about him?"

"Not that much, no."

"And you have no idea where he got the bruises?"

Snow wanted to yell at the cop to stop him asking questions. The incident happened in his office but it had nothing to do with him. He was sure Charlotte Reinhardt must be behind it. It was too coincidental that she showed up after he received the jersey, and then this little drama started playing out. But his shirt was getting damp under his armpits, and he was starting to worry that maybe some link had been discovered that tied him to the night of LeBlanc's death. But that would have come up a long time ago, wouldn't it? Snow began to wonder about the jersey that was in his trash can.

"I don't know anything about any bruises," Snow said. He tried to move nonchalantly to the side of his desk where he could see into the trash can. He wanted to make sure the jersey was covered by the padded envelope.

Charlotte marched up to him. "Is there something you're looking for, Gary?"

"No." He moved away from the desk and back to the officer, hoping Charlotte would follow. But what if she knew the jersey was in the trash can? What would she do?

The officer continued to search the intern's pockets. He pulled out a thin book. He opened it and read the first few pages. "It's his diary."

"Look," Snow told him, "I know you have a job to do, but the young man probably needs to be seen by a doctor. And what about the person who assaulted him? Shouldn't you be looking for him?"

The officer eyed him suspiciously, then went back to the diary. "This is interesting. Apparently someone named Gary has been bullying him." He flipped through the pages, scanning. "And it's been going on for weeks." He skipped to the end. "Here's the last entry. It says he plans to confront Gary about the things he's been doing."

Garrett sucked in a breath. He was starting to piece things together now. These people knew. They knew that Al had asked him to come to the barn that night, meet him alone. Or were they guessing?

"There's no diary," he said.

The officer held up the book. "Then what do you call this?"

Garrett wanted to snatch it out of his hands and check it, but he didn't want his fingerprints on it. God, he had to think. Even if they had his diary, Alan couldn't have made an entry that told what happened. Alan had *died* that night. He saw it.

"I don't believe it's a real diary."

Charlotte said, "It's as real as the scar on Gary's face."

She brought up the scar. Did they know Alan had carried a knife? Had he mentioned anything about it in the diary?

The officer didn't wait for him to respond. "Let me summarize what I've learned here. Al LeBlanc," he motioned toward the prone intern, "has bruises all over his body, which would be indicative of someone bullying him over a long time. We have witnesses to the fact that at least in part this punishment was inflicted by a large man named Gary, who was seen repeatedly knocking him to the ground. One of Gary's noticeable features is a long scar on his face. Plus, we have Al's diary which logs the continued bullying by this Gary. Is that correct?"

"What do you mean by witnesses?"

"These two ladies are witnesses to what happened."

"And we have proof," said Charlotte.

"You don't have proof of anything."

"But we do," she insisted. "We have the diary, and we have photos of the bruises which prove what Al has written in the diary."

Snow's mind raced. He thought his dad had taken care of the medical records. But what if he hadn't? Or what if the doctor had made copies? Or what if Al's parents had taken photos of the bruises? And what if they'd surfaced after all these years? If Al named him in the diary for all the things he'd done to him, and there was no reason to believe he hadn't, could they link the bullying to him and perhaps to the death?

"You don't know what happened," Snow said.

The officer was quick to counter. "But you do?"

Snow stewed about that. He *did* know what happened. And it was clear they didn't. They were fishing with this little charade, hoping to trip him up. But he hadn't killed Al that night. Not physically. Al had tried to talk to him about how he'd been hurting people and what it had made them feel like, and Al actually expected him at the end of this little lecture to show some respect. Snow had ridiculed him instead. Berated him and told him he'd never be anything more than a loser. Al had gotten so riled he'd pulled out a knife. The move caught Snow off guard, and Al slashed him across the cheek. Snow disarmed him and beat him around a bit. Dominated him. Humiliated him.

And then the damned kid ran up to the rafters where there was a noose waiting and he hanged himself while Garrett watched. A final shot at revenge.

Snow was horrified at first. But then he realized—he hadn't killed Al. Al was just weak, like so many other people he'd known. He pushed it out of his head, covered his tracks, and went home. Al wouldn't get to him.

But he knew today's world was different. Not everyone would see it the way he did. If these people could link him to Al's death with photos and a diary, it didn't matter that LeBlanc really did commit suicide. He would be as guilty of killing Al as if he had shoved his head in the noose and dropped him off the top beam.

"Let's face it," Charlotte said. "This Gary is guilty of severe bullying. And we can prove it. We have the diary. We just need to get him."

Francine wondered when this little improv skit would ever end.

"Yes," she said, thinking that she might be able to help it along. She nervously held up her iPhone. "We have the photos."

Snow gave her a scowl that made her swallow hard. Maybe she should have kept her mouth shut.

The senator bent down to talk to Charlotte. "What do you want?" he said through gritted teeth.

Charlotte looked puzzled. "What do you mean?"

"Don't be obtuse. You want something. What will it take for you to get skinny boy to a doctor and forget all about this alleged incident?"

Francine tried to stay in character. She was more baffled than ever about what was really going on, but she knew she should be shocked at the direction this skit was taking. "Are you saying you had something to do with the condition of this young man? And you're trying to bribe us?"

Charlotte gave a cough that covered what Francine thought was a laugh. She was annoyed by Charlotte's reaction, but she couldn't stop looking at Snow, whose smoldering anger was clearly building.

"I'm admitting nothing," he told her, "and you know you can't prove the thing you're trying to prove. I just want the door closed and you out of here."

Once again Francine was confused. She had no idea how to respond. *Whose line is it anyway?* she thought.

Charlotte cocked her head back and studied Snow pensively. "I'm not saying there's an answer here to past sins, Gary. But I do think you should stop trying to reinvigorate an old system that gives big schools the opportunity to bully smaller ones in the almighty name of sports."

He stared at her. Reached toward her, then stopped. And stared some more. Francine thought it was a good thing this was improv. Or that an officer was there. Or that maybe they were being filmed. Or all three.

"That's what you want?"

"So little," Charlotte responded, "for what you've done."

Snow pointed at the door. "Go."

Charlotte said, "Then you've agreed?"

"Just go."

Charlotte smiled. "Francine, let's get this boy to a doctor."

Francine already had Alan by one arm. Charlotte took the other and they walked out the Senator's door, exited the secretary's empty office and down the hall. The officer followed.

Before they got too far down the hall, Snow stuck his head out the door and said, "The IHSAA principals weren't going to change their minds anyway."

Charlotte turned around. "You legislators need to stop distracting the public with stupid issues like single-class basketball. If you want to be useful, tackle the real problems, the ones we elect you to handle."

The officer guided them down the stairs. They slowly made their way out of the Statehouse to a dark sedan waiting in the parking lot. Francine helped Alan into the backseat.

"I'm okay, really," he told Francine once he was seated.

"This is Alan Thompson," Charlotte said by way of introduction. "He's really the grand nephew of Al LeBlanc."

"And Al LeBlanc is?"

"He was my friend," the officer said. "Please hold these." He gave Francine his radio and earpiece.

They were surprisingly light. Francine turned them over in her hand. They possessed amazing detail, but they were nothing more than plastic reproductions, the kind someone who had access to film-studio props might obtain.

The officer pulled off his mustache and the hairpiece. The plentiful hair had made him look twenty-five years younger. He took glasses out of his pocket and put them on. "Mel?" Francine exclaimed. "You were the police officer?"

Charlotte's brother waved a finger at her. "Not a police officer. Impersonating a policeman would have been too risky if things had gone badly. So I tried to look like one without really being one. We figured as long as we kept Garrett off balance he wouldn't notice."

The large young man who played the young Gary skipped down the steps to the Statehouse and folded himself into the seat next to Al. "This is my friend Pete," Al said. "He and Mel went in this morning dressed like janitors."

"Why did you do this?" Francine asked.

Mel raised an eyebrow. "You know how interested you are in checking off bucket list items? I just took care of my longtime #1."

He explained that Al LeBlanc had been his friend during freshman year in high school. Both of them had been bullied by Gary Snow during Coach Crumley's dreaded PE class, but Snow had taken particular pleasure in Al's misery.

"Why did it bother him so much and not you?" Francine asked.

"Al was an athlete who was reaching puberty late. He didn't like it that Gary didn't respect him. I, on the other hand, was short, skinny, unathletic and named 'Melvin.' I'd lived with that kind of stuff all my life."

"My family made some mistakes in letting the senator's father bury the truth in exchange for helping my uncle Al cope with what Snow had done," the young Alan said. "But it was working fine until the sectional game."

Charlotte picked up the story line. "When Al had the chance to show up Coach Crumley's team, he jumped on it. He'd become a decent basketball player with a wicked outside shot. That night his shooting was inspired. But in the last minute Gary bullied him again and he fell apart." She told her about the "Snowplow."

Mel sat down in the driver's seat. "His collapse haunted him. I could never find a way to pin his suicide on Gary, but I knew he was a big part of it. Today's little victory against his pet project to reinstate single-class basketball doesn't fully satisfy, but I think it's the best revenge I'm going to get."

"And my family could get," Alan said. "I couldn't believe it when I applied to be an intern and was assigned to him. We were selling the old family farm and had just found the diary, so it was like the heavens opened. Charlotte's been like an aunt to me and she had known Al, so I went to her. She enlisted Mel."

Charlotte buckled in the passenger seat up front. "The unfortunate part was that the diary was a mixed bag. Al's writing was often illegible, and when it wasn't, it didn't make a lot of sense. You got a sense of the pain, but often he expressed forgiveness. We only knew from the last entry that he planned to talk to Gary privately. Wanted to confront him with how he was hurting people and ask for his respect. We had to work around those unknowns. If we could have gotten some kind of confession out of Snow, that would have been perfect, but we didn't expect it. He's a pretty cagey politician."

Francine buckled in next to Al's friend. "I understand why all of you are involved, but why me? Why didn't you clue me in?"

"You were our 'out,'" Charlotte said. "We needed one person who could be counted on to testify to the truth in case it blew up in our faces. We all had an agenda. You didn't. A judge would listen to you."

"And by the way," Mel added. "You were great."

Francine glared at Charlotte. "I don't feel great. I feel like I was used."

Charlotte turned to look at her from the front seat. "But just think about how Gary must feel. You were only buffaloed. He got snowplowed."

Bobby Leonard

Brenda Robertson Stewart

William Robert (Slick) Leonard played high school basketball at Terre Haute Gerstmeyer and played collegiate basketball at Indiana University under coach Branch McCracken. In 1953, Leonard hit the game-winning free throws giving Indiana the NCAA national championship. After college, he played four years for the Lakers in Minnesota and one year after the team moved to Los Angeles. He spent two years with the Chicago Zephyrs where he served as a player and coach the second year. The team moved to Baltimore and Leonard served as coach for one more year.

Leonard became coach of the Indiana Pacers, an American Basketball Association team, in 1969 and served in that capacity for 12 years, the last four after the ABA-NBA merged. He led the Pacers to three ABA championships.

In 1985, Leonard returned to the Pacers as a color commentator first on television and then on radio where he remains. In March, 2011, Leonard suffered a heart attack following the Pacers road victory over the New York Knicks and was given an indefinite period of time to recover before he returned to the radio.

Leonard is a member of the Indiana Basketball Hall of Fame and was the first person inducted into the Indiana University Sports Hall of Fame. He was honored as a member of Indiana University's All-Century Basketball Team.

Leonard's trademark phrase is "Boom, baby!"

BLEEDING PURPLE

D. L. Hartmann

Muncie, Indiana
March 20, 1954

Suellen shuddered at John's decorating. Inside their three-bedroom, bath & half ranch house, large purple ribbons decorated the lamps on end tables, the window frames, and just about everything else. A large sign in purple letters covered the mirror over the couch: "Muncie Loves Her Bearcats." But Suellen left everything in place. John would take it all down after the game; at least she hoped so.

The telephone shrilled. With a sigh, she scooped the purple ribbon up so she could hold the handset. "Hello."

"Hello, sweetie. It's your favorite aunt."

Suellen gripped the phone. "What on earth are you doin' calling me in the middle of the day?" she asked. "Is Mama all right?"

"Oh, you silly girl, don't you worry. Your mama is fine as frog hair. She's off to church cooking for a funeral dinner tomorrow."

Suellen relaxed her grip on the phone. "It kind of scared me when I heard your voice, thought maybe Mama was sick or something. So, she's still working at the church—that's good. I swear, that woman is a saint. I can't wait to see you all. I'm catching the bus in the morning, so I'll be there by dark."

"That's good, sweetie. I just called to be sure you're still coming. We're all excited to see you. How is everything there in Muncie? Your mama thought you sounded funny on the phone on your birthday."

Suellen pulled the cord to let her take the phone to the couch. "Oh, everything is okay here. Really. I shouldn't have called Mama and worried her, but I was kind of upset when we had to go to a basketball game on my birthday. You know John takes basketball real serious. Fact is, we're having a little party here tonight so he can watch the state final game with his friends. I swear, if I left right now, John wouldn't miss me until the game is over."

Mary Beth laughed. "Men. They're all alike. Your daddy was plumb foolish over baseball."

Suellen gave a little snort. "I remember." She heard the sound of a key and looked at the front door. "I got to go Aunt Mary Beth, it's John home from the bank. Talk to you later. Love you lots. Don't you worry about me, hear?"

John shoved the door shut with his hip so he didn't have to set down the case of beer. "Ready for the party," he said. He put the beer in the kitchen and returned to pull off his overcoat and hang it up. He ran his hand through his thinning gray hair and gave Suellen a quick kiss.

She started toward the kitchen, then stopped. "Where are the snacks? Did you pick up chips and pretzels to go with all that beer?"

John groaned. "I forgot. I'm sorry. I stopped by the Northwest Plaza and talked to a man about a bomb shelter and it just slipped my mind."

"I thought you gave up on that idea, John. We've got all that civil defense stuff in the basement. Isn't that enough?"

"They have a shelter that's all poured and ready. They just deliver it to your house and then drop it in a hole in the ground like a septic tank."

"Like a septic tank? What a charming picture that makes."

"Listen, honey, there are a lot of people in Muncie putting in bomb shelters. The pathologist at the hospital, the Korean one, Dr. Joon Kim. Why Dr. Ball told me he went over to visit Dr. Kim and out in the garage was this big mahogany door. Dr. Kim opened it up and they went down the stairs to a fully equipped bomb shelter right there under the garage. Dr. Ball said it was something else."

"I just don't know why Dr. Ball is encouraging you in this insanity. He's not even a psychiatrist."

"Hey, honey," John said, suddenly serious, "if there's an atomic war, I want my family to survive. What's wrong with that? We could survive for weeks in a shelter and come out when it's safe."

Suellen stared at him. They'd been over this before. "Safe? It won't ever be safe after an atomic war. The air and the water will be poisonous. We'd be in danger for years not for weeks." She took a deep breath. "And what about Sally? What if she didn't get home in time—would we go down the basement without her?—to survive by ourselves while everyone else outside dies?"

John shook his head. "I don't know what's wrong with you tonight. I wouldn't go into a shelter without Sally. For God's sake, we might even have room for some of the neighbors."

"I wish you would just think as much about an atomic war as you do about basketball."

He cut her off. "I don't need to, Suellen, I *understand* basketball."

She put her hands on her hips. "Well, I've got to run to the grocery and get some snacks before Monte and Barb get here."

She didn't speak to him again until she had her hand on the doorknob. Her smile was tender. "John, I'm sorry. I didn't mean to tease you about the game. I know how important it is to you."

He walked over to kiss her goodbye. "It will be a slaughter," he said. "At least it's Milan and not Anderson."

She stared at him. "What does that mean?"

"If you were from Muncie instead of West Virginia, you would understand that when you went to Anderson for a game in the Wig Wam, you were taking your life in your hands. Those thugs attacked us in the parking lots."

"I know. I've heard the stories. Didn't Bearcats attack the Anderson fans when they came here?"

John frowned. "That's not the same thing at all. They came here intending to cause trouble. That's why we hate them."

"Do you hate all of them, or only the team?" Suellen asked.

"You know what I mean."

She shook her head. "Yes, I know what you mean. You mean you're obsessed by basketball. Completely nuts, like most of the other people in this town." She nodded toward the sign over the couch. "Muncie loves her Bearcats."

"You don't understand because you're not a Hoosier. Basketball is important in Indiana."

"Important! It's a religion in Indiana," she said.

"It's going to be great cutting down those baskets again after the way we were robbed last year." He put the bow up under his chin and grinned at her. "Think about it—state champs in '51—state champs in '52. Should have won in '53, except for that sudden death. Now in'54, the Bearcats are back. This is a day that'll go down in history. Those poor kids from that little hick town don't stand a chance."

"Hicks? Wait a minute," Suellen said, "Didn't you lose a game to a little team from Center School?"

John glared at her, suddenly serious. "Suellen, we do not talk about that in this house."

"John, I swear if I cut you..."

He finished for her, "I know. I'd bleed purple."

She groaned and pulled the door closed behind her.

In the kitchen putting beer in the fridge, John almost didn't hear the timid knock. He laid his purple ribbon down on the table, still trying to decide where to hang it up. He walked to the front door and looked at the tall, skinny man with a briefcase standing on the porch. An unbuttoned stained overcoat revealed a rumpled suit, a white shirt with a brown tie slightly askew.

"Hi, there. Remember me? I'm Steve Wilson. I met you at the plaza when you stopped to look at the bomb shelter literature." He sounded apologetic. "I hope this isn't a bad time, but I found some additional literature you might like to look over and thought I'd stop by on my way back to the hotel."

John nodded. "Sure. I remember you." He glanced at his watch; Monte and Barb would be here in less than an hour. Courtesy fought with urgency. After a long pause, he said, "Come in."

Wilson noticed John checking his watch. "I won't take but a minute of your time, but I wanted to share this with you." He handed John a brochure.

John read aloud: "To improve your chances of surviving a nuclear attack, your primary need would be an adequate shelter equipped for many days of occupancy. The fallout protections provided by most existing buildings would not be adequate if the winds blew from the wrong direction during the time of fallout deposition. To remain in or near cities that are probable target areas, one would need protection against blast, fire and fallout. Our smallest standard model is a 6-person shelter 3 ½ feet wide, 4 ½ feet high and 16 ½ feet long. A small stand-up hole at one end would allow each tall occupant to stand up and stretch several times a day."

John frowned. "You call that a six-person shelter? Six people couldn't survive for a week in a space that small. Our pantry is bigger than that."

Wilson nodded. "The small six-person is our cheapest, but you're right, it would be pretty cramped. But we have a number of other models, with some really helpful features. See, the farther you can keep away from a source of either light or of harmful radiation, the less light or other radiation will reach you—like if fallout particles are on the roof of a building and you were in the basement, you would receive a much smaller radiation dose from those particles than if you were on the floor above you." He paused and looked around. "Do you have a basement?"

"Yes," John said.

"Well, that's good. See, you need to have food and water because after the atomic bomb goes off, radioactive iodine from contaminated food and water gets concentrated in thyroid glands and causes cancers. Besides that, fires get started from thermal radiation. If that happened here, on a clear day, serious flash burns on a person's exposed skin can occur 25 miles away."

John shuddered. "Is Muncie a target area?"

"The way I understand it, Muncie is a secondary target. I mean, there's a lot of industry here—not like Chicago or Indianapolis of course, but still, if planes couldn't bomb either of those places, they would dump their loads here or over Kokomo, Richmond, Anderson, maybe even New Castle."

"That's the whole conference!" John said.

"What?"

John shook his head. "Nothing. Nothing. It's just you named all the teams in the conference."

"Well, we sell a lot of shelters in all of those cities."

John stared at the brochure with the picture of the ruins of Nagasaki. "It really could happen here, couldn't it?"

"It could," Wilson agreed. "That's why I asked about your basement. It might be possible to do some remodeling there and create a top-notch shelter for you and your family. Could you show it to me?"

John checked his watch. He could take ten minutes.

He opened the basement door and nodded to Wilson. "This way. Go slow and duck your head. There's a low place at the bottom of the stairs."

The loud clunk told him the warning had come too late. He hurried down the steps to where Wilson lay in a heap on the cement floor. He rolled the body over to see blood gushing from a deep gash on the man's forehead. Even as he watched, the blood stopped flowing out of the wound and Wilson made a sound that chilled the room.

John wished he had a mirror so he could see if it fogged up like in a Dracula movie. He did the next best thing; he put his fingers on Wilson's neck to see if he could feel a heartbeat. Nothing.

John sat down on the bottom step with a moan. Wilson was dead. The idiot ran smack into that low rafter and knocked his brains out. Now what? He stared at the corpse—that's what it was, a corpse, a dead body lying at the foot of the basement stairs, dead as a doornail.

He kept staring at Wilson. He should go upstairs and call the police right away. He stood up, his knees suddenly weak. The police would be here and take the body away. There would be questions. He would tell them the truth. Wilson was too tall to be rushing down the stairs that way. He bashed his head in and it killed him.

At the top of the stairs he stopped. Questions. The police would come and ask all kinds of questions and he would miss the game. Not only him, but Monte and Barb would miss it too. Suellen wouldn't care, but his friends wouldn't appreciate being questioned by the police while Muncie Central was stomping Milan all over the Butler Fieldhouse. He couldn't do that. No one would know if he waited until after the game. It wouldn't matter to Wilson. He wasn't going anywhere and an hour or so wouldn't make any difference to him.

He wasn't being heartless, not really. He was just practical. He would watch the game and then call the police. He took a deep breath and walked unsteadily to the sink, turned on the water and got a drink to steady his nerves. A small dribble of water ran down his chin and dripped onto his crepe paper tie, leaving a small purple stain on his white shirt.

John almost fainted when he heard Suellen say, "I got snacks." She put two grocery bags down on the kitchen table.

She studied his face. "You okay, hon? You look pale."

Not as pale as the dead man in the basement, he thought. He forced a smile. "I'm fine, sweetie. Just fine. Let's get ready for Monte and Barb."

The doorbell rang just as they set out pretzels, chips and dip and a dish of mixed nuts. Monte and Barb handed John their coats, under which they wore matching purple and white sweat shirts with purple bows in Barb's hair.

"Love the decorations!" Barb said. "You really have the spirit."

Monte nodded. "Place looks great."

"Do you all want a coke or some coffee before the game?" Suellen asked.

"I'll take some coffee," Monte said. "It should keep me awake."

"You think the game is going to be boring?" Suellen asked.

Barb laughed. "Are you kidding? The Bearcats will mop up the floor with those farm boys. It'll be pitiful, sort of like playing Burris."

Monte grinned. "Those rich boys don't like to sweat." He noticed Suellen's frown. "Heck, girl, we just want to watch our boys cut down those nets again. This game will be a piece of cake. Why, someday they'll probably make a movie out of it to use for a training film or something."

"On how to stay humble?" Suellen asked drily.

John put his arm around her. "Don't pay any attention to her. She's not a Hoosier. She just doesn't understand."

Monte and Barb nodded sympathetically. Suellen couldn't decide if she was amused or angry and decided to relax and let it go. After all, the game would be over pretty soon and be forgotten, no sense in getting upset. Besides, she was going to West Virginia in the morning where no one cared who won a high school basketball game.

John gestured to the chairs he had moved to face the television set. "Sit down, take a load off. I got the radio ready so we can listen to Don Burton do the play by play instead of Tom Carnegie."

Barb nodded. "That's good. I hate that Tom Carnegie. He's got it in for the Bearcats. You can tell."

Monte smiled at his wife. "This is going to be a slaughter. We beat Elkhart today, 59 to 50."

Suellen stopped by the door to the kitchen. "Didn't Milan beat Terre Haute by 12 points this afternoon?" She smiled. "I'll get the drinks."

Barb stared after her. "What's wrong with Suellen? She acts real nervous or something. She sure doesn't love basketball."

John tried to smile. She would really be nervous if she knew there was a dead man at the bottom of the basement stairs. "There's nothing wrong with her," he said with forced cheer, "could be her time of the moon. She gets kind of tense then. And you guys know she's not from here. She doesn't get basketball."

Barb looked thoughtful. "Well, that's all okay, but I remember when she said she didn't care if you got her another season ticket."

John shook his head. "That was around the time her father died."

"I know, and we all understood, but she doesn't holler at the games, either. How about that? That's not 'cause her father died. It's like she's from New Castle or something, like she really doesn't want the Bearcats to win."

Monte groaned. "I never will get over New Castle winning the state the year I was a senior. I was B team, but man it was something else." He grinned. "Imagine being on a team called the Trojans." He winked. "You know what I mean."

John turned the television on. "Come on, guys. You know Suellen isn't from New Castle. She's not even a Hoosier. She just doesn't get it."

Barb gave him a weak smile. "Well, it's sad, that's all. I mean, hey, we're Bearcats, that's who we are, and here are our boys playing at the Butler Fieldhouse—that place is like a cathedral."

"I couldn't believe it when I went to the drawing and pulled out that envelope and it said, *Sorry*," Monte said, his voice hoarse.

"I was standing there," Barb said, "and I swear I thought he was going to pass out, or just break down and cry like a baby."

Monte glared at her. "For God's sake, Barb, I was just upset, that's all. I never got a sorry before. It was a shock."

Suellen came in with a tray loaded with snacks. She set the tray down on the coffee table and smiled at them, apparently over whatever non-Hoosier thing had been bothering her. "Help yourselves," she said.

John reached for a small dish and loaded it with pretzels. "You know, sometimes I wish I'd gone into teaching instead of banking. If I was a school administrator I'd be at the game tonight."

Suellen stared at him. "John, you don't even like kids."

He nodded. "I know. That doesn't matter. Lots of administrators don't like kids, but I bet most of them are there at the game. No sorries for them."

Monte reached for the potato chips. "I know a guy at the Muncie Star—typesetter—and he made his own tickets for the regional last year. Pulled a sorry and just made his own tickets. Got in, too. Just kept moving around when he was in somebody's seat. Saw the whole game."

John smiled. "That's a great idea."

Suellen shook her head. "It's against the law. You could go to jail."

John felt a clutch in his stomach. He could go to jail all right. He had a dead man in his basement, and he wasn't going to call the police until the end of the game. How's that for being a good citizen?

Time did a funny thing. Suddenly the TV showed the Butler Fieldhouse and John heard the familiar voice of Don Burton. "This is the state final basketball game on WLBC. Tonight it's the battle of David versus Goliath, the Milan Indians and the Muncie Central Bearcats."

Then he was announcing the teams, "Milan Coach Marvin Wood." Blank. John heard, "Engel . . . Cutter . . .Craft . . . Plump."

The crowd roared for the underdogs. "And for the Muncie Bearcats, Coach Jay McCreary. At Forward, Junior Jim Hinds #40, Junior Gene Hinds #20, at Guard, Junior Jim Barnes #12, Junior Phil Raisor #32 and at Center, Junior John Casterlow #50."

Screaming from the Bearcat fans and some booing made Monte yell back at the TV. "Shut up, you losers. We'll show you."

Barb patted his arm even as she nodded in agreement.

John watched the figures move on the screen like ghosts, like poor dead Wilson in the basement. He would take care of the guy as soon as the game was over. He promised. He wished he'd never let Wilson in the house, or in the doorway to the kitchen. A dead man in the doorway to the kitchen.

"What on earth?" Suellen said. She stood and went over to where a tall figure leaned against the doorjamb like a weathered scarecrow. Blood streaks ran down the man's face from a wound on his forehead. His dingy overcoat hung cockeyed over his rumpled suit.

"Who are you?" Suellen asked, reaching for the man's arm.

"Wilson," he muttered. "Fell down the stairs."

"Our stairs? Did you fall down our stairs—the basement?"

Wilson nodded. "Basement. Banged my head."

Suellen turned to John in a panic. "Help me. He needs a doctor."

"In a minute," John said. "Bobby Plump is holding the ball."

Monte and Barb nodded their heads. "We'll help him in a minute."

Suellen stared at them. "Are all of you crazy? This man is hurt. He needs a doctor. Apparently, he fell down our basement stairs." She glared at John.

"Did you know about this?"

John kept his eyes trained on the television. "I thought he'd be all right." He didn't add that he had planned to call the police as soon as the game was over. Now the corpse was up and walking around, he didn't have to do that.

Wilson blinked his eyes a few times. "Could I maybe sit down?"

Suellen groaned. "Of course, you may sit down. I'm so sorry! Let me get a cloth and clean the blood off your head." She stared down at the purple crepe paper bow he had in his hand. "Where did you get that?" she asked as she helped him into a chair next to the couch.

Wilson looked down at the bow. "I don't know," he said. "I guess I saw it on the table and picked it up. I don't know."

"Well," Suellen said as she went to get a wet cloth, "hang on to it, Mr. Wilson, you fit right in."

John, Monte and Barb stared at the television. "Jim Hinds' two free throws have put the Bearcats on top 28-26 with 7:41 remaining in the game. Now Plump has the ball. He's standing still, holding the ball. He isn't moving. He's just standing there holding the ball. The crowd is going insane. I've never seen anything like this!"

John, Monte and Barb groaned in genuine agony. "Plump has held the basketball for 4:13—that's right! Four minutes and 13 seconds without moving. Now Coach Marvin Wood calls a time out. It's about time!"

Suellen wiped the blood off Wilson's forehead. The gash didn't look too deep once the blood was gone. Gently, she cleaned his face, murmuring to him. Then he moved his head so he could see around her. When she realized what he was doing, she threw the washcloth down in his lap. "You're just like the rest of them," she hissed. "Watch the game."

John, Monte and Barb, unable to sit, were on their feet watching intently. If God had spoken they wouldn't have listened as closely as they did to Don Burton.

"The Indians are back on the floor, moving the ball. Plump misses a shot. Muncie brings the ball down court. The Indians are pressing. Oh! Muncie just threw the ball away. Ray Craft drives through the defense and makes his lay-up shot. 28 ALL!! Plump is fouled. Two free throws. One. Two. Milan is ahead 30-28. Craft's shot is in and out and the Bearcats have the ball. Flowers shoots and it's in. The score is TIED! Plump and Craft bring the ball down the court. 18 seconds remain in the ballgame. Wood calls a time out. Wood is sending in Ken Wendelman for Rollin Cutter. All four Milan players are on the left side of the court. The key is wide open!! **Five seconds on the clock! PLUMP STARTS TO MOVE. BARNES IS AFRAID TO FOUL HIM. PLUMP SHOOTS!! IT'S IN!! MILAN SCORES TO WIN 32 TO 30!!"**

The three stood in shock. Suellen watched as Monte and Barb turned to each other. John started to speak, then stopped. Big tears rolled down Barb's face. Monte hugged her, patting her back. Silently, they moved like automatons toward the coat tree. John helped them with their coats. He opened the front door. They left in complete silence—there was nothing to say.

Crowd noises still came from the radio. "I can't believe it. The Fieldhouse is going wild..."

Suellen turned off the radio.

John's voice sounded as stricken as he looked. "This is a day that will go down in infamy," he whispered.

"John," Suellen said, "It's only a ball game."

"Not to a Bearcat," he said hoarsely. "This is history."

"Amen," Wilson said. "It's historic all right." He sounded happier than John.

"What?" John asked.

Wilson smiled grimly. "I'm from Anderson. I think it's great."

Suellen was able to stop John before Wilson was really dead.

Bobby Plump
Tony Perona

Everyone in Indiana knows Jimmy Chitwood is really Bobby Plump.

Long before the main character in 1986's "Hoosiers" made a last second shot to win the game for the fictitious small town of Hickory, real-life Hoosiers knew the story of Bobby Plump, who played for tiny Milan High School in 1954. Chitwood and the story of how Hickory overcame the much larger South Bend school was loosely based on Plump and Milan. Like Chitwood, Plump scored on a jump shot in the last 18 seconds of the game to win the state championship game over a much bigger school, Muncie Central.

The Bobby Plump legend is an underdog story that gets retold every March when Hoosier Hysteria reaches it zenith with the high school basketball tournament. Though the single class tournament that made the "Milan Miracle" possible was abandoned in 1997, Plump's last shot is still on everyone's mind come March. In fact, a basketball themed restaurant in Broad Ripple named "Plump's Last Shot" is a testimony to the enduring story. (The restaurant is owned by Plump's son.)

Bobby Plump was born in Pierceville and went to Milan High School. In addition to winning the state championship for Milan his senior year, Plump received the Trester Award (given for mental attitude). He was also named Indiana's Mr. Basketball that year.

Plump attended Butler University and was coached by the legendary Tony Hinkle. During his time at Butler he set several scoring records. He played on Butler's first National Invitational Tournament (NIT) team in 1958. In 1981 he was selected for the Indiana Basketball Hall of Fame.

THE MISSING MEDALLION
M.B. Dabney

Like most hospital rooms, George Madison's had a sterile feel to it. It wasn't that it was virtually germ free. It was more than that. Little about the room conveyed any personal warmth.

His bed was inclined so Madison sat somewhat upright, with white cotton covers up to his chest. He had plastic tubes in his nostrils for oxygen, and sensors attached to his chest and right index finger.

"You feeling okay, Dad? I can have Ryan go get you something," Margie said as she tucked the covers snuggly around her father's feet at the foot of the bed. Turning to face her husband near the door, she said, "Ryan, look on the top shelf of the closet and get Dad another blanket. I think his feet are cold."

"I'm fine, Pumpkin," Madison said. His voice was hoarse, the volume low. The fact that Madison's daughter didn't hear him had nothing to do with the volume in which he spoke. So he weakly waved his arm to get Ryan's attention. "No blanket."

Ryan understood.

Margie continued to fuss. "I don't understand why you wanted to be in this hospital. It's a heart hospital. You need specialists in geriatric care."

Ryan returned to his wife's side as the door slid open and an attractive middle-aged black woman entered. She had long, salt-and-pepper hair braided down her back, and a look of authority on her face.

The woman silently acknowledged Margie and Ryan but barely took her eyes off of the patient. She walked to the end of the bed, picked up the medical chart and glanced at it.

"Dr. Chandler," she said, shaking hands with Margie and Ryan. They introduced themselves. The doctor looked down at the patient before returning her attention to Margie. "I understand he's your father."

"Yes, and we are concerned about his care at this hospital."

"Indianapolis Heart Hospital will provide him the best of care, I promise you. I'll personally see to it. I'm told he specifically requested this hospital," she said before turning to the patient and slightly raising her voice. "How are you feeling today, Mr. Madison? Are you comfortable?"

Madison rallied a bit, undoubtedly because of the extra attention. "I'm feeling pretty good for an old man." A coughing fit gripped the man and the doctor checked his heart monitor. Ryan pulled his wife close but neither spoke.

After his fit, Madison said, "The reporter?" And he coughed again.

At the word 'reporter,' a stern expression marched across Margie's face. But before she could speak, the doctor continued, "He's right outside. I wanted to check on your strength before I agreed to let him interview you."

"He's too sick to talk to anyone," Margie said, looking back and forth from her beloved father to the doctor.

"I share your concern, Mrs. McDonald," Dr. Chandler said. "But I am monitoring his condition and your father ..."

From his bed, Madison interrupted them in a stronger voice than he had displayed in some time.

"I'm not dead yet and I can make my own decisions. I want the reporter. There are some things that need clearing up. After more than 40 years, it's time. Let him in."

Surprised, the three didn't move as the depth of the old man's desire hit home. Then, Dr. Chandler walked to the door and allowed the reporter in.

"Chris Atwood, senior sports writer for the Indianapolis Star," he said as he walked in and shook hands with everyone. Atwood looked at Madison, the winningest high school basketball coach in Indiana history. "It's so nice to see you again, Coach," he said, ignoring the man's devastated physical condition.

In his heyday, Madison looked more like a burly lumberjack— broad, thick and strong. He conveyed respect, authority and control from the sidelines. But now, in his late 80s and sick in a hospital bed, he looked thin, old and frail—a shadow of his former self.

"You're lying," Madison said with humor, and once again coughed but it subsided quickly. Looking at the others, he said, "Atwood here is the biggest SOB there is. But he's always given me a fair shake. Margie, get him a chair. You guys can find something to sit on or you can go somewhere for coffee. You don't need to be here."

Margie pulled a chair closer to the bed. Dr. Chandler said, "The nurses'll be in with your meds, and I'll stop by later to check up on you before I head home tonight. But if you need me, they'll beep me."

Atwood pulled a notebook, pen, and a small digital recorder from his jacket pocket. "Mind if I record?" he asked, placing the device on the bed beside Madison's right arm.

"Go ahead. I want you to get it right," the elderly man said.

"Coach Madison, your nearly 50 years of coaching boy's high school basketball is legendary. You're a Hall of Famer, with more than 600 wins and four state championships. Then all those trophies and awards, all stolen from your home last month. That must have been hard."

"Most of it was just stuff. Good riddance," the old man said.

Atwood appeared surprised. "You don't want it back?"

"Well, the police recovered some of it. Most of it really," Ryan chimed from beside the window.

"But they are keeping it for evidence," Margie said. "No telling when he'll get it back."

"They didn't recover the thing I treasured most. A gold medallion. One from Northridge's championship in the late 60s," Madison interrupted. "We weren't supposed to win that game. One player didn't get to keep his medallion."

"Sam Wilson, you mean? The backup shooting guard who disappeared?" Atwood said.

"Gave it to me that night for safe-keeping but didn't return to school after that to claim it. I'd kept the medallion all these years. Now it's missing, part of the stolen loot," Madison said.

He paused. It was as if he were gathering the courage or the strength to continue. "Might have to give it back to the state after you print what I'm about to tell you."

He now had all their attention. Atwood leaned closer. "What is it, coach?"

"We should have forfeited the game. It was a boy's game. And Sam Wilson was a girl."

"Okay, guys. Hit the showers," Coach Madison said, dismissing the boys who had tried out for the basketball team. As all the boys but one headed toward the doors at the far end of the gym, Madison looked to his assistant coach, Randy Cox. "Who's that kid, the one with the big hair?"

"Not sure, coach. Let me see," Cox said, looking down at the clipboard with their names.

"Hey you, son. Yeah, you," Madison said, waving his massive arms. "Come on over here."

The light-skinned kid could only have weighed 115 pounds soaking wet, and that was thin for a boy 5-foot-9. The heaviest thing on him was his Afro, which was so large it was a miracle his small head was strong enough to support it. The hair was supposed to demonstrate pride in his heritage, and a flair for current fashion.

Many whites, like Madison, were mystified by the Black Power movement. It scared many, but Madison wasn't one of them.

The kid glanced over to the coaches when they called and an expression akin to fear showed on his smooth, clean-shaven face. But he sauntered over.

"Yes, coach," he said hesitantly. He barely looked up at Madison when he replied.

"What's your name, son?"

"Uh, Sam Wilson, sir," he said with a polite Southern lilt to his voice.

"I haven't seen you before. You new to the school? Where you from?"

"I just moved here from down South. A small town in Mississippi," Sam said.

"You like it here?"

The boy's face lit up at once and he seemed suddenly energized, bouncing slightly on his feet. "Yes, sir. And I'd love to make your varsity team and play for you. You're a great coach and I could learn so much."

"That so?" Cox said.

"Yeah, and Northridge is a college preparatory school now. The work is harder than at my old school."

"What all are you taking?" Madison asked.

Sam gave a list of his classes.

"What's your favorite?" It was Madison again.

"Biology 2A."

"Doctor Richards, huh? Great teacher. Probably the best biology teacher in Indiana," Madison commented before switching subjects. "You ever play organized ball before? At your old school? Maybe at the Y?"

"Some. But mostly backyard stuff," Sam said.

"He's an excellent outside shooter, wouldn't you say, Coach?" Cox said.

"I'm small," Sam said, looking between the coaches. "Can't get that close to the hoop because everybody's bigger than me. So I have to shoot outside."

"You handle the ball pretty good, too," Madison said as he started walking across the court to the cart where the boys had stacked all the basketballs. Taking a ball and bouncing it to Sam, he said, "How's your free-throw shooting? Take some shots."

Sam stood at the foul line, dribbled the ball a few times and looked up at the basket, studying it as closely as the coach studied him. He lifted off with his toes and the ball rolled off his fingertips. It hit the backboard and dropped through the hoop.

The coaches bounced ball after ball to Sam with increasing speed as he jumped and took shot after shot. Most went in. Finally, they stopped.

"Randy, get the balls," coach said to his assistant. To Sam, he said, "You think you can make a free throw without hitting the backboard? Only net."

"I think so."

50

"Try it," the coach said, bouncing Sam a ball again. Sam took one quick shot after another, hitting six of seven, with three being all net.

Beads of perspiration dotted Sam's forehead and half-moons stained the underarms of his dark blue t-shirt. Madison walked over.

"Good job, son. You've got potential. Now hit the showers."

Sam backed away, nearly panicked. "Uh, my ride's gone, I think, and it's almost time for my bus. I live on the other side of town," he said. "Uh, I don't think I have time to shower."

And with that, Sam ran off, leaving the two coaches scratching their heads.

Tryouts lasted three days. On the following Monday afternoon, Sam left an ornithology field trip with Dr. Richards' biology class and hurried down the narrow first floor hallway leading to the coach's office. Madison had promised to post the varsity team roster before the end of the day.

A group of boys, with varying expressions on their faces ranging from elation to disappointment, stood outside the office talking excitedly. On the wall next to the door was the list. Sam's name was on it. He was a backup point guard on the nine-member squad.

Practice started that day and within two weeks, they faced their first opponent.

As a backup, Sam played little but showed great leadership when he did. His long shots were on target. He was quick on fast breaks, consistently scoring two-pointers on lay-ups. He called some plays and his two, late-game assists to forward Donnie Cox, the assistant coach's son, helped lift the team to a 73-72 win over Cathedral.

But perhaps most impressive of all was the game against No. 1 powerhouse George Washington.

Playing for the injured Arthur Jones, Sam scored 16 second-half points during Northridge's 24-3 run in the team's 82-77 loss. Sam sank to the floor in despair after the final buzzer, his head in his hands. His body shook from the disappointment at the team's first loss of the season.

After shaking hands with the winning coach, Madison walked over to Sam and helped him to his feet. He put his arm around the boy's slumping shoulders as they walked off. They barely noticed the fans spilling onto the basketball court.

"You played well tonight, Sam. I couldn't have asked for more."

"But we lost."

"It would have been far worse without you."

"Small consolation," Sam said, heading off as he fought back tears.

Madison felt a tug on his plaid jacket and looked down to see his seven-year-old daughter, Marjorie. He picked her up.

"I'm sorry you lost, daddy," Margie said.

"That's alright, Pumpkin. We'll get 'em next time."

"Daddy, why does that player always wear a blue t-shirt under his jersey and the other players don't?"

Madison looked at Sam's retreating form then back to his daughter. "I don't know, sweetheart. I hadn't noticed before. Maybe I'll ask him on the bus back to school."

But, he didn't. Forgot.

He did, however, follow Sam's grades, as he did with all his players. Sam had a 3.7 grade point average, with his highest scores coming in biology.

The same could not be said for Art Jones, who returned from his sprained ankle injury but who failed two classes that fall. He was dropped from the team at the beginning of the second semester.

That left the squad with eight players. Enough, but just barely.

"You're going to get more playing time, Sam," Madison said after one practice in January. "I like the way you're improving as a player."

"Thanks, Coach. I promise not to let you down."

"I'm counting on it," Madison said. "When am I going to meet your parents, son?"

"My mom's divorced. My dad, uh, well, he's not here. And my mom works a lot to support me," Sam said, sounding somewhat embarrassed by the admission.

"Well, it would be good to see her in the stands down the stretch. It's important for parents to support their kids. Cheer them on," Madison said. "You need a ride home?"

"No, I'll make it okay," Sam said and left the gym.

Ranked seventh in the state, Northridge dominated throughout the season but narrowly escaped with close victories against Chatard, Howe and Connersville when the state tournament started. A hard-fought victory against Washington got them to the state finals. They were headed for a match-up with Gary Roosevelt, the two-time defending state champions. Roosevelt hadn't lost a game in a season-and-a-half and the smart money was on them to easily handle Northridge.

In the team's final practice, Madison was putting his players through some drills when Jesse Perkins, a player who loved hogging the ball, knocked Sam to the floor. Sam's legs were spread apart and the coach noticed something. A bright red spot in the crotch of Sam's white practice shorts. None of the others seemed to notice.

Madison walked over and pulled Sam to the side.

"Are you feeling okay, son. You hurt yourself?"

"No, Coach. Why do you ask?"

"I thought I saw blood on your pants."

Sam looked down, horrified, and ran off without saying a word. Madison found him in a closed stall in the restroom.

"You alright, son?"

"I'm fine. Go away," Sam protested.

"But if you are hurt, we need to get you to the nurse to be checked out."

"I said I'm fine. I don't need any help, so go away."

"Sam," Madison started but the boy's angry voice interrupted him.

"I said go away."

Hands on his hips outside the stall, Madison stood for 20 seconds, then turned and headed for the door.

"Come to my office as soon as you come out. I mean it. In my office."

Fully dressed 10 minutes later, Sam entered the coach's office and dropped with a thud into a metal chair across from Madison's desk.

Madison interlocked his fingers and rested his chin on his hands. "Sam, I need you this weekend. And I need you healthy. But if there is something wrong, we need to have it checked out. We can help you. I promise."

Head down, Sam examined his feet as he spoke. "I don't need any help. It happens all the time."

"What? You injured? You haven't mentioned anything to me or Coach Cox."

"No injury. It happens all the time. Once a month," he finally said, looking up. His eyes locked with Madison's. "It's my period. Girls have periods."

Madison's hands dropped to the desk and his jaw went slack. He fell back into his chair and looked at Sam as if for the first time.

The smooth face, voice with a slightly higher pitch, narrow, round shoulders, never showering, the t-shirt his daughter mentioned weeks earlier. It all added up. It was amazing he had never thought of it before.

He looked away. "Oh my goodness. You're a girl." Looking back at Sam, he said it again. "You're a girl!"

"I know I'm a girl, Coach."

"But why? Why here?"

"This is a college prep school and has good academics. I need that," Sam said. "I love playing basketball and you are the best coach there is. So, it all worked out."

Madison shook his head as the implications sank in. "I can't have a girl on the team. It's a boy's team. No girls."

Moving forward in her seat, Sam said, "Yes you can. There are no specific regulations against it. I checked."

"You're a girl. I can't play you."

"You've been playing me. What's different?" she said. "I want to play. I need to play."

"Sam, I can't," he said and stopped, as if the idea had just occurred to him. "Is that your real name?"

"Short for Samantha."

"How did you get into the school?"

"I tested in, like everyone else in my class," she said. "It's me and my mom. I told you. She works a lot. But she signed the papers for me. She wanted me to take the college prep courses and finish here. She didn't notice I only put down Sam as my name."

"How do you get to school?"

"City bus."

"You take the bus to school each day and no one sees where you live or your parents? Where do you live, by the way?"

"Fourteenth and Yandees, on the eastside."

"Samantha, I have to drop you from the team. I can't play a girl."

"If you drop me, you won't have enough players to make the squad. And you can't call up a player from junior varsity. It's too late," she said. "You'll have to forfeit this weekend. That's not fair to the other players. Do you want that?"

Madison interlocked his fingers again and rested his chin on his hands. "I'll check the regulations and if it's okay, you can stay on the team. I won't tell anyone but I can't play you. Understand?"

"Coach," Samantha said, standing up from the chair.

"There's no other way. I can't play a girl on the boy's team. That's my last word on the matter."

Defeated, she stormed out of the office.

The interior of Hinkle Fieldhouse on the Butler University campus is an imposing site under normal circumstances. But on the basketball court, add nearly 10,000 screaming people in the stands and it can be overwhelming. The air is electric, the sound is deafening.

It's Indiana basketball at its best.

Samantha practiced with the team on Saturday afternoon and dressed in the blue uniform for the game that night. But Madison kept to his word and benched her. From her seat at the end she took in the scene in the stands—a sea of Northridge's blue and white colors—and hardly noticed the basketball court, where Gary Roosevelt badly out-played Northridge in the first half.

Dejected and dispirited, Samantha walked with her teammates to the locker room at the half. And as she was passing the coach, she heard a little girl directly behind him say, "You should put Sam in. Their players are too big. We can't get to the basket."

It was a good analysis. Roosevelt had two players over 6-11, including 7-foot center Ron Sweeney, while Donnie was Northridge's tallest player at 6-foot-9. They dominated him on defense and completely covered him on offense, forcing Northridge to use up its guards with outside shots that weren't going in. They were down 35-24 at the half.

The locker room pep talk was like all pep talks to underdogs being beaten. Keep your head up. Play your game, not their game. Keep it together and we can pull it out.

But Madison was nothing if not a motivator and his small squad came out looking for bear in the third quarter. They increased the pace and started connecting with outside shooting. It wasn't pretty – they forced Roosevelt's Sweeney into foul trouble – but they cut the deficit to five, 50-45 at the end of the third.

It didn't hurt that Roosevelt's big man was on the bench for nearly three minutes on the clock.

It was a brutal barroom fight in the fourth, ending in a tied score of 70-70 at the end of regulation. Samantha had not seen a minute of playing time and even the crowd was beginning to notice. She heard shouts from the stands for her to get into the game.

It didn't happen in the first overtime period, which Northridge barely survived. Roosevelt's Sweeney was called for a technical foul for throwing a punch at Donnie and ejected from the game.

Jesse Perkins sank the foul shot for the technical with 20 seconds on the clock and Northridge held on for another tie, 79-79.

But Jesse paid the price for keeping Northridge in the game. With a minute left in the second OT, he was elbowed in the right eye under the basket, drawing another technical foul and a forced ejection. The crowd went wild as Jesse, his face bloodied, was escorted off the court by a doctor.

Northridge was still down by three.

With no one else to turn to, Madison signaled for Samantha. In the huddle, Madison laid out the plan, then looked at Samantha. "You're out there only to even things up. Nothing more."

Samantha's heart was beating out of her chest. She in-bounded the ball to another guard who took it down court under a full-court press. He got the ball to Donnie, who drove down the lane. He missed the shot but got the offensive rebound amidst a flurry of arms and elbows. He shot again and scored. Northridge, down by one.

Roosevelt tried to slow the pace but missed a shot with less than 10 seconds on the clock. Northridge had the ball and Madison called timeout.

The plan was to get the ball to Donnie under the basket.

The ball was in-bounded to forward Charlie Lyle from mid-court with only seven seconds on the clock. He was quickly covered and Donnie was doubled-teamed. Glancing back away from the basket, Charlie saw Samantha, her arms up. She was wide open and at the top of the key. Three seconds left.

He passed the ball. She faked to the right, throwing off her defender, and planted her feet for the longest shot she had ever attempted in a game. Set, eyes focused on the basket, she lifted off. The buzzer sounded less than a second after the ball left her fingertips.

The oxygen was pulled from the fieldhouse as 10,000 people inhaled at once. The arc was high and good. Samantha landed on her feet and managed to jump again in anticipation as the ball seemed to hang in the air. Finally...

Swish. All net.

Madison could barely breathe as the exhausting 45-minute interview with the reporter drew to a close. He took long, raspy breaths. Margie was crying, but Ryan and Atwood hung on every word the coach spoke.

"We cut down the net. Sam included. And we got the gold medallions with blue ribbons," Madison said.

"What happened to her, Dad?" Margie asked.

"She hugged me. Thanked me for letting her play. Gave me her medallion. Asked me to hold on to it on the way back to school. She didn't want to lose it."

"And you did," Atwood commented.

"I took it. Looked for her on the bus. She wasn't on it."

"What happened at school, Dad?" asked the coach's son-in-law. "On that Monday."

"There was a pep rally but she wasn't in school. No one could find her."

"Didn't someone look up her records in the school office?" Atwood asked. "Try to reach her that way."

"Of course. I even went to the house on Yandees," Madison said and coughed. "Empty. There's a ramp to I-65 there now."

"And no one found her? Sam Wilson. It's a common enough name but no one knows what happened to her?" Atwood said.

"It's a mystery," Madison said. "And she never got the medallion."

"Has anyone seen it?" Margie said.

"Not since that night," Madison said. "I kept it in the house."

"Did you ever mention to anyone that Sam was a girl?" Atwood asked.

"Not 'til now."

Atwood stopped recording and stood up. He reached down to take the coach's hand. The grip was weak. "I'm so sorry, Coach. For everything," he said, looking about.

The coach coughed again.

"This is a great story," Atwood said, glancing more to Margie than to her father. "I'll have to check it out, run down some other sources, of course. But I'm sure it won't take much to convince the editors to run it on 1-A on Saturday. Lead story. Even better, the boy's championship game is that night."

❖

Shortly before 4 in the morning, the coach's eyes flickered open and his sudden raspy breathing caught Dr. Chandler's immediate attention. She had been sleeping in the chair beside the bed since midnight, several hours after the reporter and the coach's family left. She rose, glanced at the monitors then back down at the man who was clearly beginning his march toward death. The end was near. The interview had taken its toll.

"What can I do for you?" she said, leaning close to insure he heard.

"The drawer ... beside ... the bed," he said, catching a breath between words. "It's ... there."

The doctor opened the drawer and inside was the missing high school basketball championship winner's medallion. Dr. Chandler reached inside and lifted out the gold object. She examined it without speaking for 30 seconds, feeling its weight in her hands, the blue ribbon hanging down between her fingers. It had been a long time.

When the doctor turned back to the old man, her eyes glistened. A single tear rolled down one cheek and into the corner of her mouth.

"It's yours ... Remember? Always ... kept it ... hidden. Didn't know if ... you wanted ... your identity ... known," the coach said with difficulty. "I should've ... played you ... that night. You were ... good. Made me ... proud ... to be ... your coach."

Dr. Samantha Wilson Chandler leaned over and kissed her former coach's forehead. One of her tears fell onto his face.

"Thank you so much, Coach. My abusive dad saw the game on TV, found out where we were. Mom packed us up and we ran. It's why I left Northridge," she said. "But that basketball season was the best year of my life. I'd've never made it without you. And this," she said, holding the medallion, "means everything to me."

"Proud," was all he said in reply. Speaking had become too difficult.

Sam reached down and took his hand. For a brief moment, the twinkle in the coach's eyes from 40 years ago was there once again. Sam smiled in return just before his eyes went dark, and the coach was gone.

Brad Stevens

Tony Perona

To love fairy tales is to love the story of Brad Stevens, head coach at Butler University.

In 2000 he left the stability of a career with pharmaceutical company Eli Lilly for a more uncertain dream career: coaching basketball. The first job he accepted after leaving Lilly was as a volunteer position at Butler. Stevens was prepared to work at Applebee's to support his passion.

Just seven years later he became head coach at Butler after spending six seasons as assistant coach. In 2010 he coached his Cinderella team to the Final Four championship game. They repeated in 2011. Though they lost both their final games, Stevens' decision to follow his dream had paid off. He'd risen to national prominence as a coach, winning or being a finalist for several prestigious awards. He'd even appeared on fellow Hoosier David Letterman's talk show.

Stevens developed his love of basketball in Zionsville. Known for being a hard worker, he made the varsity team in high school and set many school records. Having decided his basketball skills were "modest," he chose DePauw University for its academic reputation.

Stevens played basketball every year at DePauw and earned multiple all-conference and academic all-conference awards. During summer vacations, Stevens taught at Butler basketball camps. He graduated in 1999 with a degree in economics.

At DePauw he met his future wife Tracy. She played a major role in his decision to leave the secure job at Lilly. He consulted her when he was offered the volunteer job at Butler. After two hours of thinking it over, she told him to go for it. She reasoned they were only 23 and he would not have a better chance to follow his dream. They were married in 2003 and have two children, Brady and Kinsley.

HOOSIER BUSINESS
Sherita Saffer Campbell

Muncie sits on the River Bend where an early Native American said: "We moved here because of the bend in river. No tornadoes will hit here." Further residents took this to heart and moved here expecting no tornadoes. Tornadoes came as first young boys and later girls whirled around the hardwood floors of The Muncie Field House so much that entire lives were spent around basketball. The kids growing up carried basketballs under their arms everywhere, dribbled them to school, slept with them. Basketball was the tornado that blew in and swept though the town. Hoops were the official sign of being a Hoosier. Everywhere. Hung on garages, trees, houses and poles were the certification that you were a Muncie Hoosier.

The High School gym floor, scene of The Basketball Finals, was lined in a scatter pattern. Boys with purple t-shirt tops lined up against boys with white t-shirt tops. The coach blew the whistle. "Move."

"Faster." His face was turning red.

The boys rushed down the wood floor, moving in and out, the ball handler driving and weaving in between the guards on the opposing side and his own men. Guards held their hands up, bent their elbows, wiggled them, stared head on at the boys on the opposite team. Arms, legs and shoulders well muscled now.

"Faster!" He yelled again. "This is called a fast break, not a waltz." Muncie's whole livelihood depended on these boys. The boys pushed faster and harder. Eyes glowed like hot coals, minds focused on the ball, their opponents and the floor.

"They're working on their fast breaks. Them boys always do them runs up the floor...steal the ball and head to the basket. And hit it every time." Lawrence Edward, one of the janitors, rested on his broom a minute to watch the team.

"Yep, they're real Bearcats. See you're filling in today for Jesse?" Ross, the maintenance chief, asked. He was on a break from office work to watch the 'Cats practice.

"Jesse fell off the scaffold working on the skylight last night. Banged him up real good. Probably will miss the game." He shook his head. "Said I would help out so old Jess could keep his job." The other janitors nodded. Ross looked at Lawrence. He thought Lawrence always worked at the junior high. He must have a talk with the sheriff. Then the Union Hall. Something wasn't right here. Sheriff told him to call if anything changed. He owed the sheriff his job.

A little bet was exchanged between the two on little bits of paper. Lawrence looked at it. "That much of a spread?" he asked. "No way, here." He handed back his piece of paper. "They are the Muncie Central Bearcats. They grab the ball, run down the court and hit a basket at the last minute. That's why they are called Bearcats. They'll win by more than that." The other janitor nodded. He looked at the paper and wrote down another figure.

"Use the damn floor," the coach shouted. This was the only time his mind was off the bicycle shop where he worked part time. Basketball and bicycles were all he thought about, except helping the sheriff. He'd talked to him today. Was glad they got the old bikes to the garage to be fixed. He yawned. He was tired. Been up all night. It was going to work.

Paul Jefferson stood outside the gym trying to listen to the shouts and noises of practice. He was almost as tall as the sheriff. He didn't like to read much about the world but he was a good intense listener. He could watch and listen with the best of them. He heard that new man Lawrence Edward telling the guys about Jesse. He'd best tell the sheriff about Jesse. The sheriff had him watching and listening for anything that seemed out of place. If he had to, he could and would do anything the sheriff wanted him to do.

❖

After practice he walked into Orv's drive-in. This was one of Muncie's gathering places for food, Cokes, dates and information. Everyone stopped by once a day to find out what was going on. Kids were listening to the jukebox. They danced in place. You couldn't dance on the floor with a partner unless you were over 21 or the place had a special license and the license cost too much for Orv's. Paul looked at the door that led to the back where big money was made playing draw poker. Lots of money. He shook his head. It was supposed to be a big secret. The best kept one. Everyone knew.

"Hey Paul, get to work."

He nodded. Headed into the kitchen. He could see across the counter where he washed the dishes into "the dining area." He turned on the taps and watched the water fill with suds as he poured in the powder. The sheriff walked up. Handed him a glass.

"Got any water there buddy?"

Paul nodded and filled a glass from the tap. Put it on the counter with his right hand as he palmed the note he had written about Jesse getting hurt. What could this mean?

Paul felt the piece of paper slip into the sheriff's hand.

Paul kept washing dishes, rinsing them under the water, trying to pretend he was listening to the jukebox playing, "There Stands the Glass." He felt that it was going to be a long afternoon of washing dishes. The sheriff was here and so was one of the big guys in town and one man he didn't know at all. The Big Boys had landed and were sitting at the same table with the chief of police and the sheriff. No one was even pretending to go into the back room. It was an open meeting. Something they wanted folks to see. He shook his head. He didn't understand these things. Trouble ahead. Big trouble. He could smell it. He waited. He peeked out the windows that surrounded the drive-in. The sheriff got up, walked away from the direction of city hall down the street. Paul smiled. Sheriff Rawlins was going to the tobacco shop where the basketball talk would be bigger and the money flowing.

Down the street at the tobacco shop a man walked in, laid a large bill on the counter and a card. His face was flushed after a long talk with the sheriff while drinking a double chocolate soda at Orv's. Sweat started to form on his forehead. He had better produce what the sheriff wanted or else. Now he needed a drink.

"You OK? You look a mite peaked," the shopkeeper said.

"Fine. I need some special mix from back there." He nodded toward the door on the backside of the counter. The left eyebrow was the only movement he made. The man at the counter nodded, looked around, reached under the counter and pushed a button. The customer picked up a card, left the money and walked in the direction his eyebrow signaled.

The sheriff walked over to the tobacco shop after he had his little visit at Orv's. He'd left the car in the county garage right under his office when he began his rounds earlier in the day. This was a special call after his executive conference at Orv's.

He had to pay a visit on the little gambling rooms behind the salons, filling stations and tobacco shops. This included Larry's and Betty's soda shop and stationary store that placed the bets with the bookies down in Indianapolis.

"Boys is just playing a little five card or twenty-one, Sheriff Rawlins."

"Didn't think they'd be doing otherwise." He looked around. "Looks like you got both teams covered in here." He was admiring the festoons of two colors of crepe paper hanging from the ceiling.

"Well, it's only fair to show respect for the opposite side, but I know our Fightin' Bearcats are going to win. At least I hope so."

"Got any money on it?"

"A little and don't go bad mouthing me. I can't afford to gamble big."

Sheriff Rawlins nodded and then said, "Don't push that button and let them know I'm coming in there."

He spoke these words very soft. A whisper, but the look on his face and the hard stare in his eyes caused the shop owner to remove his hand from the button. "That's what I intend to speak to the gentlemen in back about. I'd appreciate if you wouldn't send forth word to any other place in town that I am on a walk and talk mission."

Sheriff Rawlins walked to the back room. The "boys" as he called them because he had grown up with them, were playing blackjack and talking, until the dealer froze while dealing the last card to a man with a 16 of hearts showing who wanted a five of any suit which the dealer had just slipped under the deck.

Rawlins said nothing and just flicked his eyes from the cards on the table to the deck, and the dealer managed to get the card back on top with no one the wiser.

"Boys, tomorrow we got the big game. A whopper. We want to treat our visitors the best we can. If you choose to play some cards or bet on the game I want you to do so in an honest and fair way." He looked at the dealer. "I also expect you not to get caught or be obvious as to what you are doing."

The boys nodded. The dealer nodded very fast and wiped the sweat off his face with a red bandana. Sheriff meant every word. He knew it was his responsibility to help keep the local games secret and honest.

"Keep a low profile with the dice and cards. Bets on the game are forbidden. It's a high school game. We're the hosts. So keep the handling of money quiet and very local. 'Know your companions' as they tell you in Sunday school. So be real quiet like. I don't want to see it. I don't want to hear about it from snitches or little old ladies, or pastors. I do not want to know about it one bit. And I do not want to be surprised by bodies, folks beaten up or crying women who have no grocery money. Is that clear?"

They nodded again.

"You leave a man money to feed the family. Pay the rent. Give to his church. Everyone keeps quiet and no trouble. Then I don't have to arrest you. Play with matchsticks. Gather up money later. This is not big time gambling. Spread the word. Do I make myself clear?"

They nodded a little faster this time.

"And gentleman." This was serious, when he said 'gentleman.' Trouble was ahead. "The Big Boys are in town, from Chicago. Black hats, black suits, big black cars. Big money guys."

They nodded with a lighting speed. Eyes getting wider as they listened.

"Stay the hell away from them. Somehow they got interested in our game. As if there wasn't enough money everywhere else. Don't let any strangers in your games. Don't let them goad you into making spread bets on the games. Report such illegal acts to me. The usual channels. In fact, anything or anyone strange."

He looked down at the cards on the table. "Remember anything strange whoever, and whatever it is. Check it out with me. Don't place bets with out of towners because..."

"Where they are, the Feds aren't far behind."

"That's true. Very true, but this game has become very high stakes and causing an interest in this town for them."

"Why are they interested in us, Sheriff?"

Sheriff Rawlings closed his eyes and wondered how some people survived without thinking. Out loud he said, "I haven't a clue." Then whispered very softly, "It's election year. And more important," he paused, "Big money. Big, big, money. And a bit of a fix is in the air. Just be careful. We are in everyone's crosshairs." He turned and left, pointing his finger at them. His parting look could have frozen the drinks rock solid in their glasses.

The bike shop began to light up as the night shift began to arrive, earlier than usual. A sure sign that events were building up.

"Look guys, the cops want these bikes for the kid's center by the end of the week. Sometime during or after the tournament to show we do more than play basketball for kids," Joe said.

There was a scramble as they tried to work faster. That lasted about seven seconds before they slowed down.

There was a bang on the side door. Joe looked out the window.

"It's Paul." He opened the door. Paul rode in on his bike, big saddlebags on each side of the bike. A huge basket was attached on the front handlebars. Rolled up newspapers were sticking out of the saddlebags like sentinels.

"How did you ride with this overloaded mess down here?" one of the workers asked.

"Sheriff said bring it down here. Unload it fast. I don't know what it is. Why you need all these newspapers? Do you know I'm not supposed to know I was even here?"

He rolled his eyes. "'Put it where you need it.' That's all he told me to say. Ever. I know nothing. You hear me?" He took a breath.

"I wasn't here." He looked around the garage. It was the first time he had been allowed in. He was not supposed to look around or stay longer than it took to unload the bike.

The head supervisor of the garage whistled and men came running and took the saddlebags off the bike, grabbed the basket's contents and rushed back upstairs.

Paul nodded. They opened the side door and he left.

"I don't like it. This whole venture was to be a secret operation to make money to help those kids that can't afford bikes get them," one of the men almost shouted. "Us, the sheriff and couple of cops. Now we got the whole police and sheriff's department, a kid and God knows who else fixing bikes for the kids and doing that other thing which will get us life in prison. I know it will."

"It will not get us into prison. Sheriff Rawlins is in charge. It will work. We need this other deal to keep fixing bikes. That costs money. Besides, part of this operation is to get the bad guys. No, it will work. Just concentrate on that. Sheriff said if we do our part. Just shut up." Joe began to work on another bike.

The first complainer hung his head. "I'm just tired. I owe that man my life. My job as one of the deputies, like all of you. It will work if he says."

Everyone went back to work while the two senior deputies talked out. They figured it was better not to know everything those two knew.

"We got tomorrow daytime, no more. We need those bikes for the day after the finals celebration. We need the bikes we got fixed for tomorrow night. Those so-called security guards are still holding that money in the Quad. Why they can't put it in the bank where it's safe I will never know," he said.

"Gambling money?"

"Yep."

"From those out of town guys?"

"Yep. Guess it mustn't see the light of day or banks."

"Well, I hope it's marked or something so that they can keep track."

"It's what they gather at the liquor stores on Friday and Saturday nights after the poker games. No markings. Plus this, my friend, is from the bets on the big game, Saturday." He kept working on the bike as he explained this project to his fellow deputy.

"How do you know so much if it's a secret?"

"Because once there was some kind of mix-up and I had to help collect. Sheriff asked me to. Could not mention the shop or us."

"I bet the Sheriff arranged for the mix-up for good reason. All that money goes to the treasurer's office?"

"All mixed up with tax money until they pay off the bets. That's so as to confuse the public. Keep it secret-like. So nobody will know."

There was a silence. The room gathered energy that seemed to cause whirling blades of light and bright circling lights. Then each person went back to work with an intense concentration and no waste of energy. There was a run tomorrow, game night. And they could still get the boys' bikes to them later and on time. Perfect cover.

Sheriff walked back to his office smiling. His walk and talk went well and he learned a great deal from the street folks.

He called his secretary.

"Yes, sir."

"I'm busy on reports. No visitors."

"Yes, sir."

Inside his office he checked the blinds to make sure they were open. Then went into the bathroom, read the message he received from Paul. Then flushed it down the toilet.

He doodled on a pad. Thought about Paul. He had to help that kid more. Had to have a walk and talk with him some day. A long one.

He went back to the window to look out on his town. Everyone was getting ready for tomorrow's game. Folks were buying party food at the Kroger's. Booze at the liquor store. He watched people stopping; saw heads nod and money slipped from hand to hand. A good healthy town. Except for that last note that Paul handed him.

A janitor having an accident? That intrigued him. It was time for another walk and talk if he had time. Need to connect with Ross. He's probably still at school seeing that it's ready for the game.

That night he drove around the town, the back roads, the mean streets, and the alleys. He was in an unmarked car, his own that he kept hidden in a rented garage. Under a fake registration. He wore the clothes that he kept for such occasions as his secret drive and look missions. That's what his deputies called them.

The first real job he ever had was at a filling station. He still wore that uniform proudly on these secret missions. He drove around the town. Watched the people gathering and talking in little groups. He looked in parking lots. Checked the out of state licenses.

Then he saw the janitor walking down the back alley behind the courthouse. Walking with a big man in a black suit. He smiled and headed back to his garage. Went to the wall phone and called *The Muncie Press*. "Give me the newsroom. Name's John Doe."

"News room. Hello there, John Doe."

"Did you get that picture of the man I asked about? Lawrence Edward?"

"Yes, sir. I sure did. And sir, Jesse is doing well. I took care of the bill like you said."

"Thank you. And any pictures of our guest in the city? A heavyset man in a black suit by chance?"

"Yes, sir. I have several pictures. I have a new box of cigars for you. Meet you at The Spot Cigar Store and Bar in five minutes."

Sheriff Rawlins smiled. Walked out of the garage around the corner to the Spot, which was so full of smoke, no one could have recognized him even if he was in uniform. As a general rule, the Spot folks never ever recognized anyone that came in.

He sat at the back table. Mac, his reporter friend, was already there. Pushed the cigars across the table to him. They both took one. Mac leaned across the table and lit the sheriff's cigar.

"They put prizes under cigars now like bubble gum cards," he whispered.

Rawlins smiled. He liked when things worked well. He walked out into the night carrying his box of cigars through a thicker haze of smoke. He went back into the garage. Changed clothes and headed back to his office.

At his desk called a number, "It's time. Tomorrow," was all he said. Sheriff Rawlins went to sleep satisfied that everything was in place.

When the deputy woke him up, he went to the window and looked out. It was time to get ready. It was important that he be in full dress uniform, standing beside the band, the flag, singing the "Star Spangled Banner," hand over his heart, even if he was in uniform. Hand over his heart went down good with the voters. Him being a veteran and all. Made him seem more patriotic. Tonight he had to make sure everyone was ready.

Just as the weatherman predicted the day started bright and clear. The town burst into activity. Cafes were serving breakfast, lunch and gallons of coffee. Bars were serving beer almost by the gallon, whisky by quarts. Radios in every home, business and car were playing loudly. Loud speakers hooked up to radios that blared out into the streets kept all the town folk, who lost in the draw for tickets, listening to the progress of the game. The announcer was giving the beginning statistics on WLBC.

It was a carnival of open-air fun with no rides, hawkers selling crepe paper pompoms and flags and almost a prayer service for the teams. It was broken only after the afternoon games decided who would play in the final. Then it ramped up.

The Congregationalist minister was inwardly praying for his team. Methodist chapel was open. The priest, a former Bearcat, was saying an extra mass for all departed Bearcats and adding all the boys playing today. He thought that was less sacrilegious. Quakers were sitting in silence, fingers crossed. The Baptists held altar calls.

The afternoon game increased the odds. The Bearcats and Badgers played the night game. Bearcats at home.

Orv's was packed with the hamburgers and shakes piling up on trays being delivered by shaky waitresses and waiters. They needed plenty of food and drink to celebrate the afternoon and get ready for the night game.

Future cheerleaders and future basketball players were practicing with all their might. Even got to stay up for the final game as night began to wrap around the city.

In the bike shop, bikes and men stood at the ready. Faces blacked, trousers and shirts black, even sock and shoes black. Lights out. Silence. No smoking.

Each of the field packs on their backs carried counterfeit money that Paul had delivered to them unknowingly. A small light blinked once. The first quarter had started. They pushed bikes back and forth, no squeaks.

The packed field house held hope for a Bearcat State Championship. It held hopes of big money for the big time gamblers who cheered for the team.

One man sat in his seat holding the warm cup of revenge laced with just enough booze to smell. He was pretending to work up a greater drunk to make sure he had been noticed. He cheered louder than anyone.

"You watch it, Lawrence Edward. You'll fall off the balcony. Then we'd have to get a new janitor."

He laughed and smiled. He had sailed close to the wind before, but not at full throttle. God, he wanted out of this town, to a paradise island somewhere with his "paramour." He liked that

word. Away from small town secrets and gossips. Rich, instead
of scrimping and kowtowing to the big bosses. Anything instead
of being a lowly janitor substitute. It had taken him long enough
to get that far. He had cleaned the floors of the poor suckers and
the rich to get to sub janitor. Them rich folks had cash money
from the taxes in that safe. The town owed him.

While he was dusting for the rich folk, he had saved every
penny. Who did they think owned some of them gambling parlors?
He'd fooled that stupid sheriff.

Pay them all back for what they did to his dad. Not lettin' him
play just because they caught him trying to fix a game. And what
about him? They never let him either because of his dad. This will
show them. He smiled. The bell sounded again.

Bodies tense, the bike shop riders eased onto streets with only
a swish of noise, pedaled and then glided down the dark streets
of Muncie. Down Liberty to Second.

Second quarter up. Had to keep going until the final gun.
Maybe since the fix was in they would have double money. Now
they rode from Charles to Walnut to the courthouse. The whole
town was as silent as Christmas Eve, right before Santa came.

Each man thought, *Santa is* sure coming tonight. The buzzer
sounded, an engulfing sound spread through the city like a dam
bursting, spreading joy through the streets and alleys.

Up the steps they pedaled. No moon, just clouds, big and
dark passing across the town like dark curtains on a stage opening
for actors. The eight men swishing by while the rest stood guard.

One man kept saying, "Into the valley of death they rode."

Opening the old courthouse doors. Wheeling up more steps
to the Treasurer's office in the dark and silent courthouse. The
safe combination expert spun the numbers on the locks. Listened
as the tumbler fell into place, opened the door and started handing
out the money.

Almost as fast as one line of men passed it down and stuffed
it into bags, the other line passed the "funny money" up to be
placed in careful piles in the safe.

It took half of a basketball quarter. They had practiced. They
coasted down the steps and sped off in twenty directions.

It was half time at the field house. The cheerleaders did their pyramid, shook their little bottoms and ponytails at the same time. Lawrence Edward went outside the field house, singing and making a scene.

"Oh, Lawrence Edward is as drunk as a skunk tonight."

"He won't last the night."

"Maybe he's celebrating all those nights of dusting."

"Must be tired of that. All the schools and the courthouse."

The janitor glad-handed the whole town, beaming and singing and laughing.

The bikers went into a tunnel a little way from the garage and entered the basement of the bike shop. Locked up the doors, took off and rolled up their clothes. Snow had started to fall. The temperature had dropped.

"I swear that WLBC is good with weather. It's a lot cooler.

"Yep, we need a fire."

"Always snows once during basketball tourney."

"Usually it's the sectionals not the finals."

They opened the big furnace and as fast as they took off the black clothes, threw them in the fire. They counted the money, placed it into piles. Each pile got the same amount. The rest went into a concealed wall safe.

"Gentlemen, a job well done. We got a cut for the shop. Sheriff gets the money for his kid program. Orphanage gets money. Schools get their share. The rest goes to the scholarship fund. And some big gang boss will wind up in the bend of the river when the big Chicago boys come through like a tornado with their counterfeit money."

Later on these same big out of town gang bosses dressed in black suits, went into the court house with empty briefcases as if they were on emergency city business that had to be conducted, walked out with a little fatter briefcases. Then climbed into a black Packard and drove swiftly away.

Lawrence Edward kept up his staggering act as he went home.

The field house doors broke open. People rushed out screaming and shouting. "We're the Mighty Bearcats." They bounded to their cars. Honked horns. Danced in the street. Filled Orv's, and all the diners, restaurants and bars. Celebrations went on all night.

The bike shop slept. Sheriff Rawlins made all the public appearances to watch over the good money left behind. Night slipped over the town as if nothing had happened.

The men in black were counting out money in their room at the Delaware Hotel before they sorted out the shares. One of men who was counting and sorting said quietly, "Stop."

"Go get that Lawrence Edward guy. There seems to be some confusion."

"Money short?"

"Money bad. Counterfeit."

While the city was ending its celebration, a big black Packard drove up the street as Mr. Lawrence Edward was walking home. Still pretending to sway just enough.

"Need a ride, Mr. Edward?" The car stopped along the curb. One man got out and held the door. Another got out of the back seat, and pointed to the empty space. He whispered in Lawrence Edward's ear, "The money was counterfeit." Then slammed the door.

Sheriff Rawlins watched from his office window as the Packard drove away.

"You know," he said to his deputy, "crime just doesn't pay."

The deputy smiled and continued to count out money and put it in big manila envelopes.

"This time it paid."

"Enough for the schools?"

"Yes, sir."

"There enough for the boys scholarships?"

"Yes, sir."

"Cheerleaders scholarships?"

"Yes, sir."

"Cheering block?"

"Well, sir, not quite enough."

The sheriff thought a minute.

"Them Jackson boys still running shine over by the big bridge?"

"Yes, sir. They are trying to."

"And are those Northern boys up by Gary still trying to muscle in on their business?"

"Yes, sir."

"And is the old-timers Basketball Tourney next week?"

"Indeed it is, sir."

"Then I think we can fix it so there's more scholarship money for the cheer block if we get busy."

"Yes, sir."

"The real tax money back in the safe?"

"Yes, sir."

Sheriff Rawlins smiled. He liked things on schedule and going smooth.

Clarence Crain: *A Former High School Hoops Player Remembers Championship Run*
M. B. Dabney

Shortridge is the oldest high school in Indianapolis. It made it to the state boys basketball final game once – in 1968 – and, according to Clarence Crain, it was a magical time. "The whole season was special," former Shortridge player Crane says decades later.

Under future ISHAA Hall of Fame Coach George Theofanis, the well-disciplined Blue Devils won the regional championship in 1968 for the second year in a row, this time against their arch-rival George Washington, with its stars George McGinnis and Steve Downing.

In the state semi-final game in the afternoon, played before a wildly cheering crowd at Hinkle Fieldhouse on the Butler University campus, the Blue Devils won 58-56 against Marion on a last second shot by Oscar Evans. But they fell 68-60 to Gary Roosevelt for the championship that night.

"It was disappointing," says Crane, who was a junior at the time. "But the seniors reminded us we'd have another "shot" the next year. And we thought we did."

Unfortunately, Shortridge players never cut down the nets in a state championship.

Despite Shortridge having its best regular season in its history (19-3) in 1969 and being ranked No. 7 in the final state press rating, McGinnis – who would be named Mr. Basketball that year – got his revenge.

Washington beat Shortridge 46-38 in the regional championship game. "We were leading until late in the game," Crain says. And, he learned a valuable lesson that he remembers from that day. "Sometimes you're playing not to lose instead of playing to win. It's not a formula for success."

Crain, who is now a program officer at Lilly Endowment, went on to play college ball at Butler, also under Theofanis, who remained a mentor and friend until the coach's death in January 2011.

And as for McGinnis and Downing, there are no hard feelings. He remains friends with them to this day.

REQUIEM IN CRIMSON
Brandt Dodson

After the expiration of the Bobby Knight years, I.U. basketball experienced a series of ups and downs that challenged the faithfulness of their most ardent fans. This was one of the up years, and March Madness was in full throttle. Indianapolis was bathed in crimson and nearly everywhere I looked, I.U. reigned supreme. Even as Mary and I sat in a booth at Johnny Rockets in the Circle Centre Mall and our server made a ketchup face on my plate, I couldn't help but wonder if she was an I.U. fan.

"How's business," Mary asked, snatching a French fry from my plate and dipping it in the smiling condiment.

"Better. The insurance work keeps the wolves from the door and..."

"And Callie?"

"Better. She's heading to college this fall."

"Lemme guess. I.U.?"

"Wow," I said. "You really are quite the detective."

"*Agent.* I'm an FBI Special Agent. *You're* the detective," she said, smiling and resting her folded arms on the table. "At least you are since leaving the bureau."

I dipped a French fry in the ketchup face.

"I didn't leave the bureau. It left me, remember?"

I had been terminated several years earlier for unprofessional conduct and although I was still considered a leper by a few in the local law enforcement community, I had managed to build a stable and growing private investigation business.

"Let's just say it was a separation and let it go at that," Mary said. "The point is you are a detective." She sighed and pursed her lips.

"Okay, what's wrong?"

"What do you mean?"

"You wouldn't ask me out to lunch and then drive all the way downtown to meet me if there wasn't a good reason."

She sighed again. "Do you remember Maurice Norman?"

"Sure. Nice guy. One of Indianapolis' best agents. He was killed in a bank holdup a few years ago."

She shifted in her seat. "I've stayed in touch with Estelle since he died. We're not close friends, but I look in on her once in a while just to say 'hi' or 'how're you doing,' that sort of thing."

"Sure." I bit into my cheeseburger.

"I saw her yesterday and I knew the minute I went into the house that something was wrong. It didn't take long before she opened up."

"And?"

Mary shook her head. "Nothing specifically and everything generally. Estelle said their son, Malcolm, isn't himself lately. He's picked up some new lingo and some new friends. *Strange* friends. And then there's the money. Lots of money. And items that he shouldn't have."

"What kind of items?"

"An iPad, a high-end cell phone. Video game systems. Expensive electronics."

"How long has Maurice been dead?"

"Three years."

"And how old is the boy?"

"Seventeen."

I began subtracting the figures in my head. I've never been good at fractions, but if simple subtraction is involved, I'm your man.

"He was fourteen when Maurice got killed," Mary said.

"I would have gotten it if you'd given me a little time."

"I only get an hour for lunch." She bit into her hamburger.

"Does Malcolm have a job? A lot of kids do at his age."

"Yes, but he's only working part time. Estelle told me she found a thousand dollars rolled in his sock drawer." She stole a fry and dipped it in my ketchup face. "He's working twenty hours a week at minimum wage."

I was tempted to run the numbers again, but decided against it.

"Maybe he's been saving."

She shook her head. "Huh uh. He's only been working for a month. Even if they didn't take out taxes, he couldn't have saved that much. Not by half."

The math was too advanced. I decided to take her word for it. "You added that up pretty fast."

"I went to college."

"Drugs?"

"No. Just college."

"Cute," I said.

She shrugged and snatched another fry. "Maybe. Drugs are always a concern."

I agreed. "Lots of kids seem to have money." I glanced around the mall, and Mary followed my eye line to the kids who seemed to dominate the establishment. Most of them were dressed in designer clothes and wearing tennis shoes that cost more than my car. Nearly all of them had cell phones, MP3 players or other electronic devices, and a majority of them were carrying more than one shopping bag from brand name stores. The bags were filled to capacity.

"I had a paper route," I said. "After collecting from the people who actually paid what they owed, I had less than twenty dollars a week."

"That was good in your day."

"It was. But I didn't save any of it."

Mary grinned. "Who was she?"

"Candace Paxton. *Candy*."

"Blonde?"

"Nope. Redhead."

"Wow. You and Charlie Brown have something else in common."

I ignored the remark. "I made sure she had all the shakes and bubble gum she could stand."

She dipped another French fry in my smiley face. All the dipping had given Mr. Ketchup a bad case of Bell's palsy.

"What do you want?" I asked. "Why tell me all of this?"

"Estelle wanted me to talk to him," she said around the French fry, "but I thought you'd be a better choice."

"Why? I haven't exactly done well in the daddy department."

She shook her head. "Callie's fine. You did well with her and when I look at Malcolm, I can see the same thing. Callie lost her mother. Her confidant. Malcolm's lost his confidant at a time when a boy needs his father the most." She ate another fry. "I thought maybe you could look into it. See where the money's coming from and help him get straightened out before it's too late."

I finished my cheeseburger and pushed the tray of fries toward Mary. "How does Estelle feel about that?"

"I haven't told her."

I gave her my best stern look.

"But I will," she quickly added. "If you'll take the case."

"What case is there to take, Mary? The kid's getting money from an unknown source, maybe drugs, maybe not, and he's too reckless to hide it from his mom. She can talk to him about it, clamp down a bit and he'll be fine."

She folded her arms. "It's more than that. He needs a man to come along side and set him straight."

"I can't replace Maurice."

"No one's asking you to. I'm asking you to look in on the kid and see what you can find out."

"And then what? Say, 'hey kid, you shouldn't be doing that?'"

She sighed and studied me by tilting her head to one side. Her hair fell over her shoulder like spun coal and her jade eyes fixed on me in a cop stare. "If that's what it takes."

I ate a fry. "Where do I find him?"

I couldn't remember a time in recent history when March Madness didn't manifest itself as much in the inclement weather as it did in fan fervor. But this year the season was unusually mild. There was virtually no snow, no ice, and very little rain. The temperature hovered in the mid-50s and nearly everyone was out and about touting the colors of their favorite team. When I reached Broad Ripple on the near north side, roving gangs of fans had congregated along the sidewalks, spilling over into the streets. I worked my way around them and found the Happy Jack's burger joint that employed Malcolm. According to Mary, Estelle said he was scheduled to work until closing at eleven, less than a half hour away.

I had never met Malcolm, so there was little chance of being recognized. But I knew his father well and the trying circumstances of his death.

Maurice Norman was an FBI agent assigned to the Indianapolis field office. In his day, he was the best of the best. But time took its toll and smoothed the edge he once had. He was killed in a bank holdup while making a deposit for his son's college fund. Feeling the invincibility that comes with years of carrying a badge, he had forgotten the cardinal rule for every police officer— always have your gun. He had left his in the car and when the robbers began shooting the customers indiscriminately, Maurice died with them.

Losing a parent is a trying event for anyone, particularly for a teenager about to blossom into adulthood and particularly if it's a boy who has lost his father. *Especially* if he loses his father suddenly and under the circumstances like those in which Maurice died.

I went into the restaurant and ordered a cheeseburger and soft drink for the second time that day. No ketchup faces here, though. Just a tray of food and a seat in the dining room.

I sat with my back to the wall, eyeing a group of teens that had gathered around an older man I guessed to be in his late twenties and who seemed to hold sway over the kids. Nearly all of them were sporting I.U. sportswear or other logo items, but the older man was dressed plainly in a leather jacket, jeans and tennis shoes. His smile, though, was infectious and the crowd hung on his every word. As the closing hour approached and the dining room began to empty, Malcolm emerged from behind his work station and approached the crowd. He smiled broadly at the older man who stood to exchange hand clasps and an embrace with the teen.

"Malcolm, my man. How are you?"

I couldn't hear the response, but it must have amused the man and the kids gathered around him. All of them laughed and Malcolm glanced at his watch.

"Later, my man," the older man said, as Malcolm left him to approach me.

"Sir, we're getting ready to close."

"Sure. Sorry. I was lost in my thoughts." I stood and handed him my empty tray. Over his shoulder, I saw that none of the kids were looking in my direction, but were once again, focused on the older man.

"Is there anything else, sir?"

I shook my head. "No. Just leaving."

I left the restaurant and drove to the parking lot of a competitor across the street. My contact with Malcolm had yielded more than I had anticipated. Now, I would wait for the rest.

It was nearly one o'clock in the morning, well after closing, before the crowd of teens that had gathered around the older man left the restaurant. Malcolm left with them and I watched as he again embraced the man and they exchanged hand clasps. Malcolm left in an older model Toyota, but it was the man I needed to know and I waited until he started his car and pulled from the lot heading south toward downtown Indianapolis. As soon as he drove out of the lot in a late-model BMW, I started my car and followed him, allowing enough room for intervening vehicles to allay suspicion. As soon as I had a make on his tag, I called Mary on my cell.

"Colton?" Her voice was raspy.

"I need you to run a tag."

"At this hour?"

"Excuse me, but didn't you want me to check up on Malcolm?"

"Yes, but..."

"No buts, Mary. Call the office and have someone run this tag."

She sighed. "Okay. I'll call you back."

I flipped my phone closed and continued following the Beamer toward Indy. The traffic was heavy and the reveling crowds remained strong, due in part to the fervor of the basketball finals as well as the mild weather. Within minutes, my phone chirped.

"It comes back to a Jamal Evans Crane." According to the address she gave me, he lived in an apartment building on north Meridian, just a couple of miles from the center of the circle city.

"He must be heading home," I said.

"There's more." Jamal had been arrested on two separate occasions for assault and once for armed robbery. He resisted arrest the last time, and an officer ended up in the hospital. There were no warrants, though, and he had a clean driving record. But although his record appeared clean, and he was idolized by a group of kids, it was clear that Jamal's relaxed demeanor was a façade, masking the heart of a very violent man.

I slept well that evening and began my day with a run around the perimeter of Garfield Park. My home lies on the periphery and the spacious area serves the residents of the Fountain Square area of Indianapolis quite well. After a significant renovation during a period of urban renewal, the drug dealers, gangs, and other ne'er do-wells vacated the Indianapolis landmark, leaving a peaceful oasis in the midst of the country's eleventh largest city.

After finishing my run, I showered, shaved, and filled my travel mug with coffee before taking the ten minute trip downtown to IMPD headquarters. I found Harley Wilkins, Captain of detectives, seated at his desk with his tie undone. It was standard fare for the man and I often wondered why he bothered to wear the thing at all.

He looked up when I approached and flashed a big grin. His hair had thinned over the years and the overhead lighting reflected off his black skin.

"Colton. And here I thought my day was getting off to a good start."

"It is," I said, taking a seat in the chair next to his desk.

"And what do you want?" He leaned back and folded his big hands behind his head.

"What makes you think I want anything?"

"'Cause you wouldn't be here otherwise."

He had a point. Although I had known and worked with Wilkins during my years with the FBI, and even though he was part of my poker group, we were not close friends. Instead, we were more like working acquaintances with a mutual respect. Most of the time.

"What do you know about a Jamal Evans Crane?"

"Nothing. Should I?"

I slipped him a note bearing Jamal's tag number. "He's befriended Maurice Norman's son. Estelle is concerned and Mary asked me to take a look."

Harley's expression darkened. "Maurice was a good man."

"Yeah."

"A good cop shouldn't die like that."

"Yeah."

He took the note from me and punched it into his computer. The NCIC homepage flashed on the screen within seconds and he entered the number. It wasn't long before he had the same information as Mary.

"I've got that," I said. "I was hoping you could tell me more."

"Like?"

I shrugged. "Anything. Something. I need to know what sway this guy has over Malcolm and his friends. If he's as bad as his record says, I need to know. If not, I need to know that too."

Wilkins sighed and picked up his phone. "I'll call records. See what we've got."

"Thank you. I appreciate it."

He shot a glance at me. "Darn straight you do."

The Indianapolis office of the FBI had outgrown its space in the Federal Building on north Pennsylvania Street and required new digs. At least that was the official story. In part, it was true. But the world had taken a decidedly different turn since 9-11, and the powers that be decided that a newer complex, one that was more isolated, would provide the extra level of security the bureau needed in the brave new world of the 21st century. So they moved into a new campus located smack dab in the center of the most densely populated section of the city.

The new FBI center was located in Castleton, the boom town of the 1980s, and was situated behind a wrought iron security fence that was manned and patrolled by the bureau's own police department, a relatively new feature that had come along since I was asked to leave.

I met with Mary Christopher at the new complex, but had to wait for her on the driveway near the guard shack. Because I was no longer a Special Agent, and because I was asked to leave under less than stellar circumstances, I was not invited inside. As soon as she was in the car I handed her one of the two coffees I had picked up at a nearby Hardees and drove around the semi-circular street in front of the FBI complex before heading back toward Castleton Square Mall where I parked in the lot and killed the engine.

"I just came from Harley's office."

"And?"

"And Jamal's a bad dude," I said, blowing on the coffee before sipping.

"His arrest record told us that."

I shook my head. "There's more. He was a candidate for a scholarship at I.U. Basketball. A full ride."

"What happened?"

"The assault. Didn't you read the details?"

She clucked her tongue. "I was asleep when you called, Sherlock. I gave you what they gave me."

"Sure. Well, apparently, he lost the scholarship when he assaulted the old woman."

"How old?'

"Almost eighty. He nearly killed her, then did a little bit of time and got out. He's been on the streets for less than a year."

She removed the lid on her coffee and blew before drinking. "What's he want with Malcolm?"

I shrugged. "Don't know. But it isn't basketball pointers."

"So where do we go from here?"

"*We?* You dumped this in my lap yesterday, remember? I don't recall there being any 'we' in this."

"Okay. What are *you* going to do?"

"I'm going to follow the FBI's standard protocol for things like this."

She shook her head. "The FBI doesn't have a standard protocol for things like this. In fact, we don't do things like this."

"I am going to follow Jamal," I announced.

She took my coffee from me and slid the cup into the cup holder between our seats. "The FBI does have a protocol on surveillance. That means no coffee."

"What goes in must come out," I said.

"And you can't watch anyone in the restroom."

I shot her a glance.

"You know what I mean," she said.

Jamal was a good ball player. I sat in my car the next evening, a few dozen yards from a schoolyard where he was shooting hoops with his friends. His athletic skills remained intact and his agility and grace were impressive. He outmaneuvered the others with ease, shot from mid-court and never missed, and could get inside for a layup before anyone even knew he had the ball.

After the last game, the crowd dispersed and Jamal picked up his jacket and water bottle before heading to the Beamer. He started the car and I followed him back to Happy Jack's where he parked in the side lot and flashed his headlights twice. Within minutes, Malcolm was exiting the restaurant from a rear entrance and slid into the seat next to Jamal. They talked briefly and then drove away with me in tow.

We drove north toward Carmel, an affluent suburb in Hamilton County, located directly north of Indianapolis. Jamal and Malcolm drove to the northern edge of the city before turning left toward the Monon trail. The trail is over sixteen miles long and follows a path that was established by the Monon railroad. The trail cut a swath through the northern edge of the city and was much preferred by Carmel's walkers, runners, and bicyclers as the place to indulge their passion. On this night it was fairly congested.

I parked several stalls away from the Beamer and sat patiently. I was rewarded within minutes when another car of kids, some who I recognized from Happy Jack's, parked alongside the BMW. Some of the occupants exited their vehicle and climbed into the back seat of Jamal's car. Nothing happened for the next twenty minutes, but then the kids climbed out of the Beamer and back into their own car before driving away.

I slid downward in my seat as they passed, but kept an eye on the driver's side rearview mirror. It was then I saw Jamal's car back out of the stall. Malcolm was driving.

I followed Malcolm as he drove back the way we came and then east toward the residential section of the city. I remained as far back as I could to avoid detection, yet close enough to make tailing him profitable. But as he crossed into an affluent neighborhood, the distance between us lessened and I eased on the brake. I was grateful to see him turn down a side street, giving me time and space to avoid detection. But then I turned the corner and saw the Beamer parked in front of a house, nose-to-nose with the car the other kids were in when they met with Jamal just a few minutes before.

I extinguished my headlights and parked a hundred yards from where Malcolm was parked. It wasn't long before I was rewarded for my efforts. The kids from the other car were running from the house, their arms loaded down with computers and other, smaller valuables. They sped away as soon as they were in their car and Malcolm followed in Jamal's BMW.

For the second time that evening, I slid downward in my seat to avoid detection.

"Was he there?" Mary was leaning across the table at McDonald's.

"Yes."

She groaned.

"He was driving."

Mary sighed and folded her hands on the table in front of her. "I got off the phone with Carmel PD just before you got here. Those kids invaded the house of an old lady. They cut off the power and then cut her phone line to keep the alarm system from going off. When they tied her up, she was disconnected from her oxygen tank. She died while they were stealing her stuff, Colton."

"Mary …"

"Colton. Don't even go there. He's as guilty as the rest of them, and now an old lady is dead."

"Mary, he didn't invade the house. He drove. His worst crime is being stupid."

"He drove the car, Colton."

I could feel my anger begin to rise. "Listen, you wanted me involved so now I'm involved. If you think this kid can be saved then I'm willing to try."

"There's nothing you can do."

"Yes there is. This Jamal has power over Malcolm and the others. I need to take him down."

"By the time you take this guy down, Malcolm will be in jail, Colton. This guy is using these kids to burgle for him and then he's selling the swag."

"Probably. He's staying away from the higher profile stuff like drugs, and keeping his profile low. But I'm not trying to save all of them. I'm trying to help Malcolm. One kid, Mary. Just one out of the lot. It's worth the effort."

"I know." She ran a hand through her hair. "That explains why Estelle keeps finding cash and high ticket items."

I agreed. "Jamal lets these kids keep some of the fruits of their labors as motivation."

We sat in silence for a while, each of us alone with our thoughts. Overhead, a TV was playing a pre-game commentary for the evening's playoffs.

"I've got an idea," I said.

"What?"

I stood. "Keep your cell phone on. If it works like I think, I'll call you."

"And if not?"

I shrugged. "Then Jamal wins."

My plan in place, I made my move.

I was sitting outside Jamal's apartment when he left the building. It was a few minutes after two in the afternoon when he fired up the Beamer and headed north along Meridian toward the Broad Ripple area. I followed, and we drove to the same basketball court at which I had seen him playing previously. He parked near the court and I drove past him parking twenty yards away on the opposite side of the street. I adjusted my rear view mirror and watched as he climbed out of the car with a water bottle in one hand and a basketball tucked under his arm. Once inside the court, he slipped out of a gray windbreaker, dropping it to the ground, and gulped from the bottle before dribbling the ball to center court where he began shooting hoops. When it was clear that he was going to be alone, I climbed out of my car and approached him. He was in mid-shoot position, ball up and eyes on the basket, when he noticed me.

"You want something?" he asked.

"Yeah? And what would that be?" He bounced the ball with one hand while keeping the other on his hip. His stance was defiant. Belligerent. A phony bravado I'd seen too many times.

"I was told you can score."

"Of course I can score. Why? You want to play old man?" He laughed.

"I'm not talking about a game. I'm talking high stakes."

His smile faded. "I don't know what you're talking about." He bounced the ball.

"Sure you do. You've been scoring houses and you've got a crew that I hear is pretty good."

"Get out of here, man." He bounced the ball and shot another hoop. The ball swished through the basket.

"I know where there's a good mark. Going to be empty, too."

"I told you to get lost." He shot the ball into the basket.

I stood closer, watching him shoot. He stopped and turned to me.

"What's your problem? Get out of here or I'll call the cops"

"Call. I don't care. But I'll bet you do."

His eyes narrowed.

"I'm not a cop," I said. "But I do know about you. I get around too."

He snorted. "Yeah, you look like you get around, White Bread." He bounced the ball and shot again. Again, the ball swished effortlessly through the basket.

"I'm getting divorced and there's no way I'm going to let my old lady take everything I've worked for," I said.

He shot again and scored.

He shot again. "I said I don't know what you're talking about."

"My wife has over a half million in jewelry and there's other stuff inside too. Real silver, some original art."

He snorted again. "Who are you man? Bill Gates?" He laughed and shot the ball again. He scored.

"I want you to take the stuff and then hold it."

"Hold it? For who?"

"For me. I'll file the claim. In sixty days you get the cash and I get to keep my stuff."

He shot the ball and missed. It bounced off the backboard and he caught it on the rebound. He turned to face me with the ball tucked under his arm.

"There'll be no one home. I guarantee it," I said. "So? You in or do I need to find someone else?"

"Striking the shepherd will scatter the sheep," I said as we sat in my car, two blocks from the target house.

"Very philosophical," Mary said.

"Isn't it though?"

I had the windows of the car rolled down and a cool breeze wafted through. It was half past one in the morning and we had been on stakeout for several hours. So far, nothing had happened.

"Whose house is this, anyway?" she asked.

"It belongs to the Chief of the Carmel PD. When I explained the plan to her, she offered the use of her house without hesitation."

"Is she going to show up tonight?" she said.

I was about to answer when Mary's phone vibrated. She flipped it open. "Yes? Great. Okay. Great. Thanks." She flipped the phone closed.

"What?"

"That was one of Harley's men. They're tailing Jamal from his apartment. He met up with the kids and they're heading this way."

"Is Malcolm with them?" I asked.

"Yes."

"Good."

She half turned in her seat to face me. "Wouldn't it be better if he wasn't? I mean, I understand your plan, but if he gets involved he will go down with the rest of them."

"This isn't just about Malcolm getting away from this current predicament. It's about him becoming a man and developing a philosophy about life. He's a kid now, Mary, and he's allowing himself to be easily led. There will be other Jamal's in Malcolm's life and going to jail for burglary isn't going to teach him how to handle them. He needs to grow a set. He needs to know when to say no." I turned to face her. "He needs a moral compass. Something that he can rely on when future Jamal's try to steer him wrong, whether it's a burglary scheme or a bad investment opportunity or insurance fraud. He needs internal boundaries."

"And how's this going to give him that?"

"If everything goes as I hope, he will see Jamal fold like a paper tiger. But if not, and Malcolm's arrested with the rest of them, he will learn that there are penalties for his actions and that sometimes the cost is very high. Either way, the lesson won't be fatal, although I admit, I'm hoping for one over the other."

She sighed and we didn't talk for the next few minutes. Then, when the Beamer turned onto the street, several blocks ahead of us, Mary sat upright.

"There. That's it, isn't it?" She said.

"Looks like it." The car passed under a street light and I could make out two people. "It's probably Jamal and Malcolm." Seconds later, the second car appeared. "That's them."

Mary and I watched patiently as the cars circled the house by rounding the block. A few minutes later, they appeared again and parked curbside. Within seconds, four figures climbed out of the car and ran along the lawn toward the house. Jamal and Malcolm sat patiently in the Beamer as the crew worked diligently at a side window. Once it was open, they climbed in, one after the other. Neither Mary nor I said a thing, each of us watching, alone with our own thoughts. A few minutes later, the kids appeared at the same window through which they had entered. They dropped several swag-laden pillow cases onto the ground and then the first of them climbed out, and began assisting the others. Once all of them were out of the house, they scanned the area and began running toward their car. Then, without warning, cops seemed to emerge from everywhere. They came from behind the house and from the bushes and shrubbery that lined other homes along the street. Flashlights exposed the kids and their frightened expressions. It was then that the Beamer started and began driving away, only to be blocked by an unmarked Carmel PD squad car with a magnetic emergency light attached firmly to the vehicle's roof.

I started my car and floored the accelerator, coming on the Beamer within seconds. Mary and I jumped out of the car and ran to the BMW. A uniformed Carmel police officer was jerking Jamal from the passenger's side of the car. I opened the driver's side door and pulled Malcolm from behind the wheel. He was crying, but when he saw Mary he seemed confused.

"Mary?"

"Malcolm, your mother is concerned about you."

He looked at me. Although he knew he had seen me before, it was obvious he couldn't recall when or where.

"Hey, man," Jamal said, "I didn't have nothing to do with this. That kid," he nodded to Malcolm, "and the others they told me they was going to check up on their grandmother. I was just along for the ride. I didn't know nothing about—"

"Save it," I said, stepping from the shadows with my hand locked firmly on Malcolm's arm.

"You?" He shook his head. "Man, I should've known."

I glanced at the officer who had helped arrange the sting.

"Go, get out of here," he said.

I maintained my grip on Malcolm and half-walked, half-carried him to my car.

"Go ahead," Jamal yelled after us. "Take that baby with you. He ain't a man. He's no better than his mommy. Go on, kid. Get out of here. I don't need you or any of your friends."

I jammed Malcolm in the back seat and slid in next to him. Mary got behind the wheel and started the car. We drove past the Beamer where Jamal was stretched over the hood as handcuffs were snapped in place. He locked eyes with Malcolm and mouthed a threat as we drove away.

Mary, Malcolm and I sat in a Denny's on 38th street. The place was quiet and Mary and I were having coffee. Malcolm was having coffee and a slice of apple pie. The pie was untouched and he sat with his folded arms resting on the table. His red-rimmed eyes were dry.

"He handed me over like I was nothing," he said.

"He was using you," I said. "That's what guys like him do, Malcolm."

Mary put her arm around him.

"I was stupid," he said.

"No," I said. "You were seventeen and you did a stupid thing. But you can recover from it. You have a second chance. Your father had big dreams for you, Malcolm. But you have to have dreams for yourself. You have to keep those close to you and never let anyone take them from you. Jamal had dreams once and could have played basketball for I.U. And who knows? He may have been good enough for the NBA. But he blew his chance and he knows it. You still have yours, but it can slip away from you if you're not careful."

He lowered his head and began to weep. I glanced at Mary and saw in her eyes what we both knew. Malcolm had crossed the threshold and returned to tell about it. He hadn't lost his dream.

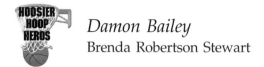

Damon Bailey
Brenda Robertson Stewart

Damon Bailey is from Heltonville, Indiana, a very small town east of Bedford. When he was an eighth grader, he was recruited by Indiana University legendary coach, Bob Knight, and drew national attention. Damon became almost a cult figure when he played for Bedford North Lawrence High School. Little old ladies formed car pools and drove to whatever city Damon was playing in. The fans supported Bailey with zeal.

Sports Illustrated listed Damon Bailey as the country's best ninth-grade hoopster in 1986. That year Damon led BNL to the state Final Four averaging over 23 points a game in the process. His team lost to two-time defending champion, Marion, in the semifinals.

Bailey was named First Team Indiana All-State that year, and every other year of his high school career. As a senior, he led his team to the 1990 state championship before a crowd of more than 41,000 people at the Hoosier Dome in Indianapolis — arguably the most people to ever attend a high school basketball game.

Bailey finished his high school career having appeared in three state Final Fours and scoring a record 3,134 points. He was named Indiana Mr. Basketball, earned McDonald's All-American honors, and was the 1990 consensus National Player of the Year. Bailey was a four year starter for Bob Knight and the Indiana Hoosiers. The team won two Big Ten championships in 1990-1 and 1992-3, and reached the Final Four during the 1991-92 season.

Damon Bailey retired from professional basketball in 2003.

GIVE AND GO
Marianne Halbert

"But what about the dead homeless guy? Or the cafeteria food poisoning?" Josie Morton said. "Interviewing Gard is just fluff. We've got nepotism in the cheerleading squad, banned books...I already *have* stories to investigate." She was getting no response, and growing desperate. "I'm even pretty confident there's something suspicious going on with those marching band kids. I mean, who would voluntarily march for hours each day unless they were under duress?"

Og Henderson shoved his way into the room, banging his knee on the door, and his tripod on the doorframe. "Hey, Mr. B.," he said, eyes focused on the equipment he was carrying, "I got some great shots at—," then he looked up. Josie drooped her head to one side, her razor-cut bangs hanging like blond daggers over her eyes. She glared at Og, seething. Og took a step back until his lanky frame bumped the wall, then stood silent. Mr. Bovine had never taken his eyes off Josie.

"When it's March," he said, "and we're in Indiana, nothing takes precedence over basketball. And there's nothing more important in basketball than a star player. Besides, he's got a great story. Raised by a single mom. Top of his class. A shoo-in for Mr. Basketball. Every college team in the NCAA is going after him. The town's dying to hear what's inside that boy's head. God willing he'll stay with the Big Ten, but he refuses to talk. I want that Gard Calway interview, and I want it by Monday."

Josie Morton stared at Mr. Bovine, unbelieving. *Some faculty advisor. What's the point of being on the high school paper if I can't do any investigative reporting? I should've stuck with volleyball.* She let out a breath, looked to the stained ceiling tiles for backup, then back to Mr. Bovine.

"Fine."

Mr. B. smiled.

Squatty old bald guys must have no idea that when seventeen-year-old girls said 'fine,' things were anything but. Josie was pretty sure Og tried to say something complimentary about her pink highlights as she stormed out, but the words he spoke were dwarfed by the ones in her head.

She slammed her locker door shut, ignoring whatever fell inside. *Seven kids sent to the hospital after eating Pot-Pie Surprise two days ago. Seven!*

Josie shoved her backpack into the corner of the bus seat, causing her window to slide down an inch. *Mrs. Dearing chooses her niece to head the cheerleaders.*

She slammed the head of broccoli onto the cutting board in her kitchen. *Dead guy found in the ravine behind the cross country track.* Chop. *On school grounds.* Chop. *But nooo.* Chop. She had to interview—

"Gard Calway?" Josie didn't like the way the smile slinked across her mom's face later as she said the name. "You two were so close in first grade. Remember that volcano proj—"

"Yes, Mom. I remember the volcano project." Josie plunked ice into two tall glasses. "And second grade when you and his mom were room-mothers together, planned all the class parties." She filled the glasses with water. "You know what else I remember?"

Her mom opened the oven door, easing her head away to avoid the heat.

"Third grade. When I was rollerblading and fell in front of his house. My knees were bleeding." She set the glasses down on the table, maybe a little too hard. "I remember how he and his friends laughed. Sixth grade, when he stole my iPod—"

"Which you'd leant him—"

"Which he denied, and never gave it back."

Her mom put the broccoli-stuffed chicken breasts on their plates, and sat down at the table. "Boys lose things: iPods, their homework, their temper. He was probably just too embarrassed to tell you."

Josie plopped down into her chair, and used her fork to pierce the chicken. Creamy sauce spilled out and pooled on the plate. Josie's voice was low, speaking more to her fork than to her mom. "Seventh grade. When I ceased to exist."

"Oh, Honey, lots of kids grow apart in middle school. But that was five years ago, and he's a big star now." She passed Josie a napkin. "And you're a star reporter," she said, almost as an after-thought. She placed her elbows on the table and folded her hands together. She closed her eyes, steam still rising from her plate. "Shall we say grace?"

Josie sat alone in the bleachers, netbook on her lap, while the team practiced on the court below. She pulled up the story from yesterday's town paper.

Student Finds Unidentified Body on School Grounds: According to officials, a freshman training for the 5K discovered a body when his attention was drawn by something shiny in the ravine that skirts the edge of the school property line. The deceased is presumed to be homeless. The cause of death remains unknown, pending an autopsy. Homicide detectives were called to the scene. Anyone with information is asked to contact the Sheriff's office.

Sneakers squeaked on the gymnasium floor as Gard's opponents scrambled toward him for the ball. Gard tossed the ball away to a teammate, then raced, unhindered, toward the basket. The ball whizzed back toward him. He caught the pass. Josie watched him. *He's not even worried they'll stop him.* It was probably only a second or two, but he took the time to plant himself, to focus on the net. His body moved, arms pulling the ball toward him before thrusting them up and out, release. The ball soared in a perfect high arch, falling through the net with a soft *swish* as she held her breath. A whistle blew. The coach used some hand gestures and another player took the ball outside the lines, bounced it a couple times, then tossed it back into play.

She read over the newspaper article again. *Why do they presume the guy was homeless?* Her eyes kept going back to the word shiny. *What did you have that was so shiny?*

The practice broke up, and she scrambled down the steps.

"Gard, wait up."

He turned, a few of his teammates giving him a look. He used a towel to wipe sweat from his face, then tossed it across his shoulder as he walked up to Josie.

"Mr. Bovine wants an interview for the school paper," she said.

Gard smiled and shook his head, with a *not this again* look. "Josie, you know I don't give interviews."

Wow, she thought as he headed toward the locker room. *He still remembers my name.* That took her off guard, just for a second. After he'd walked through the door, Josie could hear the muffled sound of good-natured rough-housing coming from the locker room, but as she stood alone on the gymnasium floor, it was the sound of the ticking clock that echoed in her ears.

"And, Gard, you know I don't give up so easily." She hefted her backpack over her shoulder, and exited through the back door, leaving the testosterone-laden boys, and the ticking clock, behind.

"They say it's because he's afraid of what they'll ask. About his mom," Og said. He sat on top of a picnic table behind the school, the sunlight making his mop of red hair seem even brighter than usual. Josie had her netbook open again, and was shuffling through photos Og had taken.

"Is that what they say?"

She continued to click through the images. The façade of the Health Department. A close-up of today's cafeteria lunch on a tray. *Were those the tips of Og's orange sneakers poking out in the background as the shot zoomed down on the tray in his hand?*

"You know," he said, "about her drinking."

Josie looked up for a moment. "She doesn't drink. I used to be fr..., I used to go to school with him. She never drank." The track kids came around the corner of the building and ran past. "I'll be right back."

She ran to catch up to Mark Santos, and came up alongside him.

"Hey, Mark. I was wondering if I could ask you a few questions. About the body."

Mark kept running, looking straight ahead. But it didn't escape her notice when he tightened his jaw. *So the rumors are true. He's Anonymous Freshman.*

"The paper said the guy seemed homeless—"

"I'm not supposed to discuss it."

"He's probably got a family somewhere," Josie said, panting. "Any details could help identify him."

Mark kept a steady pace, but glanced over for a moment, annoyed. "I didn't look too close. He had on a ratty coat. That's all I saw."

A stitch in her side was getting worse. Josie slowed, letting Mark pull ahead. She stepped to the edge of the path to allow other runners to go by. She bent over at the waist, breathing hard, then headed back toward Og. She dropped down onto the picnic table bench, her chest heaving.

"You...camera people...have the easy job," she wheezed.

Og shook his head. "No, we have to make everything around us seem more than it is. More dramatic, more sinister." He was focused on the computer screen. "More beautiful."

Josie sat up, and saw a candid shot of herself near her locker. She was in mid-laugh. He really did make her look beautiful.

Og fidgeted. "Sometimes, there's not much room for improvement." He switched the screen to another photo. "Oh, I love that one," he said, pointing at the screen. "If you do get the interview, that'll be a great shot." Josie looked back at the screen. There was Gard, brooding, leaning back against a bright red sports car. She shook her head.

"Yeah, but if he scratched that guy's car, he'll forfeit his first year's salary to pay for the paint job."

Og furrowed his red brows. He reached over, and tapped the arrow. The pictures forwarded. Gard opening the car door. Gard driving away.

"You did surveillance on him?" she said, genuinely surprised.

"I prefer to call it research."

"That's not—" she breathed, then went through the photos again. "Is that a Ferrari? That's not possible. How does a kid with a poor single mom afford a car like that?"

"He's poor?" Og said. "I just figured, you know with that car, and the club, well I just thought he was one of the richies."

Josie shut the netbook, stood up, and looked directly at Og. "What club?"

They spent the afternoon trying to find out if anyone at the club remembered seeing Gard there. After a few misses, they found a waitress that recognized him from the photos. He'd dined there for lunch with one other person. A man who flashed a bright smile and a lot of cash. And she remembered the man handing a set of car keys over to Gard as they stood up from the table, and saying "It's a deal." Og drove Josie home. They sat in his car in her driveway.

"I hate to believe it," she said. "I know every college in the Big Ten and beyond wants him. But this is illegal. If he's being courted, bribed, by some scout, we've got a scandal on our hands."

Og thumped the steering wheel a few times. "I don't know Josie. We've got no proof it was a scout. Since it wasn't a group of old men, probably not alumni. Could be a sports agent."

"Oh, please. Scout, alumni, agent? What's the difference? If he takes a bribe, he loses his eligibility. He's got to make a decision soon. The guy wines and dines him, well, maybe just dines him, but then gives him a car? My gut is telling me something is way wrong with this picture. And even with your mad skills, it's looking ugly."

"So what do we do now?"

"*We* don't do anything. *I'm* going to get him to talk."

Josie slipped the note, written on bright orange paper, through the slats in Gard's locker door. *I know your secret. I'd like to hear your side before I print the story.* He approached her in the hallway after fifth period.

"The terrace. After school."

Josie hadn't been to the terrace in years, even though it was within walking distance from her house. She couldn't even remember how it had gotten that nickname. It was just a small blacktop court, crumbling even more now than she'd remembered. There was a brick wall with a concrete top that they had walked on as kids. It had seemed so tall then, but now it didn't even come up to her waist. Disintegrating strands of string clung to the rim of the basketball hoop. A faded yellow hopscotch board was barely recognizable. Gard was sitting on the brick wall.

"How did you find out?" he asked.

"The lunches at the club. The car."

Gard slumped, as though the weight of the world was pulling him down. Josie sat down on the brick wall next to him.

"This is where I learned," he said. "Right here. Shooting over and over. And here you were, walking along this wall, arms out to your side for balance. I wanted to impress you. I wanted you to see me."

Josie's eyes scanned his face. *He's telling the truth. He...wanted to impress...me.* She had to remind herself to keep her breathing steady. *Get the confession.*

"Then there was that day," he said, his voice cracking. "Behind my garage. We were finishing sixth grade. Dad had been gone almost a year. I was listening to his favorite song on your iPod. "We Are the Champions." It was the first day of March Madness. He and I *always* watched the games together. You know, when we made our brackets, he talked about some of the players like he knew 'em. It was weird. He put them on a pedestal, but the way he talked, he was right up there beside 'em. Anyway, it was the first day of the tournament. And he hadn't come home. That's when I knew. He was never going to come home. And as that thought is settling in my gut, my mom stumbles to the curb. She'd bagged up her empties, along with all the clothes he'd left, and set them out in the trash. I pulled out a jacket, a khaki raincoat sort of thing, and slipped it on. Hung down to my knees. The sleeves swallowed my arms. I ran down that alley toward the terrace, and from the shadows, I saw you. Right here on this wall."

He shook his head, angry with himself. His lower lip quivered for just a moment.

"All those times I'd wanted you to see me. And in that moment you did. Me, tear-stained face, dirty from digging through the trash, dwarfed inside the jacket of a man who no longer existed."

Josie pulled her legs up onto the concrete and hugged her knees.

"I remember." He had run away. She followed, but he ducked into his garage, and she'd turned around and walked home. They never spoke again until this week. "Gard, I know growing up without your dad had to've been hard. But you've come so far. I just don't get why you'd throw it all away, for money, for things."

"You think it was about the money?" he spat. "I told him what he could do with his money. If he thought that would make up for what he did to me, to Mom…"

Mom?

"He was waiting for me after practice one day. Had heard what a star I'd become. Had even watched a couple of my games. Said nobody was as good at the 'Give and Go' as I was. Toss it away, move in for the easy score. The key was making sure my enemy kept his eye on the ball, and not on me. Said he wanted back in my life. Took me to a fancy lunch and gave me a car. I told him I'd accept it, on one condition. He'd shown me the good life. I brought him back to the house to show him ours. The torn screens, the stains the leaky roof left on our ceilings, the food stamps. Mom's AA tokens. I asked him to slip the jacket on. The one I'd pulled from the trash. The one I'd worn hundreds of times when I was alone. It was moth-eaten, musty."

The word *ratty* forced its way into Josie's mind.

"Only the buttons still shined," Gard said. "I'd seen to that. He hesitated but was so desperate to please me. He slipped it on."

Josie's stomach clenched. A moth-eaten jacket. Like something a homeless man might wear. With shiny buttons that might reflect the sun into the eyes of a cross-country kid.

"Gard," she breathed out. "What did you do?"

He'd been telling the story, lost in his own world. He looked into Josie's eyes. "You know what I did. You know my secret. But if you mean why? I saw the disgust in his eyes when he slipped that coat on. Disgust over who he'd been, who he'd been married to. Who I was. And it hit me. An epiphany, just like back in sixth grade. *He* was the one who'd mastered the 'Give and Go.' Tossed us away. Swept back just in time for the easy score. He hadn't come back to be my dad. Just to be a star-struck fan riding my coattails to the Hall of Fame. His fatal mistake was keeping his eye on the ball. He should have been watching me."

He pounced so swiftly, Josie wasn't prepared. He grabbed her and pulled her down on the back side of the brick wall. She tried to scream but he put his hand over her mouth.

"I'm sorry Josie. When he moved to take the coat off, I lost it. I put the body in the trunk of that fancy car of his and drove, not even thinking about where I was going. I got closer to the school and I panicked. I dumped the body."

Josie squirmed underneath him, clawing at his face. Gard kept one hand over her mouth, and put the other around her neck and squeezed. He began to sob. Apologizing. Explaining that if his mom found out what he'd done, she'd go back to the bottle, or worse. Josie struggled to push him away as her lungs burned. Gard's tears splashed onto her cheeks. Pressure was building up in her head. All she could see was the brick wall which suddenly seemed to loom over her, the sun bright overhead. Then a dark shape rose, blocking the light, and leapt down on top of Gard.

Og swung the tripod and caught Gard squarely on the back of the head. Gard went limp, and Josie shoved him off of her, gasping for air. She looked at Og, who was trembling.

"You...you...," she breathed. "Research?"

Og held a hand out to help her up. "I prefer to think of it as surveillance." He called for the police and an ambulance.

As they took Gard away, Josie knew the only ball he'd play now would be on a tiny concrete court, caged in by a tall chain-link fence. And beyond that would be walls that reached far higher than those of a neighborhood playground from a fading childhood memory. She hoped he would keep his eye on the ball, for if he raised his gaze toward the summit of those walls, all that would wink back at him would be the cold unyielding stare of razor wire.

Indiana Basketball Hall of Fame
Brenda Robertson Stewart

Indiana worships the game of basketball so it is only fitting that there be a Hall of Fame to pay tribute to the greatest figures in the sport. Indianapolis was the home of the Hall of Fame from 1970 to 1986. The building was sold in 1986 and bids were received from 13 communities and New Castle was selected for the new site. The two story structure is located on a five acre site near the intersection of Highway 3 and Trojan Lane. Highway 3 is accessible from Interstate 70.

The Indiana Basketball Hall of Fame epitomizes what visitors might call "Hoosier Hysteria." Indiana high school players and coaches, both men and women, are the focus.

In Indiana, basketball is a passion and part of the state's heritage. The 14,000 square foot museum features not only the teams and individuals who have been recognized, but it contains a number of interactive exhibits to bring the visitor closer to the action of Indiana high school basketball. There is an introductory film shown in the Marsh theater and memorabilia of all previous state championship teams is located on the ramp down to the main exhibition floor which is designed to replicate those at Butler's Hinkle Fieldhouse, where many basketball championships were played. The enshrinement hall is where each inductee is permanently honored, the John Jordan library is available for research on over 1,000 Indiana high schools, and archived game films are available to watch upon request. The gift shop has items to purchase as mementos.

Players become eligible for Indiana Basketball Hall of Fame induction 26 years after he/she played high school basketball. Coaches are eligible after 25 years of varsity coaching or 10 years after retirement from high school coaching. Anyone can make a nomination, but a state-wide board of directors oversees the process and each year there are directors appointed to represent each part of the state.

THE ODDS ARE ALWAYS UNEVEN
Sarah Glenn and Gwen Mayo

"Oh, dear, I forgot," Teddy said, scowling over her spectacles at the hotel register. "I wrote 1925 instead of 1926."

The clerk smiled at the curly-headed woman in the red coat.

"Don't worry, ma'am, I've written the same thing five times today. The new year's not even a week old."

"Did you have a big party here?"

She turned to scan the lobby and, behind her companions, the lengthening line. "Your establishment seems very popular. Was there a live band in your dining room, perhaps, people dancing, cheering as the clock hands inched towards midnight..?"

"There's no time to indulge your imagination, dear," Cornelia said. "We barely have time to dress for dinner. Young Roland will be waiting."

"Of course." She nodded to the clerk. "I'm sorry, but I have to go now."

The man fought back a grin. "Yes, ma'am. Here are the keys to your room"—he handed the set to Teddy—"and here are the keys for Mr. Pettijohn's room. Both of them are on the ground floor."

The white-bearded man puffed up. "Professor Pettijohn. I was a full professor at the University of Kentucky for forty-six years. Started back when it was still the Kentucky Agricultural and Mechanical College."

"My apologies, Professor. Please enjoy your stay."

Cornelia prepared to take charge of the baggage, but was intercepted by a young man, slender and tall.

"Allow me, ma'am. I can't let a lady carry the luggage of three people. Especially if Uncle Percy's got one of his contraptions in his suitcase."

"Roland!" Professor Pettijohn laughed and gripped the youth's shoulders. "You beat us here."

"They call me Rollo now. I came over with some buddies." 'Rollo' looked Teddy and Cornelia over. "Which one of you lovely ladies is my cousin?"

"The one built like a fire plug, of course."

Cornelia gave her uncle the same glare that had chastened entire hospital wards full of doughboys.

The old man ignored her.

Rollo was the one to tsk, though. "Really, Uncle. Now I can't greet either of them without putting my foot into it," he said. "I know, I will introduce myself."

He treated them to a grand bow, made comic by the floppy gray flannel pants he wore.

"I am Roland Gray, at your service, ladies."

Teddy gave him a little curtsy.

"I am Theodora Lawless, but everyone calls me Teddy. This is your—is he your cousin, or is he something once removed?"

"Cousin is the best term. I'm Cornelia."

The lad bowed again, this time without the exaggerated motion.

"Pleased to meet both of you."

He lifted one of the suitcases.

"Oof. This must be one of his. I'll go get a cart."

"Really," Cornelia grumbled at his disappearing back, "Do you believe these suitcases walked into the lobby on their own?" Her companions might both use canes, but she had carried her own baggage since she served under Colonel Roosevelt at the San Juan Heights.

Teddy laid a hand on Cornelia's arm. "How sweet of you, Rollo." She added, with a whisper, "Be nice, dear."

Cornelia was nice.

Uncle Percival extended the crook of his elbow to Teddy. "You look charming tonight, Miss Lawless."

Teddy's giggle hadn't changed with the years.

"And you're so dashing, Professor."

Cornelia trailed behind, watching the pair amble down the hallway like a stick insect over a pond. Teddy's arm locked with Percival's, giving the old man some support. He acted like he never needed help, but he'd claimed to be seventy-five for over ten years.

"Do you think your nephew will be wearing those silly pants again?"

"Oh, Cornelia, those are Oxford bags. They're popular with the college crowd these days."

"You are *au courant*, my dear lady."

Sounds of scuffling echoed in the nearby stairwell. Perhaps someone had brought more luggage than he could handle.

A muffled cry convinced her otherwise.

Cornelia sidled around her uncle and dashed for the door. She jerked it open and saw two men wrestling a third. The third man, tall and thin, must have been the source of the cry, since he now had a hand clamped firmly over his mouth.

It was Roland.

"Unhand him!"

She grabbed one of the men by his shirt collar and jerked it hard. A button snapped loose and ricocheted off the wall.

The thug responded by freeing one arm long enough to give her a hard shove. "Get lost, sister. You don't want none of this."

Cornelia lunged forward. This time, she slapped him sharply on the ear, producing a howl of pain.

Uncle Percival and Teddy entered the stairwell. The old man's first response was similar to his niece's: "Unhand my nephew!"

He laid into the pair with his cane, made of stout oak and topped with a silver wildcat's head.

Cornelia snatched Teddy's cane from her hand. "Excuse me, dear, but I need this." Now both of them were beating on the pair of thugs.

Teddy retreated and raised the alarm. A group of young college men poured into the stairwell, but the pair of thugs were long gone.

"Take him to the lobby where we can examine him," Cornelia ordered the freshmen bent over Rollo. "We're nurses."

"Yes ma'am," one young man said, hoisting Rollo to his feet.

A small crowd gathered in the lobby around the settee where Teddy and Cornelia attended to their patient.

"Pupils look good." Cornelia palpated his scalp. "Does this hurt?"

"Not a lot."

Teddy, grasping his wrist, checked the timepiece hanging from her necklace. "Pulse is good."

"No lumps on the head," Cornelia pronounced.

"Some contusions on the arms," Teddy reported. "Please wiggle your fingers. Yes, very good."

The students closest to the settee were pushed aside by an older man. "Sibley!"

Rollo stared up at the man, and then both broke into laughter.

"Sorry to disappoint you, Coach, it's just me."

Teddy looked from one to the other. "Disappoint him?"

"My apologies," the older man said. "Some students came running to tell me that my star player had been attacked. I should have known it was only Rollo again. So, were you robbed?"

"No, they didn't get that far. My uncle and cousin came along and rescued me. It's rather embarrassing."

"Better embarrassed than robbed. Or seriously hurt." The man nodded to the women and withdrew from the now thinning throng.

Cornelia followed the man's disappearing back. "Who was that?"

"That was Coach Dean. The basketball coach."

"What did he mean by 'only Rollo again?'"

Rollo grinned. "I'm tall and thin, and so is Frank Sibley. Our hair parts in the same place, too. A week ago, I was returning late from the library, and I was accosted by some students for breaking team curfew. They dragged me to Coach Dean, who straightened it out, and it's been a running joke."

"Does anyone ever mistake Mr. Sibley for you?" Teddy asked.

"If they do, he hasn't let on. I guess no one cares if someone from the pep band is breaking curfew."

Laughter and conversation surrounded the four in the dining room. Garlands of holly still lined the walls and poinsettias graced the side tables. The carpet was speckled in places with leftover confetti.

"Rollo, my boy," the professor said, "the expression on your face when we came to your aid was priceless. It reminded me of your grandmother when Corny—Cornelia's father—and I surprised her."

He chuckled as red crept into Rollo's cheeks. Then Pettijohn paused and stroked his beard.

"That must have been the first time your grandfather came calling. Anyway, Corny and I hid behind the settee until we couldn't hold back the giggles. Corny leapt up, pretending to be Henry, looked at me and declared his admiration. The two of us went prancing out the side door together but not before I got a good look at the stunned expression on Genevieve's face."

He chuckled at the memory.

"Of course, once that wore off, she chased us down and whaled the tar out of us."

"Grandpa Jackson wasn't put off by such unladylike behavior?"

Professor Pettijohn laughed.

"I think it was then and there that he decided he had found the right woman for him. The way I see it, Henry figured if she could handle the two of us she'd make a right fine woman to raise a family."

Rollo started to say something else, but a man at a nearby table stood. "Here's to our Wildcats and another winning year!"

Cheers came, followed by other toasts to Kentucky's success in the upcoming season.

Rollo was more skeptical. "They should worry more about the game tomorrow."

"Come, come," Pettijohn said. "Our team is without equal. Carey is the finest player in the South."

The boy arched an eyebrow, dark but shaped like the old man's. "Too bad you're not playing a southern team."

"As I recall, the Crimson are down a man."

"Not any more. Krueger is back."

"It should be an excellent match, then. One where Kentucky will prevail. I've devised a special method of celebration for the occasion."

"Oh? What have you come up with this time, Uncle?"

He winked. "You'll see."

"May I interrupt?" A tall man stood by their table.

"Of course you can, sir!" Rollo said, rising. "This is Coach Anderson, one of the assistant coaches," he added by way of introduction.

They slid chairs aside so the visitor could sit with them.

"Rollo, I've been talking to Coach Dean about what happened to you earlier, and I had a word with the police. There's a rumor that some men have come up from Newport to assure a Kentucky victory."

"I assume you don't mean by earnest prayer," Teddy said.

He chuckled. "No, ma'am. They bet heavily on one side, then kidnap members of the opposing team. Especially star members."

"You mean, they think I'm Sibley?" the youth squeaked.

"Everyone else is making that mistake. Why not them?"

"Is Roland in danger, sir?"

"Not really, Professor...Pettijohn, is it? These men usually hold the player until after the game, then drop him off somewhere miles from home. Sore feet is the most common complaint I've heard about."

"I presume you're guarding Mr. Sibley closely," Cornelia said.

"Oh, we are...but we'd like for these men to keep thinking that you're him, Rollo. We'll surround you with Sibley's pals from the football team. They'll keep watching you instead of figuring out that they've been had. Would you be willing to do that for the team?"

Rollo grinned. "Sure, Coach! Sounds like a real hoot."

The morning light cast deep shadows between the rough-hewn limestone buildings of the Indiana University campus. Snow still clung to the ground and bushes, but the pathways connecting the arc of classrooms and dorms had been cleared for students and visitors.

Beefy young men escorted Cornelia, Teddy, Rollo, and the Professor beside Dunn's Woods. Rollo wore a jacket borrowed from the team's star player and had been instructed to 'walk like Sibley.' Cornelia carried her service pistol in her purse. She'd brought it on the trip for extra protection in case their Dodge Brothers vehicle broke down and thought it might prove useful.

Teddy admired the architecture, making appreciative sounds. "Splendid stonework. Where is the Field House?"

"Over there." Rollo pointed to a hilly area beyond Maxwell Hall. "Thataway, past where those guys are talking. The court is on the second floor, up a steep flight of stairs. I'm sure I can make it there, though, with a lovely woman like you on my arm."

Cornelia fought an eye roll and lost. "Do young ladies buy the oil you churn out, cousin?"

"Oil? My mother simply raised me to be a gentleman, that's all."

She eyed his sagging flannels. "If she expects you to grow into those pants, she's going to be disappointed."

"These?" He glanced down amidst guffaws from their muscular chaperones. "They're all the rage in England."

"King George finally got revenge," she grumbled.

When the sightseeing ended, Roland and his entourage headed for the dorms. Cornelia and her companions turned onto the path leading to the hotel. Teddy wanted to change into whatever clothes were appropriate for a basketball game, and Uncle Percival had a case he wanted carried up to the gym. It was heavy as the dickens, and Cornelia knew who would be carrying it. Perhaps Teddy could prevail upon the chivalry of some of the other UK boosters staying at the hotel. She was the charming one.

The men Rollo had used as a point of reference were headed down the walk towards the trio now. One was about Rollo's age, but dressed more sensibly. The other two were older, perhaps brothers or even uncles. They joked with one another, laughing and punching shoulders.

When their paths crossed, the men parted to let their elders pass and tipped their fedoras. Cornelia nodded in return. The one had a nasty mark on his face, shaped almost like a cat's face. A round wildcat's face.

Her memory tingled and she turned, shouting a warning. She barely escaped the arms reaching from behind her. Nearby, Teddy screamed, kicking at her assailant. Percival thumped on the third, trying to get his cane free.

The youngest thug grabbed at her again. No time to get the gun out. Cornelia struck him instead with the black leather purse, made heavier with the weapon.

"Ow!" He clutched his elbow, stepping back.

She popped the bag open and freed the gun. "Get out of here, if you know what's good for you!"

He ran. Next to her, Uncle Percival fell to the ground. The other attackers had also fled. She helped him up and looked for his cane. She found Teddy's first. Unfortunately, Teddy wasn't with it.

A car roared to life on the street nearby and sped away. In the back, she spotted a struggling shape in red.

Rollo and his company were summoned to the Professor's room at the hotel, where Cornelia informed them of the revolting development.

Her uncle fumed in his comfy chair. "I should have seen this coming...I should have been prepared. Blast it all, I have a dozen devices that could have been useful, all at home on my workbench!"

"We were focused on their seizing Roland," Cornelia said. "When they saw that he was securely guarded, they took a presumed family member hostage. Good strategy. We need to meet it with our own."

She turned to the earnest young men. "If this involves gambling, then the mob is somehow involved. Where gangsters are, there is liquor. Rollo!"

"Yes, ma'am?"

"Where do your more...rambunctious classmates go for a little fun?"

"There's the movie theater, and pep rallies, and the glee—" The glare in Cornelia's eyes silenced him.

"I wasn't clear. Where do you go for a drink in this town?"

"Well—um, I, of course never—"

Professor Pettijohn broke in. "We're not talking about responsible students such as yourself, Rollo. Where would a young rapscallion go for a swell party?"

The youth flushed. "There's this place near campus..."

"That's where we'll start," Cornelia said.

"What? You can't just walk up to a speakeasy and ask if they're holding a little old lady hostage!"

He was met with glares by both his seniors.

"Teddy was injured by mustard gas during the Great War," the Professor said. "Perhaps she appears older than she is."

Cornelia growled. "Just tell us about this place."

Rollo told her about the speakeasy, located in one of the older rooming houses in town.

"What do you have in mind, Cornelia?" Percival asked, when the young man finished.

"You and I need to change our appearance," she said. "We'll never get through the door if they recognize us."

"She's right about that," Rollo said. "You'll have to lose the distinctive cane too, Uncle Percy. That guy you whacked isn't likely to forget it."

"The beard too," Cornelia said. "You'll look like a different man without the whiskers."

Professor Pettijohn was apoplectic.

"I haven't shaved since I was twenty," he protested. "And what about you? I don't see any way we can change your appearance enough to get by the guards."

"No," she said, "but my demeanor, that's another matter. I'll use Teddy's cane and borrow a few items, make myself look older and a little more frail."

The professor gave her a skeptical look that she ignored.

"Once we're inside," she continued, "a couple of these lads could create a distraction while we position ourselves near inside doors or stairways."

"Ah, places we can search," Percival said.

"Exactly. They aren't going to be holding Teddy in the barroom."

She paused and looked around at the young serious faces. These boys reminded her of the doughboys she'd watched going off to the trenches. Cornelia couldn't let them attempt a rescue while thinking this was a lark, not even for her dear Teddy.

"These men will be armed," she said. "I won't think any less of you and your friends if you don't wish to be further involved, Rollo."

Rollo thought about her warning for a moment.

"What sort of man would I be if I didn't help a lady in distress?" he said, looking at the Professor. "I can't speak for the rest of the guys though."

One of the football players said, "Shucks Rollo, Sibley would never forgive us if a lady got hurt on behalf of the team. She's not even an Indiana fan."

Cornelia turned her attention to her uncle.

"Do you have something that would create a diversion? I don't know what you've brought with you, but we need the sort of diversion that would draw the attention of everyone in the room long enough for these lads to disappear into other parts of the building."

"Rollo, fetch that heavy leather bag," the professor said.

"What have you got in there, sir?"

"A diversion. Now set it up here on the table."

The youth did so with a heavy oof.

"Gentlemen, meet Hot Tamale, the University of Kentucky mascot, or at least a replica of her. The live Kentucky wildcat is only allowed to attend outdoor sporting events."

He opened the case, revealing a life-sized bronze wildcat. With a flick of his finger, he released the key and the wildcat rose to standing height and let out a roar that made everyone but the professor jump for cover.

Pettijohn let out a great barrel laugh that sent him into a fit of coughing. When he recovered, he grinned at his niece.

"What do you think? Distracting enough?"

"Uncle Percy, you've outdone yourself. A clockwork wildcat. Who else would think of such a thing?"

"The young people can take Hot Tamale with them," Professor Pettijohn said. "When the guard asks what's in the bag it will be easy enough for them to claim to have come to celebrate liberating the Kentucky mascot."

As the professor talked, he rewound the clockwork key and set the lock to hold it in place.

"She is all ready to roar," he said. "Flip the lock off, and you'll have their attention."

Teddy, sitting in a strange bedroom, eyed her surroundings. The coverlet on the bed was thin and stained. The ewer on the nearby stand was cracked, and the furniture had seen better days. A nearby shelf held a collection of adventure novels. The room of a young man, then. Music and laughter echoed from below.

She eyed her captor, seated beside the door. "I don't believe we were ever introduced. I'm Theodora Lawless."

He snorted.

"Is this your room?"

The thug shook his head. "Don't get curious."

"It's too late for that, I'm afraid." She gestured at the floor. "Do the sounds below come from a speakeasy?"

"Don't ask."

"Too late again. I've already asked. Do they serve bathtub gin, or something of a better quality?"

He turned his chair aside and pulled his fedora further down on his face. "Lady, you're killing me. Quit yer yappin.'"

Teddy hmphed. "If you're going to hold me prisoner, especially at a party, the least you could do is provide me with refreshments. It reflects badly on the host."

"Tell him yerself. I hear him coming up the stairs. Maybe he'll give ya a glass of water."

She stood and faced the door. As an afterthought, she fluffed her white curls.

A heavyset older man entered the room. "Is this her, Grunt?" A younger man, gun in hand, blocked the doorway behind him.

"Hugo!"

He stared at her. "Do I know you, lady?"

"You should. From the infirmary at Verdun. You had a leg injury. Remember Nurse Teddy?"

The younger men gaped as Hugo pulled a pair of glasses from his pocket and squinted. "Nurse Teddy! From the War!"

"This has all been a terrible misunderstanding. I don't know why I'm being held."

"What are you even doing here, ma'am? I heard that they sent you to Arizona. After you were hurt."

"I lived there for a while. I came to see the game with Cornelia and her uncle. You may remember—"

"The Iron Petticoat is here, too?" He grinned at the young man behind him. "No wonder Tarzan here was having so much trouble."

"Ah, this must be your room, then," Teddy smiled. "The Burroughs fan."

"And she has an uncle," Hugo mused. "He must be older'n Moses. So, is Sibley your relative or hers?"

"Neither. Rollo, the young man Lord Greystoke attacked, is with the pep band."

Hugo turned now to scowl at both men. "You went after the wrong guy?"

"He looked like the picture, Boss," the man called 'Grunt' said. "Tall and a hair part near the middle. It's not like he was gonna wear his playin' togs all the time."

"Yeah, but Tarzan here was supposed to know better. He's the local guy."

"Maybe he hasn't attended many games," Teddy said. "And, really, Rollo does resemble Mr. Sibley."

"She's lying about him not being Sibley," the young man said. "She's trying to protect him."

Now Teddy frowned. "I do not prevaricate, young man. I came with Cornelia to see Kentucky play."

"He was surrounded by the guys from the football team."

"Rollo's a popular boy. He'd been attacked, so they were protecting him. It's not his fault he looks like your star player."

Grunt slapped their junior partner's head. "They sent us a ringer!"

"But she was wearin' a red coat," Tarzan whined. "Indiana's red."

"I happen to look good in red."

"Rats. Why didn'tcha look good in green?"

"I do," Teddy said, adjusting her curls. "Green wasn't in style this year."

Rollo and his elders eyed the rooming house from a distance.

"Now what do we do? Sneak in from the back?"

"Oh, no," Cornelia said. "That's how most of the clientele enter. Plus, they'll have lookouts stationed to watch for police raids."

Both men turned to stare at her.

"You seem quite the expert, Corny dear," the Professor commented.

"Teddy has a prescription for medicinal alcohol. It helps with her cough. Unfortunately, our pharmacy isn't always dependable. At home, we can turn to Mr. Scroggins, but we have to make other arrangements on the road."

"Scroggins...? I recall an old Luther Scroggins who lived your way. He served me my first drink of corn liquor. I thought he had passed away."

"This is his son." She remembered how touched Lester had been by the embroidered curtains Teddy had given him for Christmas. Poor Teddy...

"I hope his product is better. Luther's was mostly good for removing paint."

Rollo sighed. "What about Miss Lawless? How will we get her out of there?"

"Have any of your more adventurous friends ever mentioned the password?" Cornelia asked.

Rollo lowered his head and his ears reddened.

"You knock three times, pause and knock three more times. Then say 'Lil sent me' when the guy opens the peep hole."

"Rollo," one of his beefy companions complained.

Cornelia silenced him with a glance.

"Is everyone ready?"

"Cousin, I can't take you to a joint like that," Rollo said, waving in the direction of the building across the street. "Grandma Genevieve would roll over in her grave."

"My sister, God rest her, would understand the necessity of rescuing a lady in distress." Professor Pettijohn insisted.

"But..." his voice failed in the face of his elders' resolute expressions.

"You will not be taking me, Rollo," she said. "You and your friends should go ahead of us to the club. If they don't know you are with us, it will be easier to get into position. Just don't do anything until we get there."

"She's right," the Professor said. "We might be recognized, but they have never seen the three of you before. We're all safer if we're not together. If they grab us, you boys get out of there fast and let your coach know what happened."

"One more thing," Cornelia cautioned. "When we start searching, be ready to leave. Any gunplay, you lads go for the police. I would rather be in a position to let officers do the searching, but they won't investigate just because we think Miss Lawless is there. Tell them you heard a gunshot and they'll be there faster than you can blink."

"What about you?" the nearest one asked.

Cornelia chuckled. "Bless you lad. I've been through more wars than you're old enough to remember. Believe me, I know how to duck and hide when guns start going off."

"Go on now," the professor said, "and put a little swagger into your step. Stealing our mascot was quite a caper."

"Our turn, Uncle," Cornelia said, giving her uncle an admiring look. Shaving had taken twenty years off the professor's appearance.

Cornelia wanted to do just the opposite with her own appearance. She'd pulled on Teddy's crocheted hat and wrapped the matching shawl around her shoulders. Anyone watching would have been amazed at the transformation. Her body seemed to shrink in on itself. Back bent, shoulders stooped, and with a slightly trembling hand she reached out and took the professor by the arm.

Together, the professor and his niece ambled across the street. Cornelia pretended to need to pause and rest, partly to allow Professor Pettijohn to catch his breath and partly to give herself the chance to glance around the area for potential lookouts. She thought she caught sight of a curtain moving in an upstairs window of the butcher shop overlooking the back entrance. It was impossible to know if the person watching was a lookout, or merely a nosy shopkeeper. Gossip was the lifeblood of small-town society.

Once her uncle's breathing sounded less strained, and the young people were safely ensconced in the club, Cornelia thought it safe for them to approach the door.

Professor Pettijohn delivered the knock as directed and waited for the small wooden window to open.

"Lil sent me," he said when a pair of eyes peered out at him from under heavy brows.

"Aren't you a little old for this, Gramps?" a gruff voice replied.

The professor's barrel chest puffed and his chin tilted a little higher.

"I'm old enough to remember when it wasn't a crime to have an afternoon drink."

Cornelia kept quiet.

"Settle down Gramps, you'll have your afternoon toddy soon," the big man said as he closed the window.

They could hear a metal latch being thrown open. Soon they would be inside where she could begin searching for Teddy. Cornelia tried to tamp down her eagerness and keep up the pretence of being infirm. It wasn't easy. Her dear Theodora could be injured or worse. Who knew what these hooligans might do to insure victory?

When the door opened they were greeted by a hallway smelling of stale cigars and cheap perfume. Cornelia surmised that the cigars belonged to the doorman, who had the unlit stub of one clenched in the corner of his mouth.

"That way, Gramps," the man said, pointing to a door at the far end of the hallway. "Can you make it that far?"

Cornelia could feel her uncle's muscles tighten at the implication.

"Steady, Uncle," she said, holding fast to his arm.

The retired Professor had spent a lifetime designing and building fantastic machines. In her youth, she had watched him lift parts that must have weighed hundreds of pounds. Time had robbed him of physical strength, but even at his advanced age, Percival Pettijohn's keen mind made him a formidable enemy. She would never have dared speak to him in such a condescending tone.

Pettijohn straightened to his full height, tipped his hat to the roughen, and turned away.

"Come along my dear," he said, "we won't stay long in this establishment. I just need to clear the dust from my throat before the game."

Despite the rudeness of the doorman, the club was surprisingly well appointed. It must also have been well insulated against noise. A jazz band was playing, and she hadn't heard a single note until they reached the door. At the opposite end of the long room, a bartender stood behind the mahogany bar, behind him a large gilded mirror reflected the glow of some two dozen polished brass lamps lining the walls. A pair of matching chandeliers hung above the dark wood tables.

To the left of the bar, a flight of stairs appeared to be the only way out other than the door they entered through. Cornelia surmised that the owners of the establishment must be paying a handsome sum for protection, since they had no good way for patrons to escape a police raid.

She spotted the college men gathered around a table near the center of the room. The youngsters had the professor's case open and were elaborating to the flappers at an adjoining table how they had come into possession of Kentucky's mascot.

The professor paused long enough to catch Rollo's eye, then guided Cornelia towards the bar. He ordered a beer for himself and a sidecar for the lady.

When the drinks came, Cornelia drifted to the end of the bar nearest the stairs and leaned against the wall, pretending to listen to the music.

It didn't take the Professor long to engage the bartender into a rousing discussion of the game. After several minutes of pointing out the merits of various players, he ordered a second beer. While the bartender's back was turned, Pettijohn signaled Rollo.

Rollo released the lock.

The bartender dropped Professor's Pettijohn's fresh beer when the wildcat let out a bloodcurdling roar.

"What the devil was that?" he sputtered, not noticing that Cornelia was gone.

The roar did not go unnoticed upstairs.

Hugo, who had been sharing a drink with Teddy, jumped to his feet. "Tarzan, Grunt. Go down and find out what's going on." They ran out, and he stood near the door, readying his gun.

"Grunt? That's not really his name, is it?"

"Gunter the Grunt. That's what they call him."

She tittered, flush from her third Planter's Punch. "I'm not surprised. It appears to be a good portion of his vocabulary."

Another roar.

"I need to take a look," Hugo said, and opened the door. He immediately backed in again, though, as Cornelia entered, her pistol drawn.

"Sergeant Weber," she barked, "*You* helped kidnap Theodora?"

"No, ma'am," Hugo said, keeping his gun raised. "If I had been there, this wouldn't have happened."

"As soon as he saw me, he knew they'd made a mistake," Teddy said cheerfully. "You wouldn't shoot Cornelia, would you, Hugo?"

Hugo looked at the two women, then sighed. "I don't see a point to it. Sibley is probably sealed away in cotton somewhere."

Cornelia allowed herself a slight smile. "Let's go, dear."

Teddy stood and drained the rest of the alcohol from her glass. "I do hope you don't lose a lot of money on the game, Sergeant," she said. "It's been lovely to see you again."

"Take the stairs down the back." Hugo jerked his thumb in the proper direction. "It'll save you a lot of trouble."

"Thank you. Come along, Teddy."

"Kentucky still has a good chance of winning. The Professor says—"

Cornelia grabbed her hand and pulled her out of the room.

When they neared the corner of the building, the ladies discovered the rest of their party was in the process of being thrown out of the club. They quickly ducked back into the alley and waited until the coast was clear before continuing to the parking lot.

Rollo laughed and slapped his friends on the back when he saw his cousin come around the corner.

"Miss Lawless, you should have seen the looks on their faces when Uncle Percy's cat roared," he said. "Good gosh, when he came over and started shouting that we were a pack of thieves, and threatening to call the police, the place went wild."

"Uncle, did you really threaten to call the police in an illegal saloon?"

He smiled. "Worked like a charm. They couldn't get us out the door fast enough. Lucky I didn't wear my game suit though. They ripped my jacket on the way out. Speaking of the game, hadn't we all better get back and change?"

The stairs to the Field House gymnasium were challenging enough for the students, but near-impossible for Uncle Percival to scale. He waved off all help, though, save for Cornelia's strong arm. Two stout Kentucky boosters followed them, lugging the heavy case.

Teddy climbed ahead, taking advantage of their slow pace to stop and catch her breath. "You know," she said, when they all reached the doors, "we should have been carried up here in sedan chairs after everything we've been through on behalf of the opposing team."

"Our reward will be in our victory," Professor Pettijohn said, "Oh, that wind is cold on my chin. Remind me never to shave in winter again."

They'd arranged to have seats low and on the edge of the Kentucky contingent. The Professor removed his coat, revealing a custom-made suit in the brilliant blue of UK.

"Behold!" he announced, voice echoing above the murmurs of the crowd, and unveiled the Brass Tamale. Everyone oohed and aahed, even the Crimson supporters. He triggered the roar, and everyone went silent briefly before bursting into applause. Several moments went by before Cornelia persuaded her uncle to stop bowing and let everyone settle in for the game.

Kentucky's pep band played a brisk rallying cry, followed by the new fight song, "On, On, U of K." This was countered by "Indiana, Our Indiana" from Rollo's side of the gym. Cornelia's young cousin wore a red jacket and bowtie, and she noted, with approval, that his pants fit for once. His saxophone gleamed under the electric lights.

With the screech of a whistle, the match began. Everyone stood again to cheer, then retook their seats.

The first few minutes were intense. The squeaks of shoes on the wooden floor and the slap of the leather ball, passed from player to player, blended with the murmuring of the boosters. The Indiana players clapped as one basket was made, then another. The Wildcats tried to rally, but were stymied on all sides.

Teddy peered through her opera glasses. "Why are they all clustered around that one boy?"

"That's Carey they're boxing in," Percival said. "They still remember his performance against them from last year. He was all-American in high school."

The strategy seemed to be working; Indiana had eight points before Kentucky made its first basket. Kentucky coach Eklund switched out two players. The Wildcat boosters cheered.

"That's Mohney, and, good, the other's Besuden," Percival informed them. "A great player, although they are about to lose him."

"Lose him? Are there problems with his grades?"

"It's probably lack of money, dear," Cornelia said.

"Family trouble?"

"Worse. Tax trouble," Percival said. "His parents passed away, and his guardians didn't pay—there he goes!"

He flipped the key, and the clockwork wildcat's roar joined the crowd's. A basket for Kentucky.

The second half of the game was close-fought. Indiana struggled to keep its lead; the Wildcats kept pressing them hard. There were groans of disappointment when Mohney fouled one of Indiana's forwards. The two points gained through free throws widened a gap the Wildcats couldn't close before the final bell.

"Sibley scored thirteen points," the Professor said afterward. "Ah, the sacrifices we make in the name of sportsmanship. Not an auspicious start for my Brass Tamale. However," he said, pulling a Kodak from a pocket in his overcoat, "we should still commemorate the occasion."

He posed beside his invention while Teddy took a photo, then was forced to hold the pose while several other people took pictures as well, begging to hear the cat cry one more time.

After graciously excusing himself, the Professor began preparing the clockwork wildcat for transport back to the hotel, but was stopped by an admirer who had lingered on. They spoke for a moment, and Pettijohn broke into a brilliant smile.

"What did he say?" Teddy asked after the man was gone.

"He asked if I could produce a miniaturized version of my invention. He sells Wildcat memorabilia in Lexington, and thinks a joint venture would be profitable."

"Wonderful! Perhaps your reward for good sportsmanship is financial."

"Perhaps so, but wouldn't a win have made a stronger selling point?"

Cornelia patted his shoulder. "There's always another game to win."

"And a new patent to be had," he grinned.

John Wooden
Tony Perona

John Wooden is best remembered as the legendary coach of the UCLA Bruins, but he was born in Indiana and enshrined in the Basketball Hall of Fame in 1961 for his accomplishments as a player.

Wooden played high school basketball in Martinsville, where he led his high school team to the state championship finals for three consecutive years, winning in 1927. He then attended Purdue University where he helped the Boilermakers to the 1932 National Championship. He was the first player to be named a three-time consensus All-American.

After college he spent several years playing professionally. He also coached high school basketball and taught English. During WWII he joined the Navy and left the service as a lieutenant.

He returned to Indiana and coached at Indiana State Teacher's College (now Indiana State University) after the war. In 1948 he became head coach at UCLA, a position he would hold until he retired in 1975.

Wooden had immediate success at UCLA. The Bruins went from a 12-13 record to become the Pacific Coast Conference champions with a 22-7 record. In 1964, UCLA won the first of its national championships, repeating as champions in 1965. The team fell short in 1966, but in 1967 it reclaimed the national title. In 1975, Wooden retired with his 10th national championship.

Wooden married Nellie Riley in August 1932. They had a son, James, and daughter, Nancy. Nellie died from cancer in 1985. Wooden died in 2010 at age 99. Wooden was also an author, having written several books about basketball and life, including *Coach Wooden's Pyramid of Success: Building Blocks for a Better Life.*

MURDER IN THE DAWG HOUSE
D. B. Reddick

"Hurry up, Ralph," I shouted from behind the wheel of my black Cadillac Deville. "Or that damn head nurse is likely to call the cops on us again."

"Jesus, Jimmy, I'm hurrying already," Ralph Maloney said as he slid his ample frame across my front seat and closed the passenger door behind him. "Springing Tommy from this joint ain't easy. Now, get out of here."

I stepped on the accelerator. My car shot out of the circular driveway at the Golden Moments Retirement Center and fishtailed onto Meridian Street, leaving a fresh set of black tire marks in its wake. After falling in line with southbound traffic, I glanced in my rear-view mirror. Tommy Donahue was sitting quietly in the backseat, staring out the passenger window. It looked like he hadn't shaved or combed his thick crop of white hair in days.

"How you doin' Tommy?" I asked.

No answer.

"For Chrissakes, answer Jimmy," Ralph yelled as he turned and scolded Tommy.

Tommy slowly turned away from the window, looked straight ahead and said in a low voice, "Who are you again?"

I glanced over at Ralph, "Didn't take his meds today, did he?"

"Guess not," Ralph replied, shaking his head.

"How'd you sneak him past the nurses' station?"

"Only one on duty and she was busy yakking on the phone. Had her back to us."

"Charlie, the security guard?"

"Didn't see him," Ralph replied. "Probably on a smoke break. Where we going?"

"Hinkle Fieldhouse."

"What for?"

"Murder."

Fifteen minutes later we turned off of Meridian Street and onto 49th Street. Historic Hinkle Fieldhouse lay ahead on the campus of Butler University.

"Damn, I love that old building," I said, staring ahead at the twenties era structure.

"Remember our senior year at Shortridge?" Ralph asked. "We were here for the state finals. Crispus Attucks beat Kokomo, 92-54. Third state title in five years. Bill Garrett was the coach."

"Jimmy Rayl," Tommy bellowed from the backseat.

"Huh?"

"You remember him, don't you?" Ralph said, glancing at me. "Mister Basketball in 1959."

"The Splendid Splinter," said Tommy.

"How does he...?"

"Who knows?" Ralph shrugged.

The three of us had just stepped out of my car and were headed for Hinkle's main entrance when we heard a booming voice behind us. "Uncle Jimmy."

"Hey, Willie," I said after turning and watching Butler's Police Chief Willie Dutton jogging toward us. At six foot five, Willie looks like one of the starters on the basketball team.

"Is he really your nephew?" Ralph whispered in my ear.

"Naw, he's my godson," I replied. "My old partner's kid. But he's called me Uncle Jimmy forever. Got promoted to chief a few months back."

"Thanks for coming," Willie said, shaking hands all round. "Uncle Jimmy, this murder has everyone here spooked. The Bulldogs open their preseason on Saturday afternoon against Ball State. The Administration's worried nobody will show up if the murder isn't solved by then. Come inside and I'll show you the crime scene."

As we walked into the basketball team's equipment room, Willie explained how one of the players had shown up early for practice yesterday and had found the team's equipment manager lying on the floor.

"Who was he?" Ralph asked as I knelt down to take a closer look at the body outline and blood spots on the tiled floor.

"Phil Slater," Willie replied. "Nice guy. Wouldn't harm a flea."

"Who's handling from IMPD?" I asked.

"George McIntyre," Willie said.

"Damn," I replied as I stood up. "McIntyre's a good detective, but he can be a real pain in the ass. What do you want from us?"

"McIntyre hasn't talked to me since he left here yesterday," Willie said. "I've left him several messages, but he probably thinks I'm just a glorified rent-a-cop. Can you talk to him, Uncle Jimmy? The school's administrators are desperate to know what's going on."

As we left the equipment room a minute later, I turned to Ralph. "Where's Tommy?"

"I dunno," Ralph replied. "He was here a minute ago."

"There he is," Willie said, pointing ahead to the basketball court.

Tommy was wearing a white Butler ball cap and shooting two-handed free throws from the foul line. Nothing but net.

After dropping off Tommy at Golden Moments, I drove Ralph home and then headed for police headquarters in the City-County Building. George McIntyre was sitting behind a grey metal desk in the homicide squad room. I hadn't seen him in years. His dark hair now had numerous gray streaks running through it and the bags under his dark brown eyes practically drooped to his chin.

"Well, if it isn't legendary homicide detective, Jimmy Flynn," he said, looking up from the stack of papers piled high on his desk. "To what do we owe this pleasure?"

"Phil Slater."

"Larry Dutton's kid sent you, didn't he?"

I nodded.

"I'm not sure that big kid could find his way out of a paper bag," McIntyre said with a smirk on his face. "How'd he get that cushy job at Butler, anyway?"

"Watch it," I said, leaning my five foot ten frame across McIntyre's desk. I was within inches of his ugly face. "Willie's my godson."

"Alright, already," McIntyre replied.

My plan to intimidate McIntyre into giving me some information worked. Even though he's two or three inches bigger than me, he's never liked people getting in his personal space. Get too close and he begins to squirm.

"Looks like Slater died of blunt force trauma to his noggin," McIntyre began. "We won't know for sure until the coroner finishes with him later today or tomorrow. No weapon found at the scene."

"Any suspects?"

"Not yet, but we're still doing interviews."

"Record?"

"Nope. Slater was a regular Boy Scout."

"Keep me in the loop, McIntyre," I said as I turned away from his desk.

"Yeah...right."

The next day, I left my three bedroom ranch house near Ben Davis High School and drove over to the Irvington neighborhood on the near east side. Ralph Maloney lives alone in a rambling two-story Victorian that's been in his family for a couple of generations. He was waiting for me at the curb.

"Mornin,' Ralph." I said as he opened the passenger side door.

"What are we doing today?" he asked. He settled into the seat and struggled to fasten the seatbelt.

"We're picking up Tommy and then we're checking out Phil Slater's apartment building," I said.

"Wouldn't it be easier to do it without Tommy?"

"Yeah, but if we don't spring Tommy from Golden Moments, he'll end up sitting in front of his TV all day watching shows like *Jerry Springer*," I said. "That's no way to live."

"You're right. So, where did Slater live?"

"Broad Ripple. Willie called me last night with the address. Who knows? Maybe one of his neighbors will give us a lead about who killed him."

When Ralph and I arrived at Golden Moments twenty minutes later, we exited my car and walked towards the front door.

"You don't have to come inside," Ralph said. "I can get Tommy on my own."

"Think of me as backup," I replied.

Once inside, Ralph and I quickly walked through the sprawling main lobby before taking an elevator to Tommy's room on the second floor. As I had predicted, Tommy was sitting in his rocking chair, still in his pajamas, watching TV. Ralph and I helped him to dress before we headed back downstairs.

"And, just where do you think you're going?" demanded the blond-haired nurse sitting behind the nurses' station. She was as big as a Colts linebacker and just as mean-looking.

"Police headquarters," I replied, stepping forward and flashing my old police badge that I'd taken out of my jacket pocket.

"Aren't you too old to be a cop?" she said, looking at me suspiciously.

"I'm working undercover, ma'am," I said in the most persuasive voice I could muster. "We'll have Mr. Donahue back before dinner."

"I don't think so," she said, picking up her phone. "I'm calling his doctor and son. He's not going anywhere without their permission."

I turned and motioned for Ralph and Tommy to head for the front door.

"I wouldn't do that if I were you," I said, leaning across the nurses' counter. "You can't interfere in police business."

"Oh, yeah, just watch me," the nurse replied as she began punching numbers into her phone.

That was my cue to skedaddle. I jogged out the front door and headed for my car parked in the fire lane of the circular driveway.

"Hey, wait a minute," I heard a voice behind me yell.

I froze in my tracks. The nurse linebacker must have caught up to me. As I slowly turned around, Charlie, the security guard, was staring at me.

"Taking Tommy for a ride again, Jimmy?"

"Yeah, Charlie, but we'll have him back in plenty of time for dinner."

Charlie smiled. "Tommy's lucky to have good friends like you and Ralph."

Phil Slater lived in a three-story yellow brick apartment building on College Avenue just south of the main intersection in Broad Ripple.

"Follow me, guys," I said after parking my Cadillac in the tiny paved lot behind the building. "Let's get inside and see what's going on."

As we walked around to the front, I noticed an elderly woman struggling to get through the building's front door. Her walker had become stuck in the tiny alcove leading to the apartments. I rushed forward to help her.

"Have a nice day, ma'am," I said after untangling her walker from the doorway.

The woman glared at me, muttered something under her breath, and then hobbled down the front sidewalk to a Lincoln Town Car parked at the curb.

"What now?" Ralph asked.

"You're starting to sound like a broken record," I said, scanning the mailboxes in the alcove. "Let's find the number to Slater's apartment. There it is. It's on the third floor."

The building didn't have an elevator, so the three of us had to climb the stairs to the top floor. "This was a waste of time," said Ralph, gasping for air. "What now?"

"Why don't you and Tommy go check the second floor? See if anybody's home," I said. "Ask them about Slater. I'll be there in a few minutes."

Once Ralph and Tommy left, I reached into my jacket pocket and pulled out my lock pick kit and unlocked Slater's door. I was inside his apartment within seconds.

The place looked like a typical bachelor pad. Clothes were strewn all over the living room floor and a pile of dirty dishes was clogging up the kitchen sink. The only thing out of the ordinary was a stack of empty cardboard boxes that were shoved together in the far corner of Slater's bedroom.

Maybe Slater was planning to move before he was murdered. I moved closer to the boxes. The mailing labels on them said they'd come from Taiwan. Strange. What's Slater doing getting parcels from there? As I stepped back, my eyes caught sight of a white Butler ball cap on top of Slater's dresser.

Hmmm? It looked different from the one that Tommy was wearing. I had a hunch so I scooped up the hat and left the apartment.

"Any luck with Slater's neighbors?" I said after catching up with Ralph and Tommy. They were loitering in the second floor hallway.

"We talked to a couple people," Ralph replied. "They said Slater was a quiet guy. Kept to himself. What did you find?

I showed Ralph and Tommy the ball cap that I lifted from Slater's apartment.

"Where'd you get it?" Ralph asked.

"Where do you think?"

"Oh," Ralph replied.

"Tommy, let me see your hat for a second," I asked.

He took off his hat and handed it to me. I then carefully compared the two hats.

"What's wrong?" Ralph asked.

"Look at the inside of this cap," I said, handing him the one from Slater's bedroom.

"So," Ralph said.

"Now, look at the inside of Tommy's hat," I said.

"Hey, they're different," Ralph said. "How'd you know that?"

"I didn't at first," I replied. "It was the letter 'B' on the front of Slater's hat that tipped me off. Tommy's 'B' has a different typeface."

"They are different, aren't they?" Ralph replied. "But, I still don't get it."

"Was Tommy wearing his cap when we picked him up yesterday?" I asked.

"Now that you mention it, he was hatless until we found him shooting free throws," Ralph said.

"Exactly."

We both turned in Tommy's direction.

"Where'd you get your hat, Tommy?" I asked.

Tommy stared blankly at me. "I don't remember," he finally mumbled.

"Hmmm," I said. "I've got another hunch."

After dropping off Tommy and Ralph, I headed to the Lids store at the Greenwood Park Mall. I switched Tommy's hat with the one I took from Slater's apartment. I had the Lids' clerk spread his white Butler ball caps on the store's counter.

"Looks like somebody sold you a knock off," the clerk said after comparing his hat collection with Tommy's hat.

"You're right," I said, smiling.

The next day, I snuck out of the bedroom while Irene was still sleeping and left her a note on the kitchen table. Told her I was going to Lowe's. I hate lying to Irene, but she hates me playing detective now that I'm retired. Instead of Lowe's, I headed for the Indianapolis International Airport. I was looking for a U.S. Customs and Border Protection agent I once worked with on a murder investigation.

Franklin Washington's office was on the lower level near the baggage claim area.

"Flynn, right?" he said upon meeting me outside his office.

"You remembered."

"Sure. You tipped us off about that murder in the Park-Fletcher industrial park. Turns out the warehouse was storing millions in counterfeit merchandise. What can I do for you today?"

"I think I've got another counterfeit case for you."

Washington led me inside his office and listened as I spent the next several minutes telling him how I suspected that Slater had been murdered because he was involved in a counterfeit ring. To help make my case, I pulled out a plastic bag I brought and laid two hats on Washington's desk.

"That's all very interesting," he said when I finished. "One of your hats definitely looks like a counterfeit. Counterfeiting is a six hundred billion dollar business in this country, but I doubt that this guy was a big-time counterfeiter, or we'd have heard of him. I really can't help you right now. We're backlogged with dozens of other counterfeit cases."

Agent Washington and I exchanged a few more pleasantries before I shook his hand and left his office.

As I drove home along I-465, I began feeling guilty about not being able to help Willie Dutton solve Phil Slater's murder. I hoped it wouldn't cause him too much anguish. After all, it was an unsolved case that ruined his dad and my former partner. Larry Dutton and I had been homicide partners for nearly twenty years. I was devastated on the day I learned that he ate his police pistol. It took me several years to fully recover. Irene kept urging me to go see a therapist, but I refused. But I promised myself that I'd do whatever I could to keep Willie from finding himself in a similar situation.

As I turned onto Tenth Street, I suddenly had another hunch. I pulled over to the side of the road and called Ralph on my cellphone. He was sitting in his La Z Boy recliner reading Phil Dunlap's latest Western novel, but he agreed to let me pick him up.

"Where are we going?" Ralph asked after stepping inside my car a short time later.

"Slater's apartment."

"Again? What for this time?"

"You'll see when we get there."

"Shouldn't we get Tommy?"

"Not a good idea today."

After we pulled in front of Slater's apartment, Ralph reached for handle on the door.

"Whoa, Ralph," I said. "I want you to stay here."

"What? You had me come all this way to sit in your car?"

"Sorry, but you need to stay here and wait for me," I said. "If I'm not back in fifteen minutes, call IMPD on my cell and ask for Det. McIntyre. Got it?"

"What are you up to, Jimmy?"

"Just do what I ask for once, okay?"

Ralph reluctantly nodded his approval and slammed the door shut. I walked up the front sidewalk to Slater's apartment building and opened the front door to the tiny alcove, where the tenant's mailboxes are located. A red plastic tag above one of the mailboxes identified Frank Parker as the building manager. He lived in Apartment 101. I buzzed for him to unlock the door separating the alcove from the apartments. He replied without responding on the intercom. A few seconds later, I stood in front of the manager's apartment. I rapped three times.

A scruffy-looking guy in his mid-forties with a gray T-shirt and jeans finally opened the door.

"What do you want?" he growled. "And, how'd you get in here?"

"You buzzed me in."

"Right," he said. "I thought you were one of the old farts who live here. They're always forgetting their keys. So, what do you want?"

"I'm looking for Phil Slater."

"Don't you read the paper, mister?" he said. "Phil's dead."

"Hadn't heard that," I said, removing the ball cap from my head. "Damn, I was hoping to buy more of these hats from him for my little sports store in Shelbyville."

The manager eyed me and the ball cap for a few seconds before inviting me to step inside his apartment.

"The name's Parker," he said. "Frank Parker, I think I can help you. I have some hats like that over here."

Parker walked over to the corner of his living room and ripped open a box sitting on the floor. It looked like the ones I'd seen in Slater's apartment.

"Here you go," Parker said, handing me a hat. "Looks just like a Nike original, but it's not. Best knock-off out there today."

"Hey, you're right," I said, examining Parker's hat. "It's a good-looking fake. How much do you want for them?"

"How about five bucks apiece," Parker said. "You'll easily be able to sell them for fifteen bucks each."

"Great," I replied. "Phil charged me eight bucks for the one I'm wearing. I'll take ten of them."

Parker counted out the hats and shoved them into a large plastic bag. I handed him fifty bucks and left his apartment.

"What have you got there?" Ralph asked, after spotting the bag in my hand.

"The evidence to solve Slater's murder."

"These are great seats," Ralph said as he, Tommy and I sat two rows behind the Butler Bulldogs' team bench for their preseason opener. With less than a minute left before halftime, the Dawgs had pulled ahead of the Ball State Cardinals by eight points.

"Thank my godson, Willie," I replied. "They're better than the ones we used to have here."

"You're right. Say, how'd you know that Frank Parker killed Phil Slater?" Ralph asked.

"I didn't at first," I replied. "That's why I went to the Lids store at the mall the other day."

"I don't understand."

"The clerk showed me his hats. The eyelids on Tommy's hat were sewn shut, but the real ones weren't. That's when I got the bright idea to visit a Customs and Border Protection agent I knew. I suspected that Slater was caught up in a counterfeit hat ring. The agent was sympathetic, but he couldn't help me right away. And, that's when I started thinking how Slater might not have been acting alone. Maybe he had an accomplice. Somebody who lived in his apartment building and could let in the FedEx or UPS drivers."

"Frank Parker."

"Exactly," I said. "And, after he sold me those fake hats, I figured he must have had an argument with Slater over their little business venture and murdered him."

"Good thinking, Jimmy," Tommy said. "I'm glad I helped you solve the murder."

I smiled.

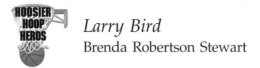

Larry Bird

Brenda Robertson Stewart

Once every generation or so, a basketball player is born who can legitimately be called a superstar, and Larry Bird was such a player. His nickname was "Larry Legend" during his professional basketball career.

Born in West Baden, Indiana and raised in French Lick, Bird's family had meager earnings, but they learned to "make-do" with what they had. Bird attended Springs Valley High School in French Lick and became its all-time leading scorer. He earned an athletic scholarship to Indiana University to play for legendary coach Bob Knight, but left because he felt somewhat lost at such a large university. The next year he enrolled at Indiana State University in Terre Haute.

In his senior year in college, Bird led the Sycamores to the NCAA championship game playing against the Michigan State Spartans and for the first time, Ervin "Magic" Johnson. The Spartans won the championship, but Bird left Indiana State with the USBWA College Player of the Year Award, the Naismith Award, and the Wooden Award. He only played for three years, but was the fifth highest scorer in NCAA history.

He was drafted by the Boston Celtics in 1978. Larry Bird, Robert Parrish and Kevin McHale formed a legendary frontline for the Celtics. Along with Magic Johnson, Bird was a key figure in revitalizing the NBA in the 1980's. Bird personified self-confidence and excellence in all areas of play. He led the Celtics to three national championships and was named the All-Star Game Most Valuable Player for three consecutive years.

When Bird retired in 1992 due to chronic back problems, he had accumulated 21,791 points over the course of his career.

Larry Bird served as coach of the Indiana Pacers from 1997 to 2000. In 2003, he became president of basketball operations for the Pacers and held that position until 2012. He is the only person in NBA history to be named Most Valuable Player, Coach of the Year, and Executive of the Year.

FALLEN IDOLS
Andrea Smith

"Are we going to need a wagon for you, too?" Detective Lenora Wise asked her partner.

Ahern's chubby face was twisted as if he were in pain as he stared down at the body. Lenora knew it wasn't the sight of a body that had shaken him; it was who the body belonged to.

"Jeez, I was at the game tonight. Saw him win it with a three-pointer at the buzzer," Ahern said. "This is gonna tear the city up."

Bryce Cooper, 'Coop' to his fans who wore his jersey number, lay on his back. His long legs and arms posed as if gliding to his famous jump shot. Lenora had seen him play once since he'd been the Indianapolis Titans' starting forward. Two years on the team and Coop was the reason the Titans were heading into game five of its first NBA playoff series.

Now he was a murder victim.

Lenora snapped on rubber gloves, knelt down next to the tech opening Cooper's bloody suit jacket.

"Finished, Joe?" the tech asked his partner, who was shooting the pics. "Need to turn him."

"Be my guest," Joe said.

The tech rolled Cooper's body over enough to be able to see his back.

"Perforating wounds. No exit wounds so bullets are still in the body," Lenora said, seeing no blood on the victim's back.

"Bingo," the tech said, laying Cooper's body on his back again. "Hard to tell how many times he was shot. Looks like close range, though."

Lenora took her flashlight from her belt, flicked a beam around the ground. "Look for casings anyway. You never can tell. Check his pockets for me."

The tech riffled through Cooper's pants pockets. Took a wallet from one, thick wad of bills from the other. Hundred dollar bills.

"Whoa," Ahern said.

The tech dropped the wallet and cash in an evidence bag. Handed it to Ahern.

"I'd say that Cosmography Daytime Rolex on his wrist is worth about $15 grand," Lenora said.

Ahern asked, "How do you know that?"

"Shopping is my second favorite pastime after this lovely job. Whoever shot him didn't want his money or his bling. Just Bryce Cooper dead. A good old-fashioned homicide."

The sound of an approaching car made Lenora turn her head. An unmarked car pulled beside the tech van. Sergeant Miller sprang from the passenger side and trotted over.

"How'd the vultures get here so fast?" he snarled. "Wish we could make it against the law for everyone except cops to have police scanners."

Lenora glanced at the TV crews crowding behind the police tape. They'd been there when she'd gotten to the scene at 2:15 a.m. She pressed her lips together to keep from laughing. Miller complained about media attention, but the reality was he never met a camera he didn't slick his hair back for. She'd quickly learned that in the two months she'd been with IMPD.

"What do you know so far?" Miller asked.

"Those ladies say they were leaving the club and saw Cooper lying here next to his Porsche. Didn't see anyone or hear anything. So they say." Lenora nodded in the direction of two women being held by uniformed officers. They wore shell-shocked expressions and short look-at-me dresses.

Lenora peeled off her gloves. "If I recall, Mr. Cooper lives — lived—in Geist. Long way to come party. Wonder why he chose this place?"

"You have hours not days to find out," Miller said.

Lenora slipped her iPhone from the case clipped to the waist of her tailored slacks. "I'll have a car pick up his widow. Better we get to her before she sees it on Breaking News."

A rumble came from the media scrum still jockeying for position along the fence. "Though we may already be too late," Lenora said.

"Good idea," Miller said. He straightened his yellow silk tie, adjusted the jacket of his pale gray suit and ran his hand over his salon cut salt and pepper hair. "Dobbs from Channel 6 is over there. He's more reasonable than most. I'll give him a few talking points to spread."

More interviews with the ladies who'd found Cooper yielded nothing. After the medical examiner gave the word and a wagon had taken Cooper's body away, Lenora and Ahern went into the Jazz Showcase to find the owner. She expected the place to be cheesy since it was located in Englewood, a poor area urban renewal hadn't hit yet. But it was actually elegant. The décor was neutral and understated. No flashy lights or wild patterned wallpaper. And the booths looked to be plush leather. The staff was doing final cleanup, their uniform of classic black slacks and white shirts wrinkled from a long night.

Lenora and Ahern talked with Bill Tapper, the owner, at a table near the long, curved mahogany bar. Lenora thought he was rather young to own a place that obviously had taken major bucks to open.

"Coop was just a great guy," Tapper said. He gripped a potent looking drink with shaking hands. "Why did this have to happen?"

"Was Cooper a regular?" Lenora asked. "I understand he grew up in this area, but lives at least 45 minutes from here."

Tapper's shoulders stiffened. "Coop didn't forget his friends when he made it. He didn't think he was too good to come back to the old neighborhood. He knew what it was like to grow up without family. Poor. So he was always looking for a way to help someone. That's why he set up his kids' foundation."

"Were there ever any problems like overzealous fans? Any issues tonight?"

Tapper looked offended. "My place is first-class. We opened in this neighborhood because it's going to boom just like downtown. We get professionals. No groupies. Coop never had trouble here."

"What about women?" Lenora asked.

Tapper gave her a blank stare.

Lenora tried again. "Was he friendly with anyone special?

Tapper squinted at her. "You asking if he was fooling around?"

Lenora waited for Tapper to answer his own question.

"No way. He was crazy about Nancy. High school sweethearts. Two beautiful kids and another one on the way. Coop didn't throw away his principles when he got that first million dollar paycheck."

Lenora gave a knowing smile. "People change. So, did Cooper dance or talk to any ladies tonight?"

Tapper arched a brow. "We had a big crowd like we always do on Friday. I didn't have my eyes on him every minute. I think he was with Dirk the whole evening. Sat right over there," he pointed to a section behind the dance floor, "at Dirk's favorite booth."

"Dirk?" Lenora asked.

"Dirk McGill. He and Coop go way back to elementary school." Tapper dropped his head. "Man, Dirk's going to be sick."

Ahern said, "I see you've got security cameras in here. How come you don't have any in the parking lot?"

Tapper looked sheepish. "I was going to have cameras installed out there in a couple months."

Ahern scowled. "We'll need your tapes."

The woman who'd served Cooper's table said he'd spent the five hours he was at the club with McGill. He hadn't danced with anyone. Had signed a few autographs and left with McGill shortly after one a.m.

After interviewing The Jazz Showcase staff, Lenora and Ahern went to the Alabama Street address Tapper had for McGill, but no one answered the door. Several calls got no answer to the cell phone number Tapper had given them. The trip being a bust, the detectives then did what every cop hates more than paperwork – met the superstar's widow at the morgue.

Petite Nancy Cooper looked too fragile to be carrying her beach ball of a stomach around. A tall man with the same blond looks seemed glued to her side.

"Troy Chambers," he said. "Nancy's brother. Hope you don't mind that I came with her." He gave his sister's shoulder a protective squeeze.

"Not at all," Lenora said, glad he'd come. She knew what it was like to lose someone. You felt as if you'd been kicked in the gut. Nancy Cooper was going to need her brother.

Ahern held the door as they filed into the sterile room, and the ME led them to a table in the corner. He looked at Lenora for her signal to uncover the body.

"Ready?" Lenora asked gently touching Nancy Cooper's arm.

Nancy Cooper nodded, and the medical examiner lifted the covering from Cooper's face. No need to show his bullet-riddled chest.

Nancy Cooper's breath caught. Her knees buckled. Lenora tightened her grip on Nancy's arm to keep her from falling.

Nancy Cooper winced. She cradled her right arm.

"I'm so sorry," Lenora said, backing away from Nancy Cooper.

Chambers sprang to his sister's side. "Can I take her out now?" he asked, irritation in his voice.

"Of course," Lenora said

Chambers gently guided Nancy Cooper from the room.

Ahern sighed. "Seems like a good time to head back to the station and do that preliminary report. Then maybe we can pay this McGill guy another visit."

Lenora and Ahern finished their police report and reviewing Tapper's security tapes as details of Cooper's death were blasted on the morning TV newscasts. All of them used Miller's sound bite, which would make him happy.

Lenora went to the ladies' room to splash water on her face, fluff her natural hair. Maybe she'd get a chance to sneak home for a shower soon.

Ahern intercepted her as she was walking back to her desk. "We don't need to search for McGill. The man has come to us. I put him in interview room No. 5."

Lenora's eyes widened. "How nice of him to save us another trip."

Dirk McGill was a walking GQ spread. Expensive dark suit. Cole Hahn shoes. Clean shaven with dark hair cut close and neat. Miller, who sucked his teeth at Ahern's Detective Colombo appearance, would approve.

McGill stood to shake her hand.

Not the usual reaction she got as a black, female detective. The year 2012 and she still had to fight for respect.

Made her BS antenna go up.

"I just got the terrible news from Bill. I figured you'd want to talk to me since I saw Coop last night," McGill said. "He was like a brother. I want to make sure you catch the SOB who killed him."

"So do we," Ahern said. "Coffee?"

"Never touch that poison," McGill said. He sat ramrod straight at the interview table. Lenora took a chair across from him with her Levenger note pad open. Ahern stood with his arms folded across his chest, rocking on his heels.

"Why did it take Tapper so long to catch up with you?" Lenora asked.

"Had my cell off for a little down time. I'd had a long day."

"You two talk about anything in particular last night?" Ahern asked. He took a toothpick from the pocket of his tan wrinkled blazer and gnawed on it. "Anything in particular on his mind?"

"Excuse me?"

"Did he seem upset?"

McGill grinned. "Did you see that game?"

Ahern nodded. "Redeemed himself in the fourth quarter."

"Then you can guess Coop was feeling pretty good," McGill said, still grinning.

"He wasn't worried about anything, as far as you know?" Lenora said.

"C'mon. What did he have to worry about? He had talent, money and was headed for a championship ring."

Ahern shifted the toothpick from one side of his mouth to the other. "You didn't say what you two talked about all those hours at the club."

McGill smiled. "The playoffs. His game. His kids." He hunched his shoulders. "The usual."

"What time did you two leave?" Lenora asked.

McGill furrowed his brow. "Don't remember the exact time. Little before or after one, maybe."

"You didn't stop to talk with anyone in the parking lot?"

"A couple of people spoke but that was all."

"Where'd you leave him?" she asked.

He leaned forward a little. "Excuse me?"

"You leave him at his car, your car? I'm just trying to understand how and where he was when you left him."

"He went to his car. I went to mine. We weren't parked next to each other so I didn't see if anyone came up to him or if he talked to someone else."

"Hard to believe people weren't camped out to catch a glimpse of the Titans' superstar, especially after a win like that."

McGill smiled. "That's why he hung out at the Showcase. People treated him like he was a regular guy."

"Then where'd *you* go for that down time?" Lenora asked, thinking about him not being home when they went to his townhouse.

McGill didn't hesitate. "Spent the night with my girlfriend."

"She have a name?"

"Veronica Barino. We were busy all night." He gave Ahern a know-what-I-mean smile. Ahern didn't return it.

"That's why I didn't hear about Coop until this morning."

Lenora put her pen away. "OK, guess that's all then. We appreciate you coming in, Mr. McGill. We assume you'll be easier to reach if we have more questions."

McGill smiled. "You bet. Whatever I can do to help, let me know. This shouldn't have happened to him."

After he left, Ahern said. "Down time my eye."

"Um hum. Shall we find out who Mr. Smooth really is?"

The background check on McGill revealed he was 28, like Cooper. Attended elementary and high school with the superstar but didn't go to college. Had never been arrested. Didn't own a gun, at least none was registered to him.

McGill bought his three-story town house a year ago and drove a black 2012 Mercedes CL550. Lenora knew the price tag for that car started at $114,000. McGill was living a pretty luxurious lifestyle for a man who had no visible income. As far as the detectives could tell, the well-dressed, high-living McGill had *never* had a job.

Lenora's neatly made bed with the four rows of pillows called her like a bowl of Haagen Daaz caramel ice cream did when she was in a funk. It took all her energy to resist, shower, dress quickly and hop on I-465 to head out to Geist where she was meeting Ahern at the Coopers' gated estate. Geist was the playground of the wealthy. Superstar athletes, CEO's, even the governor had a home there.

Nancy Copper looked even more breakable, if that was possible.

"We're hoping you can tell us something that will help us find your husband's murderer, Mrs. Cooper," Lenora said. They were in the leisure room of the stone mansion. Floor to ceiling windows brought the spectacular lake right into the room.

Nancy Cooper grimaced as she reached for a glass of water her housekeeper had placed on the table.

"Let me get it, Sis," Chambers said, popping up from his perch on the edge of the white loveseat. He placed the glass in his sister's hand. Nancy Cooper took a few sips and handed it back to him. Leaned back on the sofa cradling her arm to her side.

Lenora apparently couldn't hide her curiosity because Nancy Cooper offered, "I let the kids talk me into going on a slide in the yard and I fell. I'm lucky it wasn't that high, so I didn't hurt the baby."

Nancy Cooper dabbed at her puffy eyes with a tissue. "You asked who would want to hurt my husband. The stadium isn't big enough to hold all the people who're going to attend his memorial service because he was so loved. I just...don't understand why anyone..." The words caught in her throat, and she struggled to hold back the tears.

Chambers popped up again. Plopped beside her patting her hand. "It's okay, Sis."

Nancy Cooper closed her eyes for a moment.

"Can you tell us who he was with last night? When you last spoke with him?"

Nancy Cooper shook her head. "He always went to the Showcase to celebrate with his friends. He was feeling so good about the game."

"Was Dirk McGill one of them? What can you tell us about him?"

"Dirk? They've been friends since they were kids."

Lenora said, "We can't pinpoint what Mr. McGill does for a living."

Nancy pursed her lips in thought. "Consulting, I think. Bryce always talked about Dirk's clients. I'm pretty sure he has an investment in the Showcase."

Lenora and Ahern exchanged glances.

A little detail Tapper hadn't offered.

"Any problems with his teammates?"

Nancy shook her head. "Oh, no. They all got along well."

"What about your husband's foundation? Everything going all right there?"

She bobbed her head. "We've honored more requests than ever this year. Bryce was happy about that." She clutched her arm.

Chambers put his hand on her shoulder. During the questioning, he'd been watching his sister like a guard dog. "Maybe you should lie down."

Lenora got to her feet. "We have what we need for now. If you think of anything else that could help, please call me." She put her card on the table.

Chambers stood too. "Stay put, Sis. I'll walk the detectives out."

When they reached the foyer, Chambers told them, "I hope I'm not out of line, but you asked about Bryce's relationships with the other Titans."

Lenora said, "If you have information that could help us catch his murderer you need to tell us."

Chambers let out a huge sigh. "Jamie Simmons. He and Bryce got into it a few times."

"The point guard?" Ahern said.

Chambers glanced toward the great room where they'd left his sister. As if checking to make sure she couldn't hear him. "Nancy doesn't know this, but they had to be separated at practice the day before the game."

"You saw this?" Lenora asked.

"Yeah. Bryce had left home without his wallet. Nan asked me to drop it off."

"Well, well," Ahern said.

"Thanks," Lenora said. "We'll follow up on it."

For the first time, Chambers gave a bit of a smile. "Hope it helps."

Chamber's information sent Lenora and Ahern downtown to the Titans Fieldhouse on Maryland Street. The city had cut the ribbon on what writers called a "sparkling venue in a sparkling city" in time for the season opening. It seemed to be the good luck charm. With Cooper's hot hand, fans were convinced the Titans could go all the way.

Standing courtside, watching the team practice after this tragedy, Lenora had her doubts. She'd seen more energy at the senior facility where she volunteered.

"Commissioner wanted to postpone Sunday's game, but the guys wouldn't have it," Coach Dan Humphrey said. "The way they're looking out here I kinda wish we had. Jerry, stay in front of your man! He's gonna get around you!"

He raked chunky fingers through chunky silver hair. "See what I mean? I hope they can get it together. Coop wouldn't want his death to stop our title run."

"That was some electric finish last night," Ahern gushed. He had been giddy as a kid at the thought of meeting the legendary coach. Humphrey had a championship ring for every finger. The Titans lured him to Indy this season hoping he'd get them one, too.

So far, so good.

Humphrey's smile was wistful. "Yeah, Coop pulled it out for us." His expression turned sad. "You folks got to find out who did this."

"Cooper's money and jewelry were still on him, so robbery wasn't the motive. You notice any changes in his personality or mood? Was he getting along with the rest of the team?"

Humphrey laughed. "Coop wasn't your typical superstar— no Prima Donna who needed to be stroked all the time. Never a disagreement with a teammate. Always working to up his game. On time for practice. Just..."

"A little choir boy," Lenora finished.

Oops. Had she said that out loud?

"We heard he and Jamie Simmons had words at practice before the game."

Humphrey chuckled. "Ah, that was nothing. Nerves before the big game that's all."

"I don't see Simmons here. Wouldn't mind talking to him."

"He hurt his knee and is at rehab having it worked on. I'll let him know you want to talk to him. Armstrong! What the hell kind of pass was that?"

The guy he'd yelled at looked at him and shrugged his shoulders.

Humphrey shook his head. "Anything else you need because I really need to get back to this practice."

"Yeah, a look in Cooper's locker and at some point a few minutes with his teammates," Ahern said.

They were combing through the locker when Lenora's phone buzzed. It was Harper with the ballistics report. Cooper was shot five times at close range with a .22.

"Cooper was always relaxed when he was at the club. He could have easily let someone get close thinking they were a fan,"

Ahern said when she told him what Harper had said. "Then, again, it could have been someone he was close to. Someone like McGill. How does a guy who doesn't work drive a Mercedes and live where he lives?"

"He works. We just have to find out at what," Lenora said. "I'm wondering what Cooper did to make Simmons punch him."

Ahern stared at her. "You heard Humphrey. Wasn't anything. I wouldn't waste time chasing that."

"Don't pop a vessel," Lenora said, chuckling. "I get it. You're star struck. All I'm saying is that many shots to the heart say rage and personal."

Lenora's cell phone vibrated again.

"Is this the detective who was at the Showcase?" a woman asked with a shaky voice when she answered.

"Yes. Who's this?"

"Rhonda Blake."

Lenora searched her memory bank. "From the Showcase?"

"McGill. He's a bookie. A lowlife. He takes bets and uses the Showcase for his headquarters with Tapper's blessing." She took a deep breath after getting it out. Relieved.

"It's okay. Bets? On horses?"

Ahern paused his locker search.

"Basketball games."

"You're sure about this?"

"Check Tapper's safe in his office."

"Why tell us this now?" Lenora asked.

"Let's just say I don't like getting dumped or canned. I got both today."

Lenora smiled as she punched off the call. "We may have just learned how McGill pays his bills."

Lenora and Ahern had no trouble getting Miller to back a warrant to search the Showcase. Tapper's staff was setting up for the Saturday night crowd.

"Surprised you're not closed out of respect for your famous patron," Ahern said.

Tapper bristled. "Considered it since you haven't given me my parking lot back. But I have a business to run. Coop would understand. How can I help you?"

Lenora smiled. "Gee, you're not as friendly as you were last night. Something we said?"

Tapper glowered.

"Good thing we picked this up before we came." Lenora held up the warrant. "It allows us to go through every nook, cranny and piece of paper in this place. But we'll start with your safe."

Tapper didn't move. "My safe?"

Ahern stepped forward. "Is that a problem?"

"Now, look…" Tapper held up his hands in protest.

"We can have the officers we brought along do the honors, but I guarantee they won't be as careful as you," Ahern warned.

Tapper's eyes darted around the club. Lenora could see him thinking through his options. Deciding he had no choice, he swore and led them to his office. He pushed aside a tall bookcase to reveal the safe.

"Open it and stand back," Ahern ordered.

With shaky fingers, Tapper punched in a code on the electronic keypad.

The contents included a spiral bound business checkbook, a plastic case of DVDs and a .22 caliber handgun.

"Now see, this entitles you to be our guest at the station," Lenora said, pulling a plastic bag from her belt.

Tapper held up his hands. "You got it all wrong. I could never hurt Coop."

Lenora put the gun in the bag and handed it to Ahern. "You'll forgive us for not taking your word for it."

The detectives put Tapper in an interview room while they scanned a couple of DVDs with Jake, their IT whiz, then went in to talk to Tapper.

"The lady was right," Lenora said. "McGill keeps good records. Spread sheets seem to have everything—who placed the bets, how much. Want to tell us how you and McGill worked this?"

Tapper pursed his lips. "I don't know what you're talking about. Those belong to Dirk. I just let him use my safe."

Lenora stared at him. "Sure you want to stick to that fairytale?"

A range of emotions sweep across Tapper's face.

"Your choice," Lenora said. "We have a weapon and probable cause to arrest you."

"It's the point spread," Tapper quickly said. "You bet a team will win by a certain number of points. They take a game by less than that, you lose. Everybody was betting the Titans would run away with the game, maybe win it by 20. McGill bet Titans would pull out a squeaker."

"How much did Mr. GQ win?"

"Couple hundred thousand."

Ahern whistled.

"Bets are big during the playoffs," Tapper said.

"How could he call it so well?" Ahern asked.

Tapper clasped her hands together, lowered his head into them. Finally, he looked up. "Cooper deliberately shot off the mark to keep the point spread low then brought it out at the buzzer."

"And it was all McGill and Cooper. You had no role in it?" Lenora asked.

Tapper fidgeted in the chair. "I let Dirk keep his DVDs in my safe because Coop asked me to. Coop loaned me the money to open my club. I couldn't say no."

At that moment, the door opened and Miller stuck his head in. "You two."

In the hall, Miller said. "This guy's got some bad karma. Got another body in his parking lot."

McGill was slumped over his Mercedes steering wheel. When the techs pushed him back they saw his silk shirt crimson with blood.

"Same M.O. Shots to the chest," Ahern said.

"We know one thing. It wasn't Tapper," Lenora said.

In addition to having the perfect alibi for McGill's murder, ballistics didn't match Tapper's gun as the weapon used to kill Cooper.

"Two partners in an illegal gambling scheme dead. Has to be connected to their operation," Lenora said when they briefed Miller in his office.

"This city will explode if it gets out Cooper was fixing games," Miller said. He regarded her steadily. "How long can we keep this quiet?"

Lenora met Miller's stare. "What are you saying, Sergeant?"

"Mayor is already warning me what the city stands to lose if this gets out without us controlling the details. Just wondering if we can keep this under the radar until we nail the perp."

"You mean bury Cooper's crime," Lenora said.

"You didn't have to," Lenora said, getting disgusted.

Ahern was slouched in the chair. "I agree with the sergeant. We don't have proof Cooper was a willing participant, just Tapper's story."

Lenora rubbed her eyes. They were on fire from no sleep. "I know it's hard for you to accept that Cooper was anything other than this gifted, generous guy, but that may not be all he was."

Ahern jerked his head in her direction. "So what, now we target the victim? That how they did things when you were in St. Louis PD?"

"No, they did what you're suggesting," Lenora fired back. "Which is why I left after ten years."

Ahern turned his gaze to the wall.

Lenora directed her next words at Miller. "How can we solve this case without looking at the possibility that Cooper and McGill were murdered because of their little venture? Or that Cooper was doing something else that got him killed?"

Miller stared at them through tented fingers. "Your plan?"

Lenora looked at Ahern. "Tapper's security tapes showed nothing. We need to go over McGill's DVD files like we're mining for gold. Check Cooper's foundations. If he was willing to be a part of McGill's scheme, who knows what else he had going."

Miller looked at Ahern who avoided his gaze by studying his crinkled pants. "All right," Miller said. "But be discreet. If this embarrasses the city, my job is gone which means yours is, too."

"C'mon, Sarge—" Ahern started.

"What do you want from me?" Miller said throwing up his hands. "We needed an arrest yesterday."

Ahern bounced up from the chair. "Count me out. I won't help smear a decent guy."

Then he stormed out.

Lenora didn't mind working without a partner. She'd rather be solo than saddled with someone throwing tantrums every five minutes. So alone, she sped to Indy Sports Rehab. The timing gods were with her. Jamie Simmons was hobbling out of the building wearing a soft knee brace.

"Ouch. Are you going to be ready for tomorrow's game?" Lenora asked, showing her badge.

Simmons glanced at the shield but kept hobbling. "I'll be ready. Played with much worse."

"Can we talk?"

"I have an appointment."

"Shouldn't take long. Just tell me why you and Cooper were fighting."

She thought his hobble slowed a bit.

"Not a fight. Just a little disagreement."

"I heard it was pretty heated. You were so mad you punched him into a wall. Makes me wonder if you were angry enough to kill him."

Simmons stopped. Stared down at her from what had to be almost seven feet. He was a good-looking guy with deep chocolate skin. "That fake got what he deserved. He was a liar, a cheat and a coward."

"Tell me how you really feel. Maybe we should go to the station for a longer chat." Simmons started walking again. "Don't have time."

"I can make you take the time if I have to. This is a murder investigation."

He sliced a glance at her. "Everybody covered for Cooper. I got sick of it."

"I need details, Mr. Simmons."

She saw his jaw muscles tighten. "I used to admire the guy like everybody else. Then he hurt me on a deal. I agreed to do some events for his charity. He was supposed to return the favor. He didn't. Reneged on me three times. Cost me money; made me look like a fool."

"You confronted him?"

"He had the freakin' gall to get pissed at me. Almost broke my nose. I defended myself unlike other folks he messed over."

"Cooper had a history of violent behavior?"

Simmons said, "A long one."

Simmons gave Lenora the names of two people who'd also been on the receiving end of Cooper's rage. One was Charles Kapinski who lived in senior housing not far from the Jazz Showcase. In the kitchen of his tiny apartment, he told Lenora how he was crossing the street after taking the bus from his double shift.

"He hit me with his fancy car. Stopped just long enough to lean out and see me lying on the ground. Closed the car door and burned rubber. I was on the ground, but I saw him. Everybody knows Bryce Cooper. I couldn't believe it. Ten surgeries and I'll never walk without this cane, but at least I'm alive."

"There's no police record of this." She had checked.

"His lawyers came to see me." He looked at the floor as if ashamed. "I needed to eat, have a place to live. I took a deal and kept my mouth shut."

The other person Cooper's lawyers had paid to keep quiet was Ashley Jacobs. She'd charged Cooper with assault last year for an attack in a Carmel, Indiana hotel where she'd had a one-nighter with the "family man." She told Lenora he'd beaten her so badly, she had to have surgery to repair a cheekbone.

Cooper had everything, all right, including an ugly sadistic streak that had caused a lot of pain. Nancy Cooper at five months pregnant getting on a slide didn't make any sense. But Lenora dismissed it at the time because they'd been so focused on her grief. But now, Lenora was thinking Nancy Cooper might have been a victim of her husband's brutality, too. Women in abusive relationships often reached a point where they couldn't take it anymore.

Lenora figured she might as well not bother checking hospitals. No way Nancy Cooper would have gone to one. That would be like posting it on Twitter. The world would have known in seconds. They'd have had a doctor come to them. Maybe the team doctor.

Lenora called Humphrey and told him she had a few more questions. He was still at the fieldhouse so Lenora pushed past the speed limit down Meridian to get there.

"I'll get right to the point, so don't tip-toe around your answers to my questions. I know all about Cooper's violent behavior and the incidents you and the Titan's organization covered up. Was he beating his wife?"

Humphrey took a deep breath, a look of resignation on his face. "All right, yes, he was."

"You had the team doc treat her to cover it up."

Humphrey nodded. Then he told her every horrible detail.

"Why didn't you get the guy some help? He might be alive today if you had."

Humphrey's shoulders sagged. "I kept hoping he would get it together. I talked to Coop until my tongue was about to fall off. Nancy couldn't have done this. She loved him too much."

"Sometimes love isn't enough," Lenora said.

On her second drive to Geist, Lenora tossed around how Nancy Cooper could have killed her husband. The squad had picked her up at 3:30 a.m. Cooper' time of death was 1:55 a.m. Enough time to kill Cooper and get home. But could she drive with that arm? Shoot a gun?

Maybe she'd had help. Like from a protective brother.

The siblings greeted her with anxious expressions.

"You have news?" Chambers said.

"Actually, I need you to clarify a few things."

"Okay," Nancy Cooper said softly.

Lenora was purposely blunt. "Mrs. Cooper, I know your husband was helping McGill win bets on the games. I know he abused you and that his coach and the team covered it up."

Nancy Cooper's eyes darted at Chambers, who put a reassuring hand on her shoulder. "That, that was in his past. Bryce had changed. He never hurt me."

Lenora went on. "I know he hurt another woman last year."

Nancy Cooper swallowed hard, gave her brother a please-help-me look.

"Just what are you getting at?" Chambers said, indignation in his voice.

Lenora ignored him. "Your husband is responsible for your injury, isn't he?"

Nancy Cooper began to chew her lower lip.

"You got tired of the beatings," Lenora said quietly. "No one would blame you. But why didn't you go to the police? Why didn't you leave?"

Tears began trickle down Nancy Cooper's cheeks. "I wouldn't...He wouldn't..."

"You don't have to say anything else," Chambers ordered.

"Forget it, Mr. Chambers. Humphrey told me everything," Lenora said. "About the cracked ribs. Bad bruises. The team physician treated you."

Lenora turned to Nancy Cooper. "Women have used abuse as a successful defense before. All—"

"She's not responsible for Bryce's death," Chambers said.

Again, Lenora ignored him. "I understand. You endured so much."

Nancy Cooper began to sob.

Chambers jumped to his feet. "Stop! Just stop."

Lenora waited.

"It's me you want," Chambers finally said.

Nancy Cooper stared wide-eyed as if trying to comprehend what he was saying. Lenora saw Chambers swallow hard. His voice trembled with his next words.

"Don't say anything," Chambers ordered his sister. He said to Lenora, "I was tired of him hurting her. So I killed him."

"Troy," Nancy started.

"Everyone covered for the creep. I tried to talk to him. Threatened him even. But he wouldn't stop. Every since we were kids, I looked after her. Promised our folks that I always would. I just couldn't take it anymore. I was pissed when she called and told me he'd smacked her around again because she wanted him to stay home instead of going to that club. Some hero beating his pregnant wife."

"Where's the gun?" Lenora asked.

"What?" Chambers said, looking confused for a minute. Then said quickly, "I threw it in the Canal."

"What kind of gun was it?"

"A...uh...I have a .38."

"Oh, Troy," Nancy Cooper said, sobbing.

"What really happened, Mr. Chambers?" Lenora asked.

"I told you. I killed Bryce to stop the beatings."

"No. You didn't. Cooper was shot with a .22. You're trying to protect your sister, but—"

"You think I killed Bryce?" Nancy Cooper shouted, eyes wide with horror.

Guilt was in Chambers' eyes. "You were gone for hours. No one knew where you were."

"I had Louis drive me to the park so I could think. I could never hurt Bryce. I loved him."

Lenora could see Chambers' jaw twitch. "Is that what you call it? That's not love. That's sick."

Lenora dragged herself back to the station. Eight o'clock and folks had cleared out, including Miller. She usually avoided caffeine but needed a shot of energy so she grabbed a Coke and slunk down at her desk.

She could sleep for a week.

Three partners. Two dead. The one partner left had an alibi.

She had to find the connection.

Lenora pulled out the DVDs they'd taken from Tapper. Too bad Miller had let Ahern get away with throwing a hissy fit. These could have been reviewed.

There were at least ten. She didn't know if she could keep her eyes open long enough to go through them all.

She called Jake. He was young and single; seemed to live at the station.

"What are we looking for exactly?" he asked, as he sat down at her computer.

"Size of the bets," Lenora said. "How many. Anything."

Jake nodded. "Okay. Let's see if we can sort these files first."

She sipped her Coke. "Can we sort winners and losers?"

"Quick as a Google search." After a few keystrokes, Jake hit the print key. Fifty pages with bets ranging from $10 thousand to $400 thousand started spitting out.

"Lot of losers," Jake said.

"How else would McGill make money?"

Lenora rubbed her tired eyes, scanned the list. Most had lost a few thousand dollars. Except one. He owed McGill a bucket of money.

Jamie Simmons.

"Sorry to bother you so late," Lenora said.

Simmons looked down at her, eyes wide in surprise at her standing at the door of his West 86th Street home.

"See you're still in the brace," Lenora said.

"How can I help you, detective?"

"You can tell me about the money you lost on Cooper and McGill's gambling venture."

"Who's this, Daddy?" a tiny voice asked. It belonged to a curly-haired, chocolate-skinned boy about four years old who wrapped his arms around Simmons good leg.

"Someone I need to talk to. You go back in there with Mommy."

After his son had left, Simmons said. "I lost money. Not a crime."

"Murder is."

Simmons bristled. "I didn't kill anyone."

"I suppose you were home the night Cooper was murdered."

"I was."

"Where were you this afternoon?"

"I didn't kill anyone," he ground out.

"You lost $400 thousand dollars to McGill. You're hurt all the time. Might be your last season. I say you got desperate."

"You don't know what you're talking about."

"No? Educate me. Tell me why I shouldn't arrest you right now. The fact that you owed that kind of money to McGill gives me enough to do it."

Simmons stiffened.

"That would be horrible for your family."

He stared at her for a long time. Finally said, "It wasn't my bet."

What Simmons told her was going to hit Ahern harder than Cooper's death. He might give up basketball altogether.

From the car Lenora called Miller at home to tell him why she needed Ahern and a patrol team to meet her.

"Holy Mother. You sure about this?"

"I wish I weren't," she said. Then she had to ask, "Sergeant, you knew about Cooper's violence didn't you?"

Miller was silent for a moment then said, "Sometimes there are things beyond my control, Detective Wise."

Humphrey was getting ready for an interview with Channel 6 TV when the detectives surprised him in the station's green room.

Eyes wide, he said, "You must have news. It'll be good to have closure before the game."

"They may have to play this one without you, Coach," Lenora said.

"Come again?" Humphrey asked.

"There's a little matter of huge gambling debts you racked up with Dirk McGill who was murdered this morning."

"Gambling debts? I don't know where you got that."

"McGill kept good records. Had Jamie Simmons' name."

Humphrey arched a bushy silver brow. "Really? Doesn't surprise me. With his knee, he's through. Guess he was looking for a little insurance."

"No, Coach, he was doing you a favor."

"Me? That's crazy."

"We know you had Simmons place the bets for you."

Humphrey gave an aw-shucks smile. Looked at Ahern. "So I gamble a little. Who doesn't?"

Ahern looked like a kid who'd just learned there was no Santa Claus.

"Right, who doesn't owe $400 thousand in gambling debts?" Lenora said, laughing. "You owe bookies all over the country. You're a mess."

Humphrey set his lips in a hard line. "You don't know what you're talking about."

"Yeah, we do. Simmons told us you asked him to make the bet for you. McGill came to him to collect; he had to tell him you owed him for the loss. McGill demanded you pay up. He had to go."

Humphrey's expression was blank.

Lenora went on, "We get why McGill had to die. But why kill Cooper?"

Humphrey found the fake smile again. "You said it. Why would I kill Cooper? My star. He was the team. That would be suicidal."

Humphrey glanced at Ahern again. Got back a look of disgust.

"There's a .22 registered to you. Maybe you'll tell us where you stashed it."

Humphrey stared at her. "I'm not going anywhere. You can't prove squat, and I've got friends way above your pay grade, honey. When this is over, you'll be lucky to be working a parade."

"Did you hear that, Ahern?" Lenora asked. "Was that a threat?"

Ahern spoke for the first time, "I heard it. We need you to come with us. *Coach.*"

Ahern stepped toward Humphrey.

Humphrey sprang from the chair, reached beneath his jacket and pulled a gun. "Don't think I'll be doing that."

"First a threat, now pulling a weapon on police officers. Big, big mistakes," Lenora said.

Humphrey's eyes were hard. "Coop just needed to help me out one time. One freaking time! He owed me after all I did for him. Cleaning up his messes. Keeping his crap out of the media. Calling in favors with my police buddies. But he wouldn't do it. Said that hustler was like family."

"You really should think about what you're doing," Lenora said.

"What I think is I'm walking out of here."

Humphrey backed up to the door, reached behind to open it and backed out.

Right into the waiting patrol team.

"Those are the details," Miller told the press called to headquarters for the late night briefing.

"Just to make sure I've got this right," a reporter said. "Coach Humphrey killed Coop because he wouldn't throw the game. Then he killed this McGill character when he demanded he pay a gambling debt."

"Tragic," Miller said.

What was tragic, Lenora thought as she and Ahern watched the briefing from the back of the room, was Miller, the brass and the mayor burying Cooper's abusive behavior and his gambling scheme with McGill.

No one would know the truth about him.

That stunk.

Left Lenora wondering if trading in St. Louis PD for this was a mistake. Maybe it was time to rethink why she was even doing this job.

She slipped from the room, intending to head for the detective area.

"Lenora," Ahern called, following her out.

Lenora was a bit startled. He'd actually used her first name.

"I want to apologize for—"

She held up her hand. "Already forgotten, Jack. Going to the game tomorrow?"

Ahern shook his head. "Couldn't stand it."

The Titans, under their assistant coach, won the final playoff game in a blow-out dedicated to only one of its fallen idols.

Oscar Robertson
Brenda Robertson Stewart

Considered one of the greatest guards in NBA history, Oscar Robertson was born in Tennessee, but grew up in Indianapolis. He led Crispus Attucks High School to the state basketball championship in 1955. This was the first time an all African-American team had won a state championship. They won the title again the following season.

After high school, Robertson went to the University of Cincinnati where he was named the All-Star MVP and Rookie of the Year. He averaged well over 30 points a game for three seasons. Robertson teamed up with rival Jerry West to co-captain the 1960 Olympic team where they led the squad to a gold medal.

The Cincinnati Royals chose Robertson in the NBA draft in 1960. Other than Jerry West with the Los Angeles Lakers, no guard could match his play. Robertson became active in the player's union and eventually headed up the organization for several years working to bring player free agency to the league.

During his last few seasons, relations between Robertson and the franchise became strained and in 1970, he was dealt to the Milwaukee Bucks anchored by center Kareem Abdul-Jabbar. In 1971, the Bucks won the national championship. The Big O, as he was known, retired in 1974 as one of the basketball greats.

Oscar Robertson was inducted into the Naismith Memorial Basketball Hall of Fame in 1980 and in 2006, was inducted into the National College Basketball Hall of Fame. He was voted one of the 50 Greatest Players in NBA History.

ONE GOOD SHOT
S. M. Harding

Former sheriff Micah Barrow had just adjusted his long legs on his recliner, beer at hand, when the phone rang. "Dang it, can't a man watch a game on the television without some dangburn emergency?"

For once, he decided they could wait, at least until the first commercial break. After all, it wasn't often IU played on national TV in a run for the NCAA Tournament. Leastways, not since the Sampson debacle and Crean's having to start from scratch.

He flicked the game on with anticipation of play action. Pre-game commentary. "Pundits in politics, now I gotta listen to pundits in basketball." He hit mute.

Basketball had always been his game; he'd been tall, agile, with a damn fine eye. He remembered how the ball rolled off his fingers when the shot was just right: swish! Such a sweet moment. He'd had a wicked hook shot. Not that it would mean anything today; it was all three-pointers and slam dunks.

The phone rang again. He shoved the footrest down and walked over to the phone. "Yep."

"Sorry to disturb you at home, but I got a problem."

"Dog? You gotta drunk or a robbery or any other felony occurrence, call the sheriff."

"Askin' for your help, Micah. Got a drinker here I think is buildin' up courage."

"To do what?"

"Nothin' good. Can you come down, talk to him?"

"Dog, the game's about to start, Sarah's at work, got the house all to myself so I can cuss anytime I need to."

"It's Darby Mueller."

"Hell. OK, give me a half-hour."

As Micah drove to the Dog Pound, a biker bar turned respectable watering hole, he thought about Darby Mueller. People remembered Keith Smart because he sank the last-second shot against Syracuse that won the '87 NCAA Championship. Few remembered Darby who'd made the shot that beat LSU in the Regional. He was heading for the pros, sitting on top of the world. Until he wrapped his new Harley around a tree doing ninety. Then he became an ex-jock with a limp.

Micah pulled his truck in back of the dusty cinder block building. The only light came from the neon sign on the top of the bar. The buzz from the sign made a peculiar harmony to the exhaust fan.

He walked into the bar and spotted Dog pulling a draft beer. "Don't you look purty," Micah said. "Used to look like a walkin' bush. What's the occasion?"

"My youngest daughter's wedding," Dog said, rubbing his neatly trimmed beard. "What a man don't do for a daughter."

"Don't have to tell me." Micah pushed his cap back. "So where's Darby?"

"Snuck out. Thought he was goin' to the gents. Must've gone out the back. Stiffed me. Never done that before."

"I come all the way down here an' Darby ain't here? You ever hear of a phone? Oh, yeah, must've cause you called me to come all the way down here even though the IU game was startin'."

"You just missed him, not more 'n five minutes."

"Don't matter how much time, Dog. I ain't chasin' after him."

Dog served two guys sitting at the end of the bar. When he came back, he said, "Don't mean to piss you off, but I know he's steerin' for trouble and I thought you could head him off."

"What'd he do that spooked you?"

"Normal times, he comes in, has a beer or two with the guys an' that's it. Tonight, he orders a shot of bourbon, straight up."

"Man can't change his drink of choice without you callin' the unofficial constabulary?"

"Tonight, he comes in, don't talk to nobody. Sits in the back lookin' real broody."

"He *say* anything?"

"Talkin' to hisself more'n me. Somethin' 'bout in over his head." Dog shook his head. "Hard to remember, just mutterin'."

"*Anything* else?"

"Something 'bout the draft."

"Beer?"

"You got lint in your ears, Micah? *The* draft: NBA."

"His draft was a long time ago and ended up wrapped around a tree."

Dog threw the bar rag into sudsy water. "All I can give you is what my gut tells me. Don't think he's gonna drive into the biggest tree he can find. Think he left here on a mission."

Micah nodded, swiveled around on his stool, and got out his phone. "Sarah, I was wonderin' if you could put a BOLO out on Darby Mueller. Think he drives a older model Bronco, don't know the license."

There was a long pause. "Is this official county business, Dad?"

"Course. Wouldn't ask you for a personal favor—just like you wouldn't've asked me when I was sheriff."

"Official cause?"

"Um, suspicion of driving while intoxicated. If you spot him, call me. On my cell."

"Where are you?"

"Watchin' the game." He switched the phone off. "Now make an honest man of me, Dog, an' turn up the volume."

The call didn't come until late in the third quarter. He punched the phone on. "Reserve Deputy Barrow."

"We found your man, Dad."

A roar went up from the customers.

"Where are you?"

"Uh, watchin' with friends. Game's tied 68 to 68." He walked toward the back door. "So where's Darby?"

"Heading to the hospital. In an ambulance. Deputy Carter spotted his truck in a ditch."

"Ah, hell."

"Since this is official business that you initiated, you'll follow up?"

"Soon as the game's over."

"Dad."

"They're all tied up at 68, Sarah Anne."

"Uh, actually they're three points down now. We need a deputy at the hospital to follow up. Now. A reserve deputy will do just fine."

Micah moaned. "Yes, ma'am. Reckon it don't matter an old man might not have too many good games to watch in his future."

"Call me from the hospital."

As Micah drove back to Greenglen, he tried to pick up the game on the radio, but the radio was as old as the truck and kept fading out. "... he sets at the top of the key and shoots ... sure can pull down the boards ... IU ends the quarter ..." Micah banged his fist on the radio and it settled into static. He let loose a string of cuss words he hadn't used since 1962.

He pulled into the no parking zone by the ER doors and stomped up to the nurses' station. "Darby Mueller."

"And good evening to you, too, Micah Barrow," said a nurse without looking up from a chart.

"I apologize, Zinnia," Micah said. "All I thought I'd be doin' tonight is watchin' the game an' circumstances is conspirin' to defeat that peaceful intention."

She looked up and grinned. "Room four—but don't expect much. He got a real whack on his head."

"'Whack'—that some new medical-speak?"

"Shorthand for a concussion. Attending ordered a scan but we've been waiting for him to stabilize. Internal injuries, too."

"Can I see the possessions he came in with?"

"Came in with a wallet, change in a pocket, pack of cigarettes and a Bic lighter."

"How much cash?"

She looked at a list. "Forty-four bucks. Oh, and Deputy Carter called about five minutes ago—he's cleared the crash scene and is on his way over. Maybe he found something else in the vehicle."

"What the devil am I doin' here if he's on his way?"

"Missing the game, I'd say."

"Pah!" He pushed his ballcap back on his head. "OK if I visit with Darby?"

She nodded. "Won't do any good though."

Micah walked down the hall, saw Darby lying in bed, attached to all sorts of machines. He entered quietly, remained standing by the door. Was one shot of whiskey enough to put Darby's truck in a ditch?

"Dammit..."

Micah looked toward the bed, saw a bandaged head with one eye swollen shut. "Take it easy, Darby."

"Gotta protect him..."

"Who? Who you talkin' 'bout?"

"Toe..." Darby's good eye closed.

Micah took a seat by the bed, hoping Darby would come to again. What the hell did "toe" mean? He couldn't feel them? Or toes were causing pain?

Ten minutes of monitors beeping and Darby's senseless muttering and Micah looked up to see a deputy at the door. He rose and stepped into the corridor. "Deputy."

"Carter, sir. I doubt if you remember me."

Micah squinted. "'Bout fifteen years ago. I was sheriff and as I remember, you were a little squirt."

Carter nodded. "My brother was killed by a drunk driver. You came to the funeral, took me aside after it was over. As I remember it, you listened to me for a long time."

"Hope I said somethin' that made it a tad easier."

"Yes, sir, you did. That's why I wanted to be a cop."

"Well." Micah took his cap off, rubbed a gnarled hand through his short hair. "Uh, how'd you find Darby?"

"Got the BOLO, thought I'd best keep my eyes on the sides of the road. Intoxicated, you know?"

"So what happened?"

"Not really sure. He braked almost three hundred feet before he went off the road. The marks were real heavy, like he was standing on the brakes all the way."

Micah rubbed the back of his neck. "If his brakes was workin' good enough to lay rubber, why didn't he stop?"

"After the ambulance came, I took a good look at his truck." Carter began to pull up photos on his camera. "These are the skid marks—but they don't look like a skid to me. And look at the rear-end damage on the truck. It went hood-first into the ditch."

Micah put on his glasses, peered at a photo, then another closer shot. "You think he was pushed off the road?"

"Uh, I called the Fatal Accident Crash Team and their initial reaction was something like that. Thought I better see how Mueller is. He going to make it?"

"Got bashed round pretty good, but Zinnia didn't sound like he was on the edge. He's been talkin' a bit."

"Did he tell you who ran him off the road?"

Micah shook his head. "Too worried 'bout somebody else."

"Who?"

"Wish I knew." Micah took off his glasses, shoved them in the pocket of his shirt. "You goin' to stay here with Darby?"

"Of course, sir."

"I'm goin' to the station, so I'll clear it with Sar...the sheriff. An' send them photos in." He put his hand on Carter's shoulder. "You done a good job."

When Micah walked into the station, his scowl deepened as he saw all the smiling faces. "Good game?"

The Chief Deputy beamed. "Best end to a game since Watford's buzzer-beater against Kentucky in 2011. Real soft three-pointer just floated toward the hoop."

"We win?"

"Oh, yeah," Caleb said. "Tournament, here we come."

Micah sighed, tried to convince himself that IU basketball was ephemera.

"Miss the whole game, Dad?" Sarah asked, walking out of her office.

"Radio in the truck died."

"Or was killed?"

He snorted. "You wanna rub it in or hear 'bout Darby Mueller?"

They walked into her office and Micah reported the events of the evening. "Thing is, he took a real poundin' in that crash but he's worried 'bout somebody else. Somebody's who's in trouble."

Sarah drummed her pencil on the desk. "He was on disability a couple of years – until he went back and finished his degree. Worked for Teddy Boehm's Insurance a couple of years, then moved up to Indy."

"Come home when his momma got sick, three, four years ago. Does some coachin' at the high school, don't he?"

She nodded. "What are you thinking?"

"Just wonderin' if one of the kids he coaches is in trouble."

"Current team is clean as a whistle. No trouble from them."

"Guess I should get back to the hospital, see if Darby can fill in the who and what."

"Go home, Dad. Darby's in surgery. He won't be able to tell us anything until tomorrow."

"You got somebody guardin' him?"

"Deputy Carter's gone home to grab a couple of hours sleep— but he'll be there when Darby's back in a room."

Micah nodded.

"Dad, there's nothing we can do tonight."

"Just got a feelin' we're playin' against the clock. Darby was on the way to somewhere to act. Tonight."

When Micah got home, he went to the study and his computer. He pulled up Greenglen High School, worked his way back four years when Darby Mueller was an assistant coach, and wrote down the team members. Only a guess, but if Darby was heading out to act tonight, he had to be going somewhere close-by. Micah went to the IU basketball page and checked against his list. Two kids, one who played rarely and then a sophomore point guard who was getting a lot of floor time. Toby Mueller. Toe?

He got a well-thumbed address book from the drawer and dialed. "Is Chief Lykins on campus? Can I talk with him, please? Micah Barrow callin'."

Micah got up and began to pace. Jumpin' to conclusions, he thought. Woulda skinned a deputy for that in the old days. But it was the only course of *action*. Wouldn't cost the sheriff's department anything. Wouldn't hurt the investigation. So why was he uncertain? "Cause I shoulda told Sarah what I had in mind to do."

"What aren't you telling the sheriff, you old goat?"

"Chief—sorry I was thinkin' out loud. Old goats tend to do that."

"You call me to talk livestock?"

"Nope, called about a possible threat to two of your hoopsters." He gave the Chief the names. "Thing is, I should know more in the mornin' but I got nothin' but suspicion to give you. Thought I should give you a heads-up."

"Are you thinking protective custody?"

"More like a kinda ostentatious welfare check. Your call, Chief."

"As always, Micah, talking to you is like—"

"Heard the game was a real barnburner."

"Oh, man, it was a dream. You didn't watch it?"

"*I* was workin'. Now I'm goin' to bed."

Micah let his frustration out by slamming the nurses' station counter. "How could he be in a coma? He was talkin' last night!"

"Keep it down, Micah," the nurse said. She leaned toward him. "He had some swelling in his brain—it's pretty common now to put the patient in a medically induced coma. Let's the swelling go down from a trauma."

"For how long?"

"Hard to say. Depends on how long it takes the swelling to go down—and don't smack the counter again."

"Deputy, may I have a word with you?"

The familiar voice came from behind him. He turned to find his daughter's bright blue eyes focused on his. "Sarah Anne, I was hopin' to talk to Darby but these good folk put him asleep."

She motioned for him to follow and began to walk to the doors.

Micah turned back to the nurse. "I'm sorry for my unruly and impolite behavior." Then he followed the sheriff's retreating figure.

"You left awfully early this morning, Dad."

"Wanted to talk to Darby."

"Hoping he'd tell you who ran him off the road?"

"Nope. Was goin' to ask him who he was rushin' off to protect. The person who still needs protectin' an' Darby ain't in any condition to do nothin'."

Sarah stopped. "We need to talk. Meet you at that new coffee shop on Sycamore."

"They serve regular coffee?"

"New horizons, Dad. See you in ten."

Eight minutes later, Micah looked over the red and white striped café curtains and saw Sarah seated at a corner table. He pushed into the hiss and turbine sounds of espresso. Smelled good though.

He sat at Sarah's table and glanced at a cup she pushed in front of him. "What's this?"

"Cappuccino." She took a sip of hers. "Now, start from the beginning."

He did and told her about the call from Dog through his call to Chief Lykins at IU. "The road where Darby went off is the backdoor route to the Bloomington campus. His nephew, Toby, is there...an' Darby weren't just a coach but his uncle."

"Have you talked to Toby or his family yet?"

Micah shook his head. "Thought I'd suss it out with Darby. Didn't want to get Toby off his game."

"Oh, Lord...'off his game.' This is one of the times I think Hoosier Hysteria is *such* an understatement. We're conducting an investigation, Dad, and I don't give two hoots if Toby Mueller is off his game or not."

"*I'll* interrogate the boy if it's OK with you. Believe it or not, I remember what it's like to be young and in love with playin' basketball."

Sarah glanced at him. "And I'll find out if Darby's family knows anything. Oh, by the way, paint scratches from Darby's truck are from a GM SUV, recent model, color called raven black. We ruled out a truck from the height of the impact."

Chief Lykins led the way up to an older double in a quiet Bloomington neighborhood. He turned to Micah. "Toby said he'd stay home today except for practice." He hesitated. "Is Toby suspected of some criminal activity?"

"Don't rightly know," Micah said.

"I'll be hung from the backboard if I have to arrest him."

"How 'bout, should there be a need, I send Sarah over to do the dirty deed?"

The two men grinned. "He's all yours." Lykins turned and walked away.

Micah mounted the steps to the porch and rang the doorbell. He heard someone pound down the stairs from the second floor and the door was flung open by a tall young man who needed a shave. "Sheriff Barrow?"

"Can I come in?"

"Is my family OK? Mom and Dad? Uncle Darby?"

Micah motioned to the interior. Toby stood aside and Micah walked into a tolerably clean living room.

"You're scaring me," Toby said when they were seated.

"Far as I know, they're fine, all except for your Uncle Darby."

"Uncle Dar? He didn't show up last night after the game and ...What's happened?"

Micah decided to take it straight down the lane. "He got run off the road last night comin' up to talk to you."

"Aw, Christ."

"You want to tell me 'bout it, Toby?"

Toby buried his head in his arms. "Is he going to be OK?"

"Got banged up pretty good, but the doc said he should get through this." Micah shifted in his chair. "But you ain't. Help me get to the bottom of this an' find out who did this to Darby. He's a good man and don't deserve to suffer cause he was tryin' to protect you."

"Oh, God!"

Micah waited until Toby settled down.

Finally the boy wiped his eyes and looked directly at Micah. "I've really screwed up. I owe money to some guys and they started making threats. I asked Uncle Dar what I should do."

"Who do you owe?"

"A website—and whoever owns it."

"Start from the beginning, don't leave nothing out."

"Last year, some of the guys in my dorm were playing on-line poker. I thought it was fun and it didn't seem real—like using beans instead of cash. By the end of the year, I was down by a little over two thousand bucks."

"Lotta money for a scholarship student."

Toby brushed his hands through his short hair. "I wasn't worried because I had a job lined up for the summer that would've covered it."

"Doing what?"

"Long-haul trucking with my Uncle Brad. His business has picked up enough, he could afford to take me along. Summer before, I went up to Alaska and worked on a trawler."

"Adventure an' a lotta hard work."

"Yes, sir. But Coach got me a scholarship to the best basketball camp I could ever dream of. I only ended up working for a month or so. Then I had to pay my expenses and I ended up about nine hundred bucks short."

"You paid some?"

"Yes, sir. Didn't stop them from coming after me. I'd get e-mail almost everyday saying I'd better pay up or there'd be trouble."

"They say what kind of trouble?"

"There wasn't anything like pay by tomorrow or we'll kill you. Just these 'how can a player play with broken kneecaps?' Other stuff like that. They charged interest and now I'm into them for twenty-six hundred."

"You know who they are?"

Toby wrapped his hands around the back of his neck, the veins standing out in his arms. "Wish to God I knew."

Micah rubbed his chin. "We need to track them."

"I'll turn over my computer and passwords to you if that would help. I can't study anyway."

"Darby was talkin' 'bout a draft—yours?"

Toby nodded. "I thought if I could get drafted this spring, I'd get enough of an advance to get them off my back for good. Uncle Dar didn't want me to."

"Preciate your honesty, Toby. An' your help. I know the perfect consultant who can find these guys. In the meantime, get somebody to watch your back."

Micah called Chief Lykins and heard his sigh of relief. Then he called Sarah and gave her the basic outline. "Thought I'd take the computer to Nathan."

"Bring it in to the station and ask Nathan to meet us here. I'll get a search warrant—Judge Bragg graduated from pre-law at IU and the law school."

"Sounds like an easy three."

"Dad, I want to nab the guys who forced Darby into the hospital as badly as you do. But I want to see them stand trial right here in McCrumb County."

"By the book, yes ma'am."

He knew she was right, but he muttered all the way back to Greenglen. He walked into the department and saw Nathan Cloud's long body lounging against a file cabinet in Sarah's office. Nathan was the best tracker he knew – both in the woods and in cyber space. He tightened his grip on Toby's laptop and walked into the office.

"One computer, one consultant, one sheriff—and one warrant?" Micah asked.

"You bet—all I had to do was mention coercion of a certain point guard and we got a pretty wide-open search parameter."

Nathan repositioned a chair and opened the laptop. "You have his password?"

Micah took a folded sheet of paper from his jacket and handed it to him. "All his passwords and accounts —you know, Twits an' stuff. An' he wrote out permission for us to examine all his files."

"Nice work, Dad. Thanks."

Micah's phone rang. He looked at the caller ID and walked away from the desk. "Micah Barrow. What you need, Toby?" He nodded a couple of times. "Just now? You see the caller's number? Blocked, dang. Do yourself a favor and call the Chief right now. Don't need to say nothin' but you got a threat." He turned toward Sarah and Nathan as he pocketed the phone. "Now we know what them vermin is after—if IU gets to the Elite Eight, they want Toby to be off his game."

"Throw the game?" Sarah asked.

"Yup. The money he owes them will get forgotten 'bout if he plays ball. Bad ball, so to speak."

"Let's get to work," Sarah said. She looked over Nathan's shoulder.

"That there," Micah said, pointing to the files, "is the gamblin' site. Said a guy in his dorm last year was pushin' it. Whole bunch of guys used it. Got their names, too."

"You think he was set up in advance?"

"He was in the runnin' for Mr. Basketball his senior year. Folks knew he was on the team. Whadda you think?"

Nathan looked up from the screen. "I'd like to take this home where I've got more resources. If one of you came with, would that guarantee the chain of evidence?"

Sarah nodded, then looked at Micah. "We've got a regional list of black GM SUVs. None have come into a county shop, so we've got two deputies checking each car. But it could be imported muscle, so I've asked IMPD to keep an eye open."

"This here machine seems to be our best lead, Sarah Anne. Wanna flip a coin?"

"I've got plenty to do here, Dad. You go—but be on good behavior, both of you."

Micah had followed Nathan home, though he knew the way blindfolded. They bumped up a narrow tract to the clearing that held Nathan's cabin. Micah reckoned it was close to two hundred years old, though perfectly maintained. A tower with satellite dishes rose behind it. The kind of contradiction Nathan was.

They walked into rustic simplicity, except for the one wall covered with electronic gear. Nathan settled at a workstation and plugged in the laptop. "I want to start with the e-mails because they're easier to backtrack. I'll print them out so you'll have hard copies."

He clicked his mouse a few times and a printer began spewing out pages. Then he executed a series of commands that left Micah without a clue.

"These guys are either stupid or lazy." He pulled up a screen on another monitor, scrolled down a list, then double-clicked. "That's your threat-sender and his address."

"I'll be danged." Micah got his notebook and wrote it down. "You got documentation down for all this?"

"Hard copies coming. I wonder if the cyber casino is as sloppy? Let's take a look."

On another monitor, the poker site came up. Then the screen split and what Micah assumed was code scrolled down the left side. "How come that don't happen on my computer?"

Nathan grinned. "You don't know the magic word." His smile disappeared. "This site is sucker-rigged. High rate of success at first, then intermittent, then they lower the boom." He turned to Micah. "We're straying into federal territory. I can probably trace the site's deposits and withdrawals, but we need a federal warrant."

"To use in court. Let me make a call." Micah walked into the kitchen, held a long conversation. Finally he grinned, walked back and handed Nathan the phone. "Give him your e-mail address."

After Nathan handed it back, Micah said, "FBI friend, we go way back. He thinks we got a good chance of gettin' a federal warrant. Which he'll send to you. Until then, I guess it's time for a nap. OK if I stretch out on your couch?"

"Don't you think it'd be a good idea to call Sarah?"

"You've always looked out for her, since you two was no higher than a good stump. Good idea."

Ten minutes later, Micah was winding down the conversation with Sarah. "Thanks, Sarah. While Nathan's waitin' for the warrant, I'll pay a visit to Darby. See if he can add any information. An' if Nathan's finished with it, I'll drop the computer back at the station." He nodded a couple of times, then closed the phone.

"Nurse said it was OK for you to have a short visit," Micah said, sitting in the chair next to Darby's bed.

"Reminds me of the first time you scraped me off the pavement."

Micah looked at the bandaged head, swollen eye, and bandito bruises around his eyes. "Pretty awful time for you and your family, both times."

"My own fault the first time. I had one good shot for a great life and I blew it. I didn't want Toby to do the same thing. Talked to him just now and he said he told you everything."

"He's a good boy, just got sucker punched. The site was rigged."

"Damn!"

"You remember gettin' pushed off the road? Somethin' from that night?"

"Nope. But I do remember what I'd found out before that."

"You'd been investigatin'? On your own? Why the hell didn't you tell Sarah what was goin' on?"

"I thought if I could fix this for Toby, he could go to the NBA after he graduated. Have a great life."

Micah was silent. Dwellin' in the past, he thought, tryin' to make the past right in someone else's future was pure folly. But what man wouldn't try for redemption? He sighed. "So tell me 'bout this investigation."

"I've been to all of Toby's games—middle school through now. And I haven't missed IU's home games since I could get around after the motorcycle accident."

"I like a story as well as any man, Darby, but you need to get to the point."

Darby clenched his free fist. "Point is, I know most the regular fans. This year, when the team started practice, I saw this guy hanging around. Could've been an agent or a pervert. Not a fan."

"What'd he look like?"

"Like a bouncer from a sleazy club. He was watching Toby, so I started watching him. Name's Ward Foreman."

"How'd you get his name?"

"I'm getting tired, Micah. Just listen. Foreman hangs out with two other guys. Don't know their names, but their meetings are at Morgan's Raid. Early dinners, around 5:00."

"You know where Foreman lives?"

"Clear Creek."

"Thanks, Darby. We'll take it from here, you just use your energy to get better. Toby'd be here, but he's confined to campus. Chief'll keep him safe."

The sheriff's office had a busy forty-eight hours. The federal warrant had come in and Nathan had tracked the poker site's operators right back to McCrumb County. The warrant had also brought a conference with the DA about the feds.

They got Ward Foreman's photo from the BMV and Micah had snuck a couple of photos of the "meeting" at Morgan's Raid. Foreman's black Escalade, found in the parking lot of Edinburgh's discount mall, had front-end damage and paint scrapes that matched Darby's old truck.

The morning of the third day, Micah and Sarah were seated in her office with Cam Skillman, an FBI special agent from the organized crime unit. He handed them files. "The Las Vegas mob would be more than happy to take this scum off your hands."

Sarah looked up from the file. "Why? Does LVPD have warrants out on them? The Bureau?"

Cam shook his head. "They were minor players in the Vegas scene, but they committed the sin that can't be forgiven. They skimmed from their bosses."

"They're on the run from the mob?"

"For their lives."

"Mebbe we should just write a polite note with their addresses an' send it to Vegas," Micah said.

"Dad!"

"Hell's bells. We got nothin' to charge them two with. We got Foreman on attempted murder, maybe we can push him to roll over on them other two."

"Unlikely," Cam said.

"What about wire fraud?" Sarah asked.

"We can pick them up, get them to trial, and send them away for a couple of years," Cam answered.

"So what's your problem?" Micah asked. "You do have a problem, so spit it out, Special Agent."

"OK," Cam said, sitting back. "If we put them in prison, they'd be lucky to last a month. Even in a federal facility. And all the intel they have on the mob dies with them."

"Oh, man, I can see where this is goin'. Witness protection, bye-bye prosecution. Fly away, them devils, to a new, good life."

Cam nodded.

"All three?" Sarah asked.

"You want Foreman, he's yours. A present from the Bureau for locating them. But I'd like to coordinate arrests. 6:00 in the morning?"

Sarah nodded. "But it grieves me to let those two walk. Foreman had to be acting on their orders. Meanwhile, Darby Mueller is in the hospital where he'll be for a couple of months. Doesn't seem fair, does it?"

"If the FBI is goin' to free the men what put him in a ditch— where he woulda died if Dog hadn't been worried," Micah said, "well, least the government can do is pay his hospital bills."

"And any subsequent expenses he may incur from the attempted murder," Sarah added. "Or we could pick up those two for conspiracy."

Cam looked from one to another. "Talk about a tag team."

"Didn't know we were," Micah said. "I think in terms of basketball. Been double-teamed."

"Is that what this is about? A washed-up ex-jock?"

Micah sputtered.

Sarah glanced at him, one eyebrow raised. "It's been said, by a Butler player I think, that Hoosier basketball is a way of life. We support players on the court and after. Darby made one mistake and paid dearly for it. He was left in that ditch because he was trying to protect his nephew. To stop him from making one, big mistake. And to protect collegiate athletics from one more blow to its reputation. Since the government is going to reward gangsters, seems like the least it could do is spread the reward to an upstanding man."

"Let me make a call." Cam stepped out of the office but kept in sight. When he came back in he grinned. "Pulled in every favor owed me. It's a deal. Can't put it in writing, but you have my word. Operations at zero-six-hundred?"

"Not a second before," Sarah said. "But be warned, should Darby have financial worries from his hospitalization, you'll find out how being double-teamed can really feel."

Micah and Sarah watched Cam weave his way through the bullpen desks and out of the door.

"You gonna trust a G-man?"

Sarah put a voice-activated digital recorder on the desk. "Wouldn't stand up in any court of law, but it sure could ruin an agent's career."

Micah high-fived Sarah. "Slam-dunk, Sarah Anne."

Reggie Miller
Tony Perona

Reggie Miller didn't start out a Hoosier. Born in Riverside, California, he played for UCLA and was ranked nationally as a shooter both his junior and senior years. In 1987 he became a Hoosier when the Indiana Pacers selected him with their No. 11 draft pick. He spent the next 18 years with the organization. In the process, he became a legend in professional basketball.

When his career finished in 2005, he had made 2,560 three-point shots and was the NBA's greatest long shooter. His 25,279 career points placed him 12th on the league's all-time scoring list. But he was best known for coming through in the clutch. "Miller Time" was the catch phrase used to describe the ending stretch when Miller would take control of the game. His clutch shot made him much despised by other teams. He was routinely booed in Madison Square Garden.

In Indiana, Miller was a rock star. His rookie year he hit 61 three-pointers, more than any other rookie in NBA history at the time. In his third season, Miller led the Pacers to the NBA Playoffs. Though the team didn't survive the first round, Miller led them back again and again. They reached the NBA Finals in 2000, losing to the Shaquille O'Neal and Kobe Bryant-led Los Angeles Lakers.

Miller retired in 2005 in spectacular fashion. In his final game against the New York Knicks, he was initially booed (as usual), but near the end of the game the crowd chanted his name and gave him a standing ovation. In the closing minutes of his final game at Conseco Fieldhouse, Miller left the floor to an ovation that lasted for minutes.

Miller was inducted into the Basketball Hall of Fame in 2012.

BREAKING AND ENTERING
Sara L. Gerow

Jamie Carr took away the basketball for the third time and, as if blessed by Mercury, brought it down court with dizzying speed. Those in the field house that night went silent as Jamie dodged away from his defender just beyond the three-point line and stretched upward, lifting his arms. The basketball floated high and seemed to hang suspended in air before, as if by magic, it fell through the basketball hoop. The field house crowd exploded, stomping, screaming, then chanting, "Jamie, Jamie, Jamie." His third three-pointer that game. The bleachers shaking frightened those standing in the high rows.

Tears streamed down Molly Carr's cheeks as the noise went on. She sank back down into her seat. The friend next to her rubbed her arm. Someone behind her massaged her shoulders. It was a gift to be Jamie's mother, a gift to be raising him on her own. And doing a splendid job of it, she often told herself, for he excelled at whatever he did.

Molly could be charitable and so she stood up and applauded when another kid made a basket but her mind was on Jamie. When he was bringing the ball down the court again, she heard a familiar shout. To her left she saw his father leaning over the railing, waving his arms as if he wanted his son to acknowledge him from the basketball court. So Kevin had managed to break away from his social life in Indianapolis to drive fifty miles and arrive just before half-time. A little blond in a faux fur jacket put her arm around his waist. Molly thought she wasn't much older than Jamie. She danced and waved too but Molly figured she didn't care who won the game.

The bright lights were dim now. Old hurts smoldered. She stretched and, turning away with disgust, saw Trey Harris in the upper rows. He and his wife Kitty were neighbors and best of friends. Trey was running for mayor when autumn rolled around. Now he worked the crowd above her, shaking hands, slapping backs, handing out cards. She gave him a thumbs up when she caught his eye. He returned the gesture.

When she turned around again, Kevin waved at her and mouthed a greeting. She thought he'd come by and say hello at half-time but he didn't. Instead he and the blond claimed seats in the front row.

The Cougars won by twenty points that night and Jamie made four three-pointers. Molly stayed in her place, munching on stale popcorn, and waited for the crowd to file out. She'd meet Jamie near the locker room. Maybe they'd go to the Dairy Bar and have an ice cream. Their ritual whether the Cougars won or lost.

But Kevin and his date, with her tentative smile, were coming toward her. Before he could speak, Trey Harris came between them.

"The colleges will soon come courting," he warned, shaking Kevin's hand. They clapped each other on their backs. Stiffly Molly got to her feet and forced a smile. The blond hugged Kevin's arm as if to say, "I've got him now."

"You're looking good, Molly. I'm sorry I didn't pick up Jamie last week but—boy, am I proud of him."

Molly nodded and brushed popcorn kernels off her blue jeans. Kevin touched her arm as if there might still be something between them.

"Lisa and I want to take Jamie out for pizza."

"It's a school night." Her tone was stiff and severe.

"We'll have him home by eleven."

Molly thought Lisa's grin idiotic.

"Whatever Jamie wants," she said.

The light by the garage door was out when Molly drove into the driveway alone. She always left it on when she was gone of an evening. The light bulb must have burned out. She'd check in the morning. She cursed as she pawed through her handbag. She fumbled in the darkness in putting key to lock. As soon as she entered the kitchen she felt a disconcerting presence, as if something lurked in the darkness. It was more than Jamie not being with her or the light being out. Perhaps it was the resentment that she'd carried home from the field house. She slung her handbag onto the kitchen table and went about turning on lights. In the dining room, she switched on the chandelier and the violation was immediate. The pre-Columbian ceramic bowl that she and Kevin bought in Ecuador when they were in love was not in its place on the buffet. They had quarreled over the pre-Columbian relics during their divorce and ended up dividing the collection, Kevin snarling because he'd paid for it all.

Molly saw the chain of events. He had a key and he came into the house and took the bowl before he went to the field house. She collapsed in a dining room chair until she could control her rage and set about determining her next step. She found the ancient stone ax head, left on her family farm by a pre-historic hunter, and fondled it. Its weight and smoothness comforted her. At her elbow, sorted, aligned in rows, her collection of signed costume jewelry, pieces with the designer's name stamped on the back, gleamed under the chandelier lights. Every evening she realigned and examined her fifty-five pieces. The Miriam Haskell brooch was gone, the one with the coral flowers. As well as the pre-Columbian bowl, he'd taken her favorite piece, no doubt for that bimbo he was pursuing. She pulled herself together and put the ax head down on a pile of unpaid bills. She pulled her coat around her shoulders and marched across the street to her neighbor and best friend, Kitty Harris, who peeked between her shutters before she pulled open the door.

"Molly, what's the matter?"

She pulled Molly into her bright kitchen redolent of chocolate cake cooling on the table. Molly didn't take the seat she offered but took the glass of red wine Kitty poured for her.

"Did you see anything going on at my house tonight?"

Kitty looked surprised.

"I did see a car over there. Oh, sometime near eight o'clock. So many people come and go from your house. Jamie is popular. Someone is always stopping by."

She paced up and down Kitty's polished stainless-steel kitchen, gulping red wine.

"What did the car look like?"

"Too dark for me to tell. I'm sorry."

Molly strode into her dining room, lit only by lights set in the china cabinet illuminating Haviland china. Just as Kitty switched on the chandelier, Molly was back in the kitchen and running her hand over the granite counter top on the kitchen island.

"I'm calling the police."

"For heaven's sake. Why? What's going on?

"Kevin broke into the house before he came to the game. Well, he's got a key. He took the pre-Columbian bowl he's always thought he should have and then picked up my signed Miriam Haskell brooch. I'm sick."

"I can tell that. Trey isn't home yet. Maybe he should be with you—"

"He's campaigning, shaking hands and talking to people at the field house. I'm not waiting on him."

"I'd better come with you."

The police were at Molly's house when Kevin brought Jamie home.

"What's going on?" he shouted, coming through the kitchen, Lisa trailing him.

Molly turned on him.

"I'll bet you know what's going on. The pre-Columbian bowl is gone. And my Miriam Haskell brooch. You have them, don't you?"

"Like hell, I do."

One of the policemen re-entered the dining room.

"There's nobody else in the house. But—"

He laid eyes on Jamie.

"I heard how good you were tonight. Three three-pointers?"

"Four," Kevin shouted, "Now if you'd like you can search me and Lisa too for that matter."

Lisa jerked. She seemed ready to cry but nodded acquiescence.

"Then you can go out to my car and go through it with a fine-tooth comb. Bring in your dogs to sniff around."

He paced around the dining room, looking up and down, as if trying to spot something else missing. His Lisa huddled on a dining room chair. Molly pointed at her.

"I'll bet she knows where my Miriam Haskell brooch is?"

Lisa put her face in her hands. Kevin swung and pointed at Molly, eyes bulging.

"Thank God the other pieces from Ecuador are safe with me. The ceramic bowl is gone due to your negligence. You probably know who has it. One of those guys who traipse in and out of here all day."

Kitty stepped in front of Molly as if to shield her.

"Kev, that's unfair."

Another policeman came in through the back door.

"You're sure the door was locked ma'am? There's no sign of forced entry."

"Yes, I'm sure."

Jamie then betrayed her.

"We often forget to lock it. There's a spare in a metal box under the air-conditioner in the garden."

"Every burglar knows that hiding place," one policeman murmured.

"And I'll bet everybody in town does too," added Kevin.

As his parents shouted at each other, Jamie bent over and picked up a green thread of tinsel from near the carved leg of the dining table.

"What's this?

A policeman took it from him and studied it.

"It's excelsior," said Molly, "Packing material. You'll probably find more in Kevin's car."

"Go look," Kevin said softly.

The police did but found nothing of interest.

When they all had gone and Jamie was in his room, Kitty slipped her arm around Molly's waist. "If you'd feel better, you and Jamie can come over to my house for the night—"

"Oh, thanks. We'll be okay here. But I'm sleeping with a rifle by my bed."

The next day Mollie went about changing locks on the doors and making sure the windows were secure. One was unlocked but she saw no sign that anyone had come in through it. She picked up the signed costume jewelry and hid it all away in a safe she kept in her home office. She counted her grandmother's silver and all the vases and bowls around the house.

Two nights later she was back in the field house but all evening Jamie missed from the three-point line. The crowd groaned and the cries of "Jamie, Jamie" were sporadic. Trey went up and down the aisles again at half-time, lingering to chat with a couple who had many concerns. Kevin came in late again but without Lisa.

"He brought her along before just to taunt me," she said to no one.

Now he made a spectacle of himself by leaping to his feet and yelling when the referee called a penalty on Jamie for pushing. But again, he wanted to take him for pizza and have a chat. Molly gave in because Jamie wanted it.

The light by the backdoor was on when she got home as well as the light over the sink where she'd left unwashed dishes. A half-eaten slice of cake was on the counter.

She stopped at the dining room entrance. Annoying apprehensions gripped her. A phantom hand pulled at her. Someone had been in the house. She flicked on the dining room chandelier. The room seemed as she'd left it. She started for the hall closet and came face to face with empty picture hangers against her floral wall paper. Her five Japanese water colors were not hanging in the foyer. Another possession that Kevin coveted but couldn't claim because they were from her family. Her father had bought the collection in Yokohama at the end of World War II.

She cried aloud, then collapsed on the sofa. Her first impulse was to ring the police again. Instead she wrapped her arms around herself and sat still, as if paralyzed. Outside freezing rain pattered on the window panes. Through a gathering mist she could make out blurry lights in Kitty's living room. A light shining beside the garage told her Trey wasn't home yet. Molly got up and picked up the telephone receiver, then dropped it.

She was still sitting on the sofa when Kevin delivered Jamie to the back door. She tensed in anticipation of a meeting, but Kevin didn't come in with him. Jamie was silent, glum after a disappointing night on the basketball court. As he was hanging his jacket in the closet, he asked, "Where are your Japanese water colors?"

"I took them down and put them away. They can be seen from the street. I don't want your father tempted again."

The next week Molly dropped off Jamie at the field house, next to the bus that would carry the Cougars to the away game in Goshen. She was to ride with other team parents in the backseat of the Mellen's van. After the team bus rolled out of the parking lot, she told Connie Mellen that she'd changed her mind about the trip because she had a headache. Then she got in her own car but didn't start the motor or turn on the lights. She pretended to rearrange the clutter in the passenger seat. The Mellen van started, then pulled away into the main street. Everyone in the Mellen van was chattering, paying no attention to what was going on behind them. Molly pulled a knitted cap over her hair and wrapped her long muffler around nose and mouth. As she edged open the car door, she saw two teachers, a man and a woman, talking under the light by the field house entrance, almost on the sidewalk. The woman was Jamie's English teacher. She would recognize Molly if she walked by her. She might even strike up a conversation. All evening it must seem as if she'd ridden with the Mellens to Goshen.

A sidewalk and steps led from the rear of the field house down to the football stadium, now deserted and dark. Melting snow on the steps had probably turned to ice. The two teachers continued their talk. Molly gently closed the car door and, head tucked down, hurried in the direction of the steps to the football field. As she feared, ice glazed walkways and steps behind the field house, forcing her to make her steps short and tentative as she made her way toward the football bleachers. Her legs ached when she reached the entrance to the football stadium. With her face buried in her muffler, she stayed under the bleachers until she came to a side street. This was not the route she had intended to take home.

She avoided downtown and its brightly lit main street, instead making her way along dimmer side streets. She avoided passing homes of friends and acquaintances. She took alley ways instead, nearly falling on ice patches. By the time she got home, snow was in the air again. Her fingers were numb with cold but she managed to turn her key in the backdoor lock. She turned on no lights. Molly crept through her own house, as if she were a burglar. She passed through the living room and into the closet off the foyer where she struggled out of her parka and dropped it behind her. The flashlight was on the shelf where she'd left it, amid scarves, hats and caps. Gently she eased the door closed and waited.

The clock in the den chimed every fifteen minutes. She waited through four chimes, leaning against the soft down of her winter coat, claustrophobia choking her, imagining the horror of solitary confinement in some nameless prison. She had almost decided that the burglar wasn't coming that night when she heard movement at the back door. Molly held her breath. There came the soft creak of the back door being opened, then the sound of the kitchen door being opened. Footfalls in the kitchen. Then in the dining room. A beam of light from a flashlight darted here and there. She heard the familiar creak of her buffet door being opened.

Molly stepped out of the closet, nearly slipped on the throw rug in the foyer, and switched on the chandelier in the dining room. Now it was bright as day and she wasn't surprised to look into the startled face of Kitty Harris, holding in her hands a painted bowl belonging to Molly's great-grandmother a century ago. She might have dropped the bowl but she managed to gently place it on the table. Molly spoke first.

"What are you doing here?"

Kitty's lips shook. Her face was ashen.

"I thought I saw someone moving around in the dark over here," she stammered, "I came to see if everything is all right."

"Like hell you did."

Molly watched her across the table.

"You were about ready to take that bowl, weren't you?"

"I was not."

"Of course you were."

Molly pulled her cell phone out of her pocket. "I'm calling the police."

She flipped it open and started to call 911 but her finger tips shook. Kitty interrupted.

"No, please, Molly. Wait a minute."

Molly pressed the cell phone to her ear. Kitty came toward her as if she were going to touch her.

"I think we can work something out."

"You have my stuff don't you?"

Kitty sank into a chair and sobbed.

"I'm so sorry for this. I just watched you enjoying all your nice things and talking about them and where they all came from, who had them before you. I just wished some of those were mine to enjoy. I had to buy my treasures myself. I know now how wrong I was. So often I do things I'm sorry for."

Molly thought about how many times over coffee they'd talked about their lives and regrets. She knew about Kitty's life and what she regretted. She sat down close to the now weeping Kitty, who had so much to lose.

"Where's my stuff now?" she asked gently.

Kitty blew her nose on a tattered tissue. "It's all safe. In a box in my closet."

Molly's tone resembled a teacher with a repentant though wayward student. She stared at Kitty's down-tucked face. Her left hand tightened on the ancient stone ax head anchoring her unpaid bills.

"I haven't decided about all this. You have no idea how you've betrayed our friendship. I entrusted you with my key. You might say I was entrusting you with my life."

"And I've said I'm sorry." She stood up and tightened her scarf. "I'll go get your stuff. Everything is there. Let this be the end of it."

"No, no. Sit down. If this got out it would destroy Trey's campaign for mayor, wouldn't it?"

Kitty cried again.

"I don't ever want Trey to find out about this. He couldn't stand it. My life is in your hands."

"So it is. Here's the deal I'm willing to make."

Kitty looked at her now with renewed hope.

"I don't want this all over town any more than you do. You bring back my stuff and I'll tell Kevin and Jamie that it all showed up in a box delivered at the back door and I have no idea where it came from."

Kitty exhaled, like a defendant who'd just heard a not guilty verdict.

"You're a real friend Molly. I'll never forget this. I'll always be grateful."

"But there's one more thing."

"What's that?" she asked through the tear-saturated tissue pressed to her face.

"I want you to include your Haviland china."

Kitty visibly jerked, as if she wasn't hearing right. She gasped as if the verdict had been the gallows after all.

"But, but that belonged to my grandmother."

"I know. But it will now belong to me."

Kitty's mouth hung open. Molly thought the blood was draining from her face. That Haviland china, so elegantly displayed in her lighted china closet, was the pride of her life. Used only on special occasions. Someday Kitty would pass it on to her daughter to display in her lighted china closet.

"But Trey will notice that it's gone."

"I'm sure you'll think of something to tell him."

Kitty moved on unsteady legs. Molly thought she might fall over.

"I'll go get your stuff. But I have to think about this part."

"You have to decide now. I'm ready to call the police."

Again she flipped open her cell phone.

So Kitty agreed to the deadly exchange.

On Friday night Jamie and the Cougars were to leave from the south side of the field house for Lafayette. Molly patted Jamie's cheek and told him she was fighting a cold and would stay at home.

Before he got on the bus, he said, "Dad promised to be at this game. He's upset because I'm not making as many three-pointers as I was before. He said he expects improvement."

"Typical," said Molly.

"Lisa doesn't measure up to you, you know," he told her.

She took a deep breath of cold air.

"You don't know how good that makes me feel."

Later that evening Molly peered through her dining room window into the cold night. She saw no light at Kitty's house, and she suspected her of skulking in the dark. The light shining by the garage indicated that Trey was away. She watched from behind the curtains until she saw Kitty make her way across the street carrying a cardboard box. Molly received it at her back door, careful not to turn on the back porch light.

Neither woman said a word. Kitty stood by while Molly unpacked the box under the chandelier above her dining room table, accounting for all her rightful belongings. She examined the pre-Columbian bowl and gently placed it on the buffet. She found the Miriam Haskell brooch and pinned it to her sweat shirt. The Japanese water colors were soon hanging back in the foyer. Then she stared Kitty straight in the face.

"Now where is my Haviland china?"

"It's packed up. I'll get it."

Her shoulders drooped as she left by the backdoor. Molly waited in the darkness. In a half hour she saw Kitty crossing the street trundling the wheelbarrow she used for gardening. As she approached the back porch, Molly saw through dim light that the Haviland china had been packed in shopping bags, the china pieces cushioned with green excelsior.

She helped Kitty carry the bags into the dining room and place them carefully on the table. Excelsior fell on the table and on the oriental carpet, looking almost like part of the carpet design.

Molly uncovered one of the Haviland cups and ran her fingers over the rim.

"I really hate taking this china from you," Molly said calmly. "But my aunt took my grandmother's china after my mother died. She came in this house after the funeral and packed up what she

194

wanted. She said the china belonged to her for some reason I can't remember. My mother's will said nothing about it. Believe me, I'd never felt so violated. People are always stealing from me. Even now Kevin is trying to get Jamie away from me. Well, this time I'm the one who's doing the taking."

Then she held the Haviland cup up to the light. Kitty stood across the table, shaking, rubbing fingers that were red with the cold.

"I never will forget the time you bid against me for that curio cabinet at the Lovell's estate sale. You didn't want me to have it so you ran up the bidding and got it for yourself."

"So it's purely vengeance?" Kitty murmured.

"What did you tell Trey about this china?" Molly asked, not taking her eyes off the cup.

"I said it was going to my sister for a time. My mother's will stipulated sharing the china."

"And he accepted that?"

"His attention was on an editorial in the paper." Kitty's voice faded away.

Then she circled around the table and begged for mercy, that this penance was too great. Paying no attention, Molly examined the perfect rose bud in the center of a plate, regretting that it would be hidden away for a time. Perhaps there would be occasions when she could serve dinner on this china. She was contemplating such an occasion so she was unaware of Kitty moving behind her, unaware of her hand on the stone ax head. There was a sudden flash of pain and light as Kitty with all her strength brought the ax head down on Molly's head, not once, but three times, before Molly's legs gave way and she fell unconscious and bleeding on the oriental carpet.

Kitty then dropped the stone ax head at Molly's feet and packed her china back in the green excelsior and trundled it back across the street.

Jamie hurried into the house after his father and Lisa let him off at the back door before they left for Indianapolis. He was almost dancing because he wanted to tell his mother about another game in which he'd made four three-pointers. His game was back on track. The coach told him so.

He stopped short when he saw his mother sprawled at the foot of the dining room table, her blood soaking the oriental carpet. He took two steps back from her, then went to the telephone in the kitchen and with trembling fingers punched out his father's cell phone number.

"I'll be right there. But call 91—now," Kevin yelled after hearing Jamie's incoherent message.

Ten minutes later Kevin barged through the backdoor, trailed by Lisa, and found Jamie sitting by his mother's fallen body, her bleeding head in his lap.

"Listen to me. Did you call 911?"

Jamie mouthed something indecipherable. His mother's blood stained his hands, his blue jeans, his sweatshirt. The ancient ax head they had all handled and examined over the years lay at Molly's feet. Kevin knelt on one knee and pressed a finger against her jugular vein and got a faint heartbeat.

"Did you call 911?"

Jamie barely nodded.

Kevin gently lifted Molly's head off Jamie's lap. He took his son by the shoulders and helped him to his feet and away from Molly.

Jamie sobbed and cried, "Mom, Mom," over and over again.

Kevin gripped his shoulders and whispered close to his face, "Listen to me. I'm going to say we found her like this together. I don't want them questioning you when you're falling apart. Don't you be saying something different."

After the police arrived, Kevin explained, "Jamie has blood on him because he fell on her body, trying to revive her. He and his mother are very close."

Jamie stood aside and watched the paramedics examine his mother. Outside the winter night was bright with the revolving lights of police and ambulance. The lights bounced off the walls of the dining room. Neighbors clustered on the sidewalks around the house, huddling in heavy coats, whispering to one another.

Kevin followed the police as they went room to room, as if someone might still be in the house.

Jamie stood where Kevin told him to stand, as if he were a little boy, crying and keeping watch on his mother's battered head. Then he noticed the Miriam Haskell brooch on her sweat shirt. The coral brooch that was stolen. He couldn't remember his mother ever wearing it on a sweat shirt. Tears dried on his cheeks as he looked around the room. The pre-Colombian bowl was back in its place on the buffet, as if it had never been gone. He moved around the dining room table. No one noticed. Kevin and the police were going upstairs.

Next to the thick-soled shoe of a paramedic he saw a thread of green excelsior, reminding him of what he'd found a week ago. He crept up behind the paramedic, knelt down, and pinched the excelsior between thumb and index finger, as if they were tweezers. The attention of the paramedics stayed on his mother. Her flashlight was on the table. Jamie picked it up. The paramedics paid him no mind.

Jamie saw more excelsior near the hallway to the kitchen, on the sienna tiles on the kitchen floor. Still nobody was watching him. He heard his father and the police coming down the stairs. He passed through the kitchen. More excelsior lay on the back porch and on the back steps. With a blood stained hand he pulled open the back door and stepped out into the cold. His flashlight shone on green excelsior on the driveway, tangled on a chunk of ice, amid countless clues: boot prints, the single tire tread of a wheel barrow in packed snow. The police should cordon off the driveway, he thought.

He followed the trail of green excelsior across the street, toward the shuttered windows of the Harris's house. The light burning above their garage door told him Trey wasn't home yet. His mother's best friend Kitty wasn't at her side that night, as she was at the first break-in, as she was at every crisis in his mother's life.

The flashlight caught green excelsior ground into the icy street by a passing car. Excelsior caught in the bare twigs of a bush by the steps to the Harris's back porch. Green excelsior on the steps to the back door, the door his mother and Kitty used a dozen times a day. Revolving lights bounced off the side of the house.

There was no light in the kitchen. He rapped on the door. He couldn't see into the house through the closed shutters. He banged on the backdoor. He rattled the doorknob as Kitty's shadow fell across the window. Slowly she opened the door a crack.

"What's going on?" she murmured.

"I came to see you. I wanna come in?" Jamie wedged his foot in the doorway. His mother's blood was drying on his sneaker. Kitty pulled open the door.

"Was there another break-in? I'm not feeling well tonight."

Jamie pushed himself inside her kitchen, nearly knocking her over. The aroma of beef stew filled the room. Trey's supper probably.

"I'm calling the police," she threatened. She looked terrified in the half-lit kitchen.

"They're right across the street."

He pushed past her into the dining room. Shopping bags filled with green excelsior were all around the room. Haviland china plates were stacked on the table. A serving dish and meat platter were positioned in her china closet.

"Get out of here." She pointed to the blood on his blue jeans and sweat shirt.

"I see what I need to know," he said.

"You're getting her blood everywhere. Look at my carpet."

Jamie's head began to clear a little.

"How do you know it's her blood?"

Not waiting for an answer, he turned to retrace his steps back through the kitchen and across the street. But Kitty suddenly blocked his way. He stepped back. Then he dodged around her as he would a defender on the basketball court. She pulled a meat cleaver from the knife rack by the stove, but again he dodged away. When she came at him, the cleaver flashing in the light, he made a weaving move and pivoted, avoiding her again, but smashing into the side of the stove. The pot thudded to the floor and stew spilled across the kitchen tiles.

"You brat," she screamed.

So that's what she thought of him.

"I'm super brat," he yelled.

He almost made the backdoor when he slipped. He was on his back on the floor in pain and she was coming toward him with the cleaver. Jamie managed, as if endowed with new strength, to push himself against the backdoor and kick at Kitty. She stumbled backward but came at him again. But before she could strike, he felt movement against his leg as Trey pushed open the door. Kitty dropped the meat cleaver and pointed at Jamie.

"He tried to kill me."

Black lines swam in Jamie's vision before he passed out. When he became conscious again, Kevin was bending over him.

"Just lie there. Don't try to move."

He groaned and squeezed his father's hand.

Later that night, after the ambulance took Molly to the hospital, neighbors stood in the street and on snowbanks, oblivious to freezing temperatures, and watched a hand-cuffed Kitty Harris, supported by her husband, being led to a police car.

Molly died at the hospital early the next morning. Jamie went to Indianapolis with his father the next day. He never came back to his mother's house and never played another basketball game with the Cougars.

Steve Alford
Tony Perona

Steve Alford, now coach of the University of New Mexico Lobos, was an Indiana legend in both the high school and college basketball arena. The son of a basketball coach, Alford moved around the state as his dad changed coaching jobs. Eventually the family settled in New Castle, where his father became the high school coach and Steve attended New Castle Chrysler High School. Alford was a standout player for his father and won the state "Mr. Basketball" award his senior year. The team went to the state tournament in the quarterfinals but lost to Connersville.

Alford made the decision to play basketball at Indiana University for Coach Bobby Knight. During his career at Indiana, Alford amassed 2,438 points and became the all-time scoring leader. He was the first person to win the MVP award four times. In 1987 he helped Indiana win the national championship.

After graduation, Alford became the 26th draft pick in the NBA Draft. He spent most of the next four years with the Dallas Mavericks. When he moved into coaching in 1992, it was at Manchester College in Indiana. He quickly established himself as a winning coach, turning the Manchester program around. He spent four seasons there, then another four at Southwest Missouri State (now Missouri State). Following that, he went to coach at Iowa for another eight years.

Alford left Iowa to coach at the University of New Mexico, where he has continued his winning ways. His latest contract extension has him there until the 2019-2020 season.

Alford was a member of the 1984 U.S. Olympic basketball team, which won the gold medal and was the last fully amateur U.S. Olympic team. He and his wife Tanya have three children, Kory, Bryce and Kayla.

UNCLE VITO AND THE CHEERLEADER
M. E. May

It was time for what those Indiana relatives of mine call Hoosier Hysteria. Hysteria's right! Those people down there in Indy are nuts when it comes to basketball. Don't matter if it's elementary school, high school or college—they love it with a capital "L."

My name's Vito Mazzara and I'm a P. I. from Chicago. Ma says our ancestors are from some province called Enna in Sicily. Yeah, yeah, I know what you're thinkin.' Just because I live in Chicago and my ancestors are from Sicily don't mean I have mob connections. Sometimes I wish I did.

So what's a hot shot P. I. from Chicago doin' goin' to Indy and talkin' about basketball, you ask? I'll tell ya why, but it's a long story, so pull up a chair and relax.

My younger brother, Donatello—we call him Donnie—lives there with his wife, Theresa, and their three beautiful daughters, Maria, Katie and Gabriella. Maria is a cheerleader at North Central High School and they're playin' Zionsville in the final game of the 4A Basketball Sectional. Maria insisted I come down and watch the game. Ya see, she's not just my niece; she's my goddaughter, so how could I refuse? She's got those beautiful brown cow eyes that melt my heart like butter on a hot fryin' pan. At least it wasn't snowin' like it usually does this time of year.

So I get down to Donnie's house, we have a nice dinner, a little vino and go to the game. North Central wins. Maria's screamin' her lungs out with the rest of the cheerleaders. Her sisters are jumpin' up and down, grabbin' me around the waist, one on each side of me nearly knockin' me over onto the poor sap in front of me. My sister-in-law's wavin' her pom pom and my brother's raisin' his hands in the air shoutin' like a fool. Like I said, they don't call this Hoosier Hysteria for nothin'.

By the time we get back to Donnie's place, I've got a headache about to split my head open enough for my brains to fall out. I take two aspirin and go to bed. Next thing I know, eleven-year-old Katie's shakin' my shoulder sayin', "Uncle Vito, Uncle Vito, wake up."

I open one eye to see her worried little face and sit straight up in bed. "What's wrong, Katie?" I asked, yawnin'.

"Uncle Vito, Maria isn't home yet," she said, eyes fillin' with tears. "She should have been home by midnight."

"Time is it?" I asked, startin' to feel the same anxiety I could see in her face.

"It's 2:00. This isn't like her."

"What did your dad say?"

"I didn't wake him," she said, lookin' at me like I was nuts. "He'll be so mad at her for staying out this late."

"And you don't think I'm mad at her?"

She gives me one of those sweet little smiles of hers. "Well... it's just that you won't get anywhere near as mad as Daddy will. Besides, didn't you take a vow or something when you took the godfather job? Aren't you supposed to protect her or something?"

"That's only if your folks croak," I said without thinkin', 'cause the next thing I know she's scowlin' at me. "Okay, I'll go look for her. Got any ideas where I should start?"

"I made you a list of her friends and their addresses."

I looked at her in amazement. "You got a list for me already. How long you been up?"

"I don't sleep very well when everybody's not home," she said, lowerin' her eyes. "I'm worried something might have happened to her."

I was beginnin' to think so, too. Maria was a very responsible girl. I asked Katie to go in the kitchen and make me a cup of instant coffee to wake me up, and I got dressed. On my way to the kitchen, I heard these quiet little female voices. There was Gabriella whisperin' to Katie. Boy did these girls stick together. I never seen sisters who were so close.

"Uncle Vito," Gabriella said in a low soft voice. "You will find her, won't you? She's never been more than ten minutes late for anything!"

"Hey," I said, but they immediately shushed me.

"No disrespect," said fifteen-year-old Gabriella quietly, "but we don't want to wake Mom and Dad."

"Okay," I said quietly. "Where's my coffee?"

Just as Katie handed me the nasty instant brew, we heard the doorknob to the garage turn and saw the door open slowly. It was Maria, whose face turned to shock at the sight of us. She shut the door gently puttin' her keys and purse on the counter, cell phone still in hand.

"Where have you been?" Katie said in an agitated tone then threw her arms around her sister. Maria hugged her and Gabriella joined in. She was lookin' at me with those beautiful, but very sad brown eyes.

"Okay, break it up," I said doin' my best to sound tough. I wanted to stomp down the softy image they had of me. "This isn't like you, Maria. What's goin' on?" I put the coffee cup in the sink. No point torturin' myself with it at this point. We all sat down at the kitchen table.

"Uncle Vito, you remember my best friend, Olivia?" asked Maria.

"Sure I do. She's the blonde with the straight do that barely covers her ears. Green eyes. Cheerleader."

"Yes, that's her," she says. "Well, tonight we were all going to meet after the game at Applebee's, but she never showed. I tried to text her, she didn't answer. I tried to call her, and it just rang and rang until the voicemail answered. That means her phone is on, right?"

I nodded. This didn't sound good, but I tried to keep a calm demeanor for Maria's sake. The other two girls were lookin' at Maria in shock. Katie's eyes were tearin' again. I guess I am a softy. They was breakin' my heart.

"So what did you do?" I asked her.

"We got in our cars and went driving around trying to find her. The last text I got from the others was at 2:00 and no one saw her." She paused. I could see she was tryin' to keep from cryin'. She's like her dad; she tries to keep it under control. "I tried calling her boyfriend, Jason. He's the shooting guard on the team. Olivia said she was going to talk to him and then meet us at the restaurant."

"You get a hold of him?"

"No, his phone went straight to voicemail. Karen told me she drove by his house. It was all dark and his car was in the driveway."

Then Katie pipes up. "You don't think something bad happened to her, do you?"

"I don't know," said Maria pullin' Katie into a shoulder hug. "All I know is Brenda's boyfriend, Paul, drove by the school parking lot. Her car's still there."

"Okay," I said. "So, she meets up with the boyfriend after the game. He drive his own car to the school?"

"We all go to the games in our own cars because we have to be there at different times. Olivia wanted to talk to Jason about something important," answered Maria. "Last time I saw her she was waiting outside the locker room for him."

"Did any of you guys call her house to see if she was there?" I asked. Maria shook her head. "Don't ya think somebody should? Maybe this Jason character drove her home and she's gonna pick up her car tomorrow."

"I didn't think about that," said Maria. "We just didn't want to get Olivia into trouble."

"So, I'm gonna assume you kids didn't contact the police either," I said.

Marie shook her head her expression becomin' more frantic.

"We gotta call her parents. If she's not there, they'll need to call the police and report her missin'."

Maria used her cell to call Olivia's house. Olivia's father must have answered the phone, because Maria said, "Hello, Mr. French." After a couple of minutes, I could see he was givin' her a hard time so I took the phone.

"Hey, Mr. French," I said. "This is Maria's uncle. Apparently, your daughter Olivia was to meet up with her boyfriend after the game, and then go meet Maria and her friends at Applebee's.

Unfortunately, neither Olivia nor the boy showed and Maria's worried sick about her. Did she come home?"

I could hear a woman's voice in the background askin' what was goin' on.

"I'm sure my daughter is in bed," he said. The phone became muffled like he'd put his hand over the mouthpiece. He was probably tellin' his wife to go check Olivia's bed. Next thing I hear is a woman's very loud voice tellin' him Olivia wasn't there.

"Mr. French," I said tryin' to get his attention. "Mr. French, one of the boys went back to the school and found your daughter's car around 2:00 this mornin'."

"Why didn't they call the police?" he shouted.

"Because they thought she was with ..." I looked at Maria who mouthed the name ... "Jason." And you know kids, they were afraid they'd get her in trouble."

"Get her in trouble?" he shouted, clearly angry. "Why didn't she just go over with the group like she usually does?"

"She told Maria she had something to talk to Jason about and that's why she didn't leave with the rest of them. Since neither she nor Jason showed, they thought they'd gone somewhere together."

"I hope you don't think me rude, Mr. uh..."

"Mazzara, Vito Mazzara."

"I've got to call the police and try to find my daughter." That was it. He hung up before I could say goodbye. Can't say I blame him.

I gave the phone back to Maria whose face had fallen. I didn't have to tell her Olivia wasn't home.

"Uncle Vito?" said Maria lookin' at me expectantly. "How much do you charge to do an investigation?"

I must have looked stunned, because all three girls were lookin' from me to one another and back to me. Not sure how long it was before I spoke, but I finally asked her why.

"Because we want to hire you," she said while her sisters nodded. "You're the best private detective in Chicago, aren't you? We need the best. We're just not sure we can afford you."

"Don't you think the police should handle this one?" I said, hopin' they'd agree. Instead, I saw a trio of disappointed faces starin' at me. I had a feelin' I'd just blown my *best uncle ever* image, so I said, "I'll look for her on one condition. We have to wake your parents and tell them what's goin' on. Don't look at me like that, Maria. It's better to tell them now than to have them find out from Olivia's parents, or worse, the news media."

Maria nodded. "You're right, Uncle Vito. I'll go get them, but you will help me tell them, won't you?"

"Of course I will," I said.

I only had about four hours of sleep under my belt, but I was wide-awake now. Already I was kickin' myself for tellin' those girls I'd stay and work the case. It's not that I got a lot to do back home, there's just a certain someone from the IMPD I didn't want to run into durin' my visit.

I heard my brother grumblin' all the way down the hallway. "What's this all about, Maria? Why are you still dressed? You should have been in bed hours ago."

"Chill out, Donnie," said Theresa. "She'll explain in a minute."

"Hey there family," I said as cheerfully as I could muster.

Maria's eyes flashed from me to her father beggin' for my assistance.

"What are you doing up?" Donnie asked me.

I hesitated a moment. I promised Maria I'd tell him about Olivia, but wasn't lookin' forward to bein' the buffer between her and her father. He did have a quick temper. Theresa started makin' some coffee. She does that when she senses there won't be any goin' back to bed.

"Hey, Donnie, Theresa, ya think I could hang out for a few extra days?" I asked. "I ain't got much in Chicago needin' my immediate attention."

"What?" Donnie said, total confusion and irritation written all over his face.

"Sure, Vito," said Theresa placin' a hand on my brother's shoulder. "We'd love to have you stay, but what's this all about? You surely didn't wake us up at 2:45 in the morning to ask if you can stay a few extra days."

I glanced at the girls then braced myself. "Well, I got a few things I need to check out. I've been hired by three beautiful women to look for a missin' person."

"Really?" Donnie said raisin' his eyebrows.

"Okay, here's the thing," I said, standin' and pacin'. "Maria's friend, Olivia, went missin'. Maria, Gabriella, and Katie here hired me to look into Olivia's disappearance."

Theresa plopped down in the chair next to Donnie who sat there with his mouth gapin'. He looked from Maria to Gabriella to Katie to me. He was kind of freakin' me out.

I gave them a rundown of everything Maria had told me. When I was finished, Donnie got this stern look then instead of blowin' up, he looked at Maria with concern on his face. I was pretty sure he was thinkin' thank God it wasn't his little girl that went missin'.

"Maria, do you think Olivia would have run away or something?" asked Donnie.

"I don't think she'd do that," Maria insisted. "She wouldn't leave her family and friends."

"People do things they wouldn't normally in certain circumstances," he explained. "I guess if your Uncle Vito is willing to stick around and help find Olivia then that's a good thing."

Maria jumped up and went around the table to hug her father. "Thanks for understanding, Daddy. I'm so worried about her."

It was a beautiful scene, but if I was gonna earn my keep, I knew I'd better get goin'. Olivia's pop would have already called the cops by now and they was probably searchin' the car. This would be the best place to start. Of course, I wasn't sure what type of reception I'd get. Some cops don't like P.I.'s hornin' in on their investigations.

"Okay," I said. "I'm out of here. I'll let you know if I find out anything."

So, I grabbed my coat and headed for the school. When I pulled up, the cops had an area of the parkin' lot roped off with crime scene tape. There was a tow truck waitin' to haul the car away. A tall lanky guy was pacin', runnin' his fingers through his hair. I figured he was Mr. French

Then I saw her—one of the Indianapolis Metropolitan Police Department's finest missin' person detectives—Pepper Flannigan. Her given name is Patricia. Don't know where she originally got the nickname, but I called her Pepper 'cause I think she's hot. We had a little thing goin' one summer, probably three years ago now. I'd come down from Chicago on a case. The wife of some rich banker in Evanston had left him and went back to her family in Indy. After a few months, she disappeared and the banker got accused of disposin' of her. He hired me to prove he didn't touch the woman. Pepper and I worked together and found the wife alive and well, livin' in Florida with her new guy. She didn't want her family to know what she was doin' and claims she didn't think they'd report her missin'. Anyways, my client was off the hook and I made a pretty good buck.

So me and Pepper tried the long-distance thing for a while. Those things never seem to work. Our jobs kept us from commutin' and the flame sort of fizzled. Although, seein' her flippin' her beautiful, wavy auburn hair around, tryin' to calm down Mr. French, kind of made those old feelin's reheat. I approached her cautiously. I wasn't too sure how she'd take seein' me again.

"Hello, Pepper," I said.

"Sergeant Flannigan to you," she said, scowlin' in my direction.

Sergeant Pepper—decided I'd better not go there. She seemed a little grumpy. Maybe she should of been a firefighter since she knows how to put out a flame with a look.

"Sergeant?" I said. "Congrats on the promotion."

"What are you doing here?" she asked.

"Well, I've been hired to look into the disappearance of Olivia French."

"Who are you?" asked Mr. French.

"I'm Vito Mazzara, Maria's Uncle Vito," I said extendin' my hand. "We spoke on the phone briefly."

He took my hand. "Who hired you to look for my daughter?"

"Maria and her sisters," I answered.

"Look," said Pepper. "The police can handle this. There's no good reason for you to take your nieces' hard earned money."

"I ain't really chargin' 'em," I protested. What kinda guy does she think I am?

"I don't care. I don't want you interfering with my investigation," she spewed.

"And I don't care who is looking for my daughter," said Mr. French angrily. "I want her found. If Mr. Mazzara here wants to help, let him! I'm going home to check on my wife and see if she's found out anything from Olivia's friends." He turned abruptly walkin' towards his dark blue Beamer.

Her back was to me, her hand on her hip, watchin' Mr. French as he departed. I stood there for a minute waitin' for her to club me over the head or somethin'. I decided to speak first.

"So, there anything you can tell me about the crime scene?" I asked.

She whipped around so fast it almost made me dizzy. "There's only a minimum of information I can share with you, not that you deserve it. But I like Maria and I know this must be hard on her. Just don't get any ideas, got it?"

"Got it," I said, flame completely doused.

"First thing we did when we got the call, of course, was issue an Amber Alert."

"Did anybody find her purse, keys, anything?"

"The car was locked. Her father brought us the extra keys. We didn't find anything inside except some books, trash and a few CDs. Doesn't look like she made it back to the car, but we're taking it to the lab for a more thorough inspection."

"What about the boyfriend?" I asked. "Maria said she was meetin' up with him right after the game."

"One of my officers went over there to make sure he was home since he didn't meet the others either," she said. "Says he was home in bed by 11:30 pm."

"After winnin' the sectional?" I said skeptically. "You'd think he would be out half the night celebratin'."

"I'm going over there now to see if I can get any more info out of him," she stated. "I think the kid knows more than he's letting on. The game ended at 9:15 pm so he had plenty of time to get showered, meet the girlfriend and dispose of her before he got home."

"Can I tag along?"

"You know how the Major feels about that. Besides you're not licensed in Indiana," she said, but I noticed a softenin' of her brow. "Since you're not getting paid, I guess it makes you a concerned citizen. Of course, if you happen to show up where I am, there's nothing I can do about it."

That was more like the Pepper I knew. I got in my car and followed her to the boy's house. Pepper was right about the timeline. His house was only ten minutes from the school. But if it was him, where'd he take Olivia?

"Let me do all the talking," she said to me as we approached the door. Of course, I nodded, but I'm sure she knew it wouldn't last.

Jason Hale's father answered the door still wearin' his robe and slippers. He was tall, but much bulkier than Mr. French with sandy blonde hair and a neatly trimmed beard and mustache. He led us to the livin' room where his son and wife sat.

Pepper asked all of the standard gettin' to know you questions. Jason kept glancin' at his father before he answered. They must have had some kind of signal thing goin'. She finally asked him whether he met Olivia last night before goin' home.

"I saw her outside the locker room," he said.

"Why didn't you go out celebrating with everyone else?" asked Pepper.

"I wasn't feeling good. Too much excitement I guess," he said as he glanced at his father again. "I had a bad headache."

"Maria says Olivia had somethin' to tell you," I blurted. "What was it?"

"And who are you?" asked Mr. Hale.

"Vito Mazzara. I'm a private investigator and just happen to be Maria Mazzara's uncle."

Pepper was glarin' at me. I'd jumped in before she had the chance to work her way up to askin' the question herself. "Well, Jason," she said. "Did you and Olivia talk?"

"Yeah, but it wasn't important."

Wrong answer, I thought. When Jason said this, he looked down as if in shame. There's nothing like body language to let ya know someone's holdin' out on ya. I simply said, "Really?"

"I think my son's made it very clear he wasn't well last evening," said Mr. Hale, frownin'. "My wife and I were still awake when he came home. It was 11:00 pm. I know this because I found it odd he was home so early. Now if there's nothing else, I'd like for the two of you to leave."

"Sure, Mr. Hale," said Pepper. "I just have one more question." She turned to Jason. "Did Olivia tell you where she was going when the two of you went your separate ways?"

"She didn't say anything, just ran out," said Jason. "I figured she was going to Applebee's."

Mr. Hale escorted us unceremoniously out the door. Me and Pepper looked at one another. I was sure we was thinkin' the same thing. Why wasn't this kid more upset about his girlfriend bein' missin'? And what the h-e-double hockey sticks did she have to tell him that gave him a headache?

"Where to next?" I asked.

"Coach's house. He's usually the last to leave. Maybe he saw something."

We arrived at Coach Pratt's house approximately twelve minutes later. Nice two-story brick in one of the older neighborhoods. I remembered him from the game. Red hair in an army crew cut. Face turned beet red every time somebody screwed up or the ref made a call he didn't like. He limped slightly on his right leg. It made me wonder if he'd had some sort of accident that ruined his chances of a career playin' sports.

A cute young girl with blonde hair and bright blue eyes answered the door. She yelled, "Dad, you've got company!" and let us into the foyer.

He looked taller than he had when I was fifteen rows up in the bleachers. He invited us into the livin' room. Pepper was askin' questions before we even sat down.

"Mr. Pratt, as you may have heard Olivia French disappeared after the game last night," she said.

"I did," he said. "This is awful. I'd be devastated if it were one of my girls."

"I don't suppose you saw her waiting for Jason Hale after the game?" asked Pepper.

"No," he answered. "I was with some of the news media right after the game. By the time I went towards the locker room, Jason was getting ready to leave. Said he had a headache and was going home."

"And Olivia wasn't with him?" asked Pepper.

"Nope, and Jason didn't mention her. My only concern was Jason's headache. I knew he hadn't hit his head or been bashed by anyone during the game, so I chalked it up to him being tired." He paused for a moment. "You're not thinking he had anything to do with this, are you?"

"Until we find her, everyone she knows is a suspect, Mr. Pratt," said Pepper.

"This kid has a basketball scholarship. He's going to Purdue next year," said the coach. "He wouldn't blow this opportunity."

"Let's hope not," said Pepper. "We'll be going now. If you hear anything or remember anything, please let us know."

Once outside, I turned to her. "Somebody's lyin'. I can feel it in my bones."

"Ah, come on Vito," she said.

"I got great instincts, Pep... I mean Sergeant." I figured I'd better show her some respect if I wanted to continue in her good graces. "Maybe we should have a talk with my niece. I bet she knows more about what Olivia had on her mind than she's tellin' me."

When we got back to my brother's house, the family was just gettin' ready to go to early Mass. There were my three little angels all dressed in their Sunday best. I hated to put Maria on the spot, but we had to know what was on Olivia's mind.

"Hey!" I shouted, causin' everyone to turn their heads.

"Uncle Vito, did you find Olivia?" Maria shouted as she ran to me. I shook my head. "Maria, you remember Sergeant Flannigan?" Maria nodded.

"We need to ask you some questions," said Pepper. "Your mom and dad can be with us, if you like."

"Am I in trouble?" asked Maria.

"No. Why would you be in trouble?" I exclaimed. "We're just tryin' to figure out what was goin' on with Olivia, that's all."

Maria chose not to have her parents present, and her father agreed since I'd be with her. We went into the den and shut the door. Maria looked very nervous.

Pepper got right to it. "Is Olivia pregnant?"

The look of shock on Maria's face said it all. How could I have been so dense? What kind of serious stuff do teen-aged girls usually have to tell their boyfriends in private? Apparently, the lack of sleep and coffee had muddled my brain. I decided to let Pepper handle this one.

"Is she?" Pepper asked again.

My niece's eyes filled with tears. I figured Olivia swore her to secrecy, and at her age, friendships meant more than consequences.

"We aren't sure," said Maria. "She's late and the pregnancy test she took said yes, but she hasn't gone to a real doctor."

Pepper pursed her lips in an *I see* expression. "So I assume this is what she needed to tell Jason?"

"Yes, but Jason wouldn't have hurt her," insisted Maria. "He loved her."

"Unfortunately, sweetheart, sometimes people do hurt the ones they love," said Pepper givin' me a sideways glance. Ouch!

"One more question," said Pepper. "Was Olivia definitely going to meet you at Applebee's after she talked to Jason?"

"Yes," said Maria. "She told me she'd call me if she wasn't coming. I never got a call."

"Don't worry," said Pepper, stroking Maria's cheek. "We'll find your friend. You can go now."

Me and Pepper stayed so we could go over what we knew thus far. Olivia stayed behind to give the bad news to the boyfriend who is a potential basketball great with a scholarship to Purdue University. Boyfriend is so bummed he gets a headache so he bows outta goin' to the restaurant with her. But, did he? Was he so upset he lost it and took her somewhere to do her in?

"Sounds like Jason has motive," said Pepper. "I thought it was strange when he minimized what Olivia had to say."

"Nowadays most guys don't feel their careers are over because of a pregnancy," I pointed out. "Teenagers don't think *they have to get married* anymore."

"Still, it would put a cramp in his style if he had to get a job in order to pay child support." Pepper got up and paced. There was a knock at the door.

"Will you be joining us for Sunday dinner, Patricia?" asked my sister-in-law. Theresa always used Pepper's proper name.

"No," answered Pepper. "I need to check back with my colleagues to see if they've found her at any of her friends' houses. However, you and your husband should be prepared. The longer Olivia is missing, the more likely foul play is involved."

"Oh, dear," said Theresa. "Thank you, Patricia. It's good to see you. I just wish it was under more pleasant circumstances."

"Me, too. I'll show myself out," she said then turned to me. "I'll talk to you later."

While the family was at church, I made a couple of calls. I talked to Mr. French again to see if he'd heard anything. He said he and his wife called every friend and family member in town, but no one had seen or heard from Olivia. The search dogs they'd requested found nothin' beyond the school grounds, so she didn't walk somewhere. The second call I made was to my secretary. I know I coulda emailed her, but that's so impersonal. I left a voicemail instead. I took a nap hopin' my brain would rest enough to function properly when I woke. I still couldn't believe the pregnancy angle hadn't been the first thing to pop in my head. I slept until 2:00 p.m. when Theresa knocked on the door callin' me to dinner.

Sunday dinner was not the happy occasion it usually was. The girls weren't chatterin' endlessly about school stuff or who wore the most hideous dress to Mass. It was glum faces all around. I was the only one who cleaned all the roast beef, carrots and mashed potatoes from my plate. Donnie said he'd taken the girls for a drive to all the places Olivia hung out includin' the mall, but nobody they'd talked to remembered seein' Olivia in the past twenty-four hours. I'd left the table and was tryin' to decide on my next move when the doorbell rang. I answered it and to my surprise, Jason Hale was standin' on the front stoop. "Jason," was all that came outta my mouth.

"Mr. Mazzara," he said, Adam's apple jumpin' as he swallowed hard. "I couldn't talk in front of my parents. I don't want them to know what Olivia ..." His voice trailed off as he steeled himself to tell me everything.

"Do you want to come in?" I asked.

"Could we just go for a walk?" he asked. "I don't want to get Maria's family all worked up."

I grabbed my coat and we started to walk up the block. It took a few minutes for him to get the courage to speak again, but when he did, he confirmed Olivia's news about the pregnancy.

"I was shocked. I didn't know what to do or say so I said something stupid like how could she ruin my life. I guess I hurt her feelings because she didn't answer me she just took off running. I was going to go after her, but the coach came out and asked me what was going on."

"Wait a minute," I said. "The coach stopped you?"

"Yeah, he came out, asked me what was going on, and I said nothing that Olivia was a little upset with me. He asked me if I was meeting my friends and I told him no, I had a headache and was going home. I drove over to the park to think before I went home."

This was interestin'. Coach Pratt claimed he didn't know anything about Olivia bein' there. Why'd he lie to us? I looked at the kid and saw tears formin'. Seemed he really did care about Olivia. We walked back to his car in silence.

"Don't worry, kid. I'm gonna find her," I assured him as he got into his vehicle. He simply nodded and gave me a forced smile. Now I knew what I had to do—tail the coach! I figured the guy wouldn't make a move while his family was beggin' for his attention, so I waited until evenin' to take my place down the street just far enough to see his driveway. I'd brought my snack pack with me. A roast beef sandwich, an apple and bottled water.

I used to bring cokes or coffee with me on a job for the caffeine, but realized I had to use the john way too often. They say water is better for ya anyhow—whoever *they* are. It was startin' to get dark. Watchin' the house, I wondered if he'd overheard somethin' or if he followed Olivia to find out what was goin' on. But somethin' about this guy made me think he was a sleaze. Was the coach upset because Jason was his big chance at fame? It would blow Pratt's chance to make the headlines as the coach who inspired Jason Hale to become a star. The more I thought about it, the more I wondered if this would be a strong enough motive for Pratt to want Olivia out of the way.

About two hours later, the coach's silver SUV pulled out of the driveway. I started my car and slowly left my parkin' spot. After a few minutes, we were on Highway 31 headed north. We ventured through Carmel then Westfield until we were out in the more rural countryside. I couldn't imagine where he was goin'. Was Olivia in his SUV waitin' to be dumped in some cornfield? I only hoped he wouldn't spot me followin' him. It's harder to hide in the wide-open spaces. He took an abrupt turn onto a country road. I slowed and followed. Out here, I could watch him from afar and saw him take a left turn. If the farmhouse hadn't been painted a bright white, I might have missed seein' it since the only lights were from his vehicle. I passed by to make him think it was just a coincidence I was behind him all this time. A little way ahead, I found a short drive obscured by trees. It was probably where the farmer parked so he could work the field next to it. Gettin' out of my car, I watched the house. I could see the coach's headlights were still on. When he walked in front of his vehicle, I could see he was carryin' somethin', but it was too small to be Olivia. He went inside the farmhouse. The electricity was still workin' because lights started to go on. I darted across the yard hopin' I wouldn't stumble over branches or somethin'. My hopes were dashed as I tripped over a rock and went face first onto the ground. I felt a stick poke my cheek. I touched it to find it was bleedin', but didn't have time to worry about it. Scramblin' up, I went around the right side of the house. I found a rickety crate to stand on and peered through the grimy window into the kitchen. I saw Pratt put the box on the table and go through a door. It sounded like he was goin' down a wooden staircase. Next thing

I know, he'd pushed a young girl with short blonde hair into a chair. When she looked up, I could see it was Olivia. She raised her hands, bound with one of those plastic things. I forget what they're called. He cut her bonds and shoved the box in front of her. There was a diet coke, a sandwich of some sort and chips. She ate vigorously like she hadn't eaten all ... never mind. Since Pratt had been with the family all day, the poor girl probably hadn't eaten since he brought her out here.

When she was done, he said somethin' to her I couldn't comprehend. I ducked, fearin' one of them would see me. How was I gonna get her outta there? I'd left my gun in Chicago, not thinkin' I'd need it while I was in Indy. I heard a thud and looked in the window again. He'd pushed her up against the wall with his finger in her face. Must not have gotten the answer he wanted. He pulled out one of those plastic things from his coat pocket, rebindin' her wrists then he takes her back downstairs. A few minutes later I see Pratt throw the garbage from Olivia's meal into the box and he switches off the light. I got down off the crate and snuck around to the corner of the house. Pratt had switched off all of the lights in the house. He went to the SUV and got in. I waited a few minutes until I heard the vehicle's noise fade. Then, I put my hand in my pocket bumpin' one of those pin flashlights. What an idiot! Maybe I could of avoided becomin' a scar face had I remembered I had this stupid thing. I found the back door and to my surprise, it was unlocked. I pulled it open and crept inside. This entrance went into an old back room with pipes and electrical outlets which at one time accommodated a washer and dryer. The second door wasn't quite so easy. I pulled out my trusty tool kit and picked the lock. Baby stuff for us P.I.'s. Once inside, I realized I was in the kitchen.

"Who's there?" she shouted. "I'll do whatever you want, just let me out."

I didn't dare turn the kitchen light on in case the neighbors drove by. They might think the place was bein' vandalized and call the cops—or worse, Coach Pratt. I opened the door realizin' it led to a basement. I stepped onto the first step, shut the door and found a pull chain light above my head which was still swingin' from its recent use. I didn't see the harm in turnin' it on.

"Olivia?" I called. "It's Maria's Uncle Vito. I'm comin' down to get ya."

I heard her cryin' as I descended. I found her on a mattress up against the wall. "Hang on. I need to find somethin' to cut those," I said pointin' at her bonds. He'd put one around her ankles, too. I finally found a workbench with some wire cutters. They worked just fine. Once I had her hands and feet free, she threw her arms around my neck bawlin'. I patted her on the back, not knowin' what else to do. I asked her if she was okay to walk 'cause we needed to get to a police station. She said she could, released me, and we headed up the stairs. I took her out the same way I came in and just as we made the corner, a flash of bright light blinded us. "Where do you two think you're going?" said a deep, masculine voice.

"Please, please," Olivia pleaded. "Don't put me back in there. I'll do whatever you say."

"Hey, if it isn't the coach," I said tryin' to sound calm. The ruckus me and Olivia was makin' in the basement must of kept us from hearin' the SUV come back. "What you doin' out here?"

"I could ask you the same thing, Mazzara," he said in a not so pleasant tone. The headlights kept me from seein' him.

"So why'd you wanna torture this little girl? She gets pregnant by one of your star players and your dreams are shattered? What is it you want her to do?"

Then I heard somethin' I wasn't expectin'. "It's not Jason's baby," said Olivia almost indignantly. "It's his." She was pointin' toward Coach Pratt.

"Shut up, slut," he screamed.

"I don't understand," I said. "If it's his baby, why go to Jason? Why would you have sex with this guy?"

"He threatened to make sure Jason never got his scholarship. He said he knew how to change the grades in the computer and would make sure Jason didn't qualify. I love Jason and wanted him to succeed, so I did what Coach wanted."

"I said, shut up," Pratt screamed. Then we heard the cockin' of a shotgun. Olivia began to cry again.

"What does he want you to do?" I asked.

"Get an abortion," she squeaked. "He says it's my fault I got pregnant. I wanted to tell Jason everything, but when he said I'd ruined his life, I lost it and ran off. That's when Coach grabbed me in the parking lot and forced me into his car."

I hugged her on the pretext of comfortin' her, but whispered in her ear instead. "When I make my move, run. My car's over there in those trees. Go get help." I put my car keys in her hand.

"Break it up," Pratt shouted. "This could have been so simple. I gave her the name of a reputable doctor and was going to pay for it, but she suddenly gets a conscience. I got half way down the road and decided I'd better finish her off. Now that you've nosed in, I'm going to have to kill you, too."

I slowly moved to the right, away from Olivia. If I could divert his attention, maybe she could get away.

"Shame on you Coach," I said, continuin' to move. "You called her a slut, but look at you. Takin' advantage of a young girl like this. She's not even eighteen. How do you know she hasn't already told other people? Teenagers tend to blab, you know. You gonna shoot the whole senior class?"

I finally moved out of the mainstream of the headlights. I could see his dark figure now, gun pointed towards me. I was about to move closer to him when there were bright lights and sirens everywhere. The cops must have been comin' down the road with lights out in order to sneak up on us. I shouted for Olivia to run and took a dive for the ground. Unfortunately, before I got all the way down, he fired and nicked my left shoulder. Next thing I know, the cops are screamin' at him to drop his weapon and readin' him his Miranda rights. I look up to see an angel lookin' down on me. It was Pepper. Of course, it wasn't too long before the angel face went sour. I knew she was unhappy with me for not tellin' her what I was doin'.

"Mr. Mazzara," said a sweet, soft voice. It was Olivia still clutchin' my keys. "Thank you," she said, handin' my keys to Pepper. A female Hamilton County Sheriff's deputy put a blanket around her and took her away.

"What did you think you were doing?" Pepper said, scowlin' at me

"Just doin' what I do best." I explained how Jason Hale came to see me, assumin' the baby was his. Turned out it was Coach Pratt's baby and he intended to protect himself, not Jason.

Pepper had similar suspicions about the coach bein' involved. She told me she'd discovered Pratt owned this farm. It had belonged to his father who died six months ago. It seemed to her this would be a great place to hide a body.

Pepper demanded I get into an ambulance and go to the hospital for my petty wound. Luckily, my coat had slowed the bullet so all I had was a flesh wound. I'm sure the thirty-degree temperatures kept it from bleedin' too much. I was treated and released from the hospital a few hours later. Pepper insisted on drivin' me to my brother's house. When we arrived, it was to a hero's welcome. Theresa had made my favorite banana cream pie and told the girls no samples until Uncle Vito came home. Katie and Gabriella practically tackled me when I came through the door.

"Easy girls," said Pepper. "Your Uncle Vito's shoulder is pretty sore right now."

Maria approached me with tears in her eyes. "Oh, Uncle Vito. I'm so sorry you got hurt. You and Olivia could have been killed!"

"Don't worry about it," I said, tryin' to reassure her. "I'm a tough old bird. Besides, Olivia is home with her folks now, and she's gonna need a lot of TLC from her friends. This was pretty rough on her."

Maria nodded, a huge smile widenin' across her beautiful face. She hugged me sayin', "You *are* the best private detective in the world."

"Yeah, I know," I said pattin' her back.

Pepper gave me a stern look then rolled her eyes, shakin' her head.

"But this time I had help," I said.

At last, Pepper smiled.

Tamika Catchings
Tony Perona

When Tamika Catchings helped the Indiana Fever win the WNBA championship in 2012, it was a triumph not just over the defending WNBA champs but also over a disability that had plagued her since birth. Tamika was born with moderately severe hearing loss in both of her ears. She has learned to rely on reading lips and facial cues to compensate. Growing up with the disability was difficult. She says she wanted to fit in, but instead she stood out. She credits her parents for teaching her to try her hardest at everything, no matter what others say.

She credits her father for her athleticism. He played in the NBA for 11 years. By high school Tamika was excelling at the sport. She and her sister Tauja helped Stevenson High School to an Illinois State Championship.

Tamika played for Coach Pat Summit at the University of Tennessee. Summit told her she was a special player and could inspire kids with her accomplishments, despite the difficulties with her disability. She says she has tried to live by that mantra.

After graduating from college in 2002, Tamika was selected by the Indiana Fever and has been a Hoosier ever since. She has also been on the USA Women's Olympic Basketball Team, winning gold in 2004, 2008 and 2012. She has been an eight-time WNBA All-Star and in 2011 won the league's Most Valuable Player award.

Bringing the 2012 WNBA championship trophy home to Indiana allowed her to add the one title she longed to have in her amazing basketball resume.

Tamika says she doesn't think of her hearing loss as a disability anymore. She believes a person can accomplish anything they put their mind to, no matter the obstacles. What matters is hard work and dedication.

Catchings' story is a true inspiration.

DEADLY BET
Suzanne Leiphart

I'd resigned myself to attending three days and nights of live Indiana basketball games each and every weekend during the never-ending manic season. My feelings for my new boyfriend, Charles, had conquered any initial resistance I'd had. Charles' family for generations had been doggedly loyal high school, college and pro-ball fans. Years back, they'd even slipped in an elementary, middle school or community organization game when they could. Following Indiana basketball seemed to be a worthy and wholesome hobby, until the shocking murder.

I blamed my neighbor, Olivia Hill, partly, for my basketball conundrum. We'd met sitting next to each other at our January Lakeside Condominium Association board meeting. We lived in a gated community with a security guard, special lighting and cameras, but some residents wanted even more protection. The added expense was about to be debated.

The tall, slim young woman who had just sat down next to me tapped my arm and whispered, "I live two buildings down from you on Black Swan Lane. I'm Olivia Hill."

I turned to greet her. "Hi, I'm Marty Mayes."

She extended her hand and gave me a firm handshake.

"I really don't think we have a crime problem here, do you?"

Olivia started to answer, but the meeting was called to order. During a break she and I were able to get better acquainted. I figured I was about 10 years older at 35 than she was. We both had on sweaters and jeans. I noticed her striking face as she spoke. Deep brown eyes, high cheekbones, perfect nose and skin and straight extra-white teeth were surrounded by short mahogany hair in contrast to my long, wavy sandy-brown hair, green eyes and full cheeks.

When Olivia asked what I did for a living, I told her I was a freelance writer currently on sabbatical, and had moved here from Michigan last year after my husband died to be closer to my favorite relatives.

Olivia told me she was a physical education teacher and assistant girl's basketball coach at Indianapolis High School, commonly referred to as Indy High. She'd just started teaching at Indy High last fall, her first job after completing student teaching in a rural community about an hour from Indianapolis.

"I played high school basketball in Michigan. We weren't very good." I chuckled. "Not at all like the Indy High girls or boys basketball teams," which had each been state champions more than once the past few years.

"You should come to a game sometime." Olivia nodded her head with encouragement.

"I'd love to. Wish I could think of someone to bring with me."

"That's not a problem, Marty. There's a group of regulars that follow our games. They're friendly, all ages, married and single. You'll fit right in. There's a home boy's game this Friday night."

"A boy's game? You won't be coaching."

"No, I'll be out of town." A shadow flickered across her face. "But you'll get a chance to meet Kate, Charlie, Max and the others. You'll have a lot of fun. I'll call them and let you know tomorrow what you need to do, where you need to go."

It was exciting to go to an Indiana basketball game. I ended up sitting next to Charles March, a warm and welcoming widower of three years, who was 15 years my senior. I'd always been drawn to older men. Charlie was tall, a few inches over six feet with a large build, fair skin, full head of freshly styled smokey-gray hair, sparkling sky-blue eyes and a wide smile. A long-sleeved navy-blue Polo shirt, neatly pressed tan slacks and expensive shoes and watch completed his appealing look. He explained that he'd played basketball for Indy High and Indiana University.

"Would you like to go out for dinner sometime?" Charlie asked near the end of the game. Indy High was slaughtering Speedway.

He leaned closer, lightly pressing his muscular arm and shoulder into mine.

I cleared my throat, startled by his question and the pleasing physical contact. Why not? I thought. "Yes, I would."

"How about tomorrow night?"

Seemed a little soon, but I didn't have any plans, and I liked this man. "All right."

I watched with some anxiety as I recited and Charlie programmed my home and cell numbers into his smart phone.

Our first several dates were incredible, filled with candle-lit dinners and dancing, nature walks and cozy nights together. It was obvious that Charlie loved basketball, but I'd had no idea of his level of commitment.

One night when we were cuddling, Charlie happily let me know that from now on every Friday, Saturday and Sunday for the next several months would include going to a different basketball event. I enjoyed live basketball, but following three teams every single weekend?

Or maybe it was all the time I'd be spending with Charlie in this new relationship that made me nervous. I wasn't sure, but I knew I really enjoyed Charlie's company. Although, didn't I have other things to do? A life of my own? Not really, since I'd won some money in the lottery and decided to take a break from my work as a freelance writer. And certainly, not when I looked into Charlie's twinkling blue eyes or felt his strong, protective arms around me.

During each week Charlie and I tried to have lunch together. He had a commercial real estate business that he was grooming two of his sons to take over and manage. On one of our lunch dates, he pulled into a nondescript shopping strip and parked his Lexus at one end by a bar with pitch-black windows. Charlie didn't drink. I gave him a questioning look.

"A friend of mine owns this place," he said. "Food's pretty good."

"I never even noticed it before, yet I often drive by here."

"Nick doesn't really advertise."

"Why not?" I asked as Charlie opened his car door, stepped out and led the way. He didn't seem to hear me.

Inside, the décor was plain with worn carpeting. A handful of patrons were seated at scattered faux wood tables.

Charlie took a tall stool with a back at the bar and I followed suit. A heavy-set, gray-haired man dressed in white cook's attire with a pleated white cap at the other end of the bar made his way to us, shook Charlie's hand and slapped his shoulder as they exchanged pleasantries. Charlie introduced me to Nick. While the men talked vaguely about sports, I reviewed the menu.

"About anything you want I can fix," said Nick.

Charlie ordered a pork tenderloin sandwich with tomatoes and lettuce, and I went with biscuits and gravy, both Indiana favorites.

Nick never re-joined us, but waved from the nearby kitchen as we were leaving. He'd been on the phone almost constantly, talking in an unusually low tone.

Charlie remained silent while we drove for about a mile, holding my hand in his lap as he steered with the other. "Nick's a bookie, you know." He squeezed my hand, then let go and placed his on the steering wheel.

I turned to look at him. "How would I know that?" I knew nothing about bookmakers. Wasn't even sure what all they did.

"I like to place a bet every once in awhile." Charles stared straight ahead at the road.

I shook my head in confusion. "On what? Horse racing or something? Is that legal if you're not at the track?"

"Basketball games."

"Oh, like the Pacers. But don't you just call Las Vegas to make a legal bet there?"

"Not really."

I sighed and fiddled with the temperature controls. This was not making sense to me.

"I do bet on the Pacers sometimes," Charlie said. "Or on college ball, an occasional high school game."

"You can gamble on Indiana high school games?"

"Usually you can't, but if it's a big game with enough money interest it might qualify."

"I thought high school games would be protected from gambling. They seem so innocent, aboveboard."

"You can bet on about anything."

"Are you a compulsive gambler?" I imagined him potentially losing his home and his business.

"No way. It's just a casual hobby. Everybody does it."

"You're the first I've known. Can't you be arrested for placing bets with a bookie?"

"Theoretically, yes, but in reality, no." I shook my head in disbelief as Charlie continued. "Sometimes heat comes down on the bookie, not the bettors."

I was stunned. Who was this man, really, that I'd been dating for two months? A problem gambler?

"I'm sure you won't say anything about Nick or his business to anyone."

I took a deep breath and looked out the passenger window. Charles pulled into my drive and stopped the car. He gently turned my cold cheek toward him and gave me a warm kiss on the mouth. "Honey, don't worry about anything," he whispered. I melted into his arms. Maybe I was overreacting to the gambling, I thought, as I climbed from the car.

After I relaxed for a few minutes at home, I decided to acquiesce, at least for now, that sports betting was simply a harmless, victimless crime. But maybe I would take a look online later to learn more.

In an hour the evening news would be on television. Didn't want to miss the sports segment. I decided to take a walk before I fixed dinner. I changed into work-out clothes, winter jacket, hat and mittens and started down the street.

Olivia Hill suddenly came out of her condominium as I approached and waved to me. "Marty, how are you?" she called out.

"Just fine," I said as she came down her steps toward me bundled up in a coat and scarf.

"I have to catch a flight to New York in a few hours, but first I need to run over to the mall and pick something up at Nordstrom. I was hoping you'd water my plants while I'm gone."

"I'd be glad to help."

She handed me a key with her gloved hand which appeared to be shaking. The same dark look crossed her face that I'd noticed the night we'd met.

"Are you all right, Olivia?"

"Sure. Got to go. Thanks."

I continued on past the empty guard shack, which was only manned until 4:30, through a narrow opening next to the security gate out to the back street. I walked almost a mile to the cemetery and took the gravel path around the scenic White River setting of historic and shiny new headstones. Today there were no animal movements or sounds and sinister shadows seemed to be everywhere. Two birds of prey coasted in the twilight above. A foreboding feeling enveloped me.

Fifty minutes later I was home. I changed clothes, tossed a salad, poured a glass of milk, put them both on a tray that I set down in the family room and turned on the TV.

Breaking news beckoned at the top of the newscast. "A young woman was found dead next to her car outside Nordstrom in the mall parking lot just a short time ago!"

I caught my breath and thought of Olivia. Cause of death was not yet known, and the facts were vague. More information would be available later in the show.

Olivia had been vibrant and alive only an hour earlier, but deep down I sensed she was the mysterious victim. I choked back a tear, picked at my salad greens, then decided to go to the kitchen and add more dressing while I waited for the rest of the developing story. The chilling feeling I'd had at the cemetery had returned. The reality was that Olivia had actually seemed frightened when I'd last spoken to her.

Twenty minutes later the broadcaster announced that the dead woman had been shot and killed. No motive for murder had been determined. Her purse containing cash, credit and ID cards was found lying right near her lifeless body. Next-of-kin would be notified before the name was released to the public.

I checked online for further updates throughout the evening, gave up and thought about going to bed early, but I was restless. I stuck my head out the front door into the cold night air and decided to take a stroll by Olivia's condo.

Quickly I slipped on dark clothing including leather gloves. I checked for the keys in my left pocket along with a pen and small notepad, made sure my cell phone was off, and felt for the small .22 in my right pocket. I had a permit to carry.

The sky was death black. No stars were shining, not even a thin beam of moonlight glowed. Outdoor lighting at this end of the Lakeside complex was dimmer than on the other streets which made it easier to blend in with the blackness.

There were no sidewalks, so I stayed on the road's edge across from the homes, near the thick-trunked trees. How did Olivia, a young teacher, manage to afford a seven-figure condo at Lakeside? I wondered. People had asked the same about me, an unemployed freelance writer, including Charlie after our third date. I'd told him about the lottery money. Maybe Olivia had won the lottery, too. What were the odds of that happening to two neighbors?

I grew more focused when I spotted an SUV parked in Olivia's driveway. No lights were on in the condo. A nearby subdued street lamp might allow me to see the license plate. I moved in closer and was able to copy down the Illinois plate number on the older model SUV in my notebook.

A faint sound of Olivia's front door opening intensified my attention. I moved away fast to hide behind a huge oak across from her drive. Two bulky men were carrying something heavy down the porch stairs. They set a solid metal box down near the rear door of the SUV which must have been four feet tall, two feet wide and two deep. One man lifted up the tailgate. It struck me how no front security lights had come on outside of Olivia's and there was no interior light in the SUV. The huge men slowly raised the massive object into the vehicle. I squinted for a closer view. It looked like a safe. Why would Olivia have needed that?

The men quietly got into the car and drove out the nearby back gate which opened automatically, but only for someone leaving the complex. How did they get in? I wondered. I suppose if they're accomplished burglars no fences or card devices would be able to keep them out. Still, Lakeside was not nearly as secure as I'd declared to Olivia at the January board meeting. And my measly .22 caliber pistol wouldn't likely stop those big men.

I stepped out from my hiding place and decided to see if I could find out more as to what the intruders where doing at Olivia's. Her house key easily unlocked her door. Once inside the unlit unit I wished I'd brought a flashlight. A low light was on down a short hallway from the foyer where I stood, in what was probably the kitchen. I waited for my eyes to adjust to focus in on my surroundings. Everything looked like it was in place. I tip-toed through the front room to see if there was a back office where the safe might have been kept. I passed a couple of bedrooms that were perfectly neat and undisturbed. One more doorway stood open at the end of the hall.

Sure enough, the room contained office furniture. A few papers were scattered on the desk. Nothing seemed to be missing or out of place except that there was no computer. I noticed a closed door behind the desk to the left. It turned out to be unlocked and opened right away.

The spacious walk-in closet was much darker than the outer office had been. I waited again for my eyes to adapt to the lack of light source. At the far end of the space was an empty spot that certainly could have held the safe. Nearby file drawers were open and folders were strewn on the floor. What could they have been looking for? I bent down and picked up a handful of files with my gloves, grabbed the papers off the desk and took them to the better-lit kitchen.

The folders were filled with pages of monthly statements from banks in LA, Chicago and the Cayman Islands. I shook my head in disbelief, then wrote each account number on my note pad. Olivia's name, birth date and social security number stood out on a couple of pages which I also copied into my book.

The sound of a car horn honking outside made me freeze. The beeping finally stopped. I placed the papers back on the desk as closely as I could to where they'd been lying, and put the folders back on the closet floor, leaving the file drawers open like I'd found them. I carefully closed the closet door and silently returned to the entry area of Olivia's home. I slowly opened the outside door and listened. Nothing. I breathed a sigh of relief as I locked up and jogged back home.

Two days later Olivia's name was released on the evening news in connection with the mall murder. Shortly after, the house phone rang. It was Charlie.

"Did you hear about Ms. Hill?" he said rapidly.

"Yes. I'm shocked. And what a loss to Indy High."

"I know. A couple of my buddies called. Said it was a professional hit, maybe by the mob."

That might explain the beefy men I saw hauling the safe out of Olivia's home. "They didn't even hint at anything like that on the news. Do your friends have any idea why someone would want to hurt her?"

"No clue. I'll call you if I hear anything more. Pick you up at the usual time for the game. See if her death affects how the guys play."

I thought Charlie sounded a little too casual, but he hadn't known Olivia very well. Then it struck me, what kind of friends did he have that would know if a murder was a mob hit or not? I decided not to mention to him what I'd witnessed at her condo the other night or that I had her key.

"See you tomorrow, Charlie."

Needless to say, the crowd was lacking in its usual exuberance at Friday's Indy High basketball game. School officials had considered canceling the event due to the murder of Coach Hill, friends seated around Charlie and me said, but instead they held a short memorial before the start and had a tribute during halftime.

During the game I felt myself becoming suspicious of fans in the stands. I scanned the bleachers for burly men. Was the killer here? Were others on the hit list? The fact that Coach Hill's murder might have been mob-related was not common knowledge. Charlie and I did not mention it to anyone in the stands espousing theories about possible motives. Nor did I mention my escapade at Olivia Hill's the night before to Charlie.

The Indy High players managed to eek out a win over the rival they'd been expected to demolish. I held onto Charlie's arm tightly afterward on the way to the car as I kept glancing around, leery that the danger could be anywhere.

Indy Star online headlines the next morning reported that Olivia Hill was an alias for Candi Sparke. Photos of a slender, but muscular young woman in a low cut top, tight jeans and long blond wig were posted with the story. According to the reporter, Ms. Sparke had had drug-related arrests in Chicago, no convictions, and had worked as an exotic dancer until she admitted herself into a substance abuse treatment facility, changed her identity and moved to LA where she'd received a legitimate teaching degree in physical education.

I pondered the incredible news and wondered if Olivia had avoided drug convictions by becoming an informant. Had she been in a witness protection program in Indianapolis, albeit not a very effective one? Investigation by law enforcement continued into the high-end nightclub where Candi had worked.

Charlie and I had actually chosen not to go to a weekend basketball game and spent Saturday together running errands followed by dinner at our favorite seafood restaurant. Charlie ordered blackened salmon which sizzled when it arrived. I inhaled the delightful aroma of the garlic sauce on my giant browned scallops. We nibbled on each other's delicacies as we discussed Candi Starke's demise.

"I've hesitated about telling you this, Marty, but some of my buddies are very familiar with the club where Candi Sparke worked in Chicago. Not me, I've never been there. Not my style."

I smiled at him. "Glad to hear that."

"The place is deep in mob activity."

"Oh? So why do your friends go there?"

"They have a private gambling room. Very discreet, along with all the other services they provide."

I chewed slowly on a scallop. "You mean like prostitution?"

Charlie nodded. "Yeah. The owner's also a bookie. Some of the guys I know made bets while they were there. Classy nightclub, I guess."

"Except for all the illegal mob activity." I put down my fork and rested my hand on the table.

"Well, I mean, they said it was classy as in elegant."

"How are you involved with those types of guys? How did you meet them?"

"Business. In real estate I run into all types."

"I suppose that's true. Well, do you do other types of gambling or use call girls or drugs? You don't seem like the type, but you bet on sports and pay a bookmaker."

Charlie rested his hand on mine and looked me in the eye. "Marty, my brother was a gambler. He owed so much to a loan shark he lost his life over it."

"Oh, Charlie. I'm so sorry."

"I'm pretty sure I know who did it, but the police don't have enough evidence yet to prosecute. I've kept my fingers in gambling hoping to learn enough to help prove the case against his killer. Business, basketball and you are my addictions." He laughed nervously and squeezed my hand. "For your comfort and your safety I will cease placing any more bets. My friends will fill me in."

"What if your bookie, Nick, is involved? They probably all know each other. Online it said that bookies are also usually in the drug business and connected to the mob."

"I don't know about that. I'll agree with you that illegal betting does not make good sense. So now that I've quit my last really bad habit, maybe you'll agree to marry me in the future." He picked up my hand and kissed it.

I swallowed hard, then smiled. "Maybe. But I'm not quite ready to make that commitment."

First, I wanted to check Charlie's background thoroughly, to see if he was as truthful as he sounded, maybe have him tailed for a few months, and research Olivia's murder as much as I could. Might be able to pull together a good story to sell. I already had calls in to publications that might be interested. This story had the potential to capture national attention. But I was busy with all the ball games, and I was supposed to be on a leave of absence. The articles I'd written before were more often light human interest stories, although, before that I'd worked on one newspaper's crime beat in Michigan for a couple years.

❖

Later in the week Charlie and I went to an Indy High home game. Our team was again defeated. Since Coach Hill's death, both the Indy High boys and girls basketball teams were in a downhill slide. Nothing close to a state championship for either team would be won this year.

Olivia's case was being investigated closely by law enforcement, and the FBI had been called in, according to press accounts. A close contact of mine who was retired from the Chicago FBI office and who did private undercover work gave me information about Olivia aka Candi Sparke that had not yet been released to or discovered by the press. For a substantial fee, of course. He also recommended that I give the FBI the license plate number of the SUV at Olivia's the night of her death and the bank account numbers that I had found in her condo.

Candi had been the girlfriend of the Chicago nightclub owner where she'd danced and was well versed in all aspects of the establishment including the gambling and bookmaking operation. Her father had also been in the gambling business. Candi had loved sports in school, the private detective told me, and had become most active in the sports bet component of the club's businesses, particularly underage betting. Sometimes teens were allowed into the nightclub to gamble, but mostly they placed their bets at secret locations. Candi collected the youths' money and paid them when they won. She was basically a bookie herself with high school students working for her, via the nightclub, who took wagers from other students at two affluent suburban Chicago high schools and collected the cash for her.

After I'd spoken with my covert Chicago liaison, I received an email from an online news outlet that wanted to hire me to write an exclusive ongoing series about the Olivia Hill case. I'd written for them before. We negotiated, via email, a price for each story. I put together the first one which included a summary of the mysterious events so far along with my scoop. Wow, it felt great to be on the job again!

Charlie dropped by my home to share the latest hearsay about the death of Olivia Hill. He always had news more up-to-date than the newspapers and television stations about the hit. I told him I was working on a feature series for an online publication's crime section. He was pleased, initially.

Rumor through Charlie's grapevine was that the missing stripper, Candi Sparke, had finally been found in Indianapolis a few weeks before her death by the crooked Chicago club owner's mob associates. They were amused that she was living as a coach and teacher named Olivia Hill, but not so pleased that on the sly she was running a sports betting business at Indy High. They claimed her earnings were theirs. It had probably been a mistake for her to leave LA and move back to the Midwest near her sister, only a few hours from Chicago, Charlie surmised.

"Would you arrange a meeting for me with the club owner or someone else in the know about Candi Sparke?" I asked Charlie as he stood in my foyer.

He shook his head. "Why?"

"For my articles."

"No. It could be dangerous for you, honey."

"A phone call interview would be enough for me. You keep in touch with them."

"My buddies do. Not me."

"Then, I'd like to speak with one your buddies in the know."

"They'd never agree. You can keep asking me questions. I'll keep you informed."

"I need confirmation from a direct source."

"Sorry, Marty. Best I can do is keep telling you what I hear."

I shrugged my shoulders as I considered calling or visiting the nightclub myself.

"I'd be glad to pay your informant, but only for accurate information. They can remain anonymous. How about it, Charlie?" I stepped over close to him and rubbed his bicep. "Please?" I said as I slid my arms around him and rested my head on his shoulder.

Charlie restlessly adjusted his weight back and forth from foot to foot a few times then relaxed. He finally said, "All right. I'll try to set up something."

I gave him a slow kiss on the cheek.

Word came to me through Charlie's source a few days later via an untraceable throw-away cell phone that had been provided, to check out five affluent male Indy High School students who had attended Ms. Hill's private funeral arranged by her sister. He gave me their names. The only other student body members present at the service had been on the girl's basketball team. I discovered the five young men were not even on the boy's basketball team. Other students had only participated in the memorial at the school. Neither the media nor general public had been allowed in the funeral home.

That evening Charlie came to pick me up for the state high school finals, even though Indy High had not come close to qualifying for the play-offs. He told me in the car, while we were still in my drive, that one of his friends was frantic over the possibility that his son, Zack, had been involved in the sports betting at Indy High, along with several other students and might be harmed, even though no threats had been made.

"Zack Stoneman?"

"Yeah."

"Oh my gosh, Charlie, that's one of the names your source gave me."

"Well then, you'll really like this. I talked to Zack's dad about your stories, and Zack is willing to meet with you before he goes to the police."

I leaned over, looked into his eyes and stroked the side of his face with my fingers. "Thanks so much, Charlie. I'm touched that you set that up. You've been more supportive than I ever expected. Zack really could be helpful to my articles."

After watching one of our favorite teams, Carmel High School, win the Indiana high school basketball championship, my cheery mood disappeared the minute we arrived at my condo. I felt uneasy. I used a remote to switch on the entry light, then held Charlie's arm as we walked up to the front porch. As we neared, we both saw my storm door was ajar, and the brand new main door handle was scratched around the key area. I gripped Charlie's arm harder. I flashed on the scary men that had stolen Olivia's safe.

After we entered the foyer and decided no one had been inside, Charlie turned and grabbed my shoulders. "You've got to end the series, Marty. Someone tried to break in! It's too dangerous to keep going. I don't want you to end up like Olivia Hill."

I shook my head. "I can't. I won't. This makes me more determined to find the truth."

"I'm worried, Marty. I insist on staying here with you."

"You don't have to, Charlie. I'll be fine," I said, although I wasn't sure I believed my own words.

Charlie frowned.

"But on the other hand, I'd really enjoy having you around more."

"Then it's settled." He pulled me to him and hugged me.

I smiled in his arms. "I think I'll like having you as a roommate."

At his parents' home, Zack admitted to me that he'd been one of the five seniors at Olivia Hill's private funeral service. The five young men had all become novice gambling entrepreneurs with Ms. Hill's encouragement, Zack reported. Sports betting and bookmaking had seemed harmless to them in the beginning, Zack told me, especially since they were working for the lovely and seemingly non-threatening Ms. Olivia Hill. The boys were in charge of bringing in basketball bets from Indy High students, mostly for the pro games. They took in the money and kept records of the bets the way Ms. Hill had taught them. She'd taken a majority percentage of the proceeds, but the young men had made thousands of dollars each month.

"Did you ever work with any other bookies in Indianapolis?" I thought of Nick.

"Nope, just with Ms. Hill."

The illegal gambling enterprise, started at Indy High, had been growing and was poised to expand to other schools, according to Zack. The nightclub owner in Chicago, Ms. Hill's ex, had caught wind of the operation and paid her a visit. She'd warned the boys that the man was connected with the mob, had threatened her, and that she took his threats seriously. Out of fear, Ms. Hill quickly closed down her sports-bet business. Zack and the other four had not taken any more wagers from students, he said, for about a week before her murder. Zack hung his head and said he regretted that, even then, it'd been too late to save Ms. Hill.

Candi, aka Ms. Hill, had become greedy, according to national crime news opinion-makers, and never should have started the sports-betting business without the Chicago mob's approval, even in Indianapolis. If she'd at least shared the profits with the mobsters she might have lived. And Zack, an adult at age 18, might not have been arrested, with his life on hold, waiting for the trial.

Surprisingly, not much was said by the critics about the dangers of underage gambling or school and family values regarding gaming in general, except by the Indiana High School Athletic Association (IHSAA). Most seemed to be more interested in, even fascinated by, the mob's involvement in Olivia Hill's short, shady life.

My Chicago contact told me that the FBI had intensified their surveillance of the shady nightclub owner's activities and had pressured mob informers to squeal about the circumstances of Olivia's murder. The license plate number of the men that stole Olivia's safe, and her off-shore account numbers had likely helped their investigation, he said. Agents were about to bust a large group of Chicago mobsters.

Mob connections in Indianapolis were also being squeezed and illegal gambling operations scrutinized. Charlie had heard his brother's killer was also close to being caught for years of crimes related to loan-sharking and murder.

With the high school and college basketball seasons over, Charlie and I were at a loss as to what to do with our free time. We went to occasional Indiana Pacers games and hoped we'd be able to follow them soon to the play-offs. I'd put my new crime-writing career on hold, even after a couple of enticing employment opportunities, but was considering a lucrative offer related to writing a book about the Olivia Hill case next year. I looked forward to indulging myself with Charlie a bit longer.

After the racketeering indictments and all the media hype died down, Charlie asked me to marry him. I accepted, but only after an exhaustive background check, which I really felt was unnecessary. Until I reminded myself of my late friend, the endearing, but deceptive Olivia Hill.

Andrea Myers: Former Athletic Director at Indiana State

M. B. Dabney

When Andrea Myers was growing up in rural Dana, Indiana, near the Illinois state border, there were no competitive sports for girls at her high school. Nor were there any female coaches in boys sports. She graduated from high school in 1962, a decade before Title IX, the federal law that established a playing field – not just a level playing field – for girls sports.

Thankfully, a lot of things changed long before she retired in 2005 to play golf, travel a lot, and just relax and enjoy life.

"My first experience in competition was after I got to college," says Myers, whom everyone calls Andi, referring to her time at Indiana State University. "And I loved the competition."

She loved it so much she went on to have a four-decade career in college sports, starting with 15 years coaching women's basketball at Vincennes University, and ending with 22 years as a women's basketball coach and then athletic director at ISU, her alma mater.

Some of the high points of her career were at Vincennes, where she had an overall record of 209-95. "I started the (women's) basketball program there," she says. They offered girls scholarships as far back as 1973, and enjoyed strong teams for a number of years. She was also twice named Regional Basketball Coach of the Year.

Myers admits coaching at Indiana State was tough at first because her teams struggled. But also during her tenure she was once named Conference Coach of the Year. From 1999 to 2005, Myers was the athletic director at ISU, becoming the first woman to hold that position in the school's history.

Myers has many honors from her time as a coach and college athletics administrator, including being named the 2002 Administrator of the Year by the National Association of Collegiate Women Athletics Administrators.

But perhaps the greatest honor is having had an impact on someone's life.

"Not a week goes by when I don't hear from one of the great former athletes I've coached," she says. "And that's special."

MORE THAN THE GAME

Barbara Swander Miller

Too young to drive and too old to go looking for playmates, Tim figured he would take a walk. He headed up the gravel drive to County Road 100 West. *Nothing like walking in Chicago,* he thought. *No people... no cars...* Tim quickly scanned what was left of the little town. *Nothing interesting here.* Tim turned, noticing a weathered steeple. *Wait a minute.*

At the back corner of the lot, just beyond a thick sycamore, was a recently dug grave. Tim picked his way through the broken monuments to read the inscription.

Harold Eugene Brewster

A Friend to All, Gone Too Soon

October 1, 1933 to May 21, 2010

What! Brewster! This must be my grandpa's grave. Harold! What a name! Tim instinctively stepped back from the mound. He stared at the dirt heaped over what surely was a casket hidden beneath, his mind churning. Tim eyed the engraving. *"A Friend to All?"* He *wasn't a friend to me... or to Dad. I didn't even know him.* Tim's toe nudged the edge of the mound.

Their trip from suburban Chicago to rural Indiana had been unexpected. Tim had stayed at school late for chess club that afternoon, the day the phone call came. He had just walked into the back door when he watched his dad lose it. His strong, steady dad, crumpled against the wall in the hallway, his six-foot frame reduced to a shaking ball. The cell phone fell from his dad's right hand; a book tumbled from his left in his grief. Seeing his dad collapse rattled Tim. Not knowing what to say or do, Tim bolted for his room. He claimed he wasn't hungry later when his mom called him for dinner.

That night in his bedroom, Tim overheard his parents talking downstairs. He wondered why they didn't realize that the old gravity heat grate was a perfect conduit for their late-night conversations. If he put his head near the floor, the area rug channeled the voices straight to his ear.

"I just thought... I wanted him to see me finish," his dad choked out.

Then all Tim heard were muffled sobs. Tim let the rug fall back over the grate and climbed into bed. He pulled the warm covers over his head, trying to forget his questions.

The next day, Tim's mom updated him. "There's not going to be a funeral, Tim. Your grandpa wanted it that way. You know he and your dad didn't get along."

That was her standard answer, and Tim had never really questioned her. When he was little, he had thought maybe it was his fault that he didn't have a grandpa in his life. That was when he perfected his eavesdropping technique upstairs. Later, he had asked once when his grandpa called, but his dad had clammed up. Tim pretty much had stopped thinking about his grandpa... until now.

As soon as school was out, Tim's mom told him, the three of them were going to Roll for a week to clean, pack, and get ready for the auction of the house and all its contents.

In the first couple of days at the old farmhouse, Tim had helped his mom wash dishes and pack household items in the kitchen and in the basement. He carried box after box to the garage where the auctioneers would load them. His dad was supposed to work in the den and his grandpa's bedroom going through his father's possessions. Each night at the dinner table, Tim and his mom talked about what they had accomplished and checked off tasks on their master list, but his dad was quiet. *Why is Dad taking this so hard? He and Grandpa never talked.*

After three days, the other bedrooms had been cleared out, the living room only had furniture left; the same for the dining room. The yard was empty, and the detached garage was filling up with stacked boxes.

"Hey, need some help? Maybe we can get back home sooner if I work, too," Tim suggested to his dad who was sorting papers in the den.

"Nope. I can handle it. Go find something to do."

Tim had already noticed the lonely rim mounted on the front of the garage door, but so far there was no basketball to be found. So Tim set off to explore and ended up in the graveyard standing next to his grandpa's grave. *I wonder why everyone else thought Mr. Harold Brewster was so great when he barely spoke to his own son,* Tim wondered.

Tim wiped his forehead in the summer heat. Across the road, he heard a couple of cars crunching their way into a parking lot. The doors flung open, and some kids jumped out. Two of them sauntered up to the yellow brick building and disappeared through its double doors. The last kid stooped down to tie his shoelace. When he looked up, he spotted Tim in the churchyard and motioned him over.

It turned out that the doors opened to an old high school gym—no school in sight, just a gym. "This is cool!" Tim said to himself, as he stepped inside.

"Hey there, son!" called an older man who had a basketball resting on his hip. "Heard you were here. Wondered if you might show up." The man strode across the wooden floor and stuck out his hand. "Bob Billings," he said. "You must be Tim. I knew your grandpa."

Taken aback, Tim nodded and firmed up his grip to match the man's strong handshake.

"You play ball?" the man asked, looking at Tim closely, as if he were scouting for a college team.

"Uhh… yeah… some." Tim's eyes dropped to the floor, not sure if he was overstating his abilities.

"Well, come on." Bob tossed a ball to Tim.

The truth was that Tim had played basketball some—mostly in PE class. But he had never been on a real team. Still, he knew how to dribble and he knew how to shoot, and the extra three inches he had grown the last year couldn't hurt. So the next hour flew by as the guys split into teams and played each other under Bob's coaching and cajoling.

After a close game, the guys sprawled out on the varnished bleachers to cool off. Tim ran his fingers over the numbers in faded black paint. He turned to Bob who rested in the first row rubbing his knee. "Did you play here when you were in school?"

"Don't get him started," said Zach, laughing. Zach was the boy who had invited Tim to join the pick-up game. He wiped his forehead and grinned at the old man who owned the place now and opened it for the kids on most summer mornings.

Bob watched the boys walk across the floor to get water bottles from their bags. "Yep, I was a Roll Red Roller... and those were the days." Tim smiled as Bob's eyes settled on the stage end of the court. "Nothing else to do on Friday nights, so the whole town came to the games," he recalled. "We were stars. Everybody knew our names."

This sucks. My own grandpa could've told me these stories if I'd known him Or at least my dad could've. They both lived here.

"Yep, that Red-Roller steamroller came charging through the gym, right between lines of girls shakin' their pompoms. And then we came bursting through the door at the top of the bleachers." Bob pointed above the south bleachers. "There was a hallway right up there connected to the old school. Made a heckuva entrance!"

The other boys, who had heard Bob's stories well enough to tell them, grinned at each other and wandered back on to the gym floor to shoot free throws. But Tim was intrigued. "Did you win a lot of games?"

"We sure did. For about three years, we were the best team around." Bob paused to peer at Tim. "Had a forward that was something else. Newspapers around here called him 'The Magic Genie.' Surprised you never heard of him."

Tim shook his head and shifted on the hard bench. "Uh... my dad doesn't really talk about growing up here."

"That's a shame." The old timer shook his head. "Looked like gods, we did! All those long arms and legs." Bob leaned over closer and whispered, "Made ourselves look taller by rolling down our socks... kind of our... good luck charm." Tim nodded uncomfortably. "You know... Red *Rollers*. Magic Genie thought it up... he always liked making puns."

243

Bob held Tim's eyes for several seconds, before Tim felt uncomfortable. Then the old man looked away quickly, his eyes misting. *He must really miss those days,* Tim thought. *Maybe that's what's going on with Dad.*

"That's nice." Tim said, not sure what else to say. He glanced back to the floor where the other boys dribbled and shot.

"You gonna play some more?" his teammate called.

"Yep." Tim jumped up in relief.

With nothing else to do each morning, Tim was up by eight and out the door. After a day or two, Tim found that he was actually decent at basketball. Everyone at North Park knew him as a geek%the one whose dad was working on his Ph.D. in literature and who knew all the answers in English class. Tim had never had the nerve to try out for a sports team, but his parents had never cared. His dad always said being smart was more important than being athletic.

But it was more than the game and boredom that brought him back each morning. Tim loved the old gym and the stories about this place where his family had lived.

Each day, Bob told Tim a new one, like how one time he and Magic Genie went to May's Restaurant after the county tourney and bought all their fans pop and hamburgers. And when Bob found out that Tim didn't own a basketball, he even gave him one%he said basketball was in his blood now. Each day, more questions started gnawing at Tim. *Roll was such a neat place. Everyone here is so nice. Why did Dad want to leave?*

Later that week, an evening thunderstorm was brewing. His dad was so touchy that Tim had been avoiding him, and the muggy weather didn't help. Exhausted from a long day at the gym, Tim kicked off his Chuck Taylors and stuffed his socks inside. He could wear them tomorrow. His shirt was another story. He peeled it off, wadded it up, and shot it into the hamper.

Flashes of light filtered through the dark clouds. His dad had called it heat lightning at dinner and said it wouldn't amount to much, just "more damn heat tomorrow." That was after he had chewed out Tim for spending so much time at the gym. *I know Dad is stressed, but jeez...*

Tim rolled his shoulders a few times and got into bed. Just as he began to drift off, he thought he heard a faint thumping, almost like a ball bouncing. *Basketball really is in my blood,* he thought, and then he was asleep.

Around midnight, the heat lightning turned into a full-fledged thunderstorm. Rain pelted the screens. The chill in the air and sharp cracks of thunder woke Tim. He fell out of bed, knowing that he should close the window, and he stumbled toward it. The full-length curtains whipped out from the window frame. Cold rain shot out from the fan and quickly chilled him. He heaved up the old window frame with one hand and tugged the fan from the window with the other. The heavy window banged down as Tim set the fan on the floor and turned the dial to off. Exhausted and feeling lightheaded from his sudden exertion, Tim turned back toward his bed. Without warning, an electric terror jolted through his body.

Sitting on the edge of his bed was a young man.

Tim's feet were rooted to the floor. Even if he had wanted to scream, he couldn't have. His voice was gone. His mind was blank. He had no control. All he could do was stand and stare, his chest thumping.

The intruder ignored Tim, and in a brief flash of lightning, Tim saw that he was wearing shorts and a white tee shirt. Still not noticing Tim at the window, the young man lifted his lanky right leg across the other knee. His hands fidgeted with a small piece of cloth. After a few seconds, the young man uncrossed his legs, stood up and turned to the bedroom door, his back to Tim. Then he disappeared.

Tim shook his head to make sure he was awake. *What was that?* Tim blinked, but now there was no one in sight. He looked at his bed. *Was someone just sitting there?* Tim glanced at the door. *It's still closed. Am I dreaming? No, the window is closed, too. What the heck? Was that a ghost? Should I go get Mom and Dad?*

Tim collapsed into the old armchair, his heart still racing. He was too spooked to move. His brain swam with questions. When his heart finally slowed, Tim reached over to his bed, tugged off the top sheet, and wrapped it around himself. Somehow, he felt

245

safer covered. With his knees and the sheet pulled up to his chest, Tim was finally able to sleep again.

Dawn broke with a slight chill in the air. Tim kicked away the tangled bed sheet and stretched his legs. He knew he should get up and get dressed, but he was exhausted. Tim noticed his Chucks. *What're those on top?* Tim swung his legs out of bed and leaned closer. *That's so weird. I didn't leave my socks rolled like that.* Tim got up and went to look. *Wait a minute.... Is that what Bob meant about the Red Rollers' socks? Holy crap!* Tim stepped backward. *Was that a ghost last night? Some kid who played basketball for Roll and died?* Tim's brain flashed. *Is Grandpa's house haunted?* Tim had to get out of the house and think.

The morning stayed cool and overcast, and on the short walk to the highway, Tim debated about whether to tell the other guys and Bob about last night. *They'll probably think I'm nuts. Seeing ghosts that roll up socks!*

Down at the gym, Bob met Tim with bad news. Closin' up shop early," he told Tim. "Headed down to Hartford City. Gotta do some banking. Wish your grandpa was here to let you guys play, but..." Bob turned to leave.

Grandpa helped Bob at the gym? Hmmm.... I didn't know that. Tim pushed his thoughts aside before Bob could get away. "Could I lock up, Bob? That way, we could play for a while. We'll be careful."

Bob hesitated. "Don't usually do this." Then he tossed the keys to Tim. "Play for an hour or so, then drop 'em off. I'll find 'em."

After a close scrimmage, the guys were hot and tired. Nobody wanted to talk. The other boys headed out swigging Gatorade, while Tim jumped up onto the stage to find the circuit breakers. "See ya tomorrow," Zach called.

"Yeah, see ya," Tim called over his shoulder. He heard the old doors bang as he flicked off the breakers. Stepping back onto the stage, he smiled at the shafts of sunlight streaming through the upper windows onto the court. *I bet Bob would say they're spotlights for the old Roll Red Rollers.* Tim narrowed his eyes. The sunlight was fading, and in its place, a foggy, gray mist was settling across the floor.

Suddenly, standing under the goal were three basketball players, dressed in silky, short gym trunks and sleeveless Roll jerseys. The stocky one passed the ball to the shortest player who dribbled under the basket and tossed up an easy lay-up. Then the first one circled around to get the rebound and pass it to Number 5, the tallest one. In an obviously choreographed drill, the tall one caught it easily, loped over to the goal and did a hook shot into the waiting net. Tim knew he should be scared, but he couldn't take his eyes off Number 5, the star. *There's something about that guy,* Tim thought. *His long legs...* When the player snagged his own rebound, he flashed a broad smile at Tim, and then rocketed the ball straight at him.

"Whoa!" Instinctively, Tim's hands jerked up to catch the ball, and then he jolted. *What is going on here?* Tim blinked, but the ball… the players … and the mist were gone. Only a single sunbeam remained.

Tim slowly dribbled his faded basketball all the way home. *Am I going crazy? I just saw ghosts! Why did that guy try to pass me the ball? He had to be the guy in my bedroom. Is he that Magic Genie guy Bob talks about?*

Coming up the driveway, Tim noticed the old rim on the garage. He stopped, set himself, and tried a three-pointer. The ball sailed through the rim, hit the wooden clapboard backboard and ricocheted back to him. *Pretty good,* he thought… *for a geek.*

A geek….was this Dad's goal when he was a kid? He never talked about playing basketball. Maybe Grandpa did. Maybe Grandpa was a Red Roller. Bob never said so, but they were friends.

Tim took another shot. Moving from one place to another, pretending to dribble the ball around a non-existent defense, Tim was in The Flow. He wanted to forget about the ghosts or whatever he had seen at the gym that morning. He didn't notice another round of dark clouds rolling in.

Around noon, he heard the back door slam and his father's irritated voice behind him. "Do you mind?"

Tim stopped, his arms in mid air for a lay up. "What?" He panted and pulled the ball back down, resting it on his hip.

"I'm trying to sort through this stuff, and all I can hear is that damn basketball." Tim's dad scowled, his arms crossed on his chest.

"Well, I finished my work. And there's nothing else to do." Tim turned his back on his dad and shot again. The ball swished the hoop. "Come on, take a break, Dad. Didn't you play basketball when you were a kid?" Tim grabbed the rebound and turned to pass to his dad. But there was no point: He was already headed back into the house grumbling.

After another quiet dinner, Tim found his mom in the kitchen drying dishes. "What's up with Dad?" he asked as he took a dry bowl from her hands and put it in the cupboard.

"I think being here is bringing up some ugly memories... and maybe a little guilt. "I heard you two this afternoon. Give him some space, Tim," she said and turned back to her dishes.

What ugly memories? What's Dad got to feel guilty about? Besides never telling me anything about Grandpa. Starting up the staircase and pulling off his dirty shirt, Tim heard voices in the den. He stopped at the point where he couldn't be seen and sat on the wooden step.

"I guess this is tougher than you thought, huh?" his mother's voice began.

"Yeah, well..." his dad answered.

"Greg, you know Tim shouldn't be caught in the middle," his mother said defensively. Tim couldn't hear a response. He scooted down a step, not wanting to give himself away.

But then his mom's voice was sweet. "Maybe you should just give him the box and get it over with."

Tim's ears perked up. *Box? What box?* Tim leaned nearer to the bottom of the stairwell to hear better.

There was some muffled response.

"But why not, babe?" his mom coaxed. "The note said your dad wanted him to have it."

"I'm getting rid of it tomorrow." Tim shifted on the steps and winced when the step creaked. "It was always the same old thing with him," his dad went on. "Nothing else ever mattered. I'm not doing that to Tim."

Tim heard footsteps and then the door closed. *Crap!* Tim stood and tiptoed up the stairs and back to his bedroom.

He slipped into bed, trying to quiet his racing mind. *There's more to this stuff between Grandpa and Dad. Why won't he tell me instead of being all weird and mean about it? I'm old enough to know. I've gotta find that box.*

Tim tossed and turned, as the wind grew fierce outside his window. Before long, he hovered above himself standing on the wooden floor at the top of the stairs. Something or someone pulled him down the steps and into the darkened front yard. The wind seemed to force Tim across the yard and on to the driveway. He turned the garage doorknob and stepped onto the cement. In the middle of the floor, illuminated by a beam of moonlight, set a plain cardboard box.

Tim jolted awake. The box! He leaped from his bed, pulled on his basketball shorts, and ran downstairs. He flew through the front door and let it bang loudly. He didn't care who heard him. Tim winced when he hit the gravel driveway, dancing across it to the garage. He shoved open the door, flipped on the old overhead light. There it was, sitting in the middle of the floor: The box from his dream.

Tim lifted one flap, and all four sides popped up. On top was a folded piece of shiny red cloth. Tim hesitated and then pulled it out: A Roll Red Roller basketball jersey, number 5, red and white, and shimmering as brightly as if it were new. Tim could almost see the face of the player who had worn it—the player who had smiled at him yesterday. *Number 5!? That's the ghost! That guy must have been Grandpa! My grandpa visited me in my room and at the gym. But why? Why now?*

Tim carefully set the box on the floor and reached back inside. His hands touched canvas. Charcoal gray with rubber soles that were yellowed and peeling, but they were Chucks, the originals! Tim dug deeper. He found a trophy… and netting… newspaper clippings, … and programs from games played at the old Roll gym. Tim set them aside and pulled out a cardboard cutout photo of #5 posing in his basketball uniform, arms up as if guarding the goal. *This is my grandpa,* Tim thought looking into the young man's bright face.

"Who said you could look through this stuff?" his father snapped, stepping toward the box. Tim instinctively swept the photo to his chest and turned his back to his father who had suddenly appeared. His mother was right behind him.

"Greg," his mother started, out of breath. "Tim has a right…"

"I, uh… no one," Tim started. "I just had this dream…" *That sounds lame*, he thought. "I had to know what was in Grandpa's box. Why didn't you tell me? It was mine."

His dad moved to close the box. "Well, I guess the famous Magic Genie wins again," his dad snorted. "He can't get his own kid to play basketball, but he'll get his grandkid to. Even after he dies."

"Grandpa was Magic Genie," Tim whispered to himself, dropping the photo and carefully running his hand along the jersey's number. Tim turned on his dad.

"What is wrong with you? Why do you hate him so much? He was a star!" Tim shouted. "Everybody loved him!"

"Yeah, and he never let me forget it. Pushed and pushed me, even though I could never be the player he was. I didn't even like basketball. I hated it!" Greg yelled back, quivering with anger. "It was all I ever heard about. 'You'll get a scholarship if you just work harder.' I couldn't work harder, and I didn't even WANT a scholarship to play basketball." Defeated, Greg said, "I just wanted to study literature."

Tim's mom moved closer to her husband and stroked his back. "It's okay, honey. It's over. This is Tim, not your dad."

"No, it's not over. I tried to keep Tim from all that pressure. I couldn't handle it, and Tim shouldn't have to, either. Now Tim's got Bob and my dead dad pushing him to play ball. It'll never end."

Tim looked at his dad. "I like basketball. And I finally know my grandpa. There must be a reason I was supposed to have this box. I think Grandpa led me to it."

Greg reached down to scoop up the items on the floor, but before he could dump them back onto the container, his son yanked the box away. "There's something else in there. I want to see it."

Tim reached inside and felt tissue paper. *What else did Grandpa save?*

Tim tore away the discolored paper and tossed it behind him. In his hands, Tim held a purple-blue mortarboard. *It can't be a Roll graduation cap,* Tim thought. *It's not red.* From inside the folded fabric, a note card fell out. Tim picked it up and read the card to himself. Now it was clear. Tim understood… even if his father didn't. "Listen to this, Dad.

Mr. Harold Eugene Brewster is proud to announce
the graduation of his son,
Gregory E. Brewster,
Bachelor of Arts,
Magna Cum Laude,
from Northwestern University,
May, 20, 1975.
Please join us as we honor his accomplishments.

Tim smiled as he handed the card to his father. "You were wrong, Dad. Basketball wasn't all Grandpa cared about."

Stephanie White
Brenda Robertson Stewart

Beginning her basketball career at Seeger Memorial High School, West Lebanon, Indiana, Stephanie White averaged 36.9 points and 13.1 rebounds a game. She led Seeger to a 97-4 record over her four years, and finished with an Indiana record 2,869 points. She was named the National High School Player of the Year in 1995 and was also Indiana Miss Basketball.

White was recruited by Purdue University where she led the Boilermakers to their first NCAA title in 1999. She was named the recipient of the Wade Trophy, the National College Player of the Year, Big Ten Conference Player of the Year, Big Ten Female Athlete of the Year, consensus All-American, GTE Academic All-American of the Year, and the Honda Award as the nation's most outstanding player.

Her first year in professional basketball was spent as a member of the Charlotte Sting, but White was acquired by the Indiana Fever for their inaugural season in 2000. She retired in 2004. Subsequently, she served as an assistant coach at Ball State University, Kansas State University, the University of Toledo, and the Chicago Sky. She has also served as an analyst for ESPN and the Big Ten Network.

In 2011, White was hired as an assistant coach for the Indiana Fever. She joined Coach Lin Dunn, the former Purdue coach who recruited her. Since Stephanie White was an original Fever player, the team's winning of the 2012 WNBA title was special to her. She is a member of the Fevers All-Decade Team and has recently been elevated to associate head coach.

THE BIG SLOWDOWN
Terence Faherty

This happened a ways back, around the time I added "the Hoosier Eye" to my business cards and ads, right under my name, Harley Rensselaer. I was in Broad Ripple, a little town that had been swallowed whole by sprawling Indianapolis but never really digested. I was having lunch with a pal of mine, Albert, who's also in the profession. The private investigator profession.

You would think that when two keyhole peepers get together, they'd talk shop, but not Al and me. Yes, he razzed me a little about "the Hoosier Eye" tag, about how a man who calls himself that should be wearing bib overalls and not a sharkskin suit, but then Al was never much of a one for self-promotion. Or self-interest in general. Give him some stray-dog client who can't even pay in installments, and he's content. Throw in an occasional chance for him to talk about basketball, and he might even smile.

We were sitting on the patio of the Broad Ripple Beer Emporium, which occupied a stretch of Maple Street, a shady backwater on the northern edge of Broad Ripple's business district. It was a beautiful afternoon in early May, warm enough to eat outside but without a trace of the summer humidity that was lurking somewhere around St. Louis, waiting to pounce. And there was a breeze, too, just a shade cooler than the sunlight and delicious.

Also delicious were the Emporium's home brewed pale ale, which I was sipping, and its famous Scotch eggs, which I was eating. Those are hard boiled eggs rolled in sausage bits and bread crumbs and then fried. Cardiac specials, Al calls them, but I suspect your mouth is watering just from my brief description. Mine is, just from thinking back.

All in all, it was a perfect afternoon, except that the state basketball tournament had recently been conducted and Al wanted to talk about it. Here's the point in the story where I make a dark confession. I don't like basketball. A Hoosier—that is, a resident of Indiana—admitting he doesn't like basketball is like someone from Illinois saying he doesn't like political corruption or an Italian turning down pasta. To continue that food metaphor, it's another way of saying such a Hoosier is living in the wrong place, 'cause he's in for a lifetime supply of a dish he didn't order.

I don't care for basketball because I was never any good at it. I could shoot just fine—I excel at any kind of shooting—but I could never get more than passable at dribbling. It's true that superstars forgo dribbling altogether in favor of loping toward the basket while carrying the ball aloft like Miss Liberty's torch, but before you can be a superstar, you've got to be an ordinary player. And ordinary players dribble.

The only state I've been to that's as basketball crazy as Indiana is its southern neighbor, Kentucky. Once when I was down in Louisville on a case, I stopped for breakfast at a greasy spoon. A tableful of geezers was discussing the Kentucky-Louisville basketball game, which had been played the day before, and making it sound slightly more important to world history than D-Day. On the Thursday of that same week, I tried to breakfast in the same joint, and there were the same guys discussing the same game at the same fever pitch. I stomped out, but not before stopping by their table to deliver a sermon on the virtues of moderation.

I couldn't preach to an old buddy like Al, so I sat and listened to a recap of the final games in all four classes of boy's basketball. Before long, my mind was straying and occasionally my eyes as well. There was a particularly fetching redheaded waitress, for example, whose duties brought her in and out of my field of vision. Whenever Al looked down at the tabletop, where he was using the salt and pepper and a squirt bottle of ketchup to illustrate plays, I tried to catch that redhead's eye, though without success.

Al then moved on to the evils of class basketball. You see, until a few years ago, we only had one class of high school in Indiana, as far as the season-ending basketball tournament went. Every school in the state, whether it had fifty students or five thousand, was thrown into the same melee. If a school survived the local, sectional, and regional rounds, it was on to Indianapolis and a shot at immortality.

Basketball fanatics loved the one-class tournament, but apostles of fairness, that highly desirable and equally elusive commodity, did not. The fairness police won in the end, overriding purists like Al and ignoring a sacred precedent, the "Milan Miracle." Never heard of that one? Milan (pronounced with a long i) was a tiny high school, enrollment one hundred and sixty-one, located in a tiny Indiana town of the same name, population eleven hundred. In 1954, Milan beat mighty Muncie Central for the state championship. If that sounds like the plot of a movie, it's because it is one. They ripped it off for *Hoosiers*, a little indie you might have seen.

I knew Al would treat me to a discussion of the Milan Miracle next—all the one-class diehards swear by it—and he didn't let me down. And that's the point at which this story really starts.

"Milan had a new coach, Martin Wood," Al said, "and he taught his squad a new kind of basketball."

"Martin Wood," I repeated, like a kid who thought there might be a pop quiz coming up. Al can get you flashing back to your school days because he looks a little like a college professor: a lot of forehead and not much hair to shade it.

"He was all about controlling the ball back when most schools were only interested in shooting it."

"Ball control," I said. "Right."

I was distracted just then by the sight of a woman coming toward me down Maple Street. She was a mail carrier, and she'd taken advantage of the warm day to break out her summer shorts. I was grateful for that, because she had two of the longest legs it had ever been my privilege to see. She had a graceful, willowy stride, too, not at all like the silly walk super models use, the one where they seem to be trying to step on their own toes. She carried her mailbag like it was full of feathers and wore a sort of gray pith helmet on the back of her head like a sun bonnet.

Meanwhile, Al was lecturing on. "Wood had this four-corner offense he called the 'cat-and-mouse.' It elevated passing to an art form."

There was a lot more in that same vein, but I didn't hear it. I was trying to think of an excuse for a conversation with that mail carrier, assuming she looked as good up close as she did from a block away. I was having to exercise patience on that point, as the carrier had stopped to give directions to some guy in an oversized Colts jersey. I inferred or deduced—I can never keep those two straight—that directions were the subject by the way she was pointing back toward the cross street she'd just passed. The lost guy kept referring to a piece of paper, then dropping it, then picking it up upside down, then dropping it again.

I took his nervousness as a good omen. If the carrier could inspire that kind of Woody Allen behavior in passersby, I reckoned she must be a looker and then some.

She finally got Woody straightened out and started my way again, but she'd only managed to drop off and pick up at one business, a sign shop, before she was waylaid once more. This time it was by an altercation. A thin man and a fat woman had popped up from between parked cars to yell at each other on the sidewalk. Here again I learned something about the postal worker: She was brave. Most people would sidestep an altercation like that, but when the man pushed the woman, my willowy heroine stepped between them. It was my chance to play knight errant or would have been, if I could've caught Al between sentences.

"Milan beat Terre Haute in the morning of the state finals at Butler Fieldhouse," Al was saying, "to set up the championship game against Muncie Central."

"Ah, Al," I said, but I could see my chance had already flown.

The thin guy had backed down and quieted down almost magically. He was pointing to the bumper of a parked car, which the fat lady must have either dented or scratched. Before I could repeat my interjection, Al having ignored my first attempt, the two combatants were exchanging insurance information, using a pen provided by my lady of the mailbag.

"There was no shot clock in those days," Al said, "so Milan could just sit on its lead against Terre Haute. But against Muncie Central, a bigger and faster team, they were lucky to hang on to a tie. After three quarters, the game was knotted at twenty-six all."

I was starting to wish we had a shot clock at our table. The letter carrier was on the move again, and I was certain she'd be past me before Muncie Central and Al threw in the towel. Then, for the third time, she was stayed in the swift completion of her appointed rounds. This interruption was a woman who could have been the twin of the lady who'd scratched the fender. She was wailing over a lost little girl—they were close enough now for me to hear—and crying like a little girl herself. It was another chance for me to be Galahad, but instead of getting up, I thought to myself, "What are the odds?"

"The odds were against Milan," Al said, like he was reading my thoughts and not liking the way they were straying. "So what did Coach Wood do?"

"Punt?" I asked.

"He had his star player, Bobby Plump, hold the ball. He held onto it for four minutes and change in that fourth quarter, not even trying to score."

The lost child, who looked to be ten or so, showed up just then, smiling like she'd taken a blue ribbon for something. The relieved mother seized the mail carrier's hand and held it long enough for me to feel jealous.

Al said, "Plump then hit a fourteen-footer as time ran out. Milan won."

"Finally," I muttered, but softly, 'cause I was trying to figure out what I'd just witnessed on Maple Street, what the lost guy and the fender bender and the missing child really meant.

Then Al said, "It was Woods's decision to slow the game down that won it. 'The big slowdown,' the papers called it."

I nearly jumped from my seat. As it was, I hit the table so hard the ketchup bottle playing Bobby Plump rolled clean off.

"Al, that's it!" I said. "It's a slowdown!"

The woman and child had finally finished their thank-yous and were heading toward a sedan double-parked halfway down the block.

"Al, where's your car? Never mind." I handed him my keys. "There's my Caddy right there. Follow that Ford and call me when it lights. I think I just covered our lunch and maybe this month's rent."

Al lit out. I tossed some bills onto the table and did likewise. The mail carrier was about to enter a former house, a little frame number with that faux rustic siding, the kind where the edges of the boards still show the bends and bumps of the original tree. The business that called the cabin home was a travel agency. I would have been happier with something more substantial, like an accounting firm or a lawyer's, but I told myself that the office I was after didn't have to be this first one. It could be any one left on that block or maybe even the next block. I'd have to check every stop on the carrier's route till I found it.

The mail lady was opening the agency's front door—glass and aluminum and not rustic at all—to the buzzing of an electric bell. From somewhere in the back of the building, a voice called out, "That you, Carole?"

"Yep," she called back.

At the same time, she reached for a stack of letters on one corner of a vacant desk. That's the way things work in a small town, you see, and even in a former small town like Broad Ripple. The letter carrier waltzes in, shoots the breeze maybe, and knows right where to look for the goods.

"Just a minute, darlin'," I said before she could touch the letters.

She turned around and smiled. A lot of women won't smile when you call them darlin' or sweetheart, which is one of the reasons I do it. It's a little character insight freely offered, and a smart investigator never turns one of those down.

Carole smiled, as I said, showing a gap between her front teeth. That didn't bother me a bit. Lauren Hutton had one of those, and it never held her back. Carole might have been amused by my sharkskin suit or my Elvis hair—blond going to gray but worn like the King's, circa 1965—or by something else entirely. The mystery of that smile would have to wait.

"Just a minute," I said again. Then I dialed the volume up. "Hey back there. Could you come out a minute?"

A guy appeared whose hair also looked like Presley's. That is, it looked like Presley's had after an army barber had gotten done buzz cutting it in '58. This citizen wore a Hawaiian shirt, which might have been a trick of his trade intended to get me thinking subliminally about a big-ticket vacation.

"Yes?" he said, looking from Carole to me. I produced one of my business cards, thermographically embossed and featuring a neat little etching of an eye. I'd wanted a holographic eye that winked when you moved the card, but I'd settled for the etching.

"Harley Rensselaer," I said. "And you are?"

"Don Donaldson."

"Mr. Donaldson, before this pretty lady here takes your outgoing mail, would you check it to see if anything is missing?"

Donaldson blinked at that, but he did what I'd asked, picking up the half dozen envelopes and sorting through them.

"There is a letter missing," the agent said. "I told Susie to get it done before she went to lunch."

So I'd hit the jackpot with my first nickel. It was that kind of day. I took the letters from Donaldson and handed them to Carole, who had to have been wondering by then if she'd ever get done with Maple Street. "Thanks for your patience," I told her and got another smile in reply.

I hated to see her leave—every detective story could use legs like hers—but I knew where I could find her again on any given day. And I didn't want a representative of the Post Office on hand for the next part of the conversation.

When the door stopped buzzing behind her, I said, "Don— can I call you Don?—your secretary, Susie, finished that letter and put it here on her desk. Someone took it after she went to lunch just now."

"Took it?" Donaldson repeated. "There wasn't anything valuable in it like a check. And we never mail cash."

"A wise precaution. What exactly was in it?"

"An answer to an inquiry I received from a lady in Santa Barbara, name of Foggarty. She wanted to know the total spent on a trip I set up last year for a client, Clark Ralston. A month in Italy," he added, in case I was thinking he meant a long weekend at Dollywood, which, judging by his office, would have been a likelier bet.

"Mrs. Foggarty is Mr. Ralston's daughter and recently became his trustee. I guess he's had some health trouble since he arranged for the trip."

"Who was in your office besides Susie when you dictated the letter?"

Donaldson blinked twice this time. "How did you know there was someone with me?"

"I'm not at liberty to say," I replied, which always sounds better than "I took a guess."

It was a guess, but not a wild one. The three-act play I'd witnessed on the street had looked improvised, which suggested that the improvisers had heard about that letter at the last minute. And how else could they have heard? What's more, their presence in Donaldson's office that day had to have caused that letter to be dictated. Otherwise, the thing was too coincidental. I took a shot in the dark based on that reasoning.

"Your visitors also have a connection to Mr. Ralston."

"Yes. It was his son and daughter-in-law."

"They tried to tell you you didn't need to answer that inquiry from Santa Barbara."

"Yes. I called Mr. Ralston's contact number when I received Mrs. Foggarty's letter. I got his son."

"Who insisted on coming to see you. Something about the interview made you send a reply right away."

"Yes," Donaldson said, flat amazed. I could've sold him a used car right then if I'd had one handy.

"I never like to get embroiled in family fights," the agent said. "I mean, if Mr. Ralston wanted to treat certain members of his family to a trip and not others, that was his business."

"So he sent a group to Italy?"

"Yes, a party of five, including his son and daughter-in-law. I decided the best way for me to get out of it and stay out was to dictate the letter and get it into today's mail before anyone could strong-arm me. It was just one paragraph, giving the date of the trip and the total cost. But it got Mr. and Mrs. Ralston quite upset."

"Susie, too," I ventured, "since she had to delay her lunch to get the letter done before the mail pick-up, which she mentioned in front of the Ralstons. Lucky thing Carole was late today."

"Yes. Wait! How could you know all that?" He looked at my card again, dubious for the first time. If only I'd gotten that holographic winking eye, it might have distracted him. "What's your interest in this, Mr. Rensselaer?" he finally asked.

"I can only tell you that it's a matter of the utmost urgency." To my bottom line, I added to myself. "Tell me, did Clark Ralston set up the trip in person?"

"No, it was all done over the phone."

"That's all I need to know, I think."

"Wait! If you're saying someone snuck in here after Susie left and stole that letter, you're mistaken. I would've heard the electric bell."

I tried the door. It didn't open a foot before tripping the switch that set off the buzzer.

"Dang, you're right," I said. "No adult could get through that gap. They'd of had to have a ten-year-old girl waiting in the car. And maybe a couple of accomplices to help slow Carole down, 'cause the girl couldn't slip in here until Susie had finished and gone to lunch. So I don't blame you for doubting me, Don. I wouldn't believe it myself except for one thing."

"What's that?"

"The letter's gone. Sit tight till you hear from me. And have a nice day."

The rest, as they say in *True Detective*, was routine. Al had trailed and identified Mr. Clark Ralston, Jr., who'd played the man in the Colts jersey in need of directions, his wife Briana, the woman who'd lost her child, and their real-life daughter and letter thief, Rosemary. As a bonus, Al had also tagged the woman who'd scratched the fender, Briana's sister, Tina, and the supposed owner of the fender, Tina's husband Willie.

It didn't take me much longer to establish that those five had all been along on the famous trip to Italy. Clark Ralston, Sr., a former Eli Lilly executive who was as rich as Midas's banker, hadn't been able to enjoy the trip he'd financed or any of the other extravagant purchases recently made in his name. His health problems, a series of strokes, had actually begun before the Italy junket, not after. He was currently living out his days in a nursing home.

It only remained for me to decide whether to shake down Clark, Jr., and company or offer my services to the out-of-state daughter who had grown suspicious enough to have herself appointed her father's trustee.

I opted for the latter course. It promised to be less lucrative, but I knew it would make Al happier. And I owed Al. Also Coach Wood of Milan and Bobby Plump. And basketball in general. I told myself that I'd even take Al to a Pacers game if they won the playoff slot they were chasing just then. Luckily for me, they didn't.

Tom Crean
Brenda Robertson Stewart

Tom Crean, a native of Mount Pleasant, Michigan, was named head coach at Marquette University in 1999 after serving as an assistant coach at various universities. Under his guidance, Marquette made a number of changes to create a new team image and to compile an impressive record. Crean left Marquette after nine seasons.

Crean was hired as head coach of the Indiana Hoosiers at Indiana University in April, 2008. Due to sanctions against the university after the Sampson years and players leaving or being dismissed, Crean began with a depleted roster and a damaged recruiting record. The first three seasons saw losing records—some of the worst in the school's history.

Crean never gave up. He played like a winner stressing the Hoosier's long traditions. The recruitment of standout high school player, Cody Zeller, saw a turnabout in the acquisition of top recruits. The 2011-2012 season saw a 27-9 record with wins over #1 ranked Kentucky, #2 ranked Ohio State, and #5 ranked Michigan. Crean had guided his program from the depths of despair to one of the most remarkable comebacks in NCAA history.

For the 2012-2013 season, Indiana was ranked #1 for 10 weeks and was in the top five for all but two weeks. For the first time in 20 years, the Hoosiers won the Big Ten regular title and were a #1 seed in the NCAA Tournament.

Under Tom Crean's guidance, the magic has returned to Assembly Hall in Bloomington.

REDEMPTION

Brenda Robertson Stewart

If someone unfamiliar with Hoosier Hysteria had walked into the Needmore Hilltoppers' gymnasium on a cold February night in 1952, he might have suspected he had walked into one of Dante's circles of Hell. A full capacity crowd was writhing and yelling with purple and gold pompoms being vigorously shaken by spectators on the north side of the arena, while blue and gold pompoms were dominating the south side. With three seconds left on the clock, the basketball was knocked out of bounds. Jack Simpson in-bounded the ball to Needmore High's star player, shooting guard George Henderson. With the score tied, the Oolitic Bearcats' fans were screaming, "Defense, defense," while the Needmore crowd was shouting, "Shoot, shoot." Perspiration dripped off George's brow and ran into his eyes. His purple and gold basketball uniform was plastered to his skin. It had been a rough game. Dribbling the ball toward the basket, George lost his bearings. He headed the wrong way down the court. The Needmore crowd exploded with "No, no," while the opposing side was shouting "Shoot, George, shoot..." The Needmore fans covered their open mouths as the ball sailed through the air and swished through Oolitic's basket. George, caught up in the moment, suddenly realized he was on the wrong end of the court. The Oolitic fans clapped, cheered, jeered and stomped until the gym shook as if it were struck by an earthquake. Needmore fans shook their heads in disbelief.

George walked off the court with his head hanging low. Tears welled up in the corners of his eyes. He snuffled trying to stop the tears but they came anyway. As he walked toward the locker room, he felt lower than a sidewinder. Unable to face his team and coach, he walked down a darkened hallway to a side door. He watched fans get into their cars as he hid like a thief behind some tall shrubbery. Some laughed about Wrong-Way George. He was still hiding when he heard his father, Frank, and his grandfather, Charlie, calling for him. Covering his ears with his hands, he sobbed quietly. His family searched for him. He heard his dad say, "He's probably walking home to cool off since he'll naturally be upset. We'll pick him up on the road."

The weather was warm for February, but it was still winter in southern Indiana. That meant the temperature hovered between 32 and 35 degrees. George, freezing in his scant, wet-with-perspiration basketball uniform, knew he had to get back into the school to get his clothes. He watched his teammates and the coach leave the school parking lot. If he didn't get inside, he would be locked out and would suffer from hypothermia. Smarting from scratches inflicted by the prickly shrub, he hurried to the side door hoping the janitor hadn't locked it yet.

He shook like a tree in a windstorm, his teeth chattering. George pulled the door open and made his way to the locker room. He knew he had to hurry or be locked in the school, but he was so cold, his movements were slow and labored. Dressed in his regular clothes, he realized he hadn't worn a hat that evening. Ice crystals decorated the crew cut plastered to his scalp. He grabbed a bath towel to wrap around his ears which he couldn't feel anymore. He hoped they weren't frozen.

As George ran toward the door, he could hear the janitor whistling. He dodged the man checking the halls and locking the doors. George hurried out as fast as his freezing body would allow. He tied the towel around his head and began the two mile walk home, thinking he'd warm up if he walked briskly.

As George walked, he began to think about the tough breaks he'd had in life.

George wondered if his life would have been different if his mother hadn't died from tuberculosis when he was a baby.

The only mothering I've had is from my dad's sister—my Aunt Fanny. I love it when she cooks my favorite foods and tries to make sure I eat right.

George knew his dad loved him, but as hard as he had to work in the stone quarry, he didn't have much time to spend with him. His grandpa, himself a widower, took care of George. His dad got up before dawn to go work. When he came home in the late afternoon, his clothes were saturated with stone dust. He was either hot from the summer sun or chilled from winter's freezing cold. After he washed up in the kitchen sink using cold water from a pitcher pump mounted on the counter, Frank ate the supper his dad cooked and headed to bed.

No wonder there's no time for me, George thought. *He's exhausted just trying to make us a living.*

George thought about how much fun the weekends were in the summer. They never missed a Cincinnati Reds home baseball game. When there was no game, his dad's buddies gathered at their house to play penny-ante poker while they drank beer, ate peanuts and told tall tales.

There was no money to fix up the house which was four rooms and a path. To take baths, they'd heat water on the kitchen cook stove and pour it into a big galvanized tub they dragged into the kitchen.

I've tried to talk my dad into letting me get a job in the quarry during summer breaks as a water boy, but he says he wants a better life for me, George thought. *He's hoping I get a basketball scholarship so I can go to college. After the stupid mistake I made tonight, probably no one will want me. I do get good grades. Maybe I'll get a small academic grant*, he hoped.

George reached the dirt lane that led back to his house. He took a deep breath and tried not to cry. As he opened the front door to the house, his dad ran into the living room. "We were gettin' ready to get in the car and come look for you. We knew you'd be upset."

"I won't be getting any basketball scholarship now, Dad. The only thing I've ever been proud of being is a good basketball player. I'm nothing now."

"You hold it right there, young man," his grandpa said as he pulled the pipe from the corner of his mouth. "You're makin' too much of this whole affair. Sure, you were embarrassed by shootin' at the wrong basket, but remember one thing. It was only a basketball game. There's a lot more to life than basketball."

"I know, Grandpa. I should be happy to have a roof over my head and food to eat. Lots of kids in the world are starving."

"Don't you sass me, young man. I know sarcasm when I hear it. I'm sure it rankles more since you were playin' Oolitic."

"Which means I won't be able to go to the grocery store, gas station or burger joint since the closest ones are in Oolitic." George paced back and forth across the room. "It might be different if Needmore hadn't been playing a team five miles away and I didn't live in-between the two. I'll see those people all the time. They'll never let me live it down." He plopped down on the couch.

"George, you have more courage and determination than most people. Look at the way you've practiced every chance you've gotten on that old hoop I hung on the garage. No son of mine is a quitter." Frank jabbed the air, pointing his index finger toward George. "Sectionals are coming up in a couple of weeks and you'll be out there playing your heart out. Everyone is entitled to a mistake now and then."

George leaned his head back against the top of the couch. "I know you're right, but it hurts so much. Think I'll go fishing tomorrow and try to see some sense in this mess. Okay if I take the car?"

"It's too cold to fish. Who goes fishin' in February unless it's to ice fish, and there ain't no ice this year," his grandpa said.

"I'll dress warm. I need to be by myself."

"Take the car, George, but please be careful. I'd come with you, but it's Saturday and the boys will be comin' to play cards in the afternoon."

George heated some water and washed up in the sink. Before going to bed, he located his fishing equipment and set it by the back door so he wouldn't wake his folks the next morning. He tossed and turned most of the night. It was 6:30 a.m. when he snatched up a box of crackers and a hunk of cheese for a snack.

He backed the black, '49 Ford coupe out of the ramshackle garage, and sat for a few minutes looking at the structure while the car engine warmed up. It had three walls and a roof that sagged in the middle. *That ramshackle garage is like my life—barely able to function*, he thought.

He was undecided about where to go. Then he remembered some boys talking about a good fishing hole over on Salt Creek near Peerless. It was one of those small towns outside Bedford with a few houses that you'd miss if you blinked twice while traveling through. The morning was frosty cold, but George figured it would warm up later. As he headed east, the sun rose surrounded by pale colors ranging from yellow and orange to a small sliver of blue and lavender at the top.

The drive toward Peerless was uneventful, but Salt Creek looked like a river compared to Goose Creek where he normally fished. He found the dirt road, turned off the main road and headed toward the creek. George hadn't eaten anything before he left home and was hungry. He reached over to the passenger's seat to grab the box of crackers. Instead, he knocked the box of saltines to the floorboard. He tried to retrieve the box, but the car swerved off the road and went into the slick, wet grass and weeds. George hit the brake hard with his right foot, pushed on the clutch with his left foot. The heavy vehicle slid forward toward the creek. It seemed to have a mind of its own as it sped down the steep incline. George could hear scraping sounds on the sides and undercarriage of the car before it suddenly stopped in a copse of trees just above the cliff face that led to the creek. Some bushes were in front of the car keeping it from hurtling off the precipice.

George trembled with terror as he assessed the situation.

What have I done? George thought. *This car probably isn't even paid for and I've smashed it all up. Can my life get any worse? I've got to get out of here.*

George tried to open the door. It wouldn't budge. Trees blocked both sides of the two-door car. He rolled down the window. He tried to squeeze out the open window. The trees were still in the way and the trunks were too large to bend. George began to shake as panic set in. He tried to think.

I'll have to break the back window. No trees to block me. What can I use to break it? My tackle box is in the trunk. Maybe I can smash it with my fist. First though, I'll try to remove the back seat to get to the trunk. Maybe I can open it and get out. Nobody even knows where I am.

He slipped over the front seat into the back. He pulled and pulled, but the seat wouldn't release. He climbed up on the back seat and pounded the glass with his fists yelling, "Somebody help me! I've got to get out of here!" The car began to crawl toward the creek.

I'm going to end up in the creek. The water will be freezing. Maybe I can open a window on my way down and get out. The car's hung up on that shrub. Thank goodness. He raked his hands across his head in frustration. I'd better be still as can be. Surely someone will find me.

George's dad, Frank, and grandpa, Charlie, were playing poker with their friends. Every once in a while, one of them would look out the window. 7:00 p.m. came and went. Still no George. Charlie made ham and cheese sandwiches for the players, but he was getting concerned about his grandson. They didn't even have a car so they could go look for him. He finally called George's friends after neighbor Minnie Pierce hung up the five-party-line phone. None of the friends had seen George all day. Charlie told them to call if they saw him or heard anything about where he might be. He knew his daughter, Fanny, would lend them her old car if need be.

One of the poker players said, "Charlie, you're as nervous as a whore in church. What's the matter with you?"

"Thought George should be home by now."

"Aw, he probably got a hot date. He'll show up in a bit."

Around nine o'clock the poker game ended and the players left for home.

"Do you think we should call the sheriff?" Charlie asked.

"Yeah. I'm goin' to call. We probably should have done it before dark, but I kept thinkin' George would be home any minute."

Frank called the Lawrence County Sheriff's office and was told there was nothing that could be done until daylight, but they'd start calling volunteers to meet at the Needmore High School parking lot at dawn. The deputy told Frank he should call for volunteers also. "I heard about what happened at the ballgame. George is probably still upset and is hiding out. We'll find him in the morning. Don't worry."

Frank called friends, neighbors and relatives. He went to bed and tried to sleep, but mostly tossed and turned until near dawn.

He got Charlie up, poured some coffee in a thermos, and headed to Aunt Fanny's house to get her car.

When they arrived at Needmore High School, the parking lot was almost full of cars. Frank thought there must be at least 100 volunteers.

"With this many men, we'll find George straight away."

"I hope you're right, Dad. It's cold as a frog out here."

The sheriff divided the volunteers into groups and prepared to send them to George's favorite fishing holes. "If you find George, get to a phone and call my office. The deputy on duty will radio me," the sheriff said. "If we don't find him, meet back here at the school at dusk to make plans for tomorrow's search. Any questions?"

"No? Then let's roll."

Close to five o'clock, all the searchers returned to the school. No one had found George.

George wrapped up in the blankets that were kept in the car for the Reds' baseball games. He had eaten some cheese, but was afraid to eat the salty crackers because he was awfully thirsty.

Wish I could remember that lesson from Health class about how long a person can survive without food or water. Not long without water. Wish I'd brought a Nehi orange cola.

George found he kept fairly warm if he buried his head under the blankets. Exhausted, he slept. When he awakened, the sun had already risen. As he looked down at the floorboard, he saw a lug wrench someone had shoved under the front seat. He started to lunge for the tool, but thought better of it.

If I'm really careful, he thought, *I can break the back glass and get out of this car.*

He carefully tucked a blanket at the bottom of the glass to catch the broken pieces. Moving slowly, he raised the wrench and hit the glass with all his might. The glass didn't shatter, but the car began to ease forward again toward the edge of the cliff. For the first time, George began to sob. The car suddenly stopped. When George looked, he saw that another small shrub, suspended over the edge of the overhang, had stopped the car. But it was the last defense from the creek below.

I'm not going down without a fight. I'll turn on the lights tonight and maybe a passing motorist will see me. I should have done that last night. Wish I had something to drink and maybe a book to read.

The sky was overcast when the volunteers gathered at Needmore High School at dawn Monday morning. The sheriff said, "Frank, can you think of anyplace else George might have gone?"

"I don't have a clue. Only thing I know to do is fan out into the surroundin'areas—Mitchell, Heltonville, Peerless, Springville. You know, he might be down by Shoals at the river, though he never liked to go there alone. He says the river is too big to fish on your own."

The group was divided so each area could be searched.

The drivers headed out in their appointed directions with the same instructions they were given on Sunday morning. The stone mill supervisors even let their workers off with pay to help search.

It was almost dark when the men returned empty-handed that night.

The sheriff walked up to Frank and Charlie. "I'm awfully sorry, but I think George must have run away. We've searched everywhere we know to look. These men need to get back to work. I'm so sorry…" He couldn't finish the sentence because he choked on the words.

Frank and the sheriff had grown up together. Their children had played together. Frank walked over and patted the sheriff on the back. He thanked him and the entire crowd of volunteers.

"We're sorry we didn't find him, Frank. Don't know where else to look. If you need anything, you call us," the men said.

Frank shuffled to his borrowed car where he had left his dad. His heart felt like it did when his wife died. It might completely break this time. When they got home, Charlie was weeping. Frank had only seen his dad cry like that once in his life, and that was when Frank's mother passed away. When inside the house, Charlie went about fixing dinner, but neither man ate but a few bites. They listened to the news on the radio in the event there was any word of George, but most of the news was about the War being fought between North and South Korea.

❖

George left the car lights on Sunday night until the battery ran down, but no one came to investigate. He was so thirsty and cold that he couldn't think straight anymore. Due to hypothermia and dehydration, George slept more and more. He had been trapped for three days. Sometimes he thought he saw his mother, bathed in a glow of light, beckoning to him. He couldn't remember his mother, so he couldn't figure out how he knew it was her, but somehow he did.

No one is going to find me. I'm going to die right here on the bank above Salt Creek. I'm not sure how I got here anymore.

A short time after dawn Tuesday morning, a man on his way to work ran into the sheriff's office in Bedford shouting, "I found him! I've found, George. We'll need an ambulance, but I don't know how we're going to get him out of the car. When I turned the bend coming into Peerless this morning, I thought I saw a flash of shiny metal way down by the creek. I drove down the lane and saw tracks where George's car veered off the path and lodged in a stand of trees right on the edge of the cliff. Doors can't be opened and no way could he climb out a window. The trees have him trapped. I don't know if he's dead or alive because the windows are frosted up and I couldn't see inside the car. It's hanging on the crag by a thread. What will we do?"

"I'll call the sheriff right away. I'll call George's dad, too. Wonder why the search team didn't find the kid?"

"He's in an out of the way place. I'm sure they looked down the lane—probably drove down it, but that black car is invisible in those trees. I wouldn't have found him if the sun hadn't been shining on that spot of chrome bumper. I'm going to head back out there. Tell the sheriff I'll leave my car where he can see it."

The phone barely rang before Frank had it in his hand. He put the receiver down with a thud and ran to wake his dad. "They've found, George. Dress warm while I get us some coffee."

Thermos in hand, the Henderson's left the house ten minutes later. Frank let the car warm up while he scraped the ice off the rear window. *Darn garage needs a door*, he thought.

A few cars lined the narrow road above the dirt lane. Frank quickly parked along the road. He and Charlie took off running down the lane. The ambulance driver recognized Frank and Charlie and screeched to a stop to let them get into the back of the ambulance as it careened down the dirt lane. When they were about halfway down, the sheriff appeared and motioned the driver to stop.

"We've got to pull the car up the hill. It's hanging on a shrub above the creek. You'll be okay here. Frank, you and Charlie follow me. Be careful, this grass is slick from the frost."

There were about ten people standing at the rear of the car when Frank and Charlie got to the scene. The sheriff pointed out the danger to the car and George.

"Harley Fish is bringing his Ford tractor. If we can attach a chain to the frame of the car, we can pull it to a safer location. We can't figure out any other way to extract it and we need to get to George as quickly as possible."

Frank nodded his head in agreement.

The tractor came down the county road at full speed, engine whining. Harley Fish bounced on the seat as he drove the tractor down the hill. The sheriff stepped out and motioned for him to slow down.

"The car is barely hanging onto the cliff, Harley. Drive slow the rest of the way. The slightest jolt could send it over the edge."

Harley inched the tractor to within a hundred yards of the car. He turned it around so it was facing up the hill and backed down the hill to the car. One of the bystanders grabbed the end of the chain. Lying on his back, he slid underneath the car. The hook on the end of the chain wouldn't hold at first. It slipped off time after time. Harley grabbed the other end, pulling the chain almost taut. "Give it another whirl. Needs to be fastened to the car before I attach it to the tractor."

After a few tense moments, the man called out that the hook was in place. Another bystander held the chain taut while Harley attached it to the drawbar and eased the tractor up the incline until the chain was tight without being held. He switched to first gear and began to pull. The car seemed stuck at first, and Frank was afraid the tractor couldn't pull the car out.

The trees scraped down the sides of the car as it finally broke free with a loud crack and inched up the incline behind the tractor to level ground.

The frost on the windows had partially thawed and Frank could see George wrapped in his Cincinnati Reds' blankets in the back seat. He immediately yanked open the passenger side door, leaned in and pulled the blankets from George's face. George didn't move. Not even a sigh came from his body when his dad called his name. Frank jumped back with tears in his eyes. "I think he's dead, Dad," he said to Charlie. "I don't think he's breathing."

Charlie put his hands over his eyes and began to sob. "No, no, no. He can't be dead."

Frank had to be pulled away from the car.

George's doctor reached in and felt for a pulse. "He's alive," he yelled, "but unconscious. Get him in the ambulance and I'll start an IV. He has to be severely dehydrated. Get him to the hospital. I'll be right behind you."

Frank and Charlie started to run up the hill. Charlie slumped over and put his hand on his chest. "Are you alright, Dad?"

"I'll be as soon as I catch my breath."

Harley, the tractor driver, asked what he wanted to do with the car. Frank said he'd call a wrecker and have it pulled to a garage, but he had to take care of his son first. Harley asked who to call and what garage, and said he would take care of the car. "Get up here on the tractor and I'll take you up the hill."

"I sure hope that boy will be alright. I thought he was dead," Frank said as he turned to Charlie. "I don't know what I'd do if somethin' happened to him. He was so pale."

"I know. Ain't never seen someone alive the color he was."

George was in bad shape when he got to the hospital. The doctor told Frank and Charlie he would survive, but recovery would be slow. George surprised everyone with his will to heal quickly. The doctor gave orders for the patient to be on bed rest for the rest of the week, but George had other plans.

The basketball sectionals were less than two weeks away and George was determined to redeem himself. He began to work out slowly with the help of the head nurse on his floor, a Needmore graduate. To everyone's surprise, George was ready to go home by the end of the week. The coach was shocked when he showed up for practice the next week, but George demonstrated that he could play. No one mentioned his last game.

Needmore's team drove through their tourney opponents like Grant plowed through Richmond. The final game was between the Needmore Hilltoppers and the Oolitic Bearcats whose fans had been among the search party trying to find George. During the game, however, the old rivalry persisted as the fans taunted George, calling out wrong-way, George. To his credit, he seemed oblivious to the cheers and jeers and played harder than he had ever played in his life. The final score was Needmore, 58, Oolitic, 54. However, the Hilltoppers lost the first game of the regional the next weekend. George had played his last game of basketball.

Epilogue

George Henderson graduated third in his class the spring of 1952. No basketball scouts offered him a scholarship. No academic scholarship offers were made. Having no hope of further education, he joined the Marines. After basic training, he was sent to the frontlines in South Korea where he served with distinction until his left leg was badly wounded. George came home with a Purple Heart and a bum leg. No longer able to play basketball, George enrolled in the Indiana University School of Business under the GI Bill. Sometimes, even with a bum leg, he had to hitchhike the 20 miles to Bloomington, but people driving the route to work became familiar with George and picked him up regularly.

George graduated from college in the spring of 1957. His proud father, Frank, and his grandfather, Charlie, were on hand to see him receive his diploma. After working for the Internal Revenue Service a few years, George met the owner of one of the largest stone quarries in Indiana. They became friends and often attended sporting events together. He offered to help George start his own business and George took him up on his generous offer becoming one of the top sports agents in the country.

Eventually, he was able to build his dad and grandfather a nice house with three bedrooms, two baths, and a two car attached garage with a door. Frank attached a basketball hoop firmly above the garage door for the neighborhood kids, but he was most proud of the black Cadillac George bought him so he could drive to the Reds' games in comfort.

George was confident he had been redeemed in the community's eyes. On one of his family visits, Minnie Pierce, a now elderly neighbor, waved and yelled hoarsely as he was leaving, "Is that you Wrong-Way George?"

George grimaced and waved, got in his car and drove away.

ABOUT THE AUTHORS

Sherita Saffer Campbell is a great-grandmother, poet, mystic, psychic and mystery writer. She has been published in *Alfred Hitchcock's Mystery Magazine*, *Fate Magazine*, *Branches*, *Sagewoman*, *Humpback Barn Festival*, *Country Feedback*, and the anthologies *Racing Can Be Murder* and *Bedlam at the Brickyard*. She facilitates a poetry workshop, a Just Journaling writing group and a fiction critique group in Muncie, Indiana where she lives. "Hoosier Business," is the story of a small town sheriff who takes care of his town by protecting it from the "evil" gamblers outside of town and looking after the "good" gamblers in town. Sherita is writing a book about the sheriff.

Diana Catt teaches microbiology and does field testing in environmental microbiology. She is married and has three adult children and one grandchild. She loves to write and read. She thinks she should increase her intake of dietary fiber and stick to her exercise program. She is active in the local chapter of Sisters in Crime because the members are fun, wacky and interesting. Her fiction publication credits include: "Photo Finish," *Racing Can Be Murder*, Blue River Press, 2007; "Evil Comes," *Medium of Murder*, Red Coyote Press, 2008; "Boneyard Busted," *Bedlam at the Brickyard*, Blue River Press, 2010; "Au Naturel," Patented DNA: *A Catastrophic Clone Collection*, Pill Hill Press, 2010; "And Through the Woods," *Back to the Middle of Nowhere*, Pill Hill Press, 2010; "Salome's Gift," *Murder to Mil-Spec*, Wolfmont Press, 2010; "Slightly Mummified," *A Whodunit Halloween*, Pill Hill Press, 2010; "The Art of the Game," *Hoosier Hoops and Hijinks*, Blue River Press, 2013

M. B. Dabney is an award-winning journalist whose writing has appeared in numerous local and national publications such as *The Indianapolis Star*, *NUVO*, *Indianapolis Monthly* magazine, the *Indianapolis Business Journal*, *EBONY* magazine and *Black Enterprise.com*. A member of Sisters in Crime since 2008, his short story, "The Missing CD," appeared in the racing anthology *Bedlam at the Brickyard* in 2010. Michael's novel, *An Untidy Affair*, was a quarter-finalist in the Amazon Breakthrough Novel

Award in 2011, and he recently completed a suspense novel set in New York. He lives in Indianapolis with his wife, two daughters and their dog, Pluto.

Brandt Dodson is the creator of the Indianapolis-based Colton Parker series as well as the author of several stand-alone novels including The *Sons of Jude*, September, 2012. All his novels are available in physical as well as ebook formats. Brandt was born and raised in Indianapolis and comes from a long line of police officers on both sides of his family, extending back to the 1930's. Brandt was employed by the Indianapolis office of the FBI and served for eight years as a United States Naval Reserve Officer. He teaches and lectures at writer's conferences across the country and is a practicing, board-certified Podiatrist specializing in the surgical treatment of peripheral neuropathies. He lives with his wife and son in southern Indiana. "Requiem in Crimson," is Colton Parker's first short story appearance. Follow Brandt on Facebook and Twitter and contact him at www.brandtdodson.com.

Terence Faherty is the author of two mystery series. The Scott Elliott private eye series is set in the golden age of Hollywood and is a two-time winner of The Shamus Award, given by the Private Eye Writers of America. The Owen Keane series, which follows the adventures of a failed seminarian turned metaphysical detective, has been nominated twice for the Mystery Writers of America's Edgar Allan Poe Award. His short fiction, which appears regularly in mystery magazines and anthologies, has won the Macavity Award from Mystery Readers International. His work has been reissued in the United Kingdom, Japan, Italy and Germany. Terry lives in Indianapolis with his wife, Jan.

Sara Gerow grew up in Crawfordsville and Mishawaka, Indiana. She graduated in journalism from Indiana University. She has worked in New York and Washington D.C. as a production editor and freelance copy editor. "Breaking and Entering," is her first published fiction.

Sarah E. Glenn specializes in stories involving out-of-the-ordinary heroes and circumstances, usually with a sidecar of funny. *All This and Family, Too,* her first novel is a tale of a vampire's tribulations with her homeowner's association. Her short stories run the gamut from horror to mystery to science fiction. She contributed "New Age Old Story" to *Fish Tales,* the first Sisters in Crime Guppy anthology. Sarah has a BS in journalism from the University of Kentucky. Teddy and Cornelia, the nurses in "The Odds Are Always Uneven," were inspired by Sarah's great-great aunt who served in the Army Nurse Corps at Brest during World War I and is a family legend due to her intrepid nature and stubborn personality. Sarah belongs to the Short Mystery Fiction Society and several Sisters in Crime chapters including the Ohio River Valley Chapter, the Speed City Indiana Chapter, and the Sisters in Crime Guppies chapter. She and her co-author, Gwen Mayo, are working on a novel featuring the ladies and Uncle Percival. Follow Sarah at www.sarahglenn.com.

Marianne Halbert is an attorney from central Indiana who lives with her husband, two daughters and a chocolate Labradoodle. Her stories have been published in magazines such as *ThugLit, Necrotic Tissue*, and *Midnight Screaming* as well as anthologies from The Four Horsemen, Evil Jester Press, Wicked East Press, Pill Hill Press, Blue River Press and more. Ms. Halbert's biggest influences are The Twilight Zone, Alfred Hitchcock, Shirley Jackson and Stephen King. She was a panelist at AnthoCon 2011 and 2012, and her YA novel, *Honorable Scars*, was a quarter-finalist in the 2012 Amazon Breakthrough Novel Award Contest. She is a member of Sisters in Crime, Mystery Writers of America, The Short Mystery Fiction Society and the Horror Writers Association. Marianne recently released her first collection, *Wake Up and Smell the Creepy*, which New York Times best-selling author Rick Hautala described as "a wonderful collection...Marianne Halbert has writing chops to spare." Follow her at https://halbertfiction.webs.com or at Halbert Fiction on Facebook.

S.M Harding has had two dozen short stories published in various crime fiction publications, both on-line magazines and in print anthologies. Two of the most recent include "A Snake in the Grass" in *Spinetingler* and "Warriors Know Their Duty" in *Murder to Mil-Spec* from Wolfmont Press. She's taught classes at the Writers' Center of Indiana and participated in panels for their annual "Gathering of Writers." She edited and contributed an essay to *Writing Murder*, a collection of essays by Midwestern authors about writing crime fiction and available at indianawriters.org.

Delonda (Dee) Hartmann has written seven plays that have been produced in Indiana, including *Bells, the Musical*, a play about teachers. She wrote theater reviews for *The Muncie Star* for 15 years and got to see some great plays (and some not so great). She taught college classes for Ball State University in various Indiana prisons for 19 years. As a motivational speaker, she has spoken in 38 states and over 1,000 times at high schools. She lives in Muncie with three Yorkies. The oldest is 19, weighs four pounds, has only three legs and serves as a constant inspiration. Dee teaches English for Ivy Tech.

Suzanne Leiphart is a past president of the Speed City Indiana Chapter of Sisters in Crime. In her story, "Deadly Bet" in *Hoosier Hoops and Hijinks*, a recent Lottery winner discovers that the deadliness of the Chicago mob is interwoven with Indiana high school basketball and coaching. Leiphart's short thriller, "Roadkill," appears in the anthology, *Bedlam at the Brickyard*. Watch for her Deadly ebook series of romantic suspense including *Deadly Rich* and *Deadly Powerful*. Originally from Michigan, Dr. Leiphart is a psychologist in Indianapolis, Indiana. She has published several nonfiction and spiritual articles.

M.E. May lives in the Far Northwest Suburbs of Chicago with her husband, Paul, and their white Husky, Iris. She has spent most of her life in Indianapolis, but met her husband ten years ago and moved to the Chicago area. Her son, daughter, and four wonderful grandsons live in central Indiana. M.E. attended Indiana University in Kokomo studying Social and Behavioral Sciences. Her interest in the psychology of humans sparked the curiosity to ask why they commit such heinous acts. Other interests in such areas as criminology and forensics inspired her to write crime fiction. Her novel *Perfidy* was honored by colleagues at the Love is Murder Conference in Chicago, receiving the 2013 Lovey Award for Best First Novel. Currently she is writing a series of novels involving the IMPD which she calls the Circle City Mystery Series. M.E. is an active member of the Mystery Writers of America Midwest Chapter, Speed City Indiana Sisters in Crime, Sisters in Crime Chicago, and In Print, an affiliate of the Chicago Writers Association.

Gwen Mayo is a history junkie. Her writing is steeped in the rich history of her native Kentucky. *Circle of Dishonor*, her first published novel, and the upcoming sequel, *Concealed in Ash*, are set during the turbulent political upheaval of post Civil War Kentucky: a time when vigilantes and secret societies wielded power, and violent death was more common in Kentucky than anywhere else in the United States. She currently lives and writes in Tarpon Springs, Florida, but grew up in a large Irish family in the hills of eastern Kentucky. Gwen is a graduate of the University of Kentucky, a member of the Historical Novel Society, Golden Crown Literary Society, The Short Mystery Fiction Society, and Sisters in Crime, including the Ohio River Valley chapter, the Speed City Indiana Chapter, and the Sisters in Crime Guppies Chapter. Her stories have appeared in anthologies, at online short fiction sites, and in micro-fiction collections. In 2008 she teamed up with co-author Sarah E. Glenn to write mystery stories, one of which appears in *Hoosier Hoops and Hijinks*. They have since formed Mystery and Horror,

LLC and are collaborating on a new mystery novel set in the Roaring Twenties. Contact Gwen at www.gwenmayo.com.

Barbara Swander Miller has taught high school English for fifteen years, working with a wide range of students from remedial through honors, and 7th to 12th grades. She has taught university dual credit university classes through Ball State University and Ivy Tech Community College. Barb holds a B.A. in English Education and an M.A. in Secondary Education from Ball State University. She is currently finishing her license in High Ability Education from Purdue University. Barb is very active in the Indiana Writing Project and is a member of the National Council of Teachers of English and the Indiana Association for the Gifted. Barb is a Toyota International Teacher Program Alumnus, a Korea Academy for Educators Fellow, a US Department of State Teaching Excellence and Achievement Recipient, and a Lilly Teacher Creativity Fellow. She has traveled to Japan, India and Peru to collaborate with teachers and helped Indiana educators implement Writing Workshop in their classrooms. Barb is the author of numerous non-fiction works. She lives with her husband and three of their five children and spends much of her time grading papers and encouraging young people to write.

Tony Perona is the author of a mystery series featuring stay-at-home dad/freelance investigative reporter, Nick Bertetto, who has a knack for solving mysteries with a supernatural element. The three books in that series are *Second Advent*, *Angels Whisper*, and *Saintly Remains*. He has also written the stand-alone thriller, *The Final Mayan Prophecy*. Perona served as co-editor for the mystery anthology, *Racing Can Be Murder*, which was a finalist for the 2008 Indiana Book of the Year. Perona serves as the communications manager for the Town of Plainfield, is an elected official of Guilford Civil Township, and works as a freelance writer and editor. He is a member of Mystery Writers of America and has served the organization as Midwest Chapter President and as a member of the national board. He is also a member of Sisters in Crime.

D.B. Reddick, who also writes under the pseudonym, Joan Bruce, has had a dozen short stories published. He is a former newspaper reporter/editor and college journalism instructor who has worked for the past 15 years at a national insurance trade association in Indianapolis. He plans to retire soon and work full-time on some novels, including one about the Shortridge boys. He and his wife, Rebecca, live in Camby, Indiana where they enjoy spoiling their two grandchildren in their spare time.

Native Chicagoan **Andrea Smith** holds a bachelor's degree in journalism from Northern Illinois University in DeKalb, Illinois, and a master of arts in novel writing and publishing from DePaul University in Chicago. Smith has published four short stories featuring Chicago police detective Ariel Lawrence, including "A Lesson in Murder," featured in the mystery short story anthology *Women on the Case*, edited by Sara Paretsky and published by Delacorte. "A Lesson in Murder" earned this praise: "Of the writers introduced for the first time, American Andrea Smith stands out with her sharp plotting and terrific new Chicago police woman, Ariel Lawrence." Alison Burns, Highbury and Islington Express, United Kingdom. Smith's other short stories featuring the tenacious Chicago detective include: "Fatal Flaw," *Mary Higgins Clark Mystery Magazine*; "Elected to Die," *Mary Higgins Clark Mystery Magazine;* "Race to the Rescue," *Racing Can Be Murder*, Blue River Press; "Tarnished Legacy," *Bedlam at the Brickyard*, Blue River Press. Andrea is the current president of the Speed City Indiana Chapter of Sisters in Crime. She's also a member of Romance Writers of America, and Kiss of Death, a romantic suspense online writers group. She served on MWA's Edgar Awards committee judging the young adult mystery category.

Brenda Robertson Stewart, a graduate of Indiana University, has been an English teacher, horse breeder, professional painter, sculptor, forensic artist specializing in clay facial reconstruction of skulls, ghost writer, editor and author. *Power in the Blood*, the first in a forensic mystery series and a finalist in the St. Martin's first novel contest, was published in 2005. She has short stories published in *Derby Rotten Scoundrels*, Silver Dagger; *Low Down and Derby*, Silver Dagger; *Racing Can Be Murder*, Blue River Press, a finalist for Best Book of Indiana 2008; *Bedlam at the Brickyard*, Blue River Press; *Hoosier Hoops and Hijinks*, Blue River Press. She is the co-editor of *Racing Can Be Murder, Bedlam at the Brickyard*, and *Hoosier Hoops and Hijinks*. Brenda is a member of the United Federation of Doll Clubs, the Original Doll Artists Council of America (ODACA), the American College of Forensic Examiners, Romance Writers of America, the Short Mystery Fiction Society, the Speed City Indiana Chapter of Sisters in Crime, and the Ohio River Valley Chapter of Sisters in Crime. She speaks at many writers conferences and libraries across the country explaining and demonstrating clay facial reconstruction. Collecting primitive antiques and researching the paranormal are of particular interest to Brenda. She is a wife, mother, and grandmother and resides in central Indiana. She is one of the founders of the Speed City Indiana Chapter of Sisters in Crime.